HARBINGER OF THE STORM

DRAGONS OF THE STORM BOOK ONE

ELLE WOLFSON

CHAPTER ONE

The hoodie was going to get Vinnie in trouble. Sweat collected in her hair, making her scalp prickle, and she slid her hand under the hood, trying to scratch without dislodging the hood.

The sun glared off of the pavement and made the parade floats glitter. Most of the surrounding crowd wore shorts and t-shirts or tank tops, and here she stood covered from head to toe, including sunglasses over her eyes. She plucked at the front of the hoodie, pulling it out and in and getting some air up underneath to cool her down.

A woman in a sundress turned, her eyes roving Vinnie, a small frown on her lips. Wearing this many clothes on a hot September afternoon made her memorable.

Doesn't this make me stand out even more? No one else has a hood pulled up over their face here.

She could almost feel Hilda's exasperation through the mental connection. *It doesn't matter if you stand out — it matters if someone can recognize you later.*

Right. Okay, you're the criminal mastermind.

The connection severed abruptly. Vinnie's lips twitched but

she couldn't laugh. People would notice a weird woman in a hoodie, laughing to herself in the middle of the parade.

She stood at approximately the parade's halfway point, ready to move in either direction when Hilda told her where to go. Shaw should be somewhere nearby, but Vinnie couldn't see her. They'd chosen Shaw to lead their target away because Shaw could shift her physical appearance enough that no one would recognize her later. And she didn't need to wear a hoodie to do it.

Men on tiny motorcycles drove by tooting their horns and tossing out candy while police officers and people in lab coats meant to represent scientists carried trays of food and drinks, which they gave out for free. No wonder The Affirmation Day parade was so popular — people loved free food. The fried pastry tray the last guy had would have been tempting if she weren't frying already.

The parade ran down the street that was the unofficial boundary between The Holt, which was the poorest part of town, and the rest of the city. Vinnie stood on The Holt side, but even the feeling of home she felt here couldn't dampen the nerves twisting her stomach. When they'd decided to try to stop the crime the police couldn't, she hadn't expected to be going after mafia.

She heard TK's voice booming over a speaker just as the float he was riding came into view. He stood on top of an hourglass with the KCQT logo on the front, dark skin gleaming as he passed the microphone to his co-host and waved at the crowds.

His focus was incredible. TK was Ferr, sometimes called a blood worker, and among other things, he could find people. He had to use his power to find the person they were looking for while still entertaining the crowd.

Almost everyone in The Holt came to the Affirmation Day parade, which meant their target had to be here somewhere.

Vinnie paced the float, following the parade's direction as she made her way through the crowd. If TK had sensed the target in the other direction, she would have known. That meant they had to be getting closer, or the accountant wasn't here at all.

She relaxed her body, using her power to open her senses. Her power was unique among the Twisted. As far as she knew, there was no one else like her. There were six known types of power, but she had none of those. Instead of one kind of ability, she could borrow magic from other Twisted.

As she wove her way through the people lining the streets, she felt them. People they called Twisted because of their strange abilities. There weren't many — most Twisted had difficulty hiding their ability long-term, but it comforted her to know that if she was in danger, she could borrow their power.

There was a Zee woman was holding her child's hand as she pointed at the man dressed as a bear on the honey float, a Ferr child charming his dad into buying him cotton candy, a Wisp girl shifting anxiously from foot to foot and glancing over her shoulder every few minutes. Most had never been registered, which was illegal, but there might be a few former indentured, their tattooed hands covered or scars where the tattoo had been removed. They tattooed the backs of their hands where the mark was easy to see. That way, people knew they were dangerous. Then they implanted them with a tracking chip and hired them out to companies who could afford them.

Just ahead, some people in the crowd became agitated, voices getting louder, people shuffling away from each other. Shaw was nearby, somewhere. Her power felt stronger to Vinnie because it was more familiar. Vinnie reached out and pulled some, enjoying the soothing feeling of it washing through her for a moment before the emotions of the crowd flooded through her; happy, sad, tired. Shaw's Dancer ability also allowed her to read emotions, and that was the easiest of her abilities that Vinnie could borrow and control. The people ahead seemed irritated, not angry, but Vinnie hurried past anyway, not wanting to get caught up.

She'd fallen a little behind TK's float and was tracking along with a marching band. So much joy and excitement, Vinnie smiled and forgot how hot, sweaty, and scared she was for a moment.

Got him. Hilda's voice in her head startled Vinnie, and her stomach gave another twist of anxiety.

Where am I going?

Melville Avenue.

Not far, she was just over two blocks away. The crowds would be thicker at that intersection. Grand street cut diagonally across 63rd just past Melville, which meant the street widened, making it a popular place for the performers to stop and do their dances. Plus, there was some outdoor seating at the bus station.

Shaw could lead the accountant back down Grand to Torneo to a shop that had given them a key. Several shops had, which had been one of the trickiest things about the plan—how to get people to let them use their shop without revealing who they were.

Her hair felt soaked through with sweat, and Vinnie reached up to pull the hood down to get some relief. Her hands stilled on the edges, and she sighed, putting them back down without removing the hood.

She was almost to Melville now. The target could be on any corner of this intersection, and she didn't want him to see her until she was in the shop with her face covered.

Vinnie scanned the crowd looking for Shaw but couldn't spot her. Shaw was one of the strongest Dancers she'd ever met, could shift into so many faces she might not recognize her unless she was standing right next to her. She wouldn't recognize her with her eyes. Vinnie's power would always recognize her. Shaw's power always felt the same.

Ready, she sent the thought to Hilda, shoving the nerves deep down. They'd never taken on anything this big before.

Summer Games T-shirt, Hilda thought at her and sent a blurry

4

image she'd plucked from TK's mind. His float wasn't close enough to get a good mental image yet. Vinnie spotted the man — on the wrong side of the street. The man had a pleasant, round face. He smiled at the woman next to him, saying something and pointing at the float. The two little girls who stood in front of them looked too much like the woman not to be their children. He looked kind.

A pleasant exterior doesn't make a pleasant interior, Hilda said.

Get out of my head. That Hilda could read her thoughts without Vinnie inviting her meant she was close. Vinnie opened herself up again to see how far away the rest of the group was. *Nell's too far away. I can barely reach her. Tell her to come in. I'm going back south, there's a marching band. I shouldn't cause too much trouble crossing there. He's on the east side, with family. Where's Shaw?*

Hm. And then Hilda was gone, not just her presence in Vinnie's mind — Vinnie could no longer sense her power. The sweat beading in her hair seemed to prickle as she fought off the panic. She was not helpless, there were plenty of Twisted around if she needed power, and probably none of them could cut her off the way Hilda could.

Back down the street, the marching band had paused in the middle of the road to do a synchronized dance. Perfect. They were holding up the parade. Vinnie strode across the street.

On the other side, she pushed her way back toward their target. With her senses wide open, she could feel Nell's comforting presence getting closer. Good.

Their target smiled, a huge grin as he crouched next to the girls and pointed at the float.

Hilda? Projecting when she had no Mesmer magic was iffy, but Hilda usually caught on. This time, there was nothing but silence in her head. No answer.

Another man approached the accountant, said a few words in his ear, and pointed down the street. The accountant's face went from happy to displeasure as the man stalked off in the direction he had pointed. The accountant said something to his wife, and she pursed her lips and shook her head. He tensed, his body coiling in preparation for following the other man.

We're going to lose him.

Awareness of Hilda's magic returned. *Shaw won't do it. She's scared.*

He's going to get away. Vinnie spotted a pale blond head in the crowd, close enough that it could be Hilda.

We know what the guy looks like, we can find him again. Let's get out of here.

We've been planning this for weeks.

A gang who called themselves La Mafia controlled much of The Holt. Police were not a significant presence. Partially because it was no secret that there was a large population of unregistered Twisted, and people who tried to do something about it often disappeared. The Holt was a dangerous place. And Vinnie had never felt safer anywhere else in her life.

Still, crime was a problem. Months ago, Vinnie and her friends had decided to do something. So far, they'd only had two small requests for help, but a few weeks ago TK had gotten information that La Mafia's leader, Nieves Delgado, was getting the gang involved in human trafficking. Weeks of searching had finally led them to enough information and they formed a plan. Nieves Delgado's accountant was a sex addict. The problem? No one knew who the accountant was, not even members of the gang.

TK could track him through reading an energy signature from some paperwork they'd stolen. And while they knew his face now, they still didn't know his name. The city was large. If they lost him, it could set them back weeks or months and who knew how many people would be bought and sold in that time?

Tell Shaw we've got her. She'll be fine.

She won't do it, Vinnie. Get out of there.

Vinnie searched the crowd with her power. If she could find

Shaw, maybe she could convince her? There. At the edge of her senses, too far away for her to pull power. And the man was getting away, making his way through the people.

There was another Dancer nearby, but Vinnie had never learned to use the power to shift shapes.

That didn't mean there was nothing she could do.

I'll get him, be ready. Vinnie reached for the Dancer, pulling on the power, and twisted her own anxiety into a tight knot, imagining it in a ball in her abdomen. Then she pushed her way through the crowd, keeping her head down so no one would remember what the rude woman who shoved her way through looked like.

Don't be stupid, he'll be able to identify you. You're only there for backup.

She was already moving after his retreating form. *I'll hit him with anxiety. You plant the suggestion that he needs to follow me because he knows me, and we had good times together.*

Vinnie, it can wait. Hilda's protests seemed half-hearted. She wanted to get these guys as much as Vinnie did.

How many more will be bought and sold before we find him again? Are you ready? Vinnie was behind him now. People were glaring at them. *Do you have the suggestion?*

Her eye caught on a tall silhouette of few feet down. Hilda had come in closer, which meant she would help.

I don't know his mind like I know yours. Hilda could read minds well but was not good at manipulating them, and Vinnie was asking her to do it without touching him.

I believe in you. Vinnie grabbed the man's elbow as she passed him, pushed all the anxiety she had stored into him.

Walk, Hilda said. *He thinks you'll rat him out to Nieves if he doesn't follow.*

Vinnie walked away, glancing back over her shoulder. He licked his lips and turned to continue after the other man, not taking the bait. She dropped the link to the Dancer and felt for

TK. His float kept moving in the other direction, putting him almost out of reach, but not quite. Ferr power was trickier, less direct than Dancer or Mesmer. Vinnie paused, taking off the sunglasses and pulling back her hood just enough for sunlight to reflect off her bright green eyes.

She stepped in front of the accountant, listening for his heart-beat, trying to increase it to make him think he was excited. Then she smiled. "I'll make it worth your while."

His footsteps stuttered to a stop right in front of a man, who muttered an expletive under his breath. The accountant startled at the other man's voice and took a few steps toward her.

Vinnie skipped back a few steps. Smiling again, she tilted her head to a side street. The charm was tricky and didn't work more often than it did, but maybe with the anxiety and the suggestion...

She turned and walked down the side street, glancing back to smile at him again. The man had a sex addiction. Surely he wouldn't pass this up.

Got him, Hilda said.

Vinnie paused at the corner to make sure he followed before turning back toward Torneo, pulling her hood back up. There was no one on Torneo. The entire Holt was at the parade, except for a few entrepreneurial spirits who'd kept their shops open, hoping for some business.

The man paused, uncertain, as she crossed another intersection. Vinnie turned back and called out to him, "We're almost there."

The accountant's eyes lit up as he followed her across the street. Her destination was a small boutique clothing store sandwiched between a junk shop and a pizza parlor. Vinnie looked back at the man and pulled her hood down, giving him one more smile as she stepped into the building.

CHAPTER TWO

.

"Are you crazy? He'll be able to identify you." Nell's back was pressed against the wall near the door. She held her small body rigid, only her eyes visible through the balaclava she wore.

"He won't."

There was no time to say more because the accountant stepped through the door, smiling.

Nell turned, locking the bolt on the door.

He shifted, smile falling as he saw Nell dressed all in black. "I have powerful friends."

"Thank you for confirming that," Vinnie said.

The back door to the shop opened, and Jory stepped out, no mask covering his face. Why wasn't he wearing his ski mask? He had been the most adamant about them remaining anonymous.

Jory looked like a bouncer, square body, square jaw. He grabbed a chair that was sitting by the back entrance and carried it with one hand. He stepped behind the accountant, putting the chair down behind him. "Sit."

The accountant pulled himself up straighter, something dangerous in his eyes. "I think I'd rather stand."

Jory put a hand on the man's shoulder, and the accountant

collapsed into the chair. Jory was a Zee. He had used his body manipulating ability to weaken the accountant's muscles.

The man laughed. "Oh, you are in so much shit. A Zee? I don't know what you think you're up to, but I'm sure my boss would love to kill you anyway, even more so now that I know you're a Zee."

Vinnie met Nell's eyes over the top of the man's head. If she was as worried as Vinnie, it didn't show in her eyes.

The air changed behind Vinnie. Hilda. Vinnie opened her senses again to confirm without turning around. Her adrenaline was high, and she was having a hard time focusing on anything but what was in front of her — a man who seemed mild and amiable with his family but sat there with pure malice in his eyes. This was the man who had gone behind Nieves's back if their information was accurate.

Hilda's husky voice said, "You won't be telling anyone he's a Zee, Gerald."

"You're going to stop me?" His eyes raked over Hilda's slim body. Her suit was tight, and pale blue eyes blazed out from under her ski mask.

Nell pulled Gerald's hands behind him, duct-taping them together. He struggled, but Nell was Stone, and super strong.

"I am," Hilda said.

Gerald gasped, his eyes wide and his mouth opening and closing as he tried and failed to suck in air.

What the hell? Vinnie thought at Hilda. Where had she even learned to do that? Some people called Mesmer abilities air power, but like calling any of the abilities by an element, that was an over-simplification. As far as Vinnie had known, Hilda was only a telepath.

Gerald gasped as Hilda released him, allowing him to breathe. "Who do you think you are? Lunatics." But some of the fight had gone out of him.

"We're The Dragons," Vinnie said. "And we don't allow human trafficking in our territory."

He busted out laughing. "The Dragons? What, you think you're some kind of gang? That's the stupidest thing I've ever heard."

Vinnie's cheeks burned. She had felt a little silly saying it, but the name had been Shaw's idea. Shaw was obsessed with dragons. She wanted to shape-shift into one, but no one in this realm had ever managed that, even Shaw.

"That's rich coming from a man who works for La Mafia," Hilda said. "What is that? Some rich bitches' social gang?"

His jaw clenched. "It sounds French to me, but I don't know what you're talking about. I work for George Macon and Associates. I do know La Mafia controls this territory, not a silly bunch of Twisted."

It was Hilda's turn to laugh. "That little accounting firm in The Hills? With two other employees? You're right. You have super powerful friends. We should definitely be scared."

Gerald sat still and relaxed. If he was worried about their threats, he wasn't showing it. Vinnie opened her senses again, looking for Shaw, and found her outside the building with Cerulean. Vinnie pulled a little of her power, preparing to read Gerald's emotions when she noticed intense Stone energy.

But the power wasn't coming from Nell.

Before she could react, the sound of ripping duct tape came from behind Gerald. He launched himself at Hilda, barreling her to the ground.

"He's Stone!" Vinnie yelled.

Jory and Nell were already moving. Nell crashed into him just before his fist connected with Hilda's face.

Nieves hated Twisted. There was no way he would have hired this guy if he had known, but she should have checked.

Gerald had thrown Nell off and lunged at Hilda again.

Vinnie pulled from him, taking as much of his power as she

could hold as she intercepted his scramble, punching him in the chest. His bones crunched, but he still grasped her hand as he toppled onto his back, pulling her with him.

Vinnie rolled away from him, dropped his ability, and pulled from Shaw to give her grace as she sprung to her feet.

Jory intercepted Gerald as he tried to get up, putting his hand on the man's shoulder again, but Gerald didn't slow. His fist swung, connecting with Jory's jaw. There was another crack of bone, and Jory stumbled a few steps back.

Gerald ran for the door, sliding the bolt open. He opened it just a crack before Hilda threw out a hand, air pressure slamming it closed again.

Vinnie reached into him and pulled all the power she could hold, betting that was what had allowed him to resist Jory. Gerald collapsed.

"Get him back in the chair," Hilda said to Nell.

Nell scooped him up as if he weighed nothing and plonked him back in the chair as Hilda snatched up the duct tape.

"Vinnie, pull his power and hold it, all of it," she said as she wrapped the duct tape around his middle and the chair.

"Already done." Vinnie couldn't pull all of it — she could only draw as much as her ability allowed. When she held his power, she couldn't tell how much he had left, but Gerald wasn't moving.

"You think I won't find you?" he growled. Violence was not what she'd expected from the pleasant-faced man she'd seen smiling with his kids. "You're so bold that you tell me her name?" His eyes turned to Vinnie.

He was right, she realized with a start. Hilda had used her name, and Gerald knew her face too. And Jory wasn't wearing a mask. When they'd discussed their plan, they'd agreed to stay anonymous, and she'd already blown it. Hilda had argued that the only way to keep them safe was to kill him, but no one else had agreed.

Vinnie glanced sideways at Jory. He had a hand on his jaw,

holding it in place. Since he could control bodies, he could heal himself, but it took time. *Why isn't Jory wearing a mask?* she thought at Hilda.

Hilda seemed not to hear her as she rolled her head and shoulders and approached Gerald. "Gerald Gerald Gerald." They hadn't known his name before. Hilda had plucked it from his mind. "We know about the money, the money you kept for yourself. And the girls. Plus, you're Stone? Do you really think Nieves will let you live? Not only are you a sick fuck who is embezzling from him, but you're Twisted."

His body tensed, and his eyes looked a little wild. Finally, he was afraid. "You're crazy, bitch. He wouldn't kill me because I'm Twisted."

And we're not killing him, either, Vinnie thought. The only reason Jory would come in without a mask was if he wasn't worried that Gerald could identify him when they were finished interrogating him.

She'd been stupid. The adrenaline had gotten her on the street. The desire not to let him get away. But if Gerald could identify her, other people might find her. Her dad might find her. She drew in a breath, trying to calm her nerves. That was not worth killing someone over, though.

Hilda scoffed and addressed Gerald. "Nieves would kill us for being Twisted, but not you? You can't even keep a simple lie straight."

"I'm valuable to him. You are just vermin."

We are not killing him, Vinnie thought again.

"More valuable than the money you stole?" Hilda said. *I'm working here. Stop interrupting.*

Gerald shifted in his chair, shoving at the bonds. "He won't kill me."

Hilda turned and stalked up to Jory. "How's the jaw?" she murmured.

One corner of his lip quirked up, but he still looked grim.

Hilda spun back toward Gerald. "We won't tell him if you give us something."

"I'm not giving you shit," Gerald said.

Vinnie imagined Hilda was smiling by the crinkle in her eyes. She walked back to Gerald, crouched down, and put her hands on his. "When is the next shipment of girls coming in?" She squeezed his hands. "Oh, that's clever, doing sums in your head, so I can't read your mind. Jory?"

Again, Hilda used one of their names. She must have been talking to Jory mind to mind, and they'd agreed to kill him. She had to stop this. This was a mistake. *We are not killing him.*

We're not killing him. Hilda shot back. *Relax and stop. It's hard enough coordinating the boosts from Cer and trying to read his mind without your yammering.*

Jory put his hand on Gerald's shoulders, and Gerald jerked straight. Then his face scrunched, and he writhed at the pain Jory was sending through his body.

Vinnie swallowed nausea, and a little of the power she was holding slipped, and Gerald's writhing slowed for a second before she snatched the power back. Gerald slumped, exhausted, as Jory released him.

"When is the next shipment," Hilda said. She watched Gerald's face for a moment. "Hit him again."

Gerald's back arched out, trying to get away from the pain.

Hilda's hands tighten on his as he tried to pull them away. "Where is the trail connecting Nieves to the shipment, how do we find it?"

"Stop," Gerald croaked. "He'll kill me."

"We have evidence that you stole from him to finance your sick fantasies. He's going to kill you for that if we tell him. Tell us how to stop him and you might live."

Tears were streaming down Gerald's face, and sweat shone on every part of his body. His head shook from side to side.

Hilda's voice was low when she said, "Where is the evidence we need?"

"He'll kill me," Gerald sobbed. "He'll kill me."

"This is your only chance," Hilda said.

Gerald hiccupped and hung his head. The silence stretched out. One breath. Two, three, four.

"Got it," Hilda let go of his hands and stood.

"I'm dead," Gerald said. "My family..."

Jory's eyes were solemn. "Do it."

Hilda stepped toward Gerald again.

"Stop." Vinnie tried to get between Gerald and Hilda, but there wasn't enough room.

Hilda's eyes were hard. *This is your doing.*

Vinnie couldn't deny that she'd made a mistake. "There must be another way."

"My family." There was hope in Gerald's voice.

"She's erasing his memory," Jory said. "Not killing him. Though he doesn't deserve to live."

Vinnie's eyes stayed on Hilda. "You don't know how to do that. You said you didn't know how to do that."

"I can," Hilda said. "It's just not pretty. I might turn him into a vegetable."

Which didn't seem that much better than killing him. "No."

"What did you think would happen when you showed him your face?" Nell's voice was low and hissy.

Hilda's eyes softened. "He'll rat us out, sic Nieves on us or worse. It's not safe. Erasing his memory is the best option."

"I won't," Gerald squeaked, not sounding at all like the guy who had been raging a moment ago. "I swear, I won't."

Vinnie stepped out from between the two and looked at him as he sat there, sweating, and looking nervous. She remembered the lack of fear earlier, the rage in his eyes, the bravado.

He helped La Mafia finance the purchase of human beings for sex slaves. He raped little girls. He deserves so much worse than what I'm about to do.

Vinnie swallowed. There was evil in the world, but she wanted to stop it, not become part of it. The plan had been to give the police enough evidence they couldn't turn away — send him to prison so he couldn't hurt people.

His eyes were on her as if she would be the one to save him. "Please, Vinnie."

He knew her name. He knew Jory's name and face. He might get locked up and have no power, but he could tell others. The Holt was big, but not so big that someone couldn't find her. And if they found her, they would find her friends.

There was no trace of rage or malice on his face now, just the soft man who had watched the parade with his children.

Vinnie turned away. "Do it."

CHAPTER THREE

The day had grown dim by the time Vinnie pulled the van into the driveway outside the house they shared. TK's car was parked in the carport of the shabby old house beside Hilda's clunker, which meant they'd completed their task first.

How long did it take to turn someone into a vegetable? While Hilda had done that, Vinnie, Jory, and Shaw had gone to collect the evidence that Nell would deliver to the police.

Jory's head rolled against the seat as he turned his head to the house, the thick scar that started under his ear and disappeared into his shirt, twisting with his movement. The scar wasn't new, he'd already healed the damage from Gerald's punch. No, this was an old scar, one that should have been the killing blow. The prison guards who delivered it thought it was, and that mistake allowed Jory to escape the dead end camp. He probably could have healed the scar or made it less visible, but he'd chosen to leave it. That, and the faded remnants of the registration tattoo on his hand, unrecognizable now unless you knew what it was, stood as stark reminders of all they had to lose.

Without a word, he got out and headed for the house, leaving Vinnie to wake Shaw.

Vinnie reached over to shake her awake.

Shaw's eyelids lifted and she smiled. "We did it."

Vinnie didn't want to let her down, so she pushed away her doubts. "We did it. "

Not what she had in mind when they'd cooked up The Dragons. She'd imagined stopping thieves and bullies — maybe drug dealers selling to children. Vinnie should feel good for maybe helping to stop human trafficking, but she felt exhausted and uneasy. They'd given Gerald a bump on the head to cover for the memory loss. Vinnie tried not to think of the damage Hilda might have done.

Shaw trudged after Vinnie as she opened the gate for the low chain-link fence that surrounded the house. The house was one of those old, square, two-story buildings with a big front porch.

They trudged up the four steps — home at last. Only six of them lived here. TK had moved into his own place four months ago, just two months after he'd gotten the morning anchor job. He was on to better things.

A tingle rushed along Vinnie's skin as they got to the front door, and she tried not to sigh. The power signature coming from the house felt energizing to her, but it meant that the others had more work to do before the night was over.

The smokey odor of the house seemed stronger today. Even the delicious smell of onions and garlic coming from the kitchen couldn't completely cover it. They'd done their best to fix the place up, but it still needed a lot of work.

Nell had flopped on the couch with her arm over her eyes, her dark hair a halo above her head. "What took you so long?" she muttered without moving her arm.

"Breaking and entering isn't as easy as it looks on TV." Jory had picked the lock since Gerald hadn't had his office keys with him, and they used the alarm code he'd given them to disable the alarm. After the trouble of getting the information out of Gerald, the rest was easy. He'd kept detailed records in a password locked file.

Jory emerged from the back, already changed into faded jeans that hung loose on his hips and a paint-stained t-shirt across his broad chest. He settled himself into one recliner and picked up his phone.

The sounds coming from the kitchen were probably TK.

Cerulean stood in front of the window, facing into the room, eyes blank. She never quite got used to the empty expression he had when he'd been using his power. Blue tattoos covered his body. The one on his face curved around his left eye and crawled up the side of his nose, making him look like some deranged sports fan. Or berserker — though Vinnie imagined berserkers being big, burly, and looking like warriors. Cerulean was small and wiry, and right now, he looked almost emaciated.

Shaw slunk into the room and flopped in the second chair, curling up and closing her eyes.

"Cer?" Vinnie moved to stand in front of Cerulean. He didn't even blink as she waved her hands in front of his face. "Did anyone feed Cer?"

Nell grunted and moved her arm. "TK is cooking."

That was a no, then.

Vinnie used one foot to take off her left shoe, then repeated the process with the right, kicking her shoes under Shaw's chair as she headed for the kitchen.

TK hummed as he grabbed something from a small bowl and sprinkled it in a bubbling pot. Even here, in a relaxed place, he looked slick — pale blue short-sleeved, button-down shirt, and slacks. Even the stained white apron he wore didn't mar the image. He looked like a magazine cover of someone cooking. Stew bubbled in the pot with chunks of beef and vegetables.

"How long?" she asked. Then realized it didn't matter. Cer was too out of it for stew.

"Another ten minutes," he said. "Breadsticks are ready if you're hungry."

She was starving, but she needed to feed Cer. She went to the cabinet and pulled out the box of chocolate cupcakes and took two out.

"Vinnie," TK said, exasperated.

"Cer needs calories and probably has low motor skills right now. Soup and chewy bread won't work."

"Right," he agreed, as he moved to the cabinet to pull out some bowls. "It's been a while since I've seen him like that. Hopefully, he's just worn out."

Vinnie didn't like what he was implying. "He's been clean for a while. Where's Hilda?"

"Unknown. She took off as soon as we got here."

But he'd pulled seven bowls out of the cabinet, so he expected her to be there. "We're going to need her."

He paused, waiting for her to continue.

"Harry," Vinnie said.

"It was fine this morning."

"He's not fine now." She could elaborate later.

Back in the living room, Nell was sitting, rubbing her eyes, and Shaw was curled up on the chair like a puppy, asleep again.

Vinnie held one package in her teeth and opened the other as she approached Cerulean. When Cer used his power, it seemed to eat up his body, and sugar would help him faster than anything else. Wisps were energy and fire, and that took a harder toll than some other abilities. He'd used his energy to boost the abilities of the others. Wisps were the only Twisted that could give part of their power to someone else. And Vinnie was the only one that she knew of who could take it. Her type didn't have a name because it didn't exist.

She hated how her mind would get confused and numb from using too much Wisp energy, and Cer would burn himself up without noticing until he was a zombie. He stayed thin no matter what he ate, but if Cerulean didn't eat, he would become skeletal. That's how he'd been when she found him the second time.

She waved the chocolate cake under his nose, hoping the smell would be enough to get a reaction. His eyelids descended in a slow blink, but no other response.

"Come on, Cer." Vinnie waved it again. He did another slow blink before his eyes focused on her rather than staring off into the distance. He still looked dazed, but he saw her.

Vinnie grabbed his hand, lifted it, put the cake in, and moved both cake and hand close to his mouth.

He blinked at the cake for a moment and then smashed the cake into his mouth. Gulping, barely chewing, swallowing. Vinnie opened the second cake, and when Cer started to chew on the wrapper of the first, she tugged it from his hand and replaced it with the second.

The second cake was gone just as quickly as the first. Cerulean blinked, looking around the room, chocolate cake covering the lower half of his face and hands. Nell appeared with a glass of water, and he reached for the glass, pausing when he saw the cake on his hands but took the glass, anyway. He took a big swallow of water.

"Sorry," his light voice rasped, and he frowned at the chocolate smears again.

That was good, he was aware, which meant the daze was probably just fatigue.

He wiped at his mouth, and Vinnie wished she'd brought a napkin.

"I'll wash." He took another drink and headed for the kitchen.

"Thanks." Nell's hair swung around her face as she ducked her head. "I was so tired, I didn't think."

"That's what I'm here for."

Nell rubbed her hands on the goosebumps that had appeared on her arms, but she seemed oblivious to what she was doing.

Harry's flare was a strong one, unusual, but it had happened

21

before. The others would need to push the power back into him, so he didn't get out of control. Vinnie didn't mention it to Nell yet. Let her get some food first.

The front door creaked open, and Hilda stepped inside. Her ice-blue eyes went to Vinnie and then slid away, and she turned toward the kitchen.

Did Vinnie dare hope that Hilda at least felt bad about wanting to kill the accountant? Vinnie only hesitated a moment before following her.

In the kitchen, Cerulean leaned against a counter, eating a breadstick. They were half gone already. Good thing TK had made a giant pot of stew. He hated to eat anything he didn't cook himself, and no one complained that he usually did the cooking when he was here.

Hilda had dug into the old fridge, pulled out some turkey and cheese, and was making a sandwich. Of course, she couldn't eat with the rest of them.

She'd been hiding her abilities. What else was she hiding?

"It's ready," TK said, interrupting Vinnie's interior rant.

She stepped back out of the kitchen and told the others the food was ready.

Jory, who had been typing something on his phone, put it on a side table before reaching over and shaking Shaw's shoulder.

Back in the kitchen, TK put the pot on the table, and Cer was putting a spoon in each bowl. Hilda sat at one end with her sandwich, already eating. Vinnie went to grab the two extra folding chairs from the corner of the kitchen and wedged them in between the other mismatched chairs around their battered table.

Shaw wandered sleepily into the kitchen. "I'll get the tea."

When they were all settled at the table, TK pulled in a deep breath and smiled. His TV white teeth were a little too bright. He lifted his tea. "To our third successful hunt."

They raised their glasses. Hilda sipped hers and made a face.

"I need something stronger." Her chair scraped as she pushed back and went to the cabinet, where she had stashed a few bottles of cheap wine on the top shelf. Grabbing one, she brought it back to the table and poured wine in her glass right on top of her tea.

"Ew," Nell said.

Hilda's cheek creased in an almost smile, and everyone laughed. Everyone except Vinnie.

"It's not so bad," Hilda said. "Oh Vinnie, don't give me that look."

Jory cleared his throat and reached for the stew ladle.

Vinnie pushed down the anger and frustration. All's well that ends well. Except it wasn't.

Hilda shook her head. *I wouldn't have killed him.*

Yes, you would have. And get out of my head.

Do you really want to spoil their victory by fighting about it?

Vinnie glared across the table.

"He deserved to die," Shaw murmured, eyes glued to her stew. "After what he did."

Vinnie slammed her spoon down, splashing broth on the table. Everyone at this table had been hurt in one way or another. Either because they were Twisted who were supposed to be registered, implanted with tracking chips, and working at approved jobs only, or for other reasons. They'd somehow found each other in this stinking hole of a city, and a few weeks ago, they'd agreed to help others.

They'd agreed, even though it put them all at risk. "If Gerald had died, then the police would be after us. Maybe they wouldn't have found us, but why take that chance? How much worse would it be if he was dead?"

"If he were dead, there would be no chance he could identify you," Nell pointed out. "And the whole reason we're doing this is that the police won't do much about gang violence and other crimes in The Holt. They'd have been oh so sad, but it probably wouldn't even make the papers."

And Nell should know. She worked at the police station.

"As far as anyone knew, he was an accountant who didn't live in The Holt."

Nell waved her spoon. "Then we give them evidence of gang involvement, and no one cares."

Frustration built in Vinnie's chest. She hadn't expected Nell and Shaw to disagree with her. "He has a family. We didn't get into this to kill people."

Jory leaned back in his chair, but he pointed his fork at her. "Isn't that what a vigilante is? Taking justice into their own hands? People were bound to get hurt, Vinnie."

Jory had been the most reluctant to form The Dragons. He'd finally agreed when she pointed out that the Twisted needed a safe space too. They didn't want to draw the attention of any bigger authorities. If it was an open secret there were a lot of unregistered here, and no one did anything, then they could at least try to make it safe. As safe as any other area.

TK swallowed some stew and calmly said, "If you guys are going to get us caught, I'm out."

"Of course you are." Vinnie shoved her bowl away.

"Pluuuus, it wouldn't have been necessary to do anything if you hadn't shown him your pretty face." Hilda raised her glass in another toasting gesture and gulped down her drink.

"You didn't learn how to suffocate someone after Gerald saw my face," Vinnie said through clenched jaws. The guilt over her recklessness made her feel even worse.

TK cleared his throat. "Maybe you should all save your energy for Harry."

Hilda's smirk fell, and Vinnie noticed how haggard she looked. "Harry? I thought I felt something, and if I'm feeling it..."

Vinnie forced her hands and shoulder to relax. TK was right, they needed to save their energy.

Jory sat up straighter and went still. "I didn't even notice." Jory could also tell when the anomaly they called Harry was acting up. To the others, it just felt like a tingle or uneasiness.

Groans sounded all around the table.

"Can it wait? It was fine yesterday," Shaw whined.

Usually, that would be true. Harry's growth was often slow, taking in power over weeks and giving them plenty of warning. Occasionally, there was a quick flare like this. "It's a strong flare, feels more chaotic than normal."

Hilda picked up her plate to take to the sink. "Anyone who needs a nap, get one. Vinnie can wake us in a few hours."

CHAPTER FOUR

Vinnie stood outside the basement door in her socks, t-shirt, and lounge shorts. The edge of Harry's energy seeped through the floorboards, tickling her feet. It was close to one in the morning now. She'd waited as long as she could to let the others sleep, and her body was heavy with fatigue. Using magic took a toll on her, too, but it didn't matter, since she couldn't help with the anomaly — their harry little problem.

She'd knocked on doors a few minutes ago and heard the stir-rings of people waking before padding her way down the hall. Now Vinnie stood with her hand on the basement door, feeling the pulse of energy.

The anomalies started soon after The Rending.

The Rending. Some called it that because time was ripped and reversed for approximately eighty-eight minutes. At least, that's what the scientists had said happened. The Rending had felt like a wave of pain or anxiety for some people, depending on who you asked. Some felt as if they lived that hour and half again, but many noticed very little at all. Then the scientists said that yes, people had relived eighty-eight minutes. Vinnie had never cared to find out how they knew.

Time stopped and reversed, and some got to live that time over again, and many more never lived another minute. Some estimates said six hundred fifty thousand people died during The Rending. They collapsed and never got back up again.

Today... yesterday, Vinnie realized. It was yesterday that chronologists had affirmed that another year had gone by with no slipping of time, and the world celebrated. As far as anyone knew, there had only been two time slips. One at the original Rending in 1918 and one during The Twisted uprising in Russia in 1962. Though the second one was in doubt, as that one had been localized. Some said it was something else entirely that caused the anomaly outbreak in the years afterward that killed close to twenty thousand people. The fifty people who dropped dead could have been the heat.

Of course, if they weren't sure there had been any time reversal then, how would they know there was none each year when nothing dramatic happened?

People continued to die because of the anomalies, which started around five hours after The Rending. They were chaos that devoured people and places and, some said, time itself. The world was helpless against it, and all they could do was to avoid the areas that it sprung up. Many closed on their own, but many more didn't.

The Holt had been the scene of one of the largest and most deadly. It sprung up exactly eighty-eight days after The Rending — the timing was a coincidence — and didn't disappear until six years later.

The anomalies were the apparent result of The Rending, but it took many years before the world noticed The Twisted. It started much like rumors of aliens or bigfoot. Children with strange abilities. And then, in some places, the burnings began.

In the end, the anomalies saved the Twisted. Forty years after The Rending, they discovered that a team of each of the six types of Twisted could close the anomalies.

They couldn't kill them, they needed them to save lives, but they didn't trust them, either.

In the US, they put Twisted in separate communities for their 'protection,' and then there were gates and tattoos. Now, Twisted were put into 'training' camps as soon as they were identified. The ones that could be controlled were chipped and sent to work — the ones who couldn't be were sent to darker places.

Vinnie drew in a shuddering breath as a hand rested on her shoulder. The green remnants of a dead end camp tattoo were barely visible on the back.

"Are we going down, or are we standing here?" Jory asked.

Vinnie didn't turn around. The smart thing to do would be to shut Harry down, close him entirely, or if they couldn't, call in a crew to have it done. None of them ever brought it up, though, and she was grateful for that. The energy of the anomaly felt good, revitalizing to her. Vinnie knew it made normal people feel ill. She'd never asked the others if it felt good or bad to them, but they didn't seem to want to destroy it any more than she did.

Jory reached around her and pulled the basement door open as the others congregated in the hall behind them. There was a roar in the basement that wasn't usually there. Wind.

"Looks like it's me today," Hilda pushed past and started down the steps.

Harry's magic felt similar to the power Vinnie felt from the Twisted, but it wasn't the same. Only when Harry was acting up could she differentiate between the energies, and Hilda was right — The excess today felt like Mesmer energy, which meant Hilda would have to do a lot of the work.

Vinnie followed Hilda into the basement. The others were right behind her. She couldn't help, not that she knew of, but she wanted to be there.

The wind lifted the tendrils of her bangs and threatened to pull her hair out of its bun.

Harry was pulsing light tonight, making the center easy to

see. Hilda was first through the winds. As she got closer to the anomaly, the wind stopped tugging on her. Like a hurricane, it was calm at the center. The rest of the crew followed her into the eye, circling Harry.

The wind pushed against Vinnie, tugging on her pajamas, and raising goosebumps on her skin. This was a dangerous thing they were doing, but she was glad to be here, where the power made her feel alive. Right now, she needed to get out of the way. Vinnie backed up to the wall in the corner, out of the maelstrom.

Everyone filed into the room. Shaw paused, rubbing her eyes, and Cer stumbled into her.

"Sorry," he mumbled, as they all spread out, forming a circle around the anomaly.

Jory was the first to lift his arms so they could all join hands. A circle of Twisted didn't have to go around an anomaly, and they didn't have to touch, but the physical cues seemed to help. Plus, they fit better in the basement if they circled him.

It's not alive.

Focus on what you're doing. Do you like me so much you just can't stay out of my head?

It's not my fault you think too loudly.

Vinnie would have argued, but Hilda's movements were sluggish, and even her thoughts sounded weary. Now was not the time.

She couldn't help, and that bothered her. When she pulled power from someone else, the power worked differently for her. Often, she couldn't do as much with the power as the original owner. The difference wasn't because of raw power, because, as far as she knew, she could pull as much as they had in them. The difference was probably that they lived with the power in their bodies and therefore could understand it in a way that she couldn't.

Jory thought maybe they were stronger because their bodies were always regenerating the power. The power was a natural part of them, but if Vinnie needed more, she had to work to pull more.

Whatever the case, there was nothing she could do to help them control Harry. Vinnie couldn't even connect with the others in the circle, and they had tried different ways.

It's because you want to control every situation. In a circle, the Mesmer has to have control.

They'd been over this. Hilda didn't need to control her for them to work in a circle. The mental nudge she sent out didn't bother Vinnie at all, but Hilda insisted Vinnie was blocking her.

If she could help, she could take over if one of them was exhausted. Pulling the power was still a drain, but not as much as if they had to control it, too. If she could help, she could ease someone's burden. If she watched them enough times, maybe she could figure out what she was doing wrong.

Curling her legs under her, Vinnie snuggled into the dark corner and tried to relax her body. Feeling the power was easy enough, but she liked to see it, and that took focus. She pulled a breath in and held it for a four-count before letting it back out. After a few breaths like that, her body relaxed. Her vision shifted, allowing her to see the magic, just in time to see TK start the connection.

TK's Ferr magic was red to her sight. He could connect things. Blood calls to blood. The red thread flowed from his hands and into Shaw on his right and Cer on his left. The magic continued to flow through the group, connecting them all with a common bond.

Once they were connected, Hilda sent her magic through the connection. Pale yellow magic lit up their heads. Mesmers were air. They controlled the mental, the actual air currents, and sometimes, the refraction of light. A Ferr created a connection that allowed a Mesmer to direct the magic in a circle, but only if the owners of the magic allowed. Shaw had said it was like a nudge that helped her understand what was needed. She could refuse the nudge if she wanted. That's why a crew needed to trust each other.

Hilda's magic blazed off Shaw, and Shaw sent her own out. Shaw's ability was water. She smoothed the flow, prevented snags in the line, and kept everyone's emotions on an even keel. Being connected like that could be stressful and feel like a loss of control.

Jory, flesh and bone, he was a Zee. Zee's abilities were the least understood, but they rarely got sick, could control their bodies, and could sometimes control the bodies of other people. Jory was strong and could heal himself and others. However, there was no way to recover from the use of Zee magic except time. While others could consume something to aid their recovery, like Wisps with sugar, a Zee could only wait until they recovered. The name Zee came from the rumors that some Zee could even heal from death. Zee was for zombie, but as far as Vinnie knew, the ability to return from death was just a rumor.

Jory's green magic flowed through them, bolstering and taking away any pain, healing any small hurts, making their bodies strong enough to withstand the chaos.

Next, Nell used her stone and earth magic to ground them and give them strength. It twirled with gray, sometimes turning to brown. Nell was tiny but incredibly strong. Vinnie had even seen her grow and become larger, but that took a lot of effort.

When they were ready, stable, and anchored, it was time for Cerulean.

Vinnie's body clenched in anticipation, and her ability to see the power blinked out. Dammit. She tried to relax again but wasn't fast enough and didn't see Cer's magic hit the group, but the surge was unmistakable. Pure, raw power flooded the room, causing a frisson in her abdomen. This felt nothing like the calm of Harry's power — it was raw and wild and dangerous.

She enjoyed the thrilling feeling for a moment before trying to relax again so she could see the power. This time, she pulled air through her nostrils, following it through her mouth and down into her lungs. Her lungs expanded to capacity, and she tried to feel every inch of them before letting the air back out through her mouth.

Nothing. She wasn't calm enough. Vinnie repeated the procedure.

When the last of the air left her lungs for a second time, her eyes softened, and there was the rainbow of her friend's magic swirling together, creating a wall around Harry. When the last space in the wall filled with power, the wind in the room stopped. The sound continued behind the wall, not gone but contained. Now came the hard part. The yellow of Hilda's power broke out from the wall in little tendrils, like feelers rubbing up against Harry, trying to find the places where he caused reality to break down. Reality as they knew it anyway, and wind didn't exist in basements in this reality.

Maybe the wind belonged in another reality. The anomalies seemed to be a disturbance of space or time. Vinnie didn't understand all that. All she knew was that they opened out into other realities, which might be fun if one could go to those other realities, but people, unlike power, could only survive in their own reality. Sometimes other people or other things came through the anomalies, but they never lived long. She'd never encountered any, but Shaw had met a man who could turn into a dragon when an anomaly had opened on her family farm.

Vinnie had a nightmare once that a monster came through Harry and killed them all. Some part of her understood that keeping him down here was risky, but she didn't feel threatened.

"You would never allow a monster through, would you?" she murmured to Harry, half expecting Hilda in her head again, telling her that Harry was not alive.

But Hilda was a little preoccupied. The power that was not Mesmer flared and rose in response to Hilda's push as if it was trying to protect the air power. Tendrils of magic came from her friends and began dismantling the feelers, pushing them back.

A bright flare of orange shot out of anomaly headed straight for Hilda and Vinnie's breath caught. Cer's magic intercepted, but not before Hilda flinched back, her movement causing the wall to ripple.

TK's power rose to fortify the connection, and in a few moments, they had Harry under control again. Hilda's magic flashed out again, and the roar inside the circle died down.

The wall turned white as all the magic flowed together. Together, the team pushed, and the wall closed in around the anomaly. They held the wall there for a moment and then began dismantling their connection, energy flowing back into each individual.

As soon as TK disconnected his power, Hilda collapsed. Vinnie sprang to her feet.

"That was a baddie." Shaw's voice was thick with fatigue.

"I'll get her to bed," Nell said as she crouched down and scooped Hilda up.

"I'll get her some painkillers," Vinnie said. She hated her inability to help with containing Harry, but at least she could do this one small thing.

CHAPTER FIVE

The key grated in the lock, and Vinnie jiggled it until it turned before putting a shoulder into the door to shove it open. The comforting smell of the books washed over her. The library she ran was small, only eight shelves in a basement in the middle of The Holt, but she never stopped feeling proud of it every time she opened the door — even if the flowered wallpaper was terrible and smelled faintly of mildew and pickles.

She grabbed a wedge to keep the door from closing so that her patrons wouldn't have any trouble getting in. The weather would be colder soon, and she wouldn't be able to leave it propped open, which meant she would have to use some of the monetary donations to hire someone. That meant fewer new books, but it was necessary.

Or maybe she could get Jory to help her, but she hated to ask for more help.

To her left was the library counter Jory had helped her build. Her second-hand computer sat on top of the counter. She used the computer to check out books to the few people who cared to visit the library. The city had closed the only public library in The Holt, citing lack of patrons, years before she'd ever come here. A local dry cleaner she'd worked at had a sharing shelf that had been the only library left and that had been her favorite part of working there.

Vinnie slid behind the counter and opened the door to the sorting room, formerly a closet, maybe, where she deposited her bag on the floor. She grabbed the water pitcher off the tiny table and took it to the bathroom out front to fill it from the sink, which she used to start a pot of coffee for patrons at a little side table by her counter.

Once she'd done that, Vinnie went back to the closet to grab the returned books. Jory had also built the chute that led from the outside to a crate on an end table. The beer smell wafted up to her before she even looked in the crate. Grimacing, she plucked the empty beer bottle out of the crate, thankful that it had been almost empty, and nothing had spilled on the books. This wasn't the first time someone had used the book return as a garbage chute and probably wouldn't be the last. At least they hadn't decided it was a urinal this time. Cerulean had painted a small mural for her around the chute with whimsical creatures and label calling it a book chute, but maybe raccoons hadn't been the best animal to use. Maybe people subconsciously associated them with trash. Or they were just assholes.

Vinnie put the five returned books on the cart and pushed the cart out into the library, humming to herself.

Three of the books were romances which went on the left side, the other two books went on the right side. She took her time, putting the romances away first, then crossed to the left. The front door creaked just as she turned down the back aisle. Probably Zandia. She was early today.

The second to last book was one of her favorites and Vinnie ran her hand over the worn cover, happy that it got so much love, before opening it and reading the first few lines. She smiled to herself as she closed the book and nearly jumped out of her skin at the pair of green eyes watching her from the other side of the shelf.

The man started too, and then he laughed. "I'm sorry. I didn't mean to startle you." His voice was a gruff rumble that contrasted with the angelic halo of golden-brown hair and dimpled chin.

"Green eyes are rare," she said, then cursed herself. Idiot, what was that supposed to mean?

His eyebrow lifted at the comment. "They are. It must be doubly rare for two green-eyed people to be in the same building at the same time. Let's hope we don't rip another hole in the space-time continuum."

He was joking, she could tell from the amusement in his eyes, but it wasn't funny. She stepped back, glad there was a bookcase between them. "What can I do for you?"

He smiled, one cheek dimpling. "Are you Lavinia Forbes?"

Someone looking for her, specifically. Odd. "I am."

He pointed his finger down the aisle to show that he was walking around before striding down the aisle.

Vinnie shifted so that the library cart would stay between them, hoping that it was subtle. She didn't want to offend him if he was here to donate. Hey, it happened now and then, and something about him looked like money. Maybe it was his too perfect pores or brand new clothes that looked like they came from a middle-of-the-road department store. Money, but trying not to look like he had money.

He held out his hand. "Will."

Vinnie opened her senses to see if he was Twisted as she reached out to shake his hand — he was normal. She relaxed just a little and waited for him to say something.

After a few moments of him staring at her, she shifted from foot to foot and backed away.

"Nice meeting you, Will." Vinnie grabbed her cart.

He seemed to shake himself. "I'm sorry. You remind me of

someone I used to know. Just your chin or hair color or something."

"No problem." Pulling the cart behind her, she walked the other direction out of the aisle.

"And you're so young to be a gang leader."

Vinnie's steps slowed, and she opened her senses again, looking for other Twisted in the area in case she needed the power to protect herself. There was a Dancer a few blocks away. If it had been Shaw, her familiarity might have been enough to pull some power but pulling at that distance from a stranger would be harder. "I think you must have me confused with someone else."

"I didn't mean to upset you," he said. At her sharp look, he pointed to her hand on the cart. "You're holding that cart like you want to ram me with it."

"It's not every day someone steps in here and accuses me of being a criminal, Mr. No-Last-Name."

"Jones." And the bastard smiled again. Was he a cop? "What? Bad girls don't hang out at the library?"

Trying to be funny again. "I'm not a gang leader." If anyone was the leader, it was Jory. Maybe Nell or Hilda, but really, there was no leader. "Whatever it is you want, I can't help you." She turned her back to show that the conversation was over, and she wasn't afraid, hoping he couldn't see the tremor in her hands. They'd been so careful, hadn't they? No one should be able to find them. Yes, she'd pulled down her hood while she led Gerald away, but none of those people on the street there knew her. She ran a library. In a basement. In a section of the city where very few people read. No one knew her.

But Will Jones was not getting the message to go away. He followed her into the aisle, picking up the book on the cart before she could. "I loved this one, but the ending sucked." He put the book in the correct location on the shelf. "I'm not a cop. I heard around town that your..." He frowned. "You don't like the word 'gang.' I heard your vigilante group was available for hire and I need help."

"You heard wrong." They were not available for hire. They helped people for free. And this guy — she ran her eyes over him. If he was from around here, she'd eat one of the books.

"You're all booked up?"

"No. I think you should leave." They had two drop boxes for people to ask for help, one online, and one physical. No one was supposed to know who they were.

He finally seemed to care that he'd upset her and took a few steps back. "Maybe hear me out?"

"We're not for hire." Aaaand she'd just told him he was right, that there was a group. Vinnie turned on her heel and strode the other direction with the cart. She needed to get rid of this guy. Maybe he hadn't noticed her slip.

"So, you do have a group."

She stopped. "No." Denial was probably useless now, but she didn't know what else to do. He'd know she was lying, but she needed to make a point. "I've heard of this group, who stays anonymous. If you want to contact them, there is a physical drop box and an online one. That's what I've heard. Since you seem to know so much, maybe you've heard the same thing." Jory was going to flip out. And if Mr. Jones knew who she was, he could find the others, too. Vinnie could pass any test they had for Twisted since she didn't carry the magic around with her, but the others would not.

"I can pay very well." He had his hands up in a placating gesture.

Vinnie had made it to the front and grabbed the empty collection box off the counter and carried it into the back room. When the door closed behind her, she leaned against it and her gaze flitted to the phone in the corner. First, she needed to calm down.

He'd been in the streets. He'd heard rumors. That's all this was. Since he wouldn't leave, maybe she could find out what he knew and how he knew it.

She took one more fortifying breath before stepping out of the back room. Will was leaning on the counter, smiling at an older woman who had just come through the front door. The woman's dark face was heavily lined, but her tightly curled, close-cropped hair only had a smattering of gray at the temples.

Zandia came to the library almost every day, she'd once joked it was her second home. She turned and widened her eyes at Vinnie, eyes twinkling. "And who is this handsome man?"

That reduced her chances of getting information out of him almost to zero. The library was so small that if you were in the back corner, you could hear a conversation being held in front.

Will opened his mouth to answer Zandia but Vinnie cut in, "We don't have the book he was looking for. He was just leaving." To Will, she said, "I'll walk you out."

"Are you sure? Vinnie can find something else you might like." Zandia's tone was so suggestive Vinnie expected her to wriggle her eyebrows or start winking.

"Actually, I wasn't here for a book. I was here to talk to… Vinnie."

Vinnie clenched her jaw. Either he was socially incompetent, or he didn't mind calling her a liar in front of her patrons. She liked this guy less and less.

Zandia threw up her hands. "Don't let me get in the way. I'll just go back here." She headed toward the back of the library. "I can't even hear you."

When she'd disappeared behind the stacks, Vinnie turned toward him and said through clenched teeth. "She can still hear us."

He leaned close and murmured. "Are you always this angry?"

"I'm not—" Oh, she was angry, why deny it? She had a right to be. He came in here knowing things he was not supposed to know, not taking no for an answer, contradicting her in front of one of her regulars. She nodded her head at the door. "Outside."

Vinnie strode toward the door, jerked it open, and kicked the wedge out of the way so it would close completely. A narrow stairway led from the doorway to the alley above, and Vinnie was up the stairs and standing in the alley with her arms crossed before Will made it to the door. The amused look on his face as he came up the stairs increased her irritation.

"How did you hear about this group that helps people? Who told you I was involved and why don't you just go to the police with your problem?"

"You were on the news. The suspected mafia boss disappeared, and they think it was a vigilante group here in The Holt."

Nieves had disappeared, and that failure stung. All that they'd gone through, and he'd just disappeared before they could arrest him. Plus, as Will said, now there were rumors that The Dragons had killed him. The name they'd chosen for themselves wasn't on the news, but they had called them terrorists, and that hurt worse than failing. Maybe people would no longer ask them for help. Except for this guy. She wanted to help people; The Dragons had been her idea, hers and Cerulean's. The others had only agreed if they took precautions.

Will continued. "So, I asked around and was pointed here. The issue is not something the police can handle even if they wanted to. Isn't that why you started the group? Because the police won't help?"

The police thing wasn't hard to figure out, they'd stated that as their reason in the online drop box information. She'd kept her senses open, and the Dancer had come closer. Vinnie pulled some power and leaned closer to Will, put one finger on his chest, and glared up at him. He was not buying her denials, no use continuing. "No one is supposed to know who we are. Who told you to come here?"

His emotions were fuzzy, as if she was feeling them through a haze, but they matched the look on his face. Her anger and her refusal didn't bother him.

"I didn't know it was a secret." He eyed her hand, and she snatched it back. "Vinnie. There's a killer who is targeting Twisted. This person is moving around the country, but I believe they are here. From the patterns I've seen in other States, I have to believe the killer is also Twisted, and strong. Your local police can't handle that, even if they wanted to try. I've sent information to the Federal Investigations Department, but they won't talk to me. This is the first city with a full, experienced crew of unregistered Twisted who might be able to help."

A Twisted killer targeting other Twisted. This was big, and in spite of herself, she softened a little. If it was true, how could they not do something? When they'd agreed to form The Dragons, they'd been thinking about minor crimes — someone's house was burglarized, someone was mugging people. Then TK had brought them the La Mafia case and her friends had been reluctant. They'd done it, though, sort of. And one serial killer was less dangerous than a whole criminal gang, right?

Then the rest of what he'd said registered in her brain. He didn't just know there was a group trying to reduce crime; he knew they were Twisted. He knew there were all six types plus her. Did he know what she was? That was impossible. That must be why he thought she was the boss. She had no known ability. But how would he know about the others, what they could do? Her head was spinning, trying to come up with an answer to how he would know, but she could barely think. He knew who they were. They were in danger.

"You should leave." Her voice was breathless, weak. Vinnie stepped around him, prepared to go back into the library.

The amusement that had twinkled in his eyes disappeared, leaving him looking weary, and she felt the tiniest twinge of guilt.

She was halfway down the steps when he said, "Vinnie?"

He pulled a card from his pocket and held it out to her. The card was white, business card sized, but the only thing on it was a handwritten phone number. "Any Twisted in this city could be in danger."

Vinnie took the card in numb fingers and watched him walk down the alley and turn the corner out of sight. As soon as he was gone, she went back into the library, straight to the back room, and grabbed the phone off the wall.

CHAPTER SIX

All three cars were in the driveway when she got home. Hilda's was always there because she preferred to take the bus, but Jory's van meant he'd taken off work early, just like Vinnie had, and TK had made the drive over.

Nell had insisted that Vinnie act normal and not leave the library until closing time, but she'd closed a little early, anyway. The day had dragged. She'd used the library computer to search for serial killers targeting Twisted and found nothing. Then the draggy bus ride, and the three-block walk from the bus stop home that felt like miles.

As her hand hit the front doorknob, Vinnie opened her senses, finding exactly what she'd expected — Jory, TK, and Cerulean were here. The others were not. Straightening her shoulders, she stepped into the house.

TK and Jory sat on the couch. Two sets of worried brown eyes looked up, but TK's were wild.

"Is Cer awake?" she asked. Cer only worked odd jobs that he got through some app, and so he kept unusual hours. There were always plenty of people who needed little things fixed and didn't care if the person doing the job was licensed. Cerulean was a wizard with electrical issues.

"I don't think so," Jory said.

Vinnie trudged up the stairs to Cer's room. There were four bedrooms in the house and Cer had shared a room with TK before TK had moved out a few months ago. Jory had his own room, partly because it was his house, his name on the deed, but there were also the nightmares. Jory had loud, violent nightmares.

Vinnie shared a room with Shaw, and Nell and Hilda shared a room.

She knocked on Cer's door and waited. If it had been anyone else, she might have just opened the door and yelled in. Cerulean was twenty, only a year younger than Vinnie and one never knew what they might walk into if they opened his door unannounced.

After the third knock, Vinnie pulled a little of Jory's power and sent a leg cramp. Jory had to be touching someone for his ability to work, but maybe that was because he could use so much more power. One of the many ways the power was different for her.

Cer's gasp was loud enough to hear through the door, and Vinnie knocked again. "Cer, come on, we need to have a talk. All of us."

She waited for his mumbled reply before heading back to the living room. Just as Vinnie reached the bottom of the stairs, Hilda came through the front door. Her face, which had been tight already, hardened further.

Don't look at me like it's my fault, Vinnie thought at her.

The shake of Hilda's head was barely perceptible as she sat in one of their chairs and leaned back, splaying herself out.

"The ice queen has arrived," TK said.

"You do look like a queen. So beautiful," Cerulean said through a yawn as he scooted around Vinnie to sit on the chair next to Hilda.

Nell and Shaw came through the front door together. Vinnie hadn't been able to contact Shaw since she was a waitress, and she couldn't carry her phone while she worked. Her uniform had a black skirt, white blouse, and striped tie. The big bow that tied back her hair made her seem young, despite her height. She towered over Nell.

Shaw slunk in and sat on the couch next to Jory, eyes wide. "What's going on?"

Nell, who had paused on the threshold, waved at Vinnie to explain.

"A man approached me at the library. He knew my full name and wanted to hire The Dragons."

"Yes!" Cerulean leaped up, fist in the air. "Another job."

Jory gave him a flat look. "He knew Vinnie's name and where to find her."

Cerulean blinked and looked around the room at the unhappy faces, clearly confused.

"He wasn't from around here," Vinnie said. "He was too... something. And no one is supposed to know who we are, people knowing who we are is dangerous."

"Oh." Cerulean slumped back onto the couch. "Right. That one guy didn't get his memory erased?"

Hilda stiffened.

Nell moved into the room and sat on the arm of Cer's chair. She put her hand on his back and rubbed. "He did."

"What happened?" TK asked.

Nell shook her head. "The name Vinnie gave me was generic. There are hundreds of people named William Jones. The phone number he gave didn't lead to anything. It's unregistered. 'Face like an angel' doesn't help narrow it down. None of the databases I have access to were of any help."

"What about the murders?" Vinnie asked.

Nell shook her head again. "There's nothing in the databases about a murder investigation for a serial killer hunting Twisted.

Or a serial killer who is Twisted. Again, I didn't have much to go on. No locations, no victims that I could look for, no method of killing them." Nell wanted to be a police officer, but that would require testing to see if she was Twisted, so she settled for being an assistant which still gave her access to many police databases.

"He could be telling the truth?" Vinnie said.

"What difference does that make?" Jory asked. "We have been compromised. We don't know who he is or how he found us. Anyone could find us. The police. Anyone. We only agreed to do this if we could stay safe, and that hasn't happened. We are shutting it down. TK can take down the online drop box and Hilda and Shaw can go get the physical one."

A whimper of protest came from Shaw.

Jory hadn't been thrilled with the idea of helping people to begin with, and Vinnie wasn't surprised he wanted to shut it all down. Trying to make decisions for all of them, though? That was new.

"You can't just decide that," Vinnie said.

"We have to help people." Cer looked away, unsure of what he was saying.

"We do not," Jory said. He stood like the conversation was over.

"Hold on." Hilda sat forward. "We are not done here. Vinnie is right. You can't just decide what we do. You're not our dad."

A flash of hurt passed over Jory's eyes. "You think I'm trying to act like your dad?"

"Not MY dad," Hilda said.

"He's nothing like my dad," Vinnie said, earning another glare from Hilda. "But he still can't decide for me."

"We have to help," Cer repeated.

"What we have to do," Hilda said, "Is clean up this mess." Her pale blue eyes found Vinnie, and she looked every inch the ice queen TK had called her.

Vinnie stood straighter. "We are not turning him into a vegetable too."

"He KNEW your name," Hilda said. "You may not need to hide from the authorities the way Jory does, but we know that's not the only thing you're hiding from."

That was the second time Hilda had mentioned Vinnie's dad. Did she think he was behind this? Her dad had been controlling, though she had grown up wealthy she had lived in fear that if she didn't do exactly what he wanted he would withhold food, take her clothes and belongings to charity, lock her in closets — and that was before he found out what she was. The night he figured it out was the night she left. She had no cell phone, didn't use credit cards, didn't work using her name, out of fear he would find her. Even so, she had no fear that she'd be sent to a dead end camp, like Jory or any of the others, if they were caught in any kind of criminal activity. Dead end because you didn't get out alive. Unless you were Jory. Her ability didn't show up on tests because she had no power unless she borrowed, but she would still go to prison.

Nell's eyes widened. "Why did he give you a card with a phone number instead of just telling you to enter it in your cell phone?"

A cell phone was her biggest fear — though Cer insisted it couldn't be traced if she bought a prepaid one. Her dad was the CEO of a major telecom, and she was so used to thinking of him as all-powerful that she couldn't shake the feeling that he'd find a way. And not only had Will not offered to tell her his number, but he had a card ready with the handwritten number. "I don't think he knew enough about me to know I didn't have a phone," Vinnie said. "He was older, at least forty, maybe just one of those people who never got comfortable with new technology."

"Riiiight," Hilda said.

Vinnie knew it was a stretch, but plenty of people still wrote their numbers down. "There was a guy at The Rope a few months ago who wrote his number on a napkin."

"Possible. But why Vinnie and not one of us? He knew there were six of us." Jory had sat back down, but he was still stiff, and his words came out clipped. "Do you think it's a coincidence that you show your face and then this guy shows up? We got on the news with that crazy stunt and maybe someone with access to street feeds starts looking."

"There aren't a lot of cameras in The Holt that I know of. People don't care," Nell said. "The street cams are pretty blurry. I doubt he could have found you that way."

"Using street cams to find people is highly exaggerated anyway," TK said. "He would have also needed facial recognition software and access to a database for comparison. Or he would have needed her photo from someone else."

Vinnie's stomach lurched.

Your dad is not that powerful. It's not him, Hilda said.

He knows what I can do, and I'm sure that makes him very motivated to find me.

Out loud Hilda said, "I think your opinion of yourselves is too high. If someone had that kind of flex, why would they want a bunch of poor people in the ghetto to help them? And Vinnie's ability gives her flexibility, but she's overall weaker than any one of us. And he didn't say he knew what she could do, just that he thought she was the boss or something." She rolled her eyes.

Thanks a bunch, Vinnie thought. Though she agreed with Hilda. Unless there were other Twisted nearby, she was as helpless as a normal person.

"He found her, though," TK said. "He knows there's a full crew."

"So, we plug the leak," Hilda said.

"We're not—" Vinnie started.

Hilda held up a hand. "I'll talk to people around the neighborhood and find out if anyone knows who we are, or if anyone talked to him. I'll put out the word that we are no longer in business."

Another cry of protest from Shaw.

Vinnie felt like she'd been punched in the gut. She'd finally felt that her ability might be worth something, and they wanted to stop. "Why do we need to shut it down? He's one guy. And what if he's right, there's someone out there killing Twisted, and we could help?"

"It's not our responsibility, and it's too dangerous," Jory said. "If he found us, anyone could find us. Hilda will go figure out if anyone else knows and then we are done."

Frustration welled up in Vinnie. "And then what? Say someone else knows? Are we going to turn everyone into vegetables?"

"No one is getting turned into vegetables," Nell said. "We'll convince them it's safest if they don't talk."

Hilda scoffed. "Because people are so trustworthy. Come on, I can erase memories."

"You don't know how to do it safely," Nell snapped. "We will close the leaks. If anyone knew something or said something they probably thought they were helping."

"I just haven't had enough practice erasing memories. Let me practice on you, Vinnie. I could erase that loser you dated last year. Or your entire childhood, who knows? Maybe you'll stop being so uptight."

They weren't listening. They were acting like it was a done deal. Vinnie set her jaw. "As far as I can tell, three of us don't want to shut down the drop boxes." The only one who hadn't said anything was TK. "TK you wanted to do this. You said you wanted your future children to grow up in a safe place."

He looked her dead in the eye. "I won't have any children if I am locked up. The police may not care too much about people here in The Holt, but there will be people looking for a serial killer if there is one, no matter what your angelic visitor said about no one caring. Someone cares. I don't think we should get in the way of that. We've attracted too much attention and need to lie low. At least for a while."

That was it, then. Four to three.

"I can help ask around," Shaw said.

"Stay out of it," Jory said. "It's too dangerous."

"If Hilda can do it, I can do it."

Hilda stood and walked toward the door saying, "He's right. There's no need to risk yourself. Leave it to me. I'm expendable."

"No one said —" Jory growled. "Never mind."

Hilda was already halfway up the stairs, anyway.

Shaw pushed herself to her feet. "I'm not a child." She stormed past Vinnie and sprinted up the stairs, nearly knocking Hilda over as she brushed past her.

Jory let out a long breath. "That went well."

"She's right, she's not a child," Vinnie said. She wanted to stomp right out after Shaw. "You're taking away something important to her the least you could do is let her help." At least there was something Shaw could do to help. Vinnie was useless without the others. Completely helpless.

"You're the one who got us into this mess."

She had been reckless at the parade, but if Gerald had gotten away, they wouldn't have had the information to take Nieves down. Not that the police had caught him, but at least he wasn't running La Mafia anymore.

"You don't know that Vinnie taking off her hood had anything to do with being found," Nell said gently. To Vinnie, she said, "It is too bad you didn't ask the library guy more questions."

"I've got his number. We could call him." She knew they had already decided and wouldn't agree, but she couldn't see how calling him would do any harm.

"We are not calling him!" Jory said.

"He already knows who we are. What have we got to lose?"

This time, his entire body tensed. "Our lives."

Of them all, Jory was the only one who'd been caught. Because testing was expensive and difficult, most were only tested if there was a suspicion they were Twisted. Jory gotten in a bar fight, and if beating five guys in a fistfight wasn't suspicious enough, he'd been so angry he'd dropped several just by touching them and weakening their muscles. For being dangerous, he'd ended up in a dead end camp — maximum security, maximum abuse. Twisted died in those camps. Jory never said much about how he'd escaped, but he had almost died.

"Our freedom," TK added. "They just arrested that senator from Iowa for being Ferr. No one gets a pass."

Cer spoke in a monotone voice, "Death is easy, it's living that's hard."

There was silence for a few moments while they thought about that.

"Exactly!" TK said, a little too loudly. "I've gotta get home. Don't get us caught." He looked at Vinnie as he said the last part.

CHAPTER SEVEN

Vinnie rested her chin in her hands, one leg kicking against the stool underneath her as she stared off into the stacks.

Nell couldn't find any information about a serial killer. She'd looked for unsolved murders in the past few years, but with no information or place to start, it was hard to see a pattern. If a serial killer was targeting Twisted, the police didn't seem to know anything about it. Which didn't mean there wasn't, but unless this Will guy was working for the feds, Nell thought it unlikely he would have information the police didn't.

Hilda hadn't had any luck either. She'd talked to people around the neighborhood, trying to find someone with any information, someone who might know who they were, but most people had never heard of The Dragons. That was a kick in the ego.

Three days and they were at a dead end and TK, Hilda, and Nell had sided with Jory. They were shutting down the drop boxes. TK probably already took the online one down, and Hilda and Shaw would get the physical one tomorrow.

Vinnie kicked at her stool again and sighed. She could go get a book to read, but she just wanted to be out of here today. Last

Saturday, she'd helped stop someone who was doing horrible things and had felt good, if a little scary. She could do something, even if it didn't make the difference she had hoped. She was not the helpless little girl being locked in a closet because she disobeyed or the little girl crying her eyes out when she found out they'd taken her mom away without letting her say goodbye.

A teenage girl who had come in about fifteen minutes ago put a book on the counter.

"Name?" Vinnie asked. She didn't recognize the girl, and she knew most of the regulars. The girl told her, and Vinnie typed the name in the computer search. The girl wasn't in the system, so she took down her address and phone number and checked the book out to her.

"Thank you," the girl beamed as she took her prize out through the front door.

Starting this library was something else she'd done, she reminded herself. Not helpless. No, she couldn't have done it without help, but if it weren't for her, the library wouldn't be here. That was the sort of Rah-Rah thing Shaw would say. Go, Vinnie! You're awesome!

A few months ago, it would have been enough, because a few months ago The Holt had felt like the safest place she'd ever lived, and then Shaw had been held at gunpoint, her wallet stolen. A few days ago, the library had felt like her haven. Vinnie paused that thought. The library still felt like a haven, even though Will had come in knowing who she was and scared her. He didn't know everything about her. This was still her place, and she felt it down to her bones.

The library door thunked open, startling Vinnie out of her thoughts. Shaw came in, beaming, followed by Cerulean, looking like two teenagers up to no good.

Vinnie grinned back at Shaw. "Hi guys."

Shaw had paused just inside the doorway, and Cer pushed past her, scuffing his feet.

ELLE WOLFSON

"Hey Vin," Cer said.

"What are you guys doing here? You never come to the library."

Shaw rolled her eyes, strolled forward, and leaned on the counter. "We went out to get ice cream, and this doofus ate three banana splits and made himself sick. He didn't want to walk all the way home, and the library was nearby."

Cer shifted from foot to foot, keeping his eyes on the floor.

"There are reading chairs you can sit in," Vinnie pointed.

"I'm okay," Cer muttered.

Shaw shook her head, curls bouncing. "He wasn't okay a minute ago. Were you Cer?"

"I ate three banana splits." He rubbed his arms, eyes roving around the library as if he expected something to jump out at him. Shaw was right. He didn't seem okay. "There's a bathroom over there. Splashing water on my face helps when I feel sick."

His head swiveled in the direction she was pointing and then he was off toward the bathroom. Vinnie had seen Cer eat two boxes of cupcakes and not get sick. Three banana splits didn't seem like that much.

"He's so weird sometimes," Shaw said.

Shaw didn't mean it as an attack, but many weren't as kind. Cer was different, but he'd saved her when she'd come to the city with no money, no friends, and no idea how to survive on her own. "He's been through a lot."

Shaw's eyes had been roaming the stacks, just as Cer's had a few moments ago. Now they flitted back, landing on Vinnie. "TK thinks the drugs have permanently addled his brain."

"TK is," an asshole. "Very negative sometimes."

"Not as much as Hilda," Shaw sighed. "She scares me."

Hilda was prickly and negative. That was true. "You always know where you stand with her, but she would never hurt you."

"Oh, I didn't mean that kind of scary. Scary like maybe someday she'll call a hurricane and blow the city down. I know

54

she'd keep me safe in a cocoon when she did it." Shaw bit her lip and traced a fingertip on the counter.

"Do you think he's okay in there?" Vinnie pointed at the bathroom door.

"He's fine," Shaw breathed and then stiffened. Louder, she said, "Except for having too much cold sugar, of course. So..." She looked back down at the counter and her finger. "Do you still have that card that guy gave you?"

Vinnie, who had also been watching Shaw's finger, glanced up sharply. "Why?"

"I know you do. Can I see it? I've been experimenting with picking up emotions from objects. I can a little, but it's hazy. I wanted to see if I could get anything that would help? Since no one else can find anything," Shaw muttered the last part.

"You can pick up emotions from objects?" There were so many theories and rumors about what different Twisted could do, even over a hundred years later no one seemed to know. Or the ones who knew weren't talking.

"A little," Shaw murmured, trying to hide the excitement in her voice.

Vinnie felt a little excitement herself. The others had given up on finding anything, but if Shaw could tell Will wasn't malicious, maybe they'd consider calling him. She wanted to know. She wanted to know her friends were safe, and she wanted to know if there was someone who was a danger to others like them in the city.

Vinnie pulled the card out of the drawer under her counter and placed it on top, just as Cerulean came out of the bathroom.

"Can I get a glass of water?" he asked.

"Yeah." Maybe someday when she had piles of cash, she could get a water fountain. For now, all she had was plastic cups, which she kept in the back room. She'd tried leaving them on the counter, but people would steal the whole stack. Vinnie went to get one for him. When she returned, she handed the cup to Cer. "The bathroom faucet is the only water."

Cerulean took the cup and trudged off again.

Shaw watched him as she held the card in both hands. When he'd disappeared back into the bathroom, she put the card back on the counter. "He was afraid of something." A small frown line appeared between her eyebrows. "I think? Maybe that was you. Not like a 'monsters are chasing me afraid' More like worry."

"I was worried that he knew who I was." Vinnie tried not to droop with disappointment. Shaw couldn't even tell who the emotion was from.

"Hm," Shaw said.

"When did you learn you could read emotions from objects?" Vinnie asked.

"Cer was telling me about a Zee who could make bones dance." Shaw shuddered. "And Hilda can move air. I've tried moving water but I can't so I thought maybe I could do more with emotions. I kept trying, even though there was nothing at first. I'm getting better! I think?"

Cerulean came back out of the bathroom with his water. He took a sip and set the still full cup on the counter. "Time to go?"

"Yep." Shaw pushed off the counter. "Thanks, Vin, see you later."

VINNIE HAD a small crate beside her counter for people to return books inside the library. Periodically, she moved the books to a box under the counter. She squatted to lift the box out, grunting a little. It was almost full, and she struggled a little as she carried it to the back room.

Tomorrow the library was open for a few hours in the afternoon, but her volunteer assistant, Meg, was coming in, so she had the day off. She could re-shelve the books on Monday. Right now, she was itching to get out of here.

Vinnie went back out to lock the front door before going back for her things. She'd have to unlock it again in a minute, but she didn't want anyone walking in on her when she was changing. Pulling out her duffle bag, she grabbed her running shoes, shorts, and tank, stripped off her normal clothes, and changed. The regular clothes went back into the duffle, which she would pick up after her run. Keys, money, and ID went into the running belt. The other key, the one she'd snuck out of the kitchen drawer this morning, went in the pocket of her running shorts.

All set. When she'd first started running without a phone, she'd missed having music to listen to, but now she preferred to run in silence, feeling her body move. Plus, being more aware of her surroundings was probably safer in The Holt.

She locked the library door behind her and ascended the steps that led to the ground level. The basement opened into an alley, so she rarely saw her neighbors. No one rented the shop above the library and hadn't for as long as she'd been here, but the landlord wanted way too much for the brighter ground floor space and she couldn't afford it. Maybe she didn't want to afford it. Something about the basement just felt right.

The air was cooler today, but she'd be dripping soon enough.

When she reached the end of the alley, she looked left—the direction of home—before turning right. She ran in this direction all the time, but today's objective was more than getting some exercise. After a few minutes of brisk walking, she paused by a lamppost to stretch her calves and then started at a light jog.

Vinnie passed a man who smirked at her and shook his head. There were always strange looks when she went running down the sidewalks. Running was not a common activity around here, but she'd seen a few others in the years she'd been here. Anyone who exercised most likely did it at home or one of the cheap gyms scattered... well, not scattered. There weren't enough gyms to be scattered. As far as she knew, there were only two gyms in the area.

At the next street corner, she pushed the crossing button and flipped the hood of her hoodie up over her head, tucking the random stray hairs behind her ears. At least now she had the excuse that it was a little colder. With the running, the hood would still be too warm, but she didn't want to take the chance of being seen again.

She ran on, seven more blocks, a turn, three blocks, then a turn down a road where many of the buildings looked like they were ready to collapse. A small garage and a hardware store remained opened, sitting side by side. Vinnie opened her senses as she slowed to a walk. While she couldn't detect an ordinary person watching her, it would tell her if there were any Twisted around. For a moment, she wished she was like Hilda or Shaw, who could sense the thoughts or feelings of people nearby. Her ability wasn't much help, but it was all she had.

Vinnie stopped, sliding her hand into her pocket to finger the key. She shouldn't be doing this. Maybe if someone saw her, she could claim she was just dropping off a plea for help. That would work if they didn't see her opening the box. Anyone who knew what it was would know that she was part of The Dragons. Not that most people even knew what that was, apparently.

They'd positioned the drop box between two buildings. The two buildings were the only things left standing on that side of the street. They were twins, ugly stucco squares with tiny windows and concrete steps. The train tracks ran behind the buildings and if a train was going by, that would block the view from that direction, leaving only one way that someone could see her. The buildings were empty and had no windows on the sides that faced each other — like they had once been rival businesses and couldn't stand to look at each other.

She waited until finally she heard the rumble of a train on the tracks. Vinnie glanced both ways before stepping off the curb to cross the street. They'd scouted around and chosen this place because once you were in the back part there was no way to see what you were doing except by the mouth of the corridor between the buildings.

When she reached the corridor, the first stirring of doubt entered her mind. What would she do if someone was asking for help? Maybe she could convince the others, just this once. They'd spread the word that they would help those who needed help and then just stopped at the first sign of trouble, but if someone had already requested help before they took it down, the honorable thing to do would be to help, right?

No one had ever used the physical drop box, though. They'd gotten their two requests for help through the online drop box and Nieves Delgado through TK.

Though she knew the location of the box, this was the first time she'd seen it in place. Jory had bought one of those cash boxes with a slot in the top, bolted it to the concrete on the inside, and left it here. That she'd expected. What she hadn't expected was the painting on the side of the building above the box.

The painting depicted a dragon, sparkling purple, flying belly out toward the moon. On the ground below was a tiny, stylized fairy with deep blue dragon wings. She'd known without seeing the signature that this was his work. They were all over The Holt, on buildings and walls and the occasional small one on a pole or mailbox. Since they were all over, this one by their drop box probably wouldn't connect Cer to The Dragons.

Vinnie took one more look at the mouth of the corridor to be sure no one was there before crouching down over the box and unlocking it. Her breath caught at the small, folded piece of paper inside. Someone had used the drop box.

Grabbing the paper, she slapped the lid shut, relocked it, and stood. Her eyes darted to the mouth of the alley again before she opened the piece of folded paper.

"There's a serial killer on the loose and the police can do nothing. Please help." The same number Will had given her at the library was printed below. A small smile quirked her lips. She'd told him he should contact them through the drop box and that's what he'd done.

Vinnie shoved the note in her pocket and started for the street again.

Her muscles were warmed up now, so the run back felt smoother. When she was a block away from the library, she spotted a creepy kidnapper van parked in the street — one of those white ones with no windows in the back, and her heart sped up a little more.

The urge to run the other way and get back to the library from the other cross street was strong, but it was too late. He'd already spotted her. Jory's eyes burned into her as she approached the van.

"Where have you been?" He was not happy. She didn't need Shaw's ability to tell that.

She could feel the paper in the pocket of her shorts brushing against her thigh. He couldn't have known where she'd been. "Why are you here?"

"Shaw and Cerulean have done something." He looked at his watch. "I was about to give up on you and go without you. Get your things and I'll explain on the way."

CHAPTER EIGHT

Jory's explanation hadn't taken long. Shaw and Cerulean had taken the phone number they'd tricked her into showing them and called Will. They said they were trying to get information, but he turned it around on them and they gave him all their names and agreed to a meeting.

And they couldn't have delayed the meeting. Oh no. They were going right now. This ride was the only time they had to figure it out and so everything Vinnie wanted to say had to wait while they hashed out a rough plan.

The meeting would take place in the amusement park Shaw had worked at during the summer before she'd gotten the waitressing job. They were almost there by the time they'd decided what to do.

It wasn't enough time for Vinnie to process the hurt that Shaw and Cer had tricked her. She'd sat in front so Jory could explain things more easily. Now Vinnie turned, eyes brushing past TK who sat in one of the middle seats to the back bench seat where Shaw, Cer, and Nell sat.

"Can you read emotions from objects or was that just a lie to get the phone number?" Vinnie asked.

Shaw shifted in her seat. "I can read some emotions from objects. I didn't lie to you."

"You lied to me about why you wanted to see it."

Shaw looked away, toward the van wall.

The crunch of gravel under the tires signaled they'd arrived at the amusement park. Vinnie twisted back in her seat and stared out the front window and waited for Jory to park.

"Hey!" Hilda said as Shaw pushed past her to grab the handle of the sliding door.

"We did the right thing," Shaw said as she pulled the sliding door open. "Just because you guys were too chicken doesn't mean it was wrong."

She left the door open, and Cerulean scrambled after her.

"Will you guys let me move first?" Hilda said through her teeth.

Shaw had done what Vinnie had thought they should do. Maybe it hurt because they hadn't asked her or tried to bring her in on it. Would she have agreed? No, but they didn't even ask, and they'd given him their names? Shaw said it was a show of good faith. Hilda wanted to erase his memory like she had Gerald.

Something pressed against her leg from the pocket of her shorts as she climbed out of the van. The note. In all the excitement, she had forgotten to tell the others about the note. Would it make a difference now? Probably not. They hadn't wanted this, but now that they were here; they were going to get some answers.

The back parking lot was deserted, as the park had already shut down for the season. They would reopen for Halloween week, but that was weeks away. Shaw had stolen a key to the back gate when she worked here, which had been more shocking to Vinnie than her calling Will, as was her refusal to turn the key over to Jory.

Shaw had already unlocked the gate, and she and Cerulean waited on the other side for the rest of them to catch up.

The shop stalls were all closed, sliding boards pulled down to cover their fronts. Wood boards also covered the windows in the free-standing lots. On one of them, someone had spray-painted a nickname.

"You'd think they'd have an alarm system," Vinnie said.

"Police come by at night sometimes," Cer said.

She didn't want to know how he knew that, or if it had something to do with why Shaw had stolen the key.

Shaw had asked Will to meet them in Cowtown.

"How is he supposed to get in when he doesn't have a key?" Hilda murmured.

Shaw shrugged. "He'll find a way."

Cowtown was a mock old west town, so it seemed more fitting that it was deserted. It was like a ghost town.

They had arrived twenty minutes before the meeting was supposed to take place, wanting to be early enough they could get out of sight before Will arrived. They'd assumed he would arrive early too, and if they hadn't had to wait for Vinnie, they would have been even earlier.

The town had false store fronts, complete with front porches and swinging doors on some. Behind most of the fronts, there was nothing but a few props, usually, but the ones in the middle had risers for people to watch the old west shows and those had a large opening for people to see through.

Hilda headed straight for the saloon, followed by Jory. The others took up locations behind various fronts, leaving Vinnie standing in the middle of the street alone.

Her eyes caught movement at the end of the street, just before Will stepped around the back corner of the souvenir shop.

When he reached the front of the shop, he shifted his body, bowing his legs wide and holding his arm out like he was going to reach for pistols. When he was a few feet from her, he stopped. "This town ain't big enough for the both of us."

Trying to be funny again. Vinnie frowned.

He dropped his arms and stood up straighter. "This is a strange place for a conversation. Not even any place to sit."

Vinnie agreed. Plus facing off in the street as if this was a showdown felt confrontational. "The crew wanted to meet you somewhere neutral."

He looked at the buildings. "I suppose they're all here."

"Some," she said, wishing she could make this feel a little less like they were enemies in the wild, wild west. They'd decided Vinnie would talk to him because he already knew her face, not because she was the best interrogator. "What is it you want from us?"

"It's going to be like that, is it?"

"We're just talking," Vinnie said. "I need to know what you want before I can tell you if we can give it to you."

"We're not just talking." His head swiveled to the door of the saloon just before it swung open.

Hilda stepped out, and Vinnie tensed. *What is the point in making a plan if you're not going to follow it?*

"It is going to be like that," Hilda said, answering Will's earlier question. *I can't get a reading on him, something is off.*

His gaze swept Hilda from head to toe. She was the only person Vinnie had ever known who could look elegant in jeans and sneakers.

"You must be Hilda," Will said.

At least that answered the question of whether he knew anything about them. He couldn't have known this was Hilda if Shaw had only given him names.

Hilda sauntered down the steps. "And how do you know that?"

"I do my research," Will said.

"Hm," Hilda kept walking. She reached Will and walked

around him in a slow circle, giving him a more thorough once over than he'd given her. "And what does your research tell you, Mr.… Jo… Darrow? That's an odd name."

He'd lied to her about his name. *You got something?*

"You can read minds clearly, that's rare." Will's voice had dropped an octave, and his pose was relaxed, not concerned at all about Hilda's threatening stance. "Did you get that ability before or after you met Lavinia?"

"I've always had the ability," Hilda said, and she had. It was one of the first abilities she'd developed, and probably the only thing that had saved her as a child. "Why would it have changed when I met Lavinia?"

Some of the others did have new abilities, even it wasn't the one Will was asking about. Hilda moving air as she had when they'd caught Gerald, was new. Shaw's ability to read emotions from objects was also new, but Shaw had explained that she'd been working on that one.

Shaw says she can't get a read on his emotions. Maybe anger, but she's not sure.

That wasn't alarming. Shaw wasn't that close. *What's he thinking about?*

Last night's dinner, but not in a deliberate way like Gerald was doing sums, it's like he's actually thinking about steak and sweet potatoes.

Will grinned. "She seems like the type who would make you see new possibilities. Sometimes that's all you need."

Vinnie pulled some of Shaw's power and took a few steps until she was even with Hilda. She wanted to look into his eyes, hoping it would be enough. "You're lying." There, a tightening of his eyes, but she couldn't read his emotions. She rarely could unless she touched someone. Marching up to him and putting her hands on him seemed like a good way to announce she was Twisted too.

"Not at all. And my, you have such a pleasant personality." He was trying to goad her, the way she'd goaded him.

What's he thinking now? Vinnie thought.

Cheesecake. He's a Mesmer, it's like a record that he's playing.

He's not Twisted. There was nothing from him, not even a hint of power.

Another Mesmer planted the thought somehow, then.

That was also not an ability she'd even heard of, but maybe Hilda had.

The general store door opened, and Shaw came out, almost skipping down the steps until she was between Vinnie and Will.

We had a plan, she thought at Hilda.

The plan wasn't working.

Vinnie growled in frustration.

"There's that anger again," Will said. "At least it's not directed at me this time."

"Why wouldn't I be mad at you? You put us in danger, and you won't give a straight answer to anything."

More doors open and the crew came out. Jory from the saloon, Cer from the general store. Nell and TK from the bank. TK was wearing a ski mask, as if he had anticipated having to hide his identity.

Will smiled again. "I already know who you are, Terrance Kent."

TK stayed silent and didn't remove the mask. He followed the others as they moved to form a semi-circle facing Will. Shaw's eyes were wide, though her face was impassive. Fear rolled off her and the rest. Vinnie didn't need to feel emotions to feel that. They were panicking. The only one who wasn't afraid was Cerulean.

What are you guys doing?

Hilda ignored her. She faced Will, feet planted wide, shoulders tense. "Do you know who we all are?"

Will addressed Vinnie. "I put in a request in your metal box like you told me to, and Shaw called. I came here in good faith because your friends said they wanted to discuss helping me. Instead, I find an ambush. You've barely asked me any questions. How can I answer them? I'm the one who should be angry." He turned to Hilda. "Your friend told me your names. It wasn't difficult to figure out who was who. I was told Lavinia was the point of contact, but there was a full crew, all six types, with her as the manager as it were. Maybe my intel was mistaken?" He eyed Hilda.

"No, Vin's the boss." Hilda crossed her arms and cocked a hip as she eyed him. "You want questions? Who told you about us?"

He wasn't wrong. He'd come here thinking they were going to help him. Now they were all freaking out because Hilda and Shaw couldn't read him?

Will's eyes darted from Hilda to Vinnie, and he took a few steps back, holding up his hands. "I have obviously upset all of you, and that was not my intention. I just needed some help hunting a killer."

What had he seen in Hilda's face that made him nervous, when he had been calm before? Vinnie needed to see what was going on. All their backs were to her. She stepped through the semi-circle, feeling a frisson along her skin, and turned. Hilda's face was cold, impassive. Vinnie's eyes traveled along the circle and saw almost identical hard expressions.

Jory held up a hand and Will fell to his knees as if the strength had gone out of him. He couldn't do that. Jory had never used his power at a distance.

Hilda? What's happening?

"It's going to be like that, is it?" Will stayed on his knees. Calm seemed to have returned. "I already said that."

Vinnie wished she felt the same calm. Hilda's eyes bored into Will, and she didn't answer Vinnie's mental query.

Hilda stood up straighter. *There's a rope in the saloon on the wall. Go get it.*

What?

Vinnie!

"No," Vinnie said. "You're scaring me. What do you think you're doing?"

"He's blocking me somehow," Hilda growled.

"That's no reason to—"

Hilda broke out of the semi-circle and walked past Vinnie, wind following her wake. She put her hands on the sides of Will's head. "What's your mother's name?"

His eyes blinked heavily. "I had a mother."

"What was her name?"

Will's face twisted in pain.

"Hilda!" Vinnie started forward, but Jory caught her elbow. "Jory?"

Will was swaying like he was drunk. "It's okay, Evie, everything will be okay." He was talking to her. He seemed to be trying to focus. "Her name was Sarah."

"Liar." There was a compression in the air and Will flew back, landing on his back.

Enough. Vinnie jerked her elbow out of Jory's grasp. Vinnie tried to pull Hilda's power away but Hilda blocked her.

Hilda rounded on her — eyes wild. *You would put us all at risk?*

He hasn't done anything! Hilda's words had been strange, but Vinnie's head was buzzing, and she couldn't quite sort out why.

Take my power and look at him.

"I can't!" Vinnie yelled over the roaring in her head. "You're blocking me."

I'm not blocking you.

Vinnie felt Shaw at her back, and the roaring slowed. She reached for Hilda's power. It slammed into her, making her stumble.

Hilda's ice-blue eyes seemed to soften. She turned back to Will. A breeze lifted her hair, even though there was no wind. "How did you find out about us?"

Will's thoughts were in Vinnie's head, as clear as a movie. A man in the streets, wearing a red t-shirt over a potbelly. Will had heard a criminal was caught and did the man know? "I heard there was a crime boss caught and given to the police. I asked around."

Exactly what she had seen.

Will pushed himself into a sitting position, draping his arms over his knees, a slight tremor in his hand betraying his unease.

"You just came into a strange town and started asking about Twisted?" Vinnie asked him.

Vinnie saw a computer, and the fuzzy outline of someone before the image shifted to a news article from Providence, Rhode Island, and shifted again to fuzz.

Will sighed, lifting his hands to rub his eyes. "No, well, yes. I've been tracking the disappearances of Twisted and there are patterns, an increase in chaotic anomalies before it starts. That started here about a week ago. The Holt has a reputation of being a hotbed of unregistered Twisted. I've been unsuccessful, so I thought maybe it was time to ask for help."

While he talked, Vinnie got an image of him doing all these things, searching on the computer, walking among people, and talking to them. Too clear. She wasn't this good at reading thoughts — they usually came to her in impressions. This was what Hilda meant. The thoughts felt planted, as if someone put them in his head.

There had been a rash of anomalies popping up in the last week or two, mostly harmless, though one woman had been injured. That part of what he said was true.

She released the power back to Hilda and called up her own. Just because Will didn't have any ability didn't mean there wasn't anyone with magic. There.

He's not alone. There's a Mesmer outside CowTown, a few buildings back.

I can hear the other. It's like trying to listen through a wall with earmuffs. They must be blocking our attempts to read Will's thoughts. Now, why would they need to do that? I'm getting a boost from Cer. See if I can get past it. Her head tilted.

"One more time, Mr. Darrow, How did you find Vinnie? No one is supposed to know her name. We have procedures in place for anyone who wants to talk to us."

Will's mouth parted, and a small, confused frown wrinkled his perfect forehead. "The man at the convenience store on 52nd Street knew her name, what she was doing. If you're hiding, you aren't hiding that well."

Manny? Manny was an old man who ran a little shop. He'd had an issue with some local kids stealing things and they'd helped him. He had used the drop box to contact them.

"You're lying!" Hilda stalked toward Will.

He scrambled to his feet, hands clenched like he was about to attack, but then he released the hands and relaxed his shoulders.

"Sorry," Jory said. His voice was dull. "I can't hold him."

"I don't owe you any explanation at all," Will said. "I came here expecting a respectful conversation and you attack me." His eyes met Vinnie's. "I thought you were the good guys. This is who you associate with?"

A small jolt of guilt shot through her. She pushed it away. He had found them and refused to tell them the truth. He was neither angry nor scared about what was happening, but he wasn't resigned, either. His body was tense, like any minute he would spring into action and kick all their asses.

"You have exposed us and are lying to us. What did you expect? You want something from us but won't even give us the truth."

He took a few steps back, poised to run. It couldn't have been her words. A soft breeze lifted her hair, and she remembered being in the basement with Harry's wind. She turned.

Her friend's hands were linked, forming a small rainbow

facing her and Will. With her senses still open, she could feel their magic in the air, could feel it changing.

"What are you doing?" None of them were looking at her. The magic picked up, sounding like a hurricane in her head. She needed to get out of the circle, but she couldn't move.

Let me out of the circle. Her insides heaved.

We need you to ask how he found us. Hilda's voice in her head was flat and slow, like it was being dragged out of her.

"I'll tell you, don't hurt me," Will said. He had stopped backing away and stood frozen.

"We're not going to hurt you," Vinnie said, wishing she believed herself.

Ask

"Hilda, stop, this isn't the way. It's not even that important." Just because he'd found them didn't mean he'd tell anyone else. Their faces were all blank, eyes seeing nothing.

Ask

The power twirled and danced around her, stronger than any she'd ever felt.

Stop, whatever you're doing, stop. What if the Mesmer comes to his rescue?

Ask him, Vinnie.

Will swayed on his feet, head lolling. Maybe if she asked, they would stop. "How did you find us?" Vinnie asked. "How did you find me?"

Wind whooshed by her, ruffling Will's hair, and his arms jerked and pulled close to his body like he was being squeezed.

His head rolled from side to side, eyes blinking lazily. "I will always find you."

Her body shuddered at the words, the threat they implied, and Vinnie's bones ached. Her body called her to take it, to suck up all the power. She'd never felt that before, but her body craved the power, wanted every drop. She could just suck it up and she'd be so powerful, no one could touch her. Vinnie pushed the thoughts down. She didn't need the power. She didn't need it.

"How did you find me this time?"

His head turned away from her. "You will regret this, Lavinia. You're not the type of person who can live with this."

"I'm just asking questions." Fire burned in her back, and her anger rose.

Tell Cer to tone it down. But if Hilda heard her, there was no response. "I just. Need to know how you found us." To keep my friends, my family safe, to make this scary wild energy stop.

"I'm not a threat to you. I need you." His eyes were watering, making him look like he was crying.

"Are you reading my thoughts?" The sound of wind roared through her head now. She knew that there was no wind. Her bangs didn't tickle her forehead. Her body felt so far away from her thoughts.

"I am not like you," he said.

"What is that supposed to mean?" she yelled. "Answer the question!" Something took hold of her throat, and she couldn't feel her limbs anymore. *Hilda, back off, it hurts.*

We have to know.

And Vinnie could hear the voices of the others.

We have to know.

We have to know.

We have to stop.

What's happening, I can't stop.

Why doesn't he answer? I won't go back. It hurts so much.

Vinnie clutched her head, covering her ears as if that would make it stop, but it wouldn't stop. The voices got louder, and the wind got stronger.

STOP

We can't stop.

We have to know.

It hurts, it hurts, it hurts.

"How did you find me?" Vinnie's voice came out as a wheeze.

Will's mouth opened and he collapsed. His body lay on the ground, eyes open and staring. The wind was too strong. Vinnie couldn't tell if he was breathing. He looked dead. Was he dead? His eyes didn't blink.

They had to stop. She tried to relax, to shift her vision so she could see, but the noise was too much.

I can't hear his mind at all, Hilda's voice said. Vinnie could hear the panic, the pain. She didn't think Hilda was ever scared, but she was scared now.

Then Cer collapsed, his hands breaking the hold between Jory on one side and Shaw on the other. The sound in her head lessened and then got louder, but the sound wasn't wind. The sound was a roaring fire.

The sound shifted, growing louder, and something hit Vinnie in the chest. She stumbled.

You have to stop it, Hilda cried.

Me? But Vinnie couldn't think the words. She couldn't stop it. Nell collapsed, and the earth rumbled under their feet. Weight descended on Vinnie, dropping her to her knees.

"Stop!" A man stood over Will with a gun pointed at them, but they weren't moving, they couldn't do anything. After a few frozen moments, he seemed to realize this. He holstered his gun, knelt, grabbed Will's arm, slung it over his shoulder, and lifted.

Help. She wanted to call out to him, but they had already disappeared past the buildings.

Vinnie could feel the weight of the surrounding energy crushing her. How could she stop it? "Nell's... not... breathing," Jory's voice came through a sludge.

The power was crushing Nell.

Shaw dropped to her knees, water spewing from her mouth.

The power was all around Vinnie. Her friends had combined it but when Cer passed out, and then Nell, their power stayed in the connection, but they weren't awake to control it, it was overwhelming them.

She could feel it, though, just like she could feel the power in each of them individually. Vinnie pulled, gasping as it coalesced around her.

"Break. Connection," she told Hilda. "Break circle."

I can't just break it. It will snap back on you and kill you.

Hilda was probably right. Her thoughts cleared. *I've got it. I can take the power.*

The roaring stopped, and for a moment Vinnie thought they'd been wrong about the backlash. Then the magic hit her, shoving her face first into the ground.

If she could pull, she could push. Vinnie didn't stop to think about it, just shoved the power down into the ground.

The ground heaved and buckled. The buildings shook, parts of them crumbling and falling. When the shaking stopped, Vinnie lay on a small ridge, a foot higher than the rest of the ground.

Nell took a gasping breath.

CHAPTER NINE

The noise that everyone was making, the soft grunts and shuffling bodies, sounded like silence compared to the roaring that had been in Vinnie's head. The others were picking themselves up off the ground. All except Cerulean, who lay still and unmoving. She couldn't tell if his chest was rising and falling, but she could tell his eyes were closed. Unlike Will's.

"Did we kill him?" she asked.

Jory's head turned to Cerulean, and he reached out a hand to touch him. "Just passed out."

Hilda was on her feet, dust in her hair and a line of dirt under her nose that had clung to some snot. "I think she meant the douche."

The douche. Will had done nothing but find them and ask for help. Vinnie swallowed the pain down. He hadn't done anything wrong, had he?

"What happened?" TK said.

"I couldn't stop. I'm sorry I couldn't stop." Shaw's cheeks were wet with tears.

Nell reached over, wrapping her arms around her. "I don't think any of us could."

"Have you guys ever had that happen before?" Vinnie knew they hadn't. Unless they were practicing forming circles when she wasn't around. As far as she knew, the only time they used circles was to tamp down Harry.

"Noooo," Hilda said. "But we've never had a Vinnie push her way in before."

"I didn't push my way in. You formed the circle around me. It felt exactly like that time when we tried to put me in the circle with you guys — you trying to take over my mind. You were the one in control. What happened?" Vinnie's body was shaking. From anger or fear, she didn't know.

Hilda's face flushed. "I told you before, I wasn't trying to take over your mind. You're so paranoid. I have to guide the magic, that's how a circle works."

"Then why did you crush him?" No one had answered the question about Will.

"Guys," TK pushed the heels of his hands into his eyes. "Maybe you can save the drama for later? We need to get out of here. He could come back, and the earthquake is certainly going to attract attention."

"He's right." Jory used his foot to nudge Cer, almost rolled him over.

Cer moaned and Shaw moved into a crouch, grabbed his hand, and tugged him as she stood. Cerulean's upper body came up off the ground, but then flopped back down.

"If he won't wake up, I can carry him," Nell said.

Cer moaned again.

"Got it." She crouched, preparing to scoop him up like a bride, but he slapped her hands away.

"I'm up." He rolled to his stomach and bounced to his feet, then swayed, almost going down again.

Nell shoved her shoulder under his arm, offering support, and turned him toward the back gate. "You guys coming?"

Vinnie pushed herself up to follow. Shaw stood frozen, her

feet not budging as the rest of them started back to the van. Vinnie bumped her elbow with her own. She didn't know what else to say. Tears leaked from Shaw's dusty eyes, but she seemed unaware.

"Hey," Vinnie said. "We need to go."

"Was he dead?" Shaw wailed.

Vinnie wanted to say he wasn't because she was afraid Shaw wouldn't move, but she couldn't lie to her. "His friend will take care of him. We need to go." She tugged Shaw's elbow.

Shaw allowed Vinnie to guide her a few steps before stopping, wiping her eyes, and following the others.

When they reached the back gate, Cerulean stumbled forward and grabbed the lock, melting it.

"We have the key," Jory muttered. He pushed through the gate, and the rest of them followed.

"If we use the key, they'll know someone has one, probably someone who worked here," Nell said.

Sirens sounded in the distance as they reached the van.

"Those aren't for us." Jory slid the back door of the van open, and they climbed in.

All except Jory and Nell. She held out her hand. "I'll drive."

He handed her the key and got in the passenger side, slumping in the seat.

When they were all in the van, Nell turned to Hilda, "Can you hide the whole van?"

"Yep," Hilda said. "As long as you don't drive anywhere there might be another car, it should be safe. You can't stop at stoplights because they will try to occupy the same space, they will try to change lanes into lanes where you are. So yeah, if you don't drive on the road or anything, it will be perfectly safe."

Nell shoved the van into drive. "Do it." She pulled out, throwing gravel.

"Vinnie, take the power. You're better at air displacement than me."

If there was one thing Vinnie wanted no part of right now, it was Hilda's magic. She was right, though, Vinnie was better at it. She sat up straighter, rolled her shoulders, and pulled the power.

"Hilda was being sarcastic!" Jory said. "It's not safe. Why do we need to hide the van?"

Their voices grew more distant as Vinnie focused. She'd only done this for objects that were standing still because people could still see something reflecting light when it moved.

"They could be after us," Nell said.

Vinnie didn't know the exact mechanics of actual light reflection or displacement. She only knew it felt like pulling a cloak around an object. Now she needed to pull the air close and keep the cloak moving with them.

"That guy is not coming after us, and authorities will take their sweet time coming to look at a little rumble."

"Someone will come after us," TK said.

Nell slowed as she pulled the van onto the road. "Are we hidden or not?"

Her voice seemed to come from far away, and it took all the focus Vinnie had to answer. "Yes."

"Why are you so sure about that, Terrance?" Jory's voice was low, dangerous.

TK looked out the window. When he spoke, his voice was soft. "Dude was dead. And from the look of it, he had some powerful friends."

Dead. They'd killed him. Vinnie wasn't the only one who thought so.

Jory slumped again, defeated. "Maybe we'll just get ourselves killed before they can get to us then. Great plan."

"People can still see us," Vinnie said. "They'll just see a large shimmer and will avoid it. Later they'll think they were being paranoid."

What TK had said about Will being dead was knocking around in her mind, and she felt suffocated, squeezed into the back seat with Shaw and Cerulean. Cer squeezed her wrist. "You need a cupcake."

"Shaw, can you..." Nell said. "Maybe make people feel an aversion to where we are, to further discourage them?"

"I've never done that before," she rasped. Her eyes were wide, and her face had softened to be rounder, younger. Sometimes when she was feeling vulnerable, Shaw made her appearance more childlike, probably without even being aware.

"The danger will be minimal on the service road." Nell hunched forward, hands clenched tight on the steering wheel.

"Where are we going, Nell?" Jory asked.

"Somewhere quiet," Nell said. "Safe."

Not home, then. Vinnie tried to work up some curiosity, but she was too tired.

"Home is safe," Shaw said.

No one answered. The silence stretched on in the van until Nell broke it again. "You guys can let go of the power."

Vinnie let go of the power, leaned back against the seat, and closed her eyes.

When she opened them again, it was dusk and Nell was pulling the van up to a house in an open field. Tall grass surrounded it, but there were no trees or other houses for quite a way. Lights of a small town sat in the distance.

"Where are we?" Vinnie asked.

Nell unbuckled her seatbelt and threw it off. "Home."

By the time Vinnie was out of the van, Nell had opened the front door of the house. The house appeared faded in the dim light, but the smell of pitch in the air told Vinnie that Nell had had it re-roofed. Inside the house, the paint was fresh. There was no furniture in the small front living area, but Nell led them toward the back where there was a second living room sunk lower.

"A split-level," Jory said, as he took in the old sectional couch covered with crocheted blankets, a glass coffee table, and decorations that looked like something out of the sixties.

"This is where I grew up," Nell said.

Nell's grandmother had raised her, but her grandmother had died about three years ago. Beyond that, she didn't know much about Nell's life before they'd met.

"I'm sorry, I don't have it complete. I didn't expect to have to use it so soon. I only got permission to use it from my brother a few months ago."

"You knew we would need to hide when we started. You expected trouble." Vinnie felt stupid. Nell had seemed to believe in what they were doing as much as Shaw and Cer, but she had been preparing for the worst all along.

Being prepared doesn't mean she doesn't believe in your sweet little vision.

Stay out of my head. You don't do this to the others. Why me?

Hilda smirked at her. *Because I like you best. You're my little cupcake, all sweet and squishy and gross. Oh hey, I think I'll call you that. Cupcake.*

"It's not a good hiding place since someone could easily trace it to you," TK said

"I didn't do it to hide," Nell said. "But if we had to, it would be a good temporary place to give us room to breathe. My brother has a different last name and didn't grow up here. It wouldn't be that quick to trace the house to me. Unless you knew me or my grandmother. Or unless you're a cop. You think we're going to be running from the cops?"

"We broke into an amusement park and destroyed part of it," TK said. "We might be running from the cops."

"Then we've got bigger issues than we can solve tonight," Hilda said. *See, she didn't do it to hide, cupcake.*

Vinnie rolled her eyes. *You ever think of minding your own business?*

Hilda widened her eyes in mock surprise. "Neverrrrr," she whispered.

A laugh escaped Vinnie, earning a glare from Jory, who had been looking out the curtainless window. "Can we put something up over this?"

"I have some sheets," Nell said.

"Food?" Cerulean asked.

Nell waved toward the front of the house. "In the kitchen."

Vinnie followed Cer. She remembered the sick, roiling feeling and the way Will had looked dead. Eating was out of the question, but knowing there was food was comforting, and Cerulean certainly needed some. The others did, too. In the cabinets, she found cans of pasta and chili, saltine crackers, peanut butter, and a big jar of honey.

Cerulean grabbed the jar of honey and fished around in the drawers for a spoon. There was no way TK would eat the pasta, so Vinnie pulled out two big cans of chili, located a saucepan, and put them on the stove to warm.

Shaw had come in and was now staring at the surface of the cheap round table. "I have to go to work tomorrow."

Jory came through the doorway, followed by TK and Nell. "You'll have to call in. We all will," he said.

"We can't stay here forever," Cer said, a note of panic in his voice.

"We won't stay here forever," Nell said. "Just a few days. I'll go to work tomorrow and find out if there's anything about the amusement park being broken into and see if I can find this guy using his real name."

"If that's his real name." Hilda was leaning against the door. "His Mesmer was throwing all sorts of bullshit at me. I'd like to know how he did that."

"Is that what happened?" Vinnie asked. Vinnie didn't think it had been her power that had caused things to spiral out of control, but she couldn't be sure.

Hilda straightened. "I don't know what the hell happened."

"You just said—"

"You saw it yourself, the roast beef and cheesecake. He must have done something to our circle, too."

Oh. Vinnie had thought she meant why they'd lost control. Not the memories that weren't real. No one had given a straight answer about why they'd formed the circle.

Hilda marched toward the cabinet. "Why did you say he was in his forties? He was our age."

"Are you kidding?" Hilda was messing with her now.

"Hilda's right," TK said. "He couldn't have been more than thirty."

Vinnie tried to remember his face but just saw him lying on the ground, eyes to the sky. "Maybe it was his voice."

"Hm." Hilda had dumped several painkillers in her hand and dry swallowed them. "Whatever, I'm getting some sleep."

"I'll ride into town with Nell. She can take me to my car, and I'll bring back some groceries," TK said. He was picky about what he ate. It had something to do with when he was homeless for a few weeks before moving in with Jory four years ago.

"Risky," Jory said. "Anyone could follow you and Nell."

"Which is another good reason," TK said. "I'll be able to sense if either of the people who were out there today is near. If they are, we know it's not safe."

"Dead people don't follow you," Cerulean said. "I want to go home. I have cupcakes." He was frowning at a spoonful of honey. The jar was half empty already.

"We don't know he was dead," Shaw squeaked. Shaw's eye jumped to each of them, but no one would look at her. They all thought the same as Vinnie. He was dead.

"We're staying here," Jory grabbed the pot of chili off the stove and slammed it on the table and went to the cabinet for bowls.

The food couldn't possibly be warm yet, but Shaw, Nell, and even TK dug in without a word. Tomorrow TK would go with

Nell, in spite of Jory's protests, and most likely Nell would find nothing, and they'd all go back to their lives as if nothing had happened, but something had happened. For a moment, Vinnie longed to hear some sarcastic comment from Hilda in her mind. Anything to distract her from the memory of empty eyes, but it didn't come, and she was alone with the image playing a loop in her head.

CHAPTER TEN

Something thumped her foot — a flick of someone's fingers were smacking into the balls of her feet. First one foot, then the other. Vinnie cracked her eyes open and slanted them toward the window. The sky was pitch black.

Shaw crouched by her feet, prepared to flick again.

Vinnie curled her feet in. "Stop that."

"There's a big open field out there." Shaw stood and bounced on her toes. "We should try it."

Vinnie's entire body felt like a truck had run her over. She couldn't have slept more than a few hours. "Tomorrow." She mumbled and rolled over.

"We may not be here tomorrow night."

"Roof." They usually practiced on the roof of a nearby grocery store, which they'd found conveniently had a ladder. They could have just practiced inside the house since they were never successful, but she wasn't about to say that to Shaw.

"Viiiinnnieee," Shaw said. "You can sleep tomorrow. We'll be here all day. It's a huge field and I won't have to worry about being seen. Maybe I'll be able to relax."

Relax. Vinnie had been sleeping. Sleeping was better than

relaxing because she couldn't think about Will. The image of his lifeless eyes popped into her head, and Vinnie's eyes flew open, preventing the image from lingering.

The blanket she slept on smelled powdery, stale, and dusty, as if baby powder had gotten old and mixed with sweat. She'd been too tired to notice before, and now there was no way she was going to go back to sleep. Her body had just enough rest that her thoughts would distract her. Maybe this was a good idea. Well, not a good idea. Trying to transform into a dragon had never been a good idea.

"I can't sleep," Shaw whispered. "I keep imagining someone taking my power and controlling it, and I can't stop, and people die. He wasn't dead, was he?"

Vinnie didn't want to answer that any more than anyone else had tonight.

Groaning, she pushed the covers aside and sat. They were in Nell's bedroom, she'd opted to sleep on the floor, while Shaw and Nell shared the bed.

Vinnie grabbed her pants from the floor and pulled them on, then her t-shirt. Her shoes were in the living room.

Shaw was gone as soon as she saw Vinnie was getting up.

Vinnie passed Hilda sprawled on the couch with one arm flung over her face, on her way to retrieve her shoes and dirty socks. Shaw stood on the back patio, face turned to the sky, arms full of plastic water bottles.

"We should stay close to the house," Vinnie said as Shaw bounded off into the yard.

There was a lawn of sorts, but no one had mowed in a long time. There could be burrs. Or snakes.

"There could be snakes," Vinnie murmured, but Shaw was already skipping through the grass to the back fence. "Can we stay..." And there Shaw went, over the fence. "In the yard."

Vinnie picked her way down the overgrown path, trying to

avoid anything tall. Like grass. It was probably wicked, wicked grass hiding all sorts of deviltry.

"Are you ready?" Shaw called out just as Vinnie's feet hit the ground on the other side of the fence.

Ready? She was nowhere near ready. And Shaw dropped the water bottles and began stripping her clothes off. A shirt came flying at Vinnie and she scrambled to catch it, but it fell in the dirt. Vinnie bent to pick the shirt up just as a pair of pants hit her in the face. The pants she held with her left hand as she snatched the shirt with her right. As she tried to shake the dirt off, Shaw started doing little kicks and waving her hands. When she saw Vinnie had both things, she yanked her underwear down and unhooked her bra.

Vinnie glanced back at the house. "Do you really—?" But before she could finish, the undergarments were sailing at her too.

"I don't want to ruin them if I succeed. No one's looking, Vinnie."

When Vinnie had the clothing gathered, she opened to the power and relaxed her body. She needed to see and feel what was happening if she wanted to help.

The magic tingled around and through Shaw's body. Her legs became shorter, thicker at the top, thinner at the bottom, and bent like a cat or dog. Then Shaw's legs started turning green and the surrounding power shrunk so fast it looked like someone pulled a plug.

"Maybe don't worry about the skin, the texture change is pulling a lot of energy."

Shaw nodded and stood panting for a moment. She reached down and picked up one of the water bottles she'd brought along, draining it. Then her face screwed up in concentration as her torso thickened and her arms shone. The shrinking paused as Shaw's breathing became heavier.

Vinnie took a few steps closer. "Rest, hold up, you're over-doing it."

Shaw's head shook from side to side, and then her body suddenly shrunk, small wings sprouting on her back. Laughter escaped her lips as she looked at them. "I made wings."

Then she collapsed over on her side. Vinnie rushed forward with another water bottle, pulling it open. She knelt, lifted Shaw's shoulders, and poured water in her mouth.

The almost-dragon that was Shaw swallowed. This was not the first time Shaw had grown wings, but they looked a little more detailed this time. The form was almost right, but she was tiny for a dragon and still covered in human skin with human eyes and teeth.

"So creepy," Vinnie said.

Shaw grunted. "It'll be cool when I get it right. I got the wings."

Shaw struggled with texture. She could change her shape and appearance as a human, but she had a hard time with the texture of dragon scales, and she couldn't change her total mass like Nell could. But she was sure she'd find a way. Maybe she would. There weren't many verified instances of Dancers shifting shapes at all, but Shaw could change her appearance so much she was unrecognizable. She'd said she could even change her gender, but Vinnie had never seen her do that.

Shaw breathed in. Her body relaxed, and she reverted to her human form. This required less power because it was comfortable and familiar.

"Rats," Shaw said. "I tried to pull in more water from the environment like Nell said. She increases her mass by pulling from the earth, but I couldn't. It has to be possible."

Shaw thought transforming into a dragon was possible because she'd seen one. All sorts of creatures came through anomalies from time to time. There were animals like the ones in their world, strange things no one had heard of, and the occasional mythological creature, including Shaw's dragon. There had been at least two other dragons to come through, but who knew how many other things came through that no one knew about? The world at large didn't know about Shaw's dragon because he appeared over her parents' home in the middle of nowhere and turned into a man almost immediately. As far as they knew, Shaw was the only one to see his dragon form and so who knew how many things came through no one ever saw? Plus, anomalies blinked out sometimes just as fast as they appeared. The creatures and people who came through never lived long, and scientists thought it was because they didn't belong in this world.

Shaw's dragon had been a Dancer, like her. She said he was huge, so it had to be possible for her to increase mass, but he hadn't told her how. Only said she needed a vessel, which sounded to Vinnie like she needed to hold more power. The dragon-man hadn't been able to turn back into a dragon on their side of the anomaly.

Being naked on the dry ground apparently didn't bother Shaw, but something else was bothering her. Tears flowed down her cheeks. Vinnie didn't think she was crying because of the failed transformation.

"Let's try scales on your normal form if you have the energy," Vinnie said.

Shaw swallowed. "Okay."

She closed her eyes. Her magic swirled again, bending her skin in, and making tiny scales, starting at her feet, creeping up her legs.

Then, without warning, they rushed up her body, and a green-scaled human opened her eyes.

"Holy shit," Vinnie said. "You did it."

Shaw sat up and wrapped her arms around her raised knees. "I was scared before. But there are a lot worse things to be afraid of out there, aren't there."

Vinnie put her hand on Shaw's back. "I'm sorry."

"If you hadn't told us, we wouldn't have gone after him. If I hadn't called him... He was so convincing." Shaw turned to her, eyes shining in the night. "That power, Vinnie. So much more is possible. It was scary and out of control, but I felt like I could do anything. And you made an earthquake. Nell has never done that." She sat up straighter, eyes wide. "You try to change."

"What?" Vinnie had never tried to change her form because she didn't want to be anything other than herself.

"Yes, you made an earthquake. Maybe you can be a dragon."

"I don't want to be a dragon." She was here to support Shaw, not change herself, but Shaw was right. Something had happened out there, something they hadn't understood, and that was dangerous.

Shaw grabbed her hands. "But you can use our abilities in different ways, maybe you can do it and then you can show me how."

Shaw wanted to be a dragon so badly. The others thought it was a silly goal, useless, but Vinnie understood what it was like to want more control over your own body. "I'm more like a conduit. I don't understand your power any more than you do. And you've already used up so much tonight, I don't want to take more."

"You won't even try?" Shaw had shifted her eyes again to be larger than normal.

"Don't give me those puppy eyes. What if I can't shift back?"

Shaw snorted. "You probably won't even be able to shift at all."

Probably, and that was a scary thought. "I could too."

"Nah," Shaw said. "It's not as easy as it looks."

Was Shaw trying to comfort her into trying or taunt her? "It doesn't look easy."

"And it's even harder than that."

Vinnie snorted at the expression on Shaw's face. "You're a little button pusher."

Shaw grinned as if this were a compliment.

"Not a compliment."

"Totally was. It means I get my way. That's a good thing. And you can stop being a scaredy-cat."

Shaw had been sheltered, growing up on a farm, only allowed contact with the family, but she'd been away from home over a year and a half — long enough not to seem so innocent. "Being manipulative is not a good thing. For other people. And not for you either. And I'm not scared."

Shaw scooted forward and wrapped her arms around Vinnie. Vinnie, surprised, hugged her back. "Depends on if I use it for good or evil. You're hurting and you need to do something good, so you'll feel better, but you are scared. You don't want to do anything if you're not sure you can control it. But if you don't understand how it works, you make yourself vulnerable. I'm pushing you because I care."

Okay, scratch the innocent part. She was right. That's what had been spinning in the back of Vinnie's mind since last night. There was too much out there she didn't understand. Vinnie squeezed Shaw a little hard. "I'll try it."

Shaw squealed and bounced. She let Vinnie go and grabbed her shirt out of Vinnie's arms, pulling it on as she stood. "Pants?"

Vinnie passed her pants to her and stood up, brushing the dirt off her backside.

Shaw had her pants back on, shoved her underwear into her pocket and bra into her waistband, and waited.

All the lights in the house were still out. Vinnie wasn't as comfortable in her own skin as Shaw — or maybe she just didn't want people seeing her naked. Sighing, Vinnie pulled her shirt over her head and tossed it to Shaw.

"It won't work anyway. I'll leave my pants on."

"No one cares, Vin-nie."

"I would have to take my shoes off and there might be snakes."

"There are no snakes. I can feel animals too."

"Burrs," Vinnie said.

Shaw tilted her head and raised an eyebrow.

"Fine," Vinnie grumbled and reached down to pull her shoes off, then slid her jeans down over her hips, shimmying a little since her hips were a lot wider than her waist. When she stood back up, Shaw had her arms folded.

She couldn't really expect Vinnie to go completely buff. Anyone could look out the window. "No way, I'm leaving the underthings on. Ready?"

Shaw shrugged. "Yep."

Vinnie shook her hands and kicked her feet. This was why Shaw did it. She didn't need to warm up to use the power — it was just nerves. She closed her eyes and drew in a deep breath. Then her eyes popped back open. "Are you sure you have enough energy?"

"Vinnie!"

Vinnie closed her eyes again and pulled the power, felt it flow through her. Dancer energy always made her feel a little like her insides were being tickled. Now what? Vinnie had seen Shaw do this three or four times now but seeing wasn't the same as doing.

"Can you feel all the parts of your body? Try to feel every part, limbs and bones and veins."

Vinnie tried that. Starting with her toes, she could feel the bones in her toes, nerves, skin. This was a little creepy.

"And you just imagine it, it doesn't have to be complicated, the power knows what to do, it won't hurt you."

Imagine it, imagine what though? That her body was green and scaly? She imagined she was green and scaly. Nothing felt different, but she was too afraid to open her eyes. "Did it work?"

Shaw giggled. "No, you have to put your mind in the part you want to change. Like, your brain is not in your head, but in your knees or whatever. Oh hey, maybe make your hair grow or something since you've been growing it out, that's easier."

She was growing it out, and it was down to her shoulders

now, which made it so much easier to pull back out of the way, but if she could grow anything, Vinnie wanted bigger boobs, she'd always had a flat chest. Vinnie tried to imagine her mind was in her boobs. For Vinnie, using power was more than what happened in her mind. They all felt different in her body. Using Dancer power to read emotions felt natural, almost like she was experiencing the emotions herself. She felt them in her body, the anger, the sadness. Now the power sat in her body, and she felt a vague sense of Shaw's excitement in her chest, but she'd never tried to direct Dancer energy. Whose power had she directed? Jory. They'd practiced removing minor aches and fatigue, which meant she had to take the energy and send it out of her. Vinnie pulled at Shaw's power and directed it to her chest.

Shaw snorted and Vinnie knew by the tightness in her bra something had happened.

She opened her eyes and looked at her chest. Her A-cups were now a solid B. "But how does it know where to take the mass from?" She grabbed her new boobs. "And can I keep them?"

"Probably for an hour or two. See? It's easy. The power knows what to do, it's our minds that make it difficult. Try something harder."

What did a dragon look like? Her back legs would be shorter, and her face would be longer. She felt her face move and her heart sped up. No, no, no, that was too weird. She wanted her Vinnie face.

"Um," Shaw said.

Vinnie opened her eyes. "Whash?" Oh no, her face didn't go back. Her hands went up to her face, feeling her slightly elongated lower jaw. "Shith, shith, shith."

"Don't panic, don't panic." Shaw's magic washed over her again, soothing. "You know what your face looks like. You remember what your face looks like. And your body, it's okay. Your body knows. Let it go back to what it was."

Vinnie slowed her breathing, remembered what it felt like to be her, but nothing moved. Her breath hitched. What if she had a long face forever?

"Relax," Shaw said.

Relax. Relax. She knew how to relax. She'd had to practice for so long to keep from accidentally taking power. When she was little, her mind would just reach out and take some. People never noticed. Right now, she needed to be deliberate. Vinnie started at the top of her head and imagined that her scalp was relaxing, her forehead relaxing, her jaw relaxing. She knew what being at ease felt like. She knew what being Vinnie felt like, and the power did the rest.

When she opened her eyes, Shaw was grinning at her. "You did it. And you kept the boobs. Now for the Dragon!"

"I'm pretty sure my boobs have always been this big."

Shaw laughed.

"I think we need to get some rest. I promise I'll try again another time." The truth was, she was scared she wouldn't be able to get herself back if she did it again.

"Sure, okay." Shaw's posture said it wasn't okay, but Vinnie never wanted to be a different shape again. Except for the boobs.

CHAPTER ELEVEN

Vinnie's eyes had made it to the bottom of the page in the book in front of her, but her mind hadn't come along for the ride. She was back at the library, sitting on the stool at the counter. They'd stayed at Nell's house for two days. The police had determined the earthquake to be natural, which was ridiculous. No one had turned up dead, and Nell couldn't find anything about a Will Darrow, either, but that still probably hadn't been his name. A week had gone by, and nothing had happened.

Outwardly, everything was fine, but Vinnie's mind kept going down the same paths of guilt and worry and shame.

Zandia placed a book on the library counter. Her dark eyes looked concerned. "Are you okay? You look like you should have taken more time off."

Vinnie had told all the library patrons that she'd been sick for the two days she was gone, and she certainly looked like she could have been. Dark circles seemed to have taken up permanent residence under her eyes.

She smiled. "How would you get your books, then? I'm okay. I'm just not sleeping well. Just one today?" The book Zandia had chosen was a romance with a happy couple on the cover.

"I'm not done. I just thought I'd leave this here. Everything feels heavy today." Zandia patted Vinnie's hand and turned back to the library.

Everything did feel heavy today.

The front door opened, jingling the bell Vinnie had put up.

Carla, another regular, turned to glare at the bell. "What is that?"

"It's a bell so people can't sneak up on me," Vinnie said.

Carla hmphed, then her face softened. "That's a good idea. You never know these days. Maybe you should take some self-defense classes too."

That was… different. Carla held onto irritation like it was her job and she hated change. Unless the change was a new book.

"I don't think the neighborhood has gotten that dangerous," Vinnie said, but the response was automatic. The Holt had always been that dangerous.

"Not just the neighborhood, the whole world is dangerous." Carla ambled into the room, wide hips swaying. "My friend Martha's daughter has been missing for three days."

Vinnie uncrossed her legs and sat up straighter. Will had said that's how it started, people going missing. "What?"

Carla leaned on the counter. "Oh yeah, terrible thing. The police say she just ran away or is off on a bender or something. She was… is… she's seventeen. And she and Martha got into a big fight, but she's almost an adult. She wanted to skip school so she could see one of the Warrior Game events that were during the day. Her mom said she could watch the weekend ones, but the girl has some big crush on that Conor guy."

Vinnie didn't pay attention to sports. Particularly not ones that exploited Twisted. "That Conor guy?"

"Mm, I have a crush on Conor Hahn too." Zandia placed two more books on the counter.

"Zandia," Carla mock slapped her on the arm. "Anyway, Maddie is missing. The police say she just ran away, but

Martha says she wouldn't do that. She skipped school that day, though."

"Was she—" She couldn't ask that, though. Even if Maddie was Twisted, she was hiding it, and Carla likely wouldn't know. "There weren't any rumors, or anything strange about her, were there?"

Carla stood up straighter.

"Vinnie! In this day and age, girls can do what they want with whoever they want," Zandia chided.

"I think," Carla said. "She wants to know if there were rumors that the girl was special."

"Special?" Zandia made a face. "Oh, you mean, was she one of *them*? That would be something. Maybe they came and took her and didn't tell her parents?"

Carla glared. "She wasn't. She was perfectly normal."

"But if there were rumors…" Vinnie pressed.

"There were not, maybe once when she was a little girl, but she was perfectly normal. And even if she wasn't, they would have tested her and sent her back to her family. Honestly, Vinnie, why would you even say something so awful about a poor missing girl?" Back straight, she stalked off into the stacks before Vinnie could ask if they had tested her that one time when she was a little girl.

Carla might have been even angrier with her, but she'd know if it was a coincidence or something more.

That's what usually happened. Something strange happened, and they rounded up anyone who they suspected of doing it and tested them. They'd tested Vinnie several times, but they didn't have a way to detect her unusual ability. Yet. Both incidents had been her fault. Her fault that twice someone else had been discovered and taken away. One of them had later died. She hadn't understood her ability and used it without thinking the first time. The second time had been on purpose, and just because she hadn't thought all the consequences through didn't mean that she wasn't responsible for that death. Now, with Will, that made two people who had died because of her.

She didn't want there to be a third. If they'd tested the girl and she passed, then her disappearance was just a coincidence and not Vinnie's fault for getting in the way of someone who wanted to stop a killer.

Zandia tapped the books on the counter. "You think she was?" she said so softly Vinnie barely understood her.

"I don't think they take people without notifying the family," Vinnie said. But she wasn't sure. There were accusations, horror stories, and conspiracy theories. When her mom was taken, they talked to her at school, no secrecy. *Your mom was a Mesmer, Vinnie, did you know?* No, she'd said, and she'd believed she didn't know when she was five. Only when she was older did some of her memories of her mom make sense.

"What if she snuck off to the games without her ID? And then..." Zandia shuddered. "They took my nephew. He never hurt anyone. Works in the ORs in Nevada now. They only let us see him once a year."

ORs- Outbound Registered were Twisted that were trusted enough to work outside the camps. Most ORs had been taken as children but some who went in as adults made it into the government crews or were hired out to private companies. If he worked in the ORs, that meant he still worked for the government and not a private company.

What could Vinnie say to that? Better than the camps? She was sure it was, but that didn't mean it sucked less. "They took my mother when I was five."

"You were tested?" Zandia said.

Children of Twisted were almost always tested. They loved to get them young. Vinnie nodded. "You?"

Zandia shook her head, mouth tight.

Vinnie entered the books into the computer check-out system, glad she didn't have a scanner like the downtown libraries. She liked having the extra time to talk to her customers. After she'd bagged the books in the canvas tote Zandia had brought, she asked. "Do you need help out?"

"You know I don't," Zandia said. Despite her early complaint, Zandia was strong and fit for someone nearing seventy. "And you're going to have your hands full in a minute."

Vinnie didn't have time to wonder why she'd said that. As soon as the bell rang, signaling Zandia's exit, Carla stalked back up to the desk.

"The new releases are exactly the same as last month. None of them are new."

"Donations are down this month, and I need to save money to repair the door. We have five new books this month, but I already checked them out to other patrons."

Carla's irritation didn't wane. "The computer is down again too."

The library had one computer for a card catalog and internet access. Ordinarily, she would ask if Carla would like to donate. Carla would stalk off in a huff and find a book and check it out and that would be that, but she wanted to ask more about the girl.

"Let me look." The card catalog was on the back wall, across from the front desk. Vinnie had situated the computer so that she could see the person using it but turned to the side where she couldn't see the screen, so they'd feel like they had more privacy when searching.

When she got there, the screen was blue. She pressed the power button, holding it down until the computer began the reboot process.

Vinnie kept her eyes fixed on the screen and tried to sound casual. "You don't think the girl.... What was her name again? Ran away?"

"Maddie was afraid of her own shadow. And no wonder, her

parents hovered. Never let her do anything on her own. What do they call that? Helicopter parenting."

"But she was bold enough to skip school on her own?" That didn't quite mesh.

"Martha said she had some new friend, some troublemaker. Using Maddie. The other girl probably talked her into it."

What would she use a scared girl for? If Maddie was Twisted or had some sort of ability and the other girl found out, then it made more sense. And overprotective parents didn't mean that she was Twisted but it certainly could. Shaw's parents had gone to extremes, and they wouldn't be the only ones.

The computer booted up normally, and Vinnie entered the library password and moved out of the way.

"There you go," she said. "I hear there are people that will investigate things the police won't. Have Maddie's parents considered that?"

"No justice is better than vigilante justice." Carla sat down. "Just as likely to kill her as to save her."

Will's blank eyes, open and staring up at the sky, popped into Vinnie's head. "I haven't heard of anyone dying." Maybe Will hadn't been dead and there was another explanation.

Carla's mouth twisted as she typed in her search. "Not yet, but that's the way it works. I've seen it before. Some do-gooders decide they know best, people get hurt, and the people who caused the damage disappear."

The assessment stung, but Carla was a bitter, complaining woman. "You've seen it before?"

Carla's face scrunched. "Didn't you hear about that massacre a few years ago?"

Vinnie knew there had been some gang violence in The Holt just before she'd arrived. That was how Nieves Delgado had taken over La Mafia. She wouldn't have called him a vigilante or someone trying to do good, and all the dead had been members of the gang, no bystanders. Still, Vinnie wanted no part of anything like that.

Carla turned the computer screen away, making it clear she was done talking, so Vinnie went back to the front desk and plopped her butt in the chair.

What if the serial killer had taken this girl, and she ended up dead because of what they'd done? The thought was a new groove in the well-worn pattern of the last week. Until now, the victim had been hypothetical.

Nell couldn't find anything because the criteria were too broad. Even if there was an increase in chaotic activity and anomalies, that happened everywhere at some point. An increase in missing people also occurred where the anomalies increased because they could swallow people or people would step into them deliberately and never come back.

It should be simple enough to look for cities with an increase in chaotic activity and compare with missing persons or deaths. Nell's theory was that, if there was a killer, they chose these cities because of the anomalies — authorities would be much less likely to worry about more missing people.

What about Warrior games, though? Would anyone have noticed if there was an increase in chaotic activity any time they were in town?

The games were traveling games, moving to a different city every few months with two seasons per year. Whatever city they moved to came up with a theme, and teams of competitors competed in various sports and obstacles. The obstacles themselves were at least partially created by teams of Twisted. Vinnie had watched one a few years ago in California where the competitors raced boats, surfed, and swam through rough waters and winds created by Twisted.

Vinnie woke her computer up and typed in a search. She looked up all the cities the games had been in the last few years. Then she looked up the first one to see if there was an increase in chaotic activity and there was. Excitement tingled in her abdomen and she moved on to the next one.

The bell over the door rang, startling her out of her focus. A young man stepped in and paused. He frowned at her and the books. "Sorry, wrong door." And he was gone again.

Vinnie shook her head. The library was in a basement, with a door that clearly said it was a library, yet people still wandered in, confused from time to time.

Carla placed a book on the counter. "He is a good-looking devil."

"What?" The man had been scruffy, and a little greasy looking.

Carla nodded at the computer, and Vinnie turned back. Her cheeks warmed at a full-page spread of Conor Hahn.

"Research." She grabbed the book and changed tabs so she could check Carla out. "And what did you say Maddie's last name was?"

"Mm-hm." Carla smirked. "I didn't say." She took her book and left.

Vinnie turned back to the computer. Conor Hahn was a good-looking man. Blond hair, slightly bleached out from the sun, blue eyes, the perfect amount of eye crinkles from his huge smile.

She shook herself, clicked off the page, and went back to the next city of the Warrior Games list. That one also had an increase in anomalies. She kept searching. In every city the games had been in the last two and half years, there had been an increase in anomalies. Conor Hahn had joined the Warrior games three years ago.

Then she looked at training schedules. Once, the anomalies increased in the town where Conor Hahn's team trained, but only once. There were no missing persons or murders in the news at the same time.

But all missing people didn't make the news, right?

A quick search turned up a database of missing people and

unidentified bodies. People had gone missing in three of the four cities around the time frame that the Warrior Games were in town, and one in the city where they'd trained.

That didn't mean that it was a serial killer. People went missing all the time. But almost every town having an increase in anomalies in the last two years seemed too big to be a coincidence.

Vinnie started looking for anything unusual about the people who had disappeared, which was much harder, even in the days of people putting their entire lives on the internet. There was only one unexplained death that was strange. A young man had been missing for days and they found him hanged in an empty house with a suicide note. His family raised a stink, saying that he would never have done that and that the note didn't sound like him.

That didn't prove anything at all.

Still, Vinnie pulled open her desk drawer to pull out a pad and paused. The card Will had written his phone number on stared at her. He wasn't dead, she told herself again. He was probably out there, looking into this right now. Vinnie took out the pad and pen, wrote the boy's name, and continued her search.

Vinnie wrote all the names, the names of the missing, the names of the dead, and descriptions of unidentified bodies. There were fourteen people on the list. She wrote Maddie down, bringing the total to fifteen.

Maddie, who had wanted to go see Conor Hahn.

She put a big star next to the name of the boy and continued her search. When she'd gotten through five of them, her computer chimed, telling her it was time to go home. The property manager had the electricity on a timer, and it would turn off in half an hour. With no computer at home, she'd have to wait to continue the search.

Her hand hovered over the mouse. If Maddie was out there now, taken by a killer, how much time did she have? Vinnie clicked back to the Warrior Game's website. The home page was like a giant advertisement, and there was Conor on the front page, along with four other athletes. Vinnie clicked on his profile. Three years, she read the dates again.

That still didn't prove anything.

Definitely.

She tapped her fingers on the desk as she stared at his picture. There was an event going on right now. A stadium event, which meant not too far away, and Hilda worked close enough she could pull some magic. If she could get close enough, she might get some vague impressions. She wouldn't be able to read the thoughts clearly, but if he were thinking about anything strongly, say a girl locked up in his basement, she might get that.

That was a crazy thought and a long shot. She should just leave it alone, but what could it hurt? The worst that could happen was nothing, she'd have no new information, that's all. Decided, Vinnie shut down the computer and gathered her things.

CHAPTER TWELVE

The stadium was a marker in the middle of the city. On one side, you were in the city proper, and on the other, you were in The Holt. Vinnie stepped off the bus, still in The Holt. The stadium loomed at the end of a street a block from where she was standing. It had been the last destination of the parade, and now it was her destination.

The walk was too short, and the tiniest trickle of unease settled in Vinnie's abdomen as she crossed the street, same as it did every time she stepped out of The Holt. Maybe because The Holt was the first place, she'd felt safe since she was a child, and they took her mom away. Or maybe being surrounded by Twisted was subtly soothing to her, just like being near Harry.

The stadium straddled the line between home and 'out there.' But even on The Holt side, where there was less money, some fancier places had sprung up, like the day spa where Hilda worked as a receptionist.

The spa was about two blocks away, and Vinnie could feel Hilda among the few other Twisted moving around in the neighborhoods beyond. There was also a large cluster somewhere on the other side of the stadium — probably the crews that made the obstacles for the games.

Vinnie had arrived just as people were filing out into the packed parking lot, and the futility of being here struck her. It wasn't like she could just walk up to the stadium and demand to talk to Conor Hahn. Even if she could, what would she say? But she didn't want to go home yet.

Maybe if she walked around the stadium, she could convince herself there was nothing she could do, and that it was too late, and that feeling guilty wouldn't solve anything. She could tell herself she'd tried to do the right thing. That had never made her feel better about what happened in high school, but maybe this time.

Vinnie dodged cars and people as she made her way closer to the stadium. The last time she'd been here was two years ago for a concert, and she hadn't explored — she'd just gone in the front gate and back out when it was over. There had to be other exits for the teams, right?

She made it to the side wall of the stadium and followed it around two curves until she was on the side opposite where she'd started. Ahead, there was a fenced parking lot with buses inside. When she was close enough, she could see the buses had team names on the side. A little hum of excitement tickled her. When she was sitting in the library, it hadn't seemed that difficult, just get close to the teams and maybe she'd hear something, and here was the possibility that she would see them.

Conor played for the Tigers and, as luck would have it, their bus was the second one closest to the fence. She should be able to see them as they left the stadium.

Never mind that she could barely read thoughts up close. This would work.

Vinnie eyed the distance between herself and the nearest bus and reconsidered. There was no way this was going to work unless she got closer. There had to be a gate somewhere, right?

She walked along the fence line and came to a small, padlocked gate door. The gate where the buses got in was probably similar. There were no guards. Maybe they didn't have trouble with crazed fans climbing six-foot fences.

Only six feet. Vinnie grabbed the fence, stuck her foot between the wires, and climbed. The wire felt like it would cut through her palms, but in a few moments, she was at the top. Anyone could see her up here. The main parking lot wasn't far away. She scrambled over and dropped to the other side. The impact jarred her leg, and she winced.

This was pure idiocy. Still time to climb back over. Just as she had the thought, the doors to the stadium opened and a few people in team sweats came through.

Still time. She glanced up at the fence and back at the team. Give up or stick with the plan and try to hear something? There were wide lamp posts stationed all over the parking lot and one of them was near the front of the Tiger's bus.

Decided, Vinnie skittered toward it, hoping that no one noticed before she could hide better. When she got to the lamp pole, she reached out, found Hilda's magic, and pulled, ignoring the twinge of guilt at pulling so much energy. Hilda might have a wicked headache later. With the Mesmer power, she focused on the surrounding air until the molecules became almost visible. Then she pulled them close, making the air dense so she would be almost invisible. If she was still, no one should see her.

Now to juggle two things with the power at once, because *that* should be fun and easy. Vinnie held on to the air and tried to open the Mesmer ability to hear thoughts. Fuzzy murmurs of thoughts entered her head from the teams boarding the buses. Hunger, thirst, body pain, so vague and distant, she couldn't even tell who they were coming from.

The teams boarded the buses, some tired, head down. Others laughing and talking, but no one was thinking about kidnapping or murder. Or if they were, she certainly couldn't tell. She was an idiot, and this was a colossal waste of time. Now she had to stand here until they were all gone.

Vinnie sagged against the post. She could be home by now. After what seemed like an eternity, the first bus was at the gate, ready to pull out. Four more to go.

What are you doing? Hilda's voice startled Vinnie. She sounded angry.

There was no way she could tell Hilda what she was doing. *Hilda! Just borrowing a little. I stopped at The Rope for a quick drink after work and there's this guy —*

Hilda jerked the power away. *My power is not your toy.*

Hilda! I need — It didn't matter, though. The buses were across the parking lot. Even if someone saw her, they would just think it strange. Vinnie dreaded the climb back over the fence.

"Hi."

She whirled and stood facing Conor Hahn, five feet away, in street clothes with a duffle bag thrown over his shoulder.

"Hi?" Vinnie squeaked.

"Are you a coach? You look a little young, and I don't think I've seen you before."

Could it be that easy? But no, the way he was smiling at her. He knew she wasn't a coach. At least he looked amused? Maybe it amused him to find another victim so soon. No, he couldn't know that she was Twisted. Unless he'd just seen her appear out of thin air. Dammit.

"I—um, no, I think I'm lost?"

He took a few steps closer. "Lost, huh?" Conor's eyes traced the fence that surrounded the entire parking lot. Nope, no way anyone could get lost and end up in here.

"I—-I climbed the fence?" She tried to look sheepish.

He was still smiling, and that smile seemed more blinding than it had in photos, his eyes even more perfect. "Looking for anyone in particular?"

Say something, fast. But if she took a moment to think, he

would think she was just star-struck, right? That was better than the truth. Maybe. Ugh. She needed help. Vinnie cast her net out, searching for someone with an ability she could borrow.

There was a slight tingle from Conor that didn't feel like any kind of ability that she knew of, but it didn't feel normal either.

"I'm sorry." He stepped even closer. "That was a hard question, I see. Let's start with something easier." He held out his hand to shake. "I'm Conor."

Her hand lifted automatically and connected with his. His hands were rough, calloused, and the tingle increased.

"I'm Nia." She cringed. Vinnie hated that nickname. Why had she said that? Only her dad called her that.

He bobbed on his knees and adjusted his bag in a way that made him seem almost shy. "Nia, you don't look like a Nia."

Her smile was automatic, as if her face had a mind of its own. "It's short for Lavinia."

He smiled even bigger — how was that possible? Dimples appeared on his cheeks. "Ah, yes, that's more like it. You look like Lavinia with the dark hair and the..." He waved his hand around his face and laughed self-consciously. "And green eyes. I'm sorry. I go full dork around beautiful girls alone in parking lots."

Her smile fell. Vinnie forced her cheeks back up and held still to keep from glancing around. She was alone in a parking lot with someone who might be kidnapping and murdering people. His smile had made her forget.

If she kept him talking, maybe she could learn something. "Just women alone in parking lots?"

"Oh, my god." He covered his face with his hands. "That came out creepy, didn't it?"

She held her thumb and index finger close together. "Little bit. Why didn't you go with the rest of the team?"

"I have an errand to run, so I brought my rental car today. Hey, do you want to go with me? Maybe we could grab dinner?"

An errand. He probably wouldn't check on a girl he kidnapped if he was inviting her along.

Unless he meant to lock her up, too. Vinnie knew she was being paranoid, but Maddie had come to see him, and where he was, people went missing.

"I need to get home." She backed up. "People are expecting me and would definitely notice if I didn't show up on time. Good thing I told everyone where I was going." Smooth.

His face showed his confusion. "I'm sorry. I didn't mean... I keep apologizing, and yet you're the one in the parking lot where you're not supposed to be." He ran his hands over the back of his head. "I should go, too."

He turned away, and Vinnie felt a loss. She hadn't gotten what she needed, because she was being a scaredy-cat, but she had no protection.

"Wait," she said, and he turned back. "You're right. I'm the one who should be apologizing. I didn't want to say because—" Vinnie took three steps, put one hand on his arm, and looked in his eyes. "A friend of my little sister's disappeared a few days ago. She was a big fan of yours and last we heard she was coming to the games. I—" She looked away, trying to ignore the tingle, and wishing she hadn't seen the flash of anger in his eyes when she asked about Maddie. Conor Hahn was angry when, a few moments ago, he'd been smiling. It was all she could do not to run.

He returned to smiling and his hand came around and squeezed hers on top of his. "What was her name? I'll ask around."

Sure. Sure, he would. "Thank you. Her name is Maddie." His startled reaction was impossible to miss — the widening eyes and parted lips.

He pulled away and swung his bag around to the front and dug a marker out of the side pocket. He held it out to her, then held his hand out, palm up. "If you'll give me your number, I'll call you if I hear anything. Or maybe to see if you'll take me up on dinner another time." Her face must have been incredulous because he continued. "I know, probably inappropriate, but I think you've bewitched me with those eyes."

Yeah, she should just give her number to a potential serial killer.

His lips quirked as she stared at him.

Say something. Idiot. What harm could it do? The house number was unlisted. It wasn't like he could find her entire name or where she lived from it, right? Will had to have had some other resource that an athlete, even a professional one, didn't have. If he was a serial killer, getting closer to him might help her find Maddie.

He winced and opened his mouth to say something. Vinnie grabbed his hand in hers and scribbled the phone number for the house.

CHAPTER THIRTEEN

Vinnie stepped off the bus a few blocks away from home and wiped the smile off her face. Conor Hahn was a potential serial killer, no matter how genuine his smile looked. Even if he wasn't, she had serious things to think about. She had no time for the warmth that had curled up in her abdomen, and she needed to focus.

On the ride, she'd gone back over the day and wondered if she was seeing things that weren't there. What were the chances that one of her patrons knew a girl who disappeared a week after Will told them a serial killer was kidnapping and killing Twisted? And that the girl was going to see Conor Hahn right before disappearing. If he were the killer, would he have done something so obvious?

This was all probably nothing, but she felt better than she had in a week. If this was a lead, maybe they could help. This wasn't as dangerous as helping some guy they didn't know, and the others would see that. She'd have to apologize to Hilda for drawing power, but she'd had a good reason. Vinnie pushed the smile off her face again as she went up the front steps.

Music blared through the door, so Vinnie was prepared for

the blast of sound when she stepped inside. Shaw came sliding toward her in her socks, did a little wiggle, then ran a few steps back the other direction and slid again.

"Are you ready?" Cer called out from the back of the hall.

"Ready! You'll want to get out of the way, Vinnie!"

Vinnie side-stepped into the living room just as a tennis ball came flying down the hallway, then another and another. Shaw ducked and dodged and spun in the narrow space. Not one hit her.

"You got 'em all!" Cer came to the front as the balls bounced madly around the room. He put out a hand, slowing them down.

"Whoa," Vinnie said. "Where'd you learn that?"

He grinned. "I learned about friction. It stops stuff. That's why things can't keep going and going. Gravity makes friction and they stop."

That didn't explain how he'd stopped them. "Okay?"

"Friction is things rubbing together." He was expecting her to understand. "That's what fire is, things rubbing together, and they get angry and agitated."

Comprehension dawned. "You agitated the air around the balls?"

His smile grew and Vinnie knew that's what he'd done. Or what he thought he'd done. Wisps shouldn't be able to control air, should they?

"Did you see me move, Vinnie? I was so smooth!" Shaw said.

"Yes, you were. Smooth like water," Vinnie agreed. This was why they sometimes discovered Dancers in the martial arts, and as actual dancers.

"I gotta get ready for work." Shaw ran toward the staircase and slid, grabbing the banister to stop herself. "Oh, Vinnie!" Shaw's voice was teasing. "Conor Hahn called. He thought I was your sister. He wanted you to call him back. Something about dinner? Did you get a date with Conor Hahn?"

He'd already called. There had been a bit of a wait for the bus, but it hadn't taken her that long to get home — less than an hour.

"Why is Conor Hahn calling, Vinnie?" Hilda asked, startling Vinnie. She hadn't heard the door open with all the noise. Hilda closed the front door behind her. "Did you bump into him at the bar?"

"I... um..."

Hilda pushed past her. "Can you turn that music off? Or Down?" she shouted.

Cer scrambled over to the old-fashioned stereo by the side wall, clicking it off before hunkering down on the couch and grabbing the headphones attached to the video game console.

Jory's head poked out of the kitchen, and Hilda brushed past him too. "What's going on?" he said as he pulled his head back into the kitchen.

Shaw had already disappeared to get dressed for work, which left Vinnie facing Jory and Hilda alone. She straightened her shoulders, hung her bag on the coat tree, and marched down the hall.

Hilda turned just as Vinnie came through the door, a glass of wine in her hand. She leaned against the counter, waiting.

"I wanted to see if I sensed anything at the stadium. I ran into him. He asked for my phone number."

"Why did you say you were at the bar?"

"I was hiding. I didn't want to spend ten minutes trying to explain."

Jory was gathering some sketches up off the table with stiff movements. He worked in construction but was taking some online architectural drawing classes. His eyes darted between the two of them as he put the drawings in his portfolio.

"You can explain now," he said.

Her earlier hope that they'd change their minds and agree to look into the disappearance vanished with the look on their faces. "One of my regulars has a friend whose daughter is missing. She might be Twisted."

"Jesus, Vinnie." Hilda unfolded her arms. "This is about that guy again. I thought we agreed to let it go."

"Is this about amusement park guy's theory?" Jory said. He'd sat back down at the table, but he seemed poised to leap back up. The scar on his neck bulged with tension.

Vinnie swallowed. "You guys shut down The Dragons. I never agreed to stop trying to figure out why he contacted us, and I think he was right, something is going on."

"You're basing this on a teenager running away?" Jory asked.

Hilda dropped her arms and leaned forward. "If he was right, then let him handle it!"

Jory's question was valid, but Hilda's response made Vinnie angry. "He's dead, Hilda! He's dead because of us. How can he handle it?"

Shaw appeared in the doorway. "I have to go to work," she said, her voice barely audible. And she slid away, head down.

"You've upset Shaw," Jory said, a dangerous note in his voice. His fingers curled into fists.

Vinnie reminded herself that he would never hurt her, no matter how angry he got. All the scars on his hands were not from his time in the dead end camps. Some were from fists colliding with people's faces. Some in The Holt called him the preacher, but Jory was no saint.

Despite her reassurances to herself, Vinnie felt some tension ease when Nell came into the kitchen. She'd just gotten off work, too, and was still in her black slacks and heels.

Vinnie kept her eyes away from Jory's scarred hands as she sat at the table. "Jory, there may be a serial killer killing Twisted. The girl skipped school to go to the games. She wanted to see Conor Hahn. For the last two years, any city that hosts the Warrior Games sees an increase in anomalies. Conor joined the games three years ago. People go missing in the months the games are in town."

"People go missing all the time, and the games are usually in big cities." Nell sat at the table next to Jory. "But the rest of that sounds strange. I can look into it."

"No," Hilda said.

"Excuse me?" Nell half stood, tensed as if she was ready to fight.

Jory uncurled his hands, splaying them on the table. "Vinnie went to the stadium, somehow bumped into Conor Hahn, and gave him our phone number. He called."

Nell's mouth opened and closed. Then she grinned. "Conor Hahn called you?"

"This is not something to smile about," Hilda said. Nell had relaxed her stance, but Hilda looked like she was ready to brawl. "Someone went into the library and told Vinnie a girl was missing and she went off on her own and gave what she thinks is a serial killer our phone number. She's as bad as Shaw and Cerulean."

That wasn't fair. "I'm not putting anyone in danger. He doesn't know who we are. He doesn't even know my last name. And it's not like I'm going to return his call."

"You put *yourself* in danger," Jory said. "Do you think that doesn't matter to me? To any of us?"

Vinnie opened her mouth. Hilda and Nell were looking at her, waiting for her to say something. Were they all worried about her? Would she be angry if one of them had done what she had done? She hadn't been angry at Cerulean and Shaw because she understood the need to help. She didn't want her friends to get hurt. She'd hurt enough people in her lifetime without adding to that, but she couldn't just do nothing.

She'd just said that she wouldn't call Conor, but she would. Vinnie had already decided she would. How could she make them understand?

"I can't sleep at night," she said. "I see Will's face when I close my eyes, and in my dreams, there are bodies everywhere. And if he was right, then…. I just want it to stop. More people could die because of something I did. I have two dead because of me already. I don't want more."

"We don't know that he was dead. People can get knocked out and look like that," Nell said.

Jory's shoulders relaxed, and he rubbed his hands down his face, suddenly looking much, much older than his twenty-nine years. "The high school bully wasn't your fault, either. Maybe we screwed up, but this is not something we can fix."

Hilda put her empty wineglass on the counter. "Are we forgetting that Vinnie gave this guy our number? He *can* find us, and unlike Miss My-ability-can't-be detected, all of ours can."

"He can't find us easily," Jory said. "I think Vinnie's right about there being no danger there, but we need to leave this alone."

Hilda lowered her eyelids. "We should just kill him."

"We are not killing him!" Vinnie said. "What is WRONG with you?"

"One less douche in the world seems like a win-win."

"We aren't killing anyone," Jory said.

"Mm, bummer," Hilda said. "But hey, you can have a hot date, Vinnie. How long's it been?"

Jory stood, placing his palms flat on the table, and leaned toward Hilda. "If someone associated with the games is killing Twisted, she is staying as far away from him as possible."

It was like he hadn't even heard her.

Hilda strolled forward, placing her hands on the table, mirroring his pose. "I'm pretty sure you are not her father, or boss, which means you have no say in what she does or does not do, and if you didn't notice, Vinnie already said she was going to do something. I'm guessing that means she will call this guy even though she just told us she was not."

Vinnie would have been warmed at the defense, but Hilda wasn't defending her, just arguing with Jory.

"Are you guessing or are you reading minds without permission again?" Jory asked.

Vinnie looked at Nell, whose eyes were darting between Jory and Hilda. "Should we do something?" Vinnie mouthed.

Nell shook her head, pointed at the kitchen exit, and mimed walking out with her fingers. She was joking, of course.

Had Vinnie really thought they would help once she told them what happened? It seemed silly now. The people who'd agreed to form The Dragons all those months ago were an illusion she'd believed. Of course, they wouldn't help. Even though Will was gone, and this was their screw-up and their responsibility, they didn't want to do anything.

Hilda's stormy eyes turned to Vinnie. "Because it wasn't our fault. Don't you get it? We have never lost control of our abilities like that. How strong was that Mesmer with Will?"

"What did we miss?" Nell said.

"Vinnie is shocked the rest of us don't want to fall on our swords and kill ourselves because something went wrong. Just because she wants to off herself doesn't mean the rest of us should." Her eyes flashed toward Jory. "And no, I can't always turn off my abilities at a time that's convenient for everyone. Blocking thoughts takes energy too, and Vinnie is LOUD."

She was serious. Vinnie thought she was joking all those times she said her thoughts were loud.

"No one is falling on their swords!" Jory said. "Vinnie is letting this go."

But she wasn't. He assumed she would, just because it's what he and Hilda and TK wanted, but they didn't get to decide what she did.

"Even if it wasn't my fault, even if he is still alive. I know something or might know something, and maybe I can do something. I thought we all agreed that we wanted our home, our neighborhood, to be a safer place. That was my mistake. We are not safe if there is someone out there killing our kind."

"You don't know—" Jory started.

"I don't know that there isn't," Vinnie said. "And neither do you. If there isn't a killer out there, then there's no risk. If there is, maybe there's something I can do. If you don't want to help, fine, but I'm not asking for anyone's permission. I will do what I can. I will keep you all out of it. I won't even mention your existence, so you can stay safe in your hiding places."

She stood, eyeing them, waiting for one of them to say something, but no one did.

"I can help." Cer had abandoned his video game and was standing in the doorway, his hands limp at his sides. His blue eyes were luminous, and he seemed a little dazed in the way he often did when he used a lot of power.

"Thank you, Cerulean." Vinnie brushed her hand down his arm as she passed on the way to her room.

CHAPTER FOURTEEN

Vinnie had called Conor from the library phone this afternoon and he'd called right back, saying he found something, and he'd show her. He had a team meeting today, but he asked that she meet him in at The Roundhouse, and now here she was at the stadium for the second time in two days.

The Roundhouse sat on the opposite side of the stadium, across the street. Vinnie walked around the edge of the parking lot, which was still crowded today, and crossed the street at the light.

The round building was unmistakable. Vinnie had seen it before but had never really thought about its purpose. Conor said it was like a clubhouse. It had a gym and meeting rooms. Inside the building, the air had that sterile feeling, much like a hotel. There was a short hall and a large man in a tracksuit sat on a stool, looking bored.

His eyes flicked toward her as she approached.

"I'm here to see Conor Hahn," she said.

"Nia?" he asked.

She nodded, and he waved her through. "Have a seat. He'll be out when he's showered and changed."

The hall opened into a large, round room. A few people lounged on a large circular sofa in the middle of the room that looked like it could seat at least thirty people. Others sat at one of the tables and chairs in the middle of the circle. Around the perimeter of the room were doors with team names on them, and between the doors against the round wall were more small tables.

Vinnie sat at the large outer ring of couches, tucking her bag up against her side. Were the Twisted crews also in this building? Most likely they kept them separate, wouldn't want the star athletes mingling with the scum, but it didn't hurt to check and if she could use the power, that would help.

She opened her senses and registered that the crews were nearby for a moment before the power overwhelmed her senses. The room spun with sensation, even though she hadn't drawn any of the power. Voices filled her mind. Too many to make sense of. Emotions made her shake. Vinnie could hear the blood rushing through her veins, and her body tingled.

She gasped, trying to control the sensations flooding into her, trying to shut it off, but she couldn't think, she couldn't breathe. Just like at the amusement park. Will's blank eyes popped up in her head.

"Vinnie?" The voice boomed and echoed, and something touched her, searing pain along her arm.

She needed to shut it out, find her center in the storm. Vinnie found a small dark space inside and focused hard. The voices and sensations faded, and in a few more breaths, she shut off the ability to detect power.

When the room came back into focus, she was curled on her side on the couch, panting, sweat beading her forehead. Conor hovered over her, a look of concern on his face.

Vinnie closed her eyes, hoping maybe it would shut out the embarrassment.

"Can I get you something? Water?"

Nope, not being able to see him looking at her didn't help.

She opened her eyes and pushed herself up. "Water would be great, thank you."

As he walked away, her eyes drifted down his broad shoulders, to his tapered waist and—

A throat cleared. Vinnie jerked her eyes away. Two women hovered over her. One had dark hair and was wearing sweats with the Tiger's logo on them. The other was in jeans and a pale blue polo. She had fake red hair and a sharp nose, which made her look a little like a fox.

"It is a marvelous view," the woman in the sweats said. She held out her hand. "I'm Lou, and this is Kara, one of our trainers."

Vinnie shook her hand. Kara didn't offer hers — just plopped down on the couch next to Vinnie.

Conor reappeared with a glass of water, handing it to her, before sitting on her other side. "Are you okay?"

Three pairs of eyes were on her. She needed an explanation. "I — had a panic attack. I'm not used to all the people." That part was true. "I'm fine."

He put a warm hand on her shoulder and rubbed. "Hey, it happens."

"I've never had a panic attack," Lou said. She was still standing there, hovering over them. Weird and awkward.

"I knew a guy in high school who had them," Kara said. "Have you tried exposure therapy?"

"Um." What was she supposed to say? She didn't know what exposure therapy was.

"Come on guys, now is not the time. I'm sure Nia has done what she can," Conor said. "Do you prefer Nia or Vinnie? Your sister called you Vinnie."

Shaw, of course. Vinnie was grateful that she was not a blusher, because her cheeks would be on fire. "Either is fine," she lied.

"I confess, I like Vinnie better." His eyes were still smiling at her, even though his mouth was not. "And you came here for information about your sister's missing friend. I have a picture, can I send it to you?"

She gave him the email address of the library.

"Cell number would be easier. You can tell me right away if it's her."

Lou had gone to a center table and pulled a chair closer, and Vinnie fought back irritation. At least she wasn't hovering.

Kara leaned over Vinnie and said in a stage whisper, "She's sitting right next to you, you could just show her. If you were going to send it to her, you could have just sent it to her wherever she was and spared her the panic attack."

Lou laughed. "But he wouldn't have gotten to see her pretty face."

Kara rolled her eyes and flopped back.

"I thought maybe she would want a copy." Conor leaned close and held his phone toward Vinnie. There was a picture of him with a girl with thick-framed glasses and frizzy brown hair on one side and a blond girl with freckles on the other. The frizzy-haired girl was Maddie. Vinnie had done some social media stalking this afternoon, found a Martha on Carla's friend list, and from there found a picture of Maddie. "I don't keep pictures, but Lou reminded me there's a fan site that posts pictures they've gotten with the teams."

"He's been asking everyone if they saw anything," Lou said. "Give the boy a mystery, and he's got to annoy everyone."

"Anyway," Conor said. "I remembered Maddie because the girl she was with was pushy and used her name every other word. Have the police talked to that girl? I know it's not much, but she was here."

"It's not anything at all," Kara said. "You think some teenager kidnapped her? They probably ran away." She put her hand on Vinnie's arm. "I'm so sorry he wasted your time. Can I give you a ride home?"

It was true, this had been such a waste of time. "Yes, thank you," Vinnie said.

Conor tensed beside her. "Pizza will be here soon. Stay and eat with us, at least."

"I should get going and let you guys eat. I need to get home." The room was stifling, and Vinnie's limbs felt heavy.

"Aww," Lou said. "You should stay and eat with us, there's—" She looked at the doorway and barked a little laugh. "Not enough food, but people will manage."

Two men had walked into the room carrying around ten pizza boxes each.

"You should stay," Conor said. "You just had a panic attack. You need time to recover."

"And Conor needs more time to ogle you," Lou said.

He laughed. "Lou, be nice."

Kara's voice was sharp. "There's plenty of women for Conor to ogle. I'm sure he has better things to do."

"Gah, Kara, no need to get your panties in a twist. I was kidding." Lou winked at Vinnie. "You should stay. It gets boring with the same old people here all the time."

Ruddy spots had bloomed on Conor's cheeks.

He was not at all like she thought a semi-famous athlete would be. Shouldn't he be suave? He didn't seem like a serial killer, but isn't that what people always said about serial killers? 'He was such a nice young man.'

"So!" Conor stood. "What kind of pizza do you like, Vinnie?"

Her disappointment that he hadn't had more information faded under his bright blue stare. What had she expected? She'd come out here without a plan, except to ask questions, and she hadn't even done that. Yet, she had been willing to give up a moment ago. Vinnie chalked it up to feeling out of her league. "Mushroom?"

"Uh, there's probably not just mushroom. I'm sorry."

There never was. "Cheese is good."

"Okay, be right back." He trotted off toward the center tables where the delivery driver had placed the pizza boxes.

"I'll help." Lou stood.

Kara's eyes followed him for a moment. "Be careful," she murmured. "He's not what he seems. We should move to a table."

Kara had already stood and moved to sit at the nearest table before Vinnie could react to her words.

Vinnie followed, sitting beside her, and had just opened her mouth to ask what she meant when Conor and Lou returned.

Conor put a plate with two slices of cheese pizza down in front of her.

Lou had already stuffed pizza in her mouth and was chewing by the time she sat. "You know what we do. What do you do for a living, Vinnie?"

"I run a library."

Lou's eyebrows rose. "A librarian. You don't look like a librarian."

"Librarians can look like anything," Conor said.

"I'm not technically a librarian." She'd never been comfortable calling herself that. "I don't have a degree or whatever they have to have. And I never worked at one or had training. I — it's a charity library, not an official one. I get donations to keep it going."

"Oh, that's amazing," Conor said. "I have a nonprofit foundation too."

The library wasn't a nonprofit foundation. It was more like a money-under-the-table foundation, but she wasn't about to say that.

"What type—" Vinnie started.

"Where is this library located?" Kara broke in. "I love books."

Vinnie's mouth opened to answer, but she caught herself. She'd come here because she thought Conor might have killed people. Telling them how to find her probably wasn't a good idea.

"It's tiny, no public funding," she said. "There's a much larger library just a few blocks north of here. You can't miss it."

Lou's lips quirked. "Yeah, Miss Designer Jeans, maybe you should stick with the fancy library." To Vinnie, she said, "That's cool of you to run a library for free."

"Yes, how noble of you." Kara's voice was flat, disbelieving. She leaned forward. "Conor's foundation isn't nearly as noble."

Lou swallowed the last of her food. "Don't start. We don't need to get into that in front of guests. Three things you don't talk about in polite company: Politics, religion, and Twisted."

Twisted. Vinnie put her pizza slice down and wiped her hands on the napkin. This might be the opening she was looking for. "I'm not polite company at all. What does your foundation do?"

Conor glanced at Kara like he was expecting a fight. "Research. It's a research foundation. We're trying to find ways to more easily identify Twisted."

The residual cheese in her mouth felt waxy, and Vinnie was glad she had already swallowed. "More easily identify them?" she said, impressed at how steady her voice was as she tried to push images of her friends being taken away out of her head.

"Yeah," Conor said. "Right now, it's so cumbersome and expensive to test. Anyone could be a Twisted and you wouldn't know, unless you work in an industry like ours, which tests everyone, or they've gone through testing and have the hand tattoo. We're trying to make it easier to test everyone. No surprises."

Easier to test everyone. Then they could all be locked away in facilities, tattooed, and controlled.

"Conor wants every Twisted to be a slave," Kara said.

Lou snorted. "They are not slaves. It's not like they're out working fields and being beaten."

"They have very little choice about where they go and what

they do, and most have no choice at all. I think that is the definition of a slave. It's disgusting." Kara pushed her plate away.

"Why would you want to identify them?" Vinnie said. And why did she feel betrayed? She didn't even know him. He'd just flirted with her. That didn't make them anything to each other.

"I don't want anyone to be a slave," Conor said. "How they're treated or not treated is a different issue. They are dangerous and have an unfair advantage over people and can hurt them. I just don't want them out there hurting people."

She shouldn't say anything. She was here to get information. "Some people are smarter than others," Vinnie said. "Should we tattoo that on their forehead? 'Smarter than you and could outwit and take advantage of you'. What about people who take martial arts classes. They should be tattooed and locked up because any minute they could beat someone up and even kill them with their bare hands."

Kara's lips quirked as she took up the argument. "Stronger than someone else? Better put a mark on them. And what about extremely good-looking people? Oh no, they could talk you into sex you didn't want to have."

"You guys are ridiculous," Lou said. "That's not the same thing at all. They can't read your mind or break your bones just by touching you."

Couldn't someone who was stronger break bones? "People can break your bones with a tire iron or pull a gun out and kill you. We don't go around locking everyone up."

"Twisted are not like normal people!" Lou said. "They were born evil. That's why they're called Twisted."

Vinnie put her hands in her lap so they couldn't see them clenched in rage. There was nothing she could do to convince someone like that, and it made her feel helpless. She couldn't let it get the better of her, though, because she was here for a reason. "What about that crew member who died a few years back? Was she evil? Did she deserve to die?" That's what Vinnie had found in today's research. Not much, but it didn't look good.

Lou looked her dead in the eye. "If you expect me to mourn her loss, you'll be waiting a long time."

"Lou," Conor shifted in his seat, eyes glued to the floor.

Vinnie held herself in check, just barely, as she glared back at Lou. Should she feel better that at least Conor was uncomfortable? Good, she hoped he stayed uncomfortable.

"That's right," Lou said. "Conor feels guilty because he wanted her fired."

Maybe he also felt guilty for killing her.

"That was a misunderstanding," Conor murmured.

Kara smirked. "Sure, but you still don't want them anywhere near you, right Conor?"

He stood, putting his hands on the table. "I'll walk you out, Vinnie."

She was finally getting some information, though Vinnie didn't know what good it did her. "I didn't realize I was leaving."

"I'm sorry." He offered her his hand. "I don't think this is what you came for, and I have somewhere else I need to be."

This was exactly what she came for, but what could she say? She took his hand and allowed him to pull her up before following him.

They walked out the way Vinnie had come in. When they were almost to the door, he said. "I'm sorry. I guess this wasn't so much fun."

"Your friends are passionate," she said.

"Not my friends, though I would be happy to introduce you to my friends if you ever speak to me again."

She'd thought he was trying to get rid of her, but maybe she was wrong. Might as well see how much he was willing to say.

"What was the misunderstanding?" she asked.

"She was in a training area when she wasn't supposed to be.

She was a Ferr, one of the team had a heart attack while she was there. Only twenty-eight. It looked like she had done it."

"I don't remember hearing anything about a team member dying."

Conor shook his head. "He didn't. And it turns out there was a family history of issues."

Vinnie hovered by the door. "And you don't want Twisted around you." She didn't want him to say yes. She wanted him to deny it.

"I don't hate them, but I'm not comfortable around them." He opened the door, and they stepped out onto the street.

Right, and he tried to get a member of the Twisted crew sent back to the camps based on zero evidence. "That must be awkward, considering it's your job."

"We don't have a lot of contact with the crew."

No, wouldn't want to risk their precious athletes. "Thank you for the information about Maddie."

"I don't suppose I can still convince you to give me your cell phone number? Or is my discomfort a deal breaker?"

Meaning he hoped he could convince her of his point of view. She didn't want to talk to him anymore, but she might get more information from him. "I don't have a cell phone. I'll call you."

CHAPTER FIFTEEN

I t was almost full dark as Vinnie's feet carried her away from the stadium. She didn't slow as she approached the bus stop and walked past it. Maybe she should go home, but that would mean facing her failure. As long as she was out, she could pretend she still thought she had a hope of being able to find Maddie.

She could go to The Rope, her favorite dive bar, and pretend she was listening to conversations even though it was Wednesday and there would only be five to ten other people. None of them would even know Maddie existed, but, hey, that wasn't much worse than her first plan.

Even if Conor wasn't a serial killer, he still wasn't dating material. He never was, she reminded herself. In a few months, the Warrior Games would move on, and Conor Hahn would move on with them. And she hadn't been there to flirt, right?

Vinnie stepped off a sidewalk into the street, jumping as a car honked. She'd been too lost in thought—too many conflicting emotions — failing to find a serial killer, being flattered that someone handsome was flirting with her.

She was still trying to absolve Conor Hahn of being a poten-tial murderer, to make excuses for him not stepping up and defending the Twisted against Lou's accusations, for being uncomfortable around Twisted, and for having a foundation to identify them. Vinnie wanted to absolve him. She wanted to believe he was good. After all, she understood being afraid.

"Stupid," she muttered. Just because some handsome guy was paying attention to her, that didn't make him a good person.

She wanted him to be, though.

Vinnie stopped walking and blinked in confusion at the wall that had appeared in front of her. This was not The Rope. First stepping in the street and now she'd walked down a blind alley because she wasn't paying attention. That was dangerous in The Holt. Not recognizing where she was was worse. She'd been down every street and every alley in these blocks. How could she not know where she was?

Vinnie turned. A figure loomed at the mouth of the alley. He stepped closer, into the light burning down from a nearby building, and she recognized him as the Mesmer who had carried Will away.

Her reaction was automatic. Opening her senses, she pulled from his ability and sent a push of air at him that did nothing but ruffle his hair.

"Miss Forbes —" he began.

Vinnie cast out, looking for a different power, and found a Zee. Her lucky day. She pulled from the Zee, sending two leg cramps at the goon, and ran straight toward him. If she could just get around him, she could probably outrun him.

He doubled over in pain, and Vinnie darted past, down the sidewalk. As soon as she was out of the alley, she knew where she was and turned, heading for home.

Her luck continued at the next intersection where the cars were stopped, allowing her to run across the street without pausing. Her feet had just touched the sidewalk on the other side when the air went out of her lungs. She doubled over, trying to draw air in, but it was thick and impossible to breathe. The last thing she saw before passing out was the Mesmer looming over her.

VINNIE WAS SITTING in a cushioned chair with something soft wrapped around her neck. Her arms were pressed against her body, telling her something was also holding her in the chair. A blip of fear in her abdomen told her to struggle, to run, but that was useless unless she knew the situation, so she pushed it down and cleared her mind so she could evaluate.

She cracked her eyes open a slit and could see that her head rested against one of those u-shaped neck pillows. Rope held her against the chair and each wrist was handcuffed to a chair arm. Her hair fell over her face, so if anyone else was in the room, they wouldn't be able to see her eyes, so she opened them fully.

The motel room was cheap, with a faded bedspread and stains in the corner of the carpet. The rope was loose enough she could almost wriggle out of it, but the handcuffs that attached her wrist to the chair were a different matter.

No one else was in the room. She could pick up the chair and waddle to the door, but if someone was waiting nearby, she wouldn't get far.

And she was not in The Holt anymore. Sometimes she forgot what it felt like to be outside of it until she had to leave the boundaries. The stadium was close enough that she could still feel home, and she was far from home right now.

The heavy drapes were open, with only the gauzy ones still covering the window. Through the film, she saw the motel sign, lit up in the night. Mostly lit up, the O had burned out.

If she screamed or banged on the window, maybe someone would hear her?

"Don't scream," said a voice from the bathroom. Even if she hadn't had the clue of the same Mesmer kidnapping her, she would have recognized Will's voice. He stepped out of the bath-room, holding his hands up like she had a gun and was robbing him. "I'm sorry, this was the only way to get you here."

Her hands tightened on the chair arms as anger warred with relief. Should she be glad they didn't kill him now that he'd kidnapped her?

He'd been dead. She was almost sure of it. If he was a Zee, she would know, and she didn't think Zee could actually come back from the dead, though there were rumors. The rumors were probably about people like Jory, who had been close to death but not dead.

"There was no other way besides knocking me out and hand-cuffing me to a chair?" Funny how people who took away your freedom always made excuses.

"You attacked Greg first, he only wanted to talk."

She'd seen his face. He hadn't just wanted to talk. "I presume that's the name of your thug? He did a lot more than talk." Presume. She sounded like her dad. Now, that was upsetting.

"You attacked first."

Her first thought was that was true, but was it? She knew her way around her neighborhood. How had she ended up in that alley? "It is not your decision or his whether I talk to you, it's mine and you took that away from me. And I won't stand in an alley waiting while an angry Mesmer, who trapped me there, tears me apart. If he wanted to talk — if you wanted to talk — maybe you should have come yourself and not have someone trick me and make me feel threatened."

"He wasn't threatening you."

"There are no dead-end alleys in that section of the city. And you were dead. I had plenty of reason to believe he would want some revenge."

"Do I look dead to you?"

He was trying to confuse her, make her feel like this was her fault. Would she still see his lifeless eyes in her dreams now that she knew he was alive? She opened herself up, and according to her senses, he was as normal as he had been the first time. Not Twisted, but he didn't know she knew that. "You're a Zee."

"Have you ever been around a Returned before? And you know that I'm not, you can sense that I'm not."

A Returned. He thought it was possible, and he knew about her power, or he wouldn't know she could sense Zee. "How would I be able to do that?"

He sat down, looking a little weary. "Your friends are extraordinarily powerful, which I didn't expect. It's been a long time since I've seen a full crew in the wild. I'll uncuff you if you'll promise to hear me out."

"You still won't answer a direct question." Would being uncuffed do her any good when Greg could drop her again? She didn't sense him nearby, so she might have a chance.

"You can sense other people's abilities and you can borrow them. I'll answer your questions and much more, but I would rather do it on equal footing."

She searched his face, looking for some sign of insincerity, but if he was lying, she couldn't tell. Vinnie could promise and then run. What did she owe to someone who had kidnapped her? Nothing. But if he was willing to talk, it wouldn't hurt to listen. And then run. She held up her wrist as far as they would go.

He stood, fishing in his pocket for a key. When he leaned over her, she took a big breath, trying to catch a whiff of rot. If a Zee could bring themselves back maybe they could bring someone else back too? Maybe one could have brought Will back.

"It's just hotel soap," he said, lips quirking. "I think it smells okay. But not so good you'd want a big sniff."

"You were dead."

He stood back, eyes narrowing. "Was I?"

At the hint of anger, Vinnie's shoulders relaxed a fraction. Anger was a normal reaction, not like the calm when things were going crazy at the amusement park or his almost jovial mood a few moments ago. He had no right to be happy.

Vinnie rubbed her wrist as he untied the rope. "Yes."

Let him deny it. Maybe she would learn something.

"Or maybe there are some things out there that you don't know about or understand. The world doesn't know about your kind, do they, Vinnie?" He sat on the edge of the bed and put his feet out in front of him. His posture reminded her of her high school English teacher when he was about to explain the symbolism in their latest reading material. "You didn't think you were the only one who could use other people's power, did you?"

She'd never heard of anyone like her. Not even a rumor. It had been over a hundred years since The Rending. Surely it would have come out by now. Twisted seemed to be getting more powerful, and Vinnie's private theory was the magic was warping and creating new types of abilities. If he was right, then people with these capabilities were out there all along, and there could be more with abilities she didn't know about. He could be one of them.

If she wanted to know, she depended on his willingness to share. "What do you mean by my kind?"

His face became almost solemn, and he stood and paced to the television before turning back to her. "The history you've been told is wrong. The common story is time stopped, the world broke etcetera etcetera, and the anomalies warped our DNA, and children were born with abnormal abilities." He paused. His eyes lit up with energy. "But The Magiera were here before The Rending. In fact, they may have caused it. They were not out in the open but lived in secret because if the world knew... well, you see what happens when they know. People are scared, and rightly so. The Magiera could rule the world. There weren't enough before The Rending. They were stronger back then, but much fewer. Now the energy is spread out, but maybe they are more powerful in greater numbers."

He was insane. Definitely insane.

"That's not possible. They noticed the power in children a little over twenty years after The Rending. If there were adults, why didn't they step in then, help the kids? Hide them?"

"The information I've been able to dig up suggests it was a rebirth. They blamed many of the deaths that day on the time shift. When time stopped and reversed, their bodies couldn't take the shock. But those who died that day may have been all the existing Magiera. Whatever caused the time warp, and the world warp... killed them. The resulting surge sent the power back out, but it was too much for the world to contain and created the anomalies. I think there were always Magiera being born to normal families, but now there was no one left to hide them. That the first were so weak suggests that might be the answer."

Vinnie communicated her disbelief with a twist of her lips. He laughed, which made him seem younger, and she studied him. Her friends were right. He looked young, but his voice and manner made him seem older to her.

From his face, she would have said they were the same age almost.

"That's probably what I looked like when they first told me that," he said. "I don't know exactly what happened, but one thing is certain, people with special abilities existed before. I've found enough records, diaries, etcetera to know that much is true. And people like you—" He pointed at her. "Were among them."

People like her. She wasn't sure how she felt about that. "If that's true, where are the rest of the people like me?"

"It was always a rare talent. They called them Vasum, and people could go their entire lives without even knowing they had the ability. It takes a certain mental state to activate the power."

A certain mental state. The first time Vinnie used her ability, she was eight. She was swinging at school, eyes closed, feeling the mesmerizing back-and-forth rhythm. She felt the power well up in her, not knowing where it came from. Then she felt hot, the burning welling up inside her. In a panic, she had stopped the swing and stumble out to the ground just as a nearby trash can caught on fire. And then the government came, and they had taken away Michael to a training camp. She didn't feel the power again until she'd started learning to meditate in high school.

The second person to get caught because of her, Lauren, hadn't been as lucky as Michael. Lauren had been a troublemaker and a bully at school. She'd ended up in a dead end camp and hadn't survived. Vinnie's father told her about Lauren's death to taunt her. He hadn't known about Vinnie's ability. Or she'd thought he didn't know.

"If you know about people like me, there must be other people who do too." What would they do with someone like her if they took her to a work camp? What would they use her for?

"I'm sure they do, but as I said, the ability is rare to have and hard to find unless you out yourself. Or one of your friends does."

"I didn't out myself, and neither did my friends. No one else knows what I can do and so no one else could have told you. Are you going to tell me how you know? You said you'd answer my questions if I didn't run."

He ran his hands through his hair. "I did. The domain name for the Dragons is registered in the domain company's name, instead of a person, but hacking into their client databases isn't difficult. Once I knew the website belonged to Terrance Kent, I found known addresses for the last few years and lo, a group of people living in the same house, exactly six. Coincidence? No. From there, we asked questions around the neighborhood. Sometimes people know things they don't know they know. If you pay attention and know what to look for, you can learn many things."

The path sounded simple when he laid it out. Except... "Hacking into client databases is easy? You work for someone? Some government agency?"

"No, I work for myself."

"You're just going after dangerous criminals from the goodness of your heart?"

He snorted and looked away. There was something dangerous in his expression, some deeply buried rage. "No, I don't have any goodness left in my heart. Someone was taken from me, and I intend to find out why."

Revenge, then. Another honest emotion. That made him more dangerous than she'd thought. "What is it you think I can do? My friends won't agree to help, and I'm nothing without someone else's power."

Will stood up from the bed, walked over to his suitcase, and pulled out an envelope. He walked back over to the table and sat opposite from her before opening the envelope and rifling through the pages. He seemed to find what he was looking for and after looking at it for a moment, he put the photo on the table in front of her.

Vinnie glanced down and jumped up from the table. "I don't want to see that. My nightmares are bad enough."

The photo he'd placed on the table was of a girl with her eyes burned out.

"There are eight more. I don't think you're the type of person to walk away from that when you could have done something."

"How do you have those? I have a friend with access to police databases who didn't find anything like that."

"Resources."

Back to being vague. She should just walk out now, but he was right. If there was someone out there burning people's eyes out and she could help, Vinnie didn't think she could just walk away. "You have high level Twisted working for you and access to 'resources' who can give you that." She pointed to the folder. "Again, why do you need me?"

He rubbed his hands down his face. "I have some Magiera on my payroll. What you can do increases the power exponentially.

I've been chasing this killer for almost two years now, but I don't know where to look in this city. I know the pattern, but I don't know how to find him. You can do that. It would be better if you had your crew and not mine, but even if they would help, I don't trust them for obvious reasons."

"You don't trust them," she snorted. Hilda insisted she hadn't been in control, but something outside of them. Vinnie had seen some of what Greg could do, him causing the incident seemed possible, but what would be the point of that? The possibility that neither side knew what had happened disturbed her. "I think you're confused. I can only use the power to a lesser extent than the original person. I mean, I can switch, which makes me flexible, but I'm not nearly as strong as they are individually."

Will blinked in surprise. "You can… switch?"

"Yes, drop one, pick up another. It's not that hard."

"No, why would you switch? Just hold both until you need them." He scratched his chin. "If you hold more than one, then you can combine them, which makes you way more powerful than any individual."

Combine powers? No, that wasn't possible. "No, I can only hold one at one time."

"You should be able to hold them all."

"At once?" He was crazy. "I can't."

He rubbed his hands on his face again. "I'm sorry. I may have wasted both our time. I'll have Greg take you home."

The declaration stunned Vinnie. This guy had gone to all this trouble to find her, and just because she thought she couldn't do what he thought she could he was dismissing her? And, she realized, he might be her only hope of finding Maddie. If he had the resources he said he had, then maybe they could do something. She'd let her self-doubt get in the way and had potentially lost an opportunity. Not only to save someone but to learn more about her ability.

"There's a girl missing already, did you know?"

"There have been no missing persons reported to the police."

They hadn't even reported it?

"But sometimes parents don't report it because they are afraid for their children," he continued. "If they are Twisted. Afraid they'll be found out. That doesn't change that without being able to combine abilities you can't do anything for me I can't do for myself. Go home, stay safe."

"You haven't had any luck finding or stopping the killer before. I can still help."

He gave her a doubtful look.

"You seem to know more about my ability than I do. I'm not sure I've even tried. If you tell me how it's done, maybe I can."

Will looked thoughtful for a moment before nodding. "I'll see what I can find out about the girl. Give me a day. We can try to combine abilities tomorrow."

"Do we have a day?" Maddie was missing now, had been for a few days.

"We can't work miracles. I'll have Greg contact you."

CHAPTER SIXTEEN

Vinnie stared across the street at the plain brown building that looked like police stations everywhere. The last time she'd been in one, she was five, the year they took her mother away. When all his money would do nothing to save mom, her dad had dragged her to the police station. He presented Vinnie, wide-eyed and crying, to appeal to their sense of compassion. At least let her say goodbye to her daughter, he'd said.

They hadn't. What had he hoped to accomplish? The display hadn't been for her benefit. Her father didn't care about Vinnie so long as she did what he said, and what he said was always changing. Sometimes he never said what he wanted, just expected her to know. She'd spent her entire childhood and teen years trying to guess and getting it wrong.

Vinnie shook herself. Nothing bad would happen just because she walked into a police station. She was supposed to meet Will soon, but she wanted to talk to Nell first. Nell had said she would help before the others had jumped in. Maybe she still would. Vinnie needed to talk to someone because she wasn't sure how she'd gone from being tied up yesterday to offering to help.

The walk across the street was shorter than she wanted it to be, and the inside of the station was quieter than she expected. No people in handcuffs sitting on benches, and the only uniform was the woman at the front desk directly in front of the doors. To the left was a room with cubicles, and to the right, what looked like a hallway of offices leading toward the back of the building.

The woman at the desk met her eyes and curved her lips as Vinnie approached.

"I'm here to see Nell Anderson," Vinnie said. She had a moment of doubt about whether they would even let her see Nell at work. If nothing else, maybe they'd send her out to Vinnie.

"Is she expecting you?"

"No, I'm a friend. I just need to talk to her about something."

"Name?"

"Vinnie."

The woman picked up the phone and dialed a few numbers. "Nell, Vinnie is here to see you." Her eyes had already turned back to her computer before she responded to Vinnie. "She'll be up in a minute."

Vinnie nodded her thanks. She wandered to the bulletin board near the door and skimmed the wanted posters, not paying much attention. Halfway down the wall, she paused at a familiar face. He was much younger in the photo, and she couldn't see the hair color because it was black and white, but she knew that face.

"Vinnie!" Nell stood in the wide entrance in front of the cubicle room, looking much happier to see her than Vinnie had expected her to be. "This way."

Nell wasn't a policewoman — was one of those jobs that required testing — but she dressed in black slacks and a white button-down shirt and almost looked like one. The heels she wore to make herself taller made her almost as tall as Vinnie. They clacked on the tile floor as she walked past rows of cubicles until they got to the back. Nell's desk was one over from the corner and she grabbed a chair from her neighbor, plunking it down next to her desk.

She sat in her chair and waited for Vinnie to sit in the borrowed one.

Vinnie pointed back the way they came and murmured. "Samuel Chabanik?"

"Yeah..." Nell said. "He looked a lot rounder when he was young. The tattoos were probably a terrible idea because they make people look twice."

"Or maybe a good idea. People look away when they see the tattoos all over his face." The photo on the wall had been Cerulean. Wanted for murder. Cerulean's power hadn't manifested until he was fourteen. His home, with his parents in it, had burned down hot and fast. So hot, there'd been nothing left, no bodies, nothing. "I thought they had declared him dead along with his parents?"

Nell nodded, eyes staring off into nothing. "They're getting smarter, using Twisted. I'm surprised it's taken them so long. The fire itself was suspicious. They knew it had to be unnatural. How they decided it was the kid, I don't know."

Vinnie knew other countries used Twisted in sensitive positions like law enforcement and medical professions, but most Americans were against the use of Twisted to do those jobs. "Hatred runs deeper than common sense," Vinnie said. There were so many ways the Twisted could help make the world a better place, but if people wanted to use them, there was no guarantee they would ask nicely any more than they did now.

Nell grunted, eyes refocusing. "So... It's close to quitting time?"

Her voice was a question. Nell had agreed to help, but after the argument, maybe she'd changed her mind. Vinnie looked around, craning her neck. This part of the office was empty. "I went to see Conor, met some of his crew. I can't picture him as a killer." And Will, with all his 'resources', didn't seem to know anything about it. Surely he would have made that connection already if there was one.

Swiveling back to her computer, Nell said, "Maybe this will help." She tapped on something, pulled up a screen, and logged in. Typed some more to pull up a different screen. Vinnie leaned forward to read when Nell turned the screen to her.

The screen showed a police report. When he was seventeen, they had arrested Conor Hahn for assault. The man he'd beaten up was hospitalized.

"No one pressed charges," Vinnie read aloud.

There was something in Nell's eyes Vinnie couldn't identify. Pity? "You think that negates him almost beating someone to death?"

Vinnie shook her head. He was violent. She should stop fighting her mind so hard and admit it was possible. "It's just his teammate Lou seemed so anti-Twisted. If anyone was killing them, it just seems like it would be her."

"Louann Henders." Nell turned back to her computer. "Old money. Serial killers are rarely women."

"That doesn't mean they can't be."

That pitying look again. Nell typed something else on her keyboard. She pulled up a news article, one that Vinnie had already seen about the Twisted crew member who had died.

"It was an accident," Vinnie said.

"No one looked too close because all the Crew are lifers."

Lifers were Twisted who were identified and taken as small children. Many considered them more reliable because they'd been raised to be obedient. Working for people was the only life they'd known, and they had no families they knew. The lifers at the games were anonymous, they kept them hooded in public, told no one their names. No one knew who they were.

"You think it was Conor? He said there was a misunderstanding when one of their teammates had a heart attack. What about that team member?" If they'd found this much in a few days, why didn't Will seem to know about the connection to the games? This could be just another thing he wasn't telling her, or he could have a blind spot. The only reason she'd made the connection was because she knew about Maddie, which Will also hadn't found, despite his supposed connections. That part, at least, was easy to explain if her parents hadn't reported it. She hadn't asked Will about the other bodies. Possibly they were in cities where there were no Warrior Games, but he hadn't given her any information that she could check.

"I can look into it but none of this is evidence," Nell said. "We have some missing people and two who have shown up dead."

Those were just the ones Vinnie found. Nell had access to more resources. "You didn't find any more around the times the games were around?"

Nell shook her head. "People disappear all the time. Dead people are news, missing people are not always. There are quite a few missing that aren't reported to the missing person sites. Maddie's parents haven't reported her missing. There was a strange kidnapping, probably nothing..."

Vinnie sat up straighter.

"There was a boy, almost a child prodigy in ballet. Seven years old, extremely talented. He disappeared, was missing for three days, and when he came back, he couldn't dance. The parents claim it was trauma, but there was a rumor that his talent was unnatural."

"This happened in a city where the games were?"

"You betcha." Nell punched a button on the keyboard with one finger for emphasis.

There were rumors about this boy with unnatural talent. The killer took him and returned when they discovered he was normal? "What did he say about the time he was missing?"

"He couldn't remember," Nell said.

Vinnie let out a frustrated breath. "Possibly a Mesmer."

"He's a kid, could just be trauma."

That was true. "You have access to some high-level databases, and that's all you found."

"Hey, I tried. The databases I have access to aren't that high level. Just some normal ones that all police have access to. I don't get any special privileges. That requires more.... clearance."

By clearance, she meant it required being tested for power. Who was Will that he could get it then? "Who would? FID?"

Nell's head tilted as she thought about that. "Maybe, the Federal Investigations Department investigates serial killers, but didn't that guy say the government wouldn't get involved or didn't know?"

"You trust him now?"

"No," Nell said. "Seems like a strange thing to lie about, but he knew your name. I've thought it through. No one should be able to find our names unless they have very sophisticated systems. More sophisticated than this." She pointed to the database she was searching. "I have as much clearance as any officer, but we're talking much higher and more sophisticated. The federal government makes sense."

But if she could trust what he said, he hadn't used technology to find them. He had that other information that Nell couldn't find. If he wasn't lying to her about that. She'd come here to ask Nell what she thought, but what came out was, "If he was working for the government, wouldn't they have come after us?"

"Unless they still want to use us. He had a Twisted with him. But we're thinking like them." She waved at the station. "He could have gotten your name straight out of your head. Found us from the magical signature on Gerald's clothes using a Ferr."

Which still didn't explain the case files he had, but Nell didn't know about that. "Did either of the two dead have burned out eyes?"

"No," Nell frowned at her.

Maybe it was all a lie. "Do you think we made a mistake? Should we have heard him out?"

Nell sighed, swiveling back to her computer. "I don't like what happened. But he was shady, Vinnie. Really shady. He might be the killer, or working with him, and was casing us out. What happened was too strange. I think Hilda's right, but I don't know why his team would want to kill him."

She hadn't heard Hilda say his own people killed him, but it sounded like her. They hadn't killed him, though, and after what she'd felt when she'd opened her senses with all those Twisted around, Vinnie thought her friends might have lost control. Linking up like that was risky. They trained the anomaly teams to handle the power, but her friends had no training. At least, none other than working with Harry.

But last night she'd turned down that blind alley that didn't exist, even though she'd walked home that way hundreds of times. Greg was strong enough to confuse her mind when she was distracted, so it was possible he could have confused them all when the power got out of control. She needed to talk to someone about this.

"Last night—" Vinnie started.

"Hey." A man's face appeared around the corner. "Sorry to interrupt, do you have that report I asked for?"

"Yes, I gave it to Stan," Nell replied.

"Ah, he's gone for the day. Don't forget to go home yourself." The man disappeared again.

"Careless," Nell said under her breath. "We shouldn't be discussing this here." She started gathering her things and shutting down her computer.

"You don't think he heard anything, do you?" Vinnie murmured. She went back over the conversation in her mind, trying to decide if they'd said anything incriminating as she pulled her chair back to the neighboring cubicle.

They walked out of the building together. The blast of cooler evening air felt good on Vinnie's overly hot, nervous body.

"I'm sorry for bringing this here," Vinnie said.

Nell pulled a light sweater over her shoulders as they walked to the bus stop. "I get it. You want to help, but Vinnie, this is way over our heads."

Will hadn't thought it was over their heads. He thought she was the key.

"Maybe if it was just one person," Nell continued.

"You think it's more than one?"

"It—" Nell started, but she didn't seem to know how to finish it. "I do. I don't care what anyone says. If Twisted were being killed systematically, someone would look into the deaths, unless there were someone powerful enough to make them look the other way."

"What reason would a group have for killing a bunch of u — Twisted." They'd made it to the bus stop.

"Hate groups can hate enough they'd want to eliminate Twisted. Or kill them just for fun." Nell shuddered.

"It seems very organized for people running on hate. I don't like to think of them as being that smart." Vinnie had never been the direct target of any hate because no one knew what she was. Being Twisted wasn't something easy to see, though some had common characteristics. The Wisps, like Cer, were often small, but there were small people in the world so that didn't single people out.

"I hear ya there." After a glance at the other person waiting for the bus, Nell murmured, "I hope we killed him. I know that's awful, but I feel safer knowing that someone who knew what we are is gone. What if it was him?"

Now was her last chance to say something, but Nell had just said she was happy they'd killed him. She might try to talk Vinnie out of going to see him, and it didn't matter. Vinnie knew she would go back out to the hotel no matter what Nell said. "Then Maddie wouldn't be missing. I have an errand. See you back at the house."

CHAPTER SEVENTEEN

T he door opened before she could knock. Will, looking exhausted, with his hair sticking out at weird angles and wearing rumpled sweats, stepped back to let her in.

"Sorry I'm late." Only about twenty minutes late, but she couldn't control the bus schedule. She'd declined Will's offer to have Greg pick her up. That guy gave her the creeps.

"No problem. Would you like a drink? I have Dr. Pepper. Or I guess I can get you a cup of water."

The wastebasket next to the small table was overflowing with Dr. Pepper bottles. That couldn't be healthy. The table itself was covered in papers. One was a badly printed photo of Maddie.

Will grabbed a bottle of Dr. Pepper from the mini-fridge and came over to the table. "Two people have gone missing. One reported to the police today, and your missing girl." He tapped Maddie's photo. "But I think you were right. This is the one the killer took. She was strong, possibly Stone, and the killer seems to prefer younger victims."

"Younger, unregistered Twisted are more numerous because they've had less lifetime to get caught. Older would be more cautious and harder to catch off guard. That doesn't mean the killer didn't go for the older one this time. Do you have another reason besides past patterns?" Vinnie said. Nell had told her that the most likely time for a Twisted to get caught was if they came into their power in childhood when they couldn't control it or when they were teenagers and got reckless.

"I talked to a friend of hers, says they skipped school, but Maddie was meeting someone and took off. The friend was uncomfortable about who she was meeting. And I have a feeling."

A feeling. Right. "Do you know who it might be?"

"Not yet, but I'm hoping you can help with that."

If she'd spotted a pattern with the Warrior Games, surely he could have, too, especially since he seemed to have more information.

"You've never seen any reason for the cities that the Twisted were killed in?"

"I didn't say that. About half in the past two years have happened in cities where The Warrior Games are, which would narrow it down, but the killer is likely Twisted and all the employees who work for the games are tested. The killings started four years ago, with one death, then there was a lag until two years ago unless I missed some which is possible. That leaves three happening in the last two years with no connection to the games. Still, that and the increased anomaly action are the closest things to a pattern that I've found."

Some of the deaths not being near the Warrior games would explain why they hadn't found some of them. Nell said there was no pattern to the deaths. "Four years ago... how do you know these are all the same killer when there's no pattern?"

His face was blank for a moment like he didn't understand the question. "Ferr," he said. "There's a trace energy pattern that's the same. We've gone through all the murders in the last few years and look for things like how they died. It's different but similar — someone rumored to be Stone crushed by rocks, a Mesmer suffocated — things like that. Then we go see if we can find the same trace of energy, which is incredibly difficult if it's been a while. There may be more we didn't find."

He had so many more resources than she had. How had she expected to do this on her own?

Will took a swig of the drink and sat. "I got some of the girl's things from the school. You can try to locate her." He rummaged around the table and pulled something out from under some paper.

The circular object looked like it had been an old telephone cord if telephones came in shimmering blue. Vinnie recognized the brand of ponytail holder because she had some herself.

"Your Ferr could do that," Vinnie said.

"You think I should drive a Ferr around the city until I get a ping? The clock is ticking."

That would be time consuming. "You'll drive me and a Ferr around the city then? Because I can't do it without pulling the power."

"Just trust me."

"Why would I do that? You haven't given me a reason to, and you tied me up."

"You're not the first Vasum I've met. I know what your kind is capable of, and I know more about what's possible than you do. For example, it is possible to hide one's ability from a Vasum."

Hide ability? Vinnie opened her senses. "Mesmer." Another damn Mesmer. He'd blocked her so completely that she hadn't even known what he was. Hilda was the strongest Mesmer she had met, and she couldn't do that. That explained a lot of what had happened. Maybe almost all of it. Would someone who could do that have been able to take control of their circle at the amusement park? Maybe he fought back, and Hilda lost control.

"Lying to me makes me want to trust you even less."

"I thought you wanted to save this girl before she gets hurt?" He moved to the bed, where he crawled to the center and sat cross-legged. "The Vasum also explained to me, in great detail, how his ability worked, and I can show you." He nodded to the bed, inviting her to sit down.

He dangled knowledge and guilt in front of her like a toy. Here, little girl, I have some candy if you'll just sit on this bed with me. Of course, she wanted to find Maddie and learn more about her ability. He was a Mesmer, so he probably knew that.

At some point when he was talking, a Ferr and a Wisp had entered the range of her ability and were in the room above them. A Wisp could boost the Ferr power, but not enough to search the entire city. Yet, he seemed to think it was possible.

Curiosity and the desire to help won. Vinnie crawled onto the bed and sat facing Will.

He placed the ponytail holder in her hand. "There's something else of hers in this room. Can you find it?"

She reached out to the Ferr and tried to pull. Vinnie had practiced enough that pulling power was easy, but this was like pulling power through sludge. Her eyes popped open.

"Narrow your bandwidth. The Ferr has some shields," Will said.

He was watching. Somehow, he was watching her use the power and knew. Vinnie pushed the discomfort down. "I don't know what that means."

"You're pulling wide open, focus, like pulling a rope through a hole. It will snag if you pull too hard."

Why, why would it snag? "Why can't the Ferr just drop the shields?"

"They're hard to reestablish," Will murmured in a voice that said he was concentrating on something else.

That something else was probably her. Vinnie buried the discomfort again and did as he'd said. She released the power back to the Ferr, then felt around the edges. The power had always just come to her — it was there, and she drew it, so it took her a few moments to feel the difference of just trying to take a small stream of it, of controlling it when it was outside of herself.

Will was right. The power flowed to her without as much resistance, but it was still slow.

Ferr energy made her very aware of her heartbeat. The hair tie lay coiled her palm and Vinnie felt for the pulse of her blood there, focusing on it until she could feel the energy signatures of the people who had touched it. Then, she loosened her attention to make it more open to the environment until her skin was alive with all that was around her.

The sensations of energy were vaguer for everything she wasn't touching, but stronger up close. The strongest energy signature was, of course, Will. She ignored him, filtering and sifting through the energies. Vinnie had practiced this with TK but while he could sense signatures for a full city block, she had trouble with just a room.

"You're afraid of the energy, try pulling a little more."

"I'm not afraid."

He sighed. Vinnie knew disappointment when she heard it. He was wrong, though. She wasn't afraid of anything she could control. What she had less control over was taking too much power and hurting someone else. She dug back into the power to reorient herself, pulled more power, then sent feelers out again. "It's in the bathroom."

"Good, how far can you reach?"

"The rooms next to us." Which was farther than she'd ever been able to reach.

"How far can you feel with your ability?"

Vinnie thought back to when she'd tried to pull power at a distance. "Best guess, almost a mile. If I know the person, even farther."

Will made a grunting sound. "Do you feel everyone or just Twisted?"

The question surprised her enough that she opened her eyes. Will was watching her face. Creepy. "Just Twisted."

He shifted on the bed so that he was facing her again. "Most people don't realize, but everyone has a small spark of what gives Magiera their power. Otherwise, Magiera babies would never be born to normal parents. You should be able to sense all people. Try that."

She dropped the Ferr energy so she could use her own ability.

"You can't even use your magic, and another?" he said.

Her face got hot, and she opened her eyes. "It's easier to focus with just one."

"Pick up the Ferr energy again."

Vinnie did as he asked.

"Your power is part of your body, your DNA. You don't have to think about it, it's just there, right? You're the glass, and the power is the whiskey. If you hold the Ferr power, you're still a glass and it shouldn't take any extra power to do what you were made to do."

"I'm the bottle and the power is the Dr. Pepper. Got it."

He grinned. "I like my analogy better."

Vinnie pulled the Ferr power into her again, feeling it in every molecule. Then she let go and the power flowed back out. "Maybe you should have your Vasum friend come and explain it to me because it doesn't feel possible."

Will's eyes hardened. "She's dead."

She? "You said it was a man earlier."

"The Vasum was a man, the person who allowed me to under-stand was a Mesmer woman. This is not something simple to explain or do. Here." He held out his hands. "Take my hands."

He smelled soapy and clean, despite his rumpled appearance, but she didn't want to touch him. The memory of his eyes, blank and staring at the amusement park popped into her head, and Vinnie fought back a shudder.

"Please. Trust me," he said. "It will make this so much easier."

"Maybe if you told me what you were going to do, I would trust you."

He wiggled his fingers. "I'm just going to give you the map."

He was talking about taking over her mind. Before she realized what she was doing, she'd scooted backward off the bed and was on her feet at the foot. "The map?"

He looked startled. "Yes, I can just put the information in your mind."

"So... what? You take over my mind?"

Understanding seemed to dawn on his face. "No, I will just insert the pattern at the right time."

Was this what he meant by a Mesmer woman helping him understand? "Insert the pattern. And I have no control over what that pattern is? You just put it in my head? Sounds like mind control to me."

Will's mouth opened. Then closed. Then he pinched the bridge of his nose and rubbed into the corner of his eyes. "You work with a Mesmer. She never assists you?"

Vinnie tensed. The time they'd tried to include Vinnie in the circle, it felt like Hilda telling her what to do, giving her no choice. That's what he wanted to do. "No, she doesn't 'assist' me."

"I can keep trying to explain, but it will be slow. We might not be able to find the girl tonight."

"It won't take me all night to figure it out." Instead of getting back on the bed, Vinnie sat in the hotel chair. He wanted her to hold on to Ferr power like it was her own. When Shaw had been helping her, she said the power knew what to do. Vinnie had never experienced it like that. She'd always needed to think about what she was doing and direct the power. This time instead of pulling the energy, she just tried to feel it, the way she felt the signatures in the ponytail holder. What did Ferr energy feel like while it was still in someone else's body?

The power sat in her body, her blood becoming a little richer. The feeling that she was holding power diminished, but she could tell it was still there. Vinnie let go with her mind, and for a moment she thought it hadn't worked. Then her mind caught up with what her body knew. She could still feel Will's energy signature as a human and not just his Mesmer power.

She laughed. "I told you I could do it."

"Okay, well, you're a quick learner. Reach out and see how many you can feel."

And she did. She reached out with her mind and felt for the people nearby and she found she could sense them, their innate abilities. Most were very weak, but Will was right, everyone had something. People having a tiny amount of ability allowed her to use the Ferr power and her own to feel them, and her mind made a map based on distance and feel.

"I can stretch a few blocks. I think I'm getting a restaurant in the distance." There were a lot of people in one place, but they weren't moving much, as if they were sitting.

"Good, Now pull the Wisp energy that's close by."

Vinnie closed her eyes, so she could focus on what she felt instead of what she was seeing. The Wisp energy was easy to pull, but she could only tell she was still holding onto the Ferr energy because she could still sense Will. This was easy. Why had he thought he needed to be in her head?

A rush of white noise started in her mind. Blood pounded in her ears and her breath rasped out of her.

"Lavinia, relax, you're okay."

She wasn't okay. She was losing control, just like at the amusement park. Just like at the clubhouse with Conor. This was too much power, too much something, and it would swallow her whole.

"Vinnie!"

And she was plunged into darkness, all feeling left her limbs, the light coming through her eyelids was gone. All that was left were her thoughts and the sound of her breathing. Then even her thoughts were slipping away. Vinnie tried to fight the blackness, but she couldn't feel her movements.

"Stop!" Will's voice pierced the darkness.

She froze.

"Breathe."

How could she breathe when she couldn't feel anything? Her lungs pulled in a deep breath without her thinking about it. Sensation returned to her arms and legs, and her heart rate slowed. A thought scrabbled against the back of her mind — she hadn't chosen to breathe deeply. Someone was controlling her body. She wanted to panic — she wanted to rage, but she couldn't. He was holding her with his mind.

"Let me go." Her voice came out a rasp.

"We're just trying to keep you from throwing fireballs at us. Calm now?"

Tears pricked her eyes. Everything was dark, and she was trapped. "Let me go."

"I'm not holding you. I gave your mind a nudge and your subconscious made you breathe. It happens all the time, you breathe without thinking, you were just letting your thoughts take over."

Her limbs loosened and light began filtering through her eyelids again. She opened her eyes to find Will sitting on the bed still, he'd moved to the edge and looked as tired as his voice sounded. There was an expression she couldn't quite read, but it looked like worry. Nothing at all like the smug look that would be on her dad's face when he let her out of the closet he'd locked her in.

Did that make it better? "I told you to stay out of my head."

Will rubbed his eyes, his jaw clenched. "You could have killed yourself. This will not work if you don't trust me. At least a little. We are dealing with dangerous magic. Something could go wrong, but if you panic, it will be harder to fix."

"I'm not panicking." But she was. The power, the sound. He'd been hurt, they could have killed him, and she could die doing this.

He held up a hand. "Most of the Bad things that could happen,

I can stop, but you have to trust me. And use that training you did to learn your ability to keep you calm. Do you think you can do that? Because if not, I will try to find the girl another way and I may not be fast enough."

Vinnie wasn't sure she could do it. She'd lost control again, just like at the amusement park. It was her fault. Hilda had been right the first time. "Why does it do that? The sound, the rush?"

"You don't just hold power, you magnify it, and your senses aren't used to it. When you hold only one it's not that obvious but if you hold more than one the growth is exponential, so you, plus the one power is not two but four, and then add another, it's eight. If you give the power back when you're done some magnification remains."

"That's why the others are stronger." When he'd asked if Hilda had gotten stronger since she'd met Vinnie, that's what he meant.

"Yes, they won't keep getting stronger forever, it's more like they're reaching their potential."

That was a lot to process, but knowing the cause made her feel a little better about the sensation. "I can stay calm. Don't make things dark again. Please. If you do —" What? She'd run like she'd run away from her dad? Stop trying to stop a killer who was threatening the only real home she'd ever had? "Just please don't."

For a moment she thought he might refuse, but then he said, "Okay, ready to try again?"

Vinnie nodded and closed her eyes.

How far could she stretch with the Wisp boost before she even ran out of energy? "There's no way I can stretch far enough. I'm not sure how far I've gone. There's so much noise."

She could feel Will shifting on the bed before he said, "This is a long shot, but the best we can do quickly. Try searching in sections, make the energy flow down a narrow corridor."

That was like asking her skin on the back of her body to stop feeling, her power was an extension of herself. "It's part of me, it's not part of me, make up your mind."

"You can direct your voice."

"But people behind me can still hear it." When she pulled, she didn't pull from everywhere, so it should be possible to direct it, too. Maybe she needed a target. She found someone in the stadium's direction and focused her attention them. While holding that she tried to expand her awareness — like seeing things in her peripheral vision without looking at them. It worked, she could read the people around the area, but it took a lot of focus. Vinnie chose another person farther out and focused on them.

Eventually, she couldn't feel any more people farther out. "I think I'm past the city," she said in wonder, finding it hard to talk. Vinnie let go of the energy and started another search. By the time she got to the edge of the city again, she could feel her mind getting fuzzy with fatigue.

"Are the Twisted okay? I'm not pulling too much?" Her voice was slurred.

"They're okay, but I think you may be done."

"One more, I have a good feeling."

Vinnie sent her thoughts along the pathway, pausing several times at signatures that were similar. Her power stretched and strained. And then she felt the signature. "I've got her."

She tried to fix the location in her head, but it slipped away. The rushing in her mind stopped and her body slumped. She couldn't stop her descent as she slid right out of the chair onto the floor and lay there limp and boneless. Maybe she could just stay here for a moment.

When she opened her eyes Will was standing over her with a bottle of Dr. Pepper. He held it out to her.

"I don't drink that stuff," She mumbled.

"The sugar will help." He sat on the floor and held out his arm, offering to help her sit up.

Vinnie ignored the arm, pushing herself up, disturbed by how much her arms shook. She knew he was right — she'd helped Cer through this enough times to know sugar helped with Wisp power depletion, but she hated Dr. Pepper. She took it and drank anyway because she would need all the help she could get to pinpoint the exact location. "I need iron, too. For the Ferr depletion. I found her, but I need one more time to find her exactly."

Will shook his head. "You won't make it through another round. We have an approximate location. We can find her."

"How long will that take? I've seen the reports. The killer might torture her, and it's only a matter of time before she's dead. I can do this."

"You won't do anyone any good if you're dead."

Vinnie scoffed. "Dramatic much?"

"Look at your pants."

"What have my pants—" She looked. Her jeans, which had been snug a few hours before, hung loosely. No wonder she felt light-headed. And no wonder Cer was so skinny, even though he ate constantly. Did that mean he was constantly using his power?

"We'll find her," Will said. "You know approximately, and I can drive a Ferr around and get a ping. Then we'll go get her."

"Me too?" What did it matter if she went as long as Maddie was okay? But she wanted to be there. She still didn't trust Will.

"If you're able by the time we find her." He handed her another Dr. Pepper. "Greg will drive you home and you can get some rest."

CHAPTER EIGHTEEN

The smell of sugar tickled her nose, and Vinnie twitched but didn't open her eyes. Greg had brought her home last night, and she'd barely made it to her mattress before crashing. Even now, she felt as if she was being crushed by air. Not because of a Mesmer — her body was just heavy with exhaustion. Her stomach rumbled, and she dragged her eyes open.

Cerulean sat on the floor, a box of chocolate cupcakes in his lap. He didn't stir when she opened her eyes, just continued staring at a point on the wall behind her bed.

"Cer?" Vinnie croaked.

He blinked and refocused his eyes on her and then held out the box.

"I'd rather have a sandwich or something." She tried to sit up, but her head spun, and she flopped back.

Cerulean reached into the box, pulled out a cupcake, opened it, and handed it to her. "You have to eat, or Hilda will re-fry my brain. And whatever you did, you're an idiot."

The last words were Hilda's. Cer was just repeating them, and of course, his idea of food was sugar, but that was what her body needed even if her mind would prefer a sandwich. She'd had a bunch of marshmallows and some sweet tea with an iron pill when she got home, but it hadn't been enough. The taste of chocolate and cream burst in her mouth, and she almost moaned with relief. Vinnie finished it and reached for the box, pulling out another and devouring it too. The last few bites stuck in her mouth.

"Tea?" she said.

Cer uncurled from his position on the floor and left. He returned a few minutes later with a glass of sweet tea. By that time, Vinnie had already eaten two more cupcakes.

He put the glass on the floor beside her. "I'm going to go fix a light switch."

Vinnie pushed herself up and this time her head didn't spin as much, though her chest felt a little tight. Someone must have turned off the alarm on her clock because she was late getting to the library.

After drinking half the tea in a few swallows, she stood on wobbling legs and made her way to the kitchen to call Meg. Meg could take care of the library today. After doing that, she dialed Will's number, letting it ring and ring, until it finally clicked over to voicemail.

She hung up the phone, grabbed some chips from the cabinet, and went back to bed.

LAVINIA. The voice in her head was gruff and masculine and not one that she recognized.

The room was dark, and Shaw was curled up on her bed, sound asleep.

Who is this?

Greg. Are you ready to get the girl?

Greg? That was not his voice. Could they change how their

voices sounded in a person's head? Vinnie made a mental note to ask Hilda as she sat up in the bed.

She'd had so much sugar today, she half expected her teeth to fall out, but it seemed to have helped. Vinnie felt almost human. From the dresser, she grabbed jeans, a long sleeve t-shirt, and socks. She wiggled into the jeans and threw the t-shirt on as she walked, pausing at the landing to slide one sock on and then the other. After going down the stairs, she grabbed her key and shoes and stepped out onto the front porch.

Greg had parked his silver SUV a few houses down. Vinnie put on her shoes as she walked, laces slapping the sidewalk. As she reached the side of the SUV, the passenger door opened, interior light showing her that Greg was alone in the vehicle.

"What's the plan?" Vinnie had called Will several times today and gotten no answer. She'd begun to think he'd ditched her after she helped find Maddie.

"I'll explain on the way."

The clock on the dash showed just after one in the morning. Vinnie tried to stifle a groan. The library was supposed to be open tomorrow and she couldn't call Meg in again. The exhaustion from the recent use of power was bad enough, now she was missing sleep too. But she'd wanted to do this.

They'd gone several blocks and Greg hadn't said a word. "You were explaining?"

"We've been watching the house all day. The girl seems to be in there, but no one else has come in or out. We need you to check for other Magiera in the area."

"You and Will are both Mesmers. You should be able to tell if there was a mind inside there."

"The killer may block abilities, but it's likely they don't know about your kind and wouldn't be blocking you."

Will was blocking her ability the first time they'd met, which meant he'd known or suspected what she was before he walked into the library. He said that people knew things they didn't know they knew but he could have just gotten it straight from her mind. That thought was chilling, that any Mesmer could pluck that information just by reading her thoughts. That was a risk she should have considered but hadn't.

Greg still hadn't told her the plan, but if all they needed was for her to see who was in there, that was easy enough. "If the killer is gone? How will we stop him?"

"We need to know what we're dealing with before we go after the killer. We just want to get the girl out and safe for now."

She thought of Hilda, always saying they should just kill people. "Or we could just shoot the killer. Then it doesn't matter what we're dealing with. Unless they're Ferr. Or can stop bullets." A Mesmer could probably make an air shield. Cerulean had stopped those balls with friction. What else?

Greg chuckled, but he didn't sound amused. He'd pulled into a neighborhood — two-story houses, maybe three to four thousand square feet. Not as nice as the neighborhood she'd grown up in, but above average. He stopped in front of a brick house like all the rest and hopped right out.

As he walked around the front of the van, a figure stepped out from the shadow of a tree. Vinnie waited until she recognized Will before getting out herself. Will pressed a styrofoam cup into her hand and the smell of coffee wafted up to her.

"This is the house?" she asked as she pulled the lid off to check the temperature. The heavy smell of sugar assaulted her nose and Vinnie winced. She preferred her coffee black, plus the thought of more sugar made her want to gag. But she probably needed it. The coffee tasted as bad as it smelled, and she made an unhappy sound as she swallowed some.

"You don't like Dr. Pepper and you don't like coffee?"

"I don't like sugary drinks. Except for Sweet Tea."

"Hm." He pointed his coffee at a for sale sign a few houses down. "That's the house."

They were drinking coffee in the middle of the night while

contemplating rescuing someone. "We're just going to stand here in front announcing our presence to anyone who looks out a window?"

"No one looks out their window at one in the morning."

Had he ever done anything like this before? Maybe that was something she should have asked sooner. He had some resources, yes, but he'd said he was just after this killer, which meant maybe he didn't know what he was doing. "You didn't return my calls."

"You needed your rest."

"I would have rested a lot better knowing what was going on."

"I was busy." The light from a nearby streetlight lit up the green in his eyes. "Can you feel the energy around the house? We need you to figure out if she's in there."

Vinnie opened up her senses and focused on the house. Immediately, she felt something, but it was confusing. "Whoever is in there has Dancer ability. Only one person. But there's something else. It feels like power but not a person."

"A power object?"

A what? He was probably going to say there were things out there she didn't know about again, but she had to ask. "Objects can have power?"

Will frowned at her. "Do you think anomalies are people?"

"Those aren't objects. They're energy. I thought you meant magic swords or something."

"Is this the time to educate, boss?" Greg asked.

"Right, no."

Vinnie suppressed her flash of irritation. They needed to focus on getting Maddie out, but an answer wouldn't have taken that long. She dropped a little deeper into her power so she could see the power, but the house remained black. Whatever she felt was not visible on the outside. "I can't tell what it is without being able to see it. There might be an anomaly in there."

"And there's only one person? I can tell the girl is there."

"Unless they can block my power like your super snowflake self."

Greg chuckled again, the sound grating on Vinnie's nerves.

Will grunted in frustration. "I'm going to have to take Vinnie in with me, so I know what I'm dealing with."

He hadn't planned on taking her with him. She supposed she should be grateful for that since this was a potentially dangerous situation, but she hated being left out.

Will put his cup on the ground and started for the house.

"The best plan is no plan," Vinnie muttered as she put her cup down and scrambled after him.

Will strode right up the sidewalk to the front door.

Okaaaay. Vinnie ducked her head in case there were cameras and followed, wishing she'd grabbed her hoodie so she could hide her face.

Will held his hand a few inches from the door frame and traced the line of it.

"Got the alarm?" Greg said from behind them.

Will nodded and stepped back. Greg held his hands over the doorknob and the deadbolt for a second. The deadbolt thunked. Greg turned the knob, pushed the door open, and stepped back as Will entered the house.

Vinnie followed Will, but Greg turned and retreated down the sidewalk.

The house was quiet and had the dusty smell of a place that had been empty for a while.

"Do you feel anything else?" Will asked. "Where's the girl?"

The Dancer energy was still faint. "This way." She skirted around a formal dining room and followed the energy signature down a hallway. As they drew closer, Vinnie could tell something was off. The power felt like a muffled thrum.

"There's an anomaly. I think it's in there with her." The hairs on her arms were standing straight up. The feeling of it was not comforting, like Harry, the anomaly in their basement.

Will tugged the door open. Vinnie had just enough time to hear his breath hiss through his teeth before she stepped through after him and the power hit her. A loud screech like a train stopping too fast hit her in the ears and she stumbled back, clutching her head.

The sound dulled to a roar, and she heard Will saying something about the anomaly. The room was a large, cavernous master bedroom, unfurnished. A soft glow came from the corner, seeming harmless. Vinnie would have thought it was pretty if it weren't making her eyes water.

Will nodded to the corner where a young woman lay on her side, arms bound in front of her, gagged, but her wide eyes were staring at them.

Forgetting her pain, Vinnie darted forward and kneeled in front of Maddie. She tried to untie the knots, but they were tight, and she couldn't get a hold on them.

She wanted out of here. "Do you have a knife?"

Will, who hadn't moved from his spot by the door, said, "I'll check the kitchen," and disappeared out the door.

Maddie whimpered and tried to say something through the gag. Vinnie pulled it off just as air slammed into her, pitching her forward into the wall. One hand landed on Maddie's midsection, and she shoved off to the side just in time to see a woman step away from the anomaly. The woman was dressed entirely in black, including something wrapped around her head.

Something hit to the ground near the doorway. Will was back, and he'd dropped the knife and threw a blast of air at the woman, who put up her hands to block and stumbled back two steps before slinging what looked like a ball of water at Will. The ball slammed into his chest, throwing him against the wall.

It had been air she'd thrown at Vinnie, hadn't it? Vinnie opened her senses again — the woman read as both Dancer and Mesmer — air and water, and something else that Vinnie couldn't get a read on. That wasn't possible.

Will and Vinnie had both gotten back on their feet. Vinnie reached into the woman, trying to get a grasp on her power, but she couldn't latch onto it. It didn't feel quite the same as when Hilda blocked her from taking power, the power just felt... slippery. The woman threw another ball at Will, hitting him in the face. His head slammed back into the wall, and he slumped to the ground.

The woman turned back to Vinnie, her arms raised to attack.

Vinnie reached for Maddie's power and got another shock. She couldn't pull it either. It was like smoke or a whisper.

The woman raised her arms to throw something, and Vinnie leaped to the side, narrowly avoiding the ball of ice as it cracked into the wall, making a large hole. Another ball of ice came flying at her and Vinnie rolled, avoiding it again. The last one didn't seem to be as powerful. Maybe if she kept dodging, she could get to the knife.

She was close, Vinnie dove for the knife but something invisible wrapped around her middle, pinning her arms to the side. In desperation, she reached for whatever was hiding inside the woman. Ferr. Vinnie pulled the power. She could feel the blood in her opponent's body, and she moved some of it up, giving the woman a head rush.

Then the bonds loosened, and the woman staggered, woozy.

Vinnie snatched the knife off the floor and charged, knocking her to the ground. She pressed the knife to her throat. "Be still." The woman's pulse beat steadily under the arm Vinnie was using to pin her down. What had she been thinking? She couldn't kill this woman, and a knife was no match for someone with two abilities, but the woman had to be running out of power. She lay limp under Vinnie, way too calm.

Vinnie opened up, trying to see if she could sense how much she had left. The power flared, and she shifted deeper again, able to call up the vision for a second before the woman's eyes flashed.

Instinct had Vinnie rolling to a side as a large spike of ice flew from the woman and embedded itself in the ceiling.

She scrambled back, away, unsure what to do next. Will was still out cold, and Greg hadn't come in.

The woman was on her feet already, the fluidity of a Dancer helping her.

The woman pulled back, throwing another ball at Vinnie. It smacked Vinnie in the chest, knocking her back against the floor and knocking the wind out of her. Her head spun, and she tried to move. She had to move, or the woman would kill her. She could make out the woman preparing to throw something else at her through her blurry vision.

Then, a fireball came from the doorway, hitting the woman on the shoulder. Her clothes ignited.

Vinnie recognized Cerulean's energy without needing to look. She pushed herself up just as a spike of ice hit Cer in the shoulder and he went down. The woman had already put the fire out.

Vinnie pulled power from Cer and sent another fireball at her.

The fireball fizzled around the woman, but she dropped to her knees. They were wearing her out. They could catch her. Before she completed the thought, a concussion of air clapped around her head. Her back hitting the floor again was the only way she knew she had fallen.

Her body hurt, every part of her body hurt, but she had to get up. She couldn't convince her body to get up. A ringing started in her ears, reached a high pitch, and stopped. Vinnie rolled onto her side, shaky arms pushing herself up as she got her feet under her again and stood, swaying.

Her eyes focused just in time to see the woman carry Maddie into the anomaly.

CHAPTER NINETEEN

Vinnie swayed. Her ears felt cold and wet. She touched one, and her hand came away with something dark and sticky. Blood. The soft glow that lit the room had diminished, but the anomaly was still there. She could go after the woman and Maddie, but would she be able to come back?

Cerulean moaned. Vinnie stumbled over to where he lay slumped against the wall, humming to himself and staring off into space.

"Cerulean?"

His eyes rolled toward her, looking eerily lit from within. "I closed it, it's okay."

The anomaly was still there, and he couldn't close it by himself, anyway. "Closed it?"

"The hole." The ice spike lay melting beside him, its tip dark. The thing was huge. How was he still alive?

She wanted to crouch down, but she wasn't sure she could stand back up. Growling in frustration, Vinnie reached over and flipped the light on. Not like she needed to worry about the killer discovering them now. With more light, she could see his shoulder, covered in blood, but there was no hole.

ELLE WOLFSON

"You used your magic to cauterize the wound." That might not be enough. She needed to get him to Jory.

His smile looked feral for the second it was on his face. "Is the man dead again?"

Vinnie turned. There was a bloodstain on the wall where Will had hit, and he lay on his side on the floor. At least his eyes were closed this time.

Greg? She didn't know if he would hear her. It wasn't like talking to Hilda, who she could trust to pick up on her sent thoughts, and he hadn't responded before.

Greg. Will is injured. Knocked out.

There was a rumble in her head before the thought came through, faint. *Is it safe?*

The killer was here, but she's gone through an anomaly. The woman had come out of it and gone back in. She needed to get Cer out of here.

Greg poked his head into the room. "Clear?"

Freaking coward. "Where were you? We could have used your help."

"I'm not a fighter, and Will has instructed me to stay out of dangerous situations. I am not to risk my life."

She stood, incredulous. "You'll risk his? You don't think he'd want you to save him?"

"No," he said simply and went to Will, crouching to check for a pulse. He grunted, reached under Will, and lifted him, straining under the weight. "I'll give you a ride if you can't drive."

Her jaw dropped as he carried Will to the door. "That's it? You drag me out here to help, I nearly die. My friend nearly dies, and that's the best you can do? Offer a ride?"

Greg was halfway down the hall already. He paused and glanced over his shoulder at her. "I'll send someone to close the anomaly."

Cerulean huffed a pain-filled laugh. "Everyone's a user, Vinnie."

She guessed she better get moving, or Greg might just leave them. "Wait, how did you get here?"

"Hilda always leaves her key in her car. There's a pocket in the glove box she thinks no one will find. Even though it's in the glove box."

"You stole Hilda's car," Vinnie breathed. At least they didn't need to hurry. Let Greg wait out there for nothing. Or not. Her eyes darted to the anomaly. No, they still needed to hurry. A surge of rage made her hope the woman stepped back through as if her anger would be enough to win this time. Vinnie was no match for her. Not without help.

She crouched down and held her arm out so Cer could put his good arm over her shoulder. Once she had her arm around his waist, they stood. His weight made her careen into the wall, but they stayed upright.

Walking back through the house felt a little surreal. Vinnie kept expecting the woman to show up and attack again.

Outside, she could see that Greg had waited for them. That was something, at least.

The kid parked a car down the street. Can you drive? He thought at her from the driver's seat.

Yes. Of course, he had to have seen Cerulean arrive while he was sitting out here like a creeper.

Greg started the SUV and was gone before they even made it down the walkway.

"Jerk," Vinnie muttered. "Could have offered to help."

"I'm light as a feather." Cer waved one arm out to the side like he was trying to fly, the movement causing them to wobble.

"And I'm weak as a kitten," Vinnie said. Her breath came out in a tired rasp.

Cer said, "It's hard to get enough cupcakes."

Together, they hobbled down the sidewalk. She got Cer settled in the passenger seat, then went to the tree to pick up the styrofoam coffee cups. Cerulean was right — she needed the energy, and she didn't want to leave evidence behind. Evidence of what, she wasn't sure. Vinnie leaned against the tree as her head swam.

When the dizziness passed, she pushed off and trudged to the car. She slid into the driver's seat with both cups, and with shaking hands, she pulled the lid off the one she hoped was hers, and passed the other cup to Cerulean, who was zoning out. Good thing he wasn't squeamish about drinking after other people.

"Key?"

He leaned back, stretching his leg out so he could get the key out of his front pocket. His head lolled again after she took the key. The cup held loosely in his hands.

"Drink." She reached out and nudged his hand until he lifted the cup to his mouth. As far as she knew, he'd never thrown a fireball before, it had to have taken a lot out of him, plus whatever it took to heal the wound.

Cerulean took a swig and made a face. "Bitter."

"Better?" she asked.

"Bitter," he repeated.

Vinnie smiled. "I meant do you feel better?"

"Yes, thank you, ma'am."

She snorted at the ma'am and started the car. "We're the same age." Practically. "What were you doing there?"

"You left. You needed help."

"You could have gotten yourself killed."

Vinnie glanced at the dash as she drove, but the clock in Hilda's car was out. The attack had happened so fast. They walked into the room and the killer, the person who was probably the killer, arrived before they could do anything. She'd had more than one ability, and they were slippery. Was that what Vinnie's ability looked like?

"They'll be mad," Cerulean said.

She'd made it out of the neighborhood and onto the main

roads. All she could think about was making sure Cerulean was okay. She hadn't considered the fallout. Yes, their friends were going to be mad that they'd gotten hurt.

"You could have died," she repeated.

He laughed, sounding a little manic. "Wisps are good at dying."

The lights from the dash reflected off his gaunt cheeks. From this side, she couldn't see his face tattoos. A thin leather band hung off his wrist, and under that was a brand-new tattoo Vinnie hadn't seen. In the dim light, it looked like a scaly serpent coiling around his protruding bones, but the wings gave it away — a dragon — more detailed than any of the other tattoos that covered his body.

Wisps are good at dying, he'd said. Most Wisps died young, their power used a lot of energy, and they were forced to use it in work crews. But Cerulean was not in a work crew. If he didn't use the power, it wouldn't take such a toll, would it?

"Green light," he said.

Vinnie tore her eyes away and drove, glad she didn't need to look at him when she asked the next question. "Are you using again?" She didn't mean the power. Cerulean had a drug problem for years, but he was clean now. He had to be clean now.

He sighed and rolled his head away, and Vinnie's heart sunk.

"Cer, you have to stop that. You know it means you can't control your power. It will burn you up." Aside from the other risks, but she wasn't sure Cer cared about those.

He stared out the window, watching the lights go by. "You don't understand."

She didn't understand. She absolutely didn't understand. "No, I don't understand, and you won't tell me. I ask. I'm here, but you won't talk to me. Why would you kill yourself? You can't control the power if you are using. You have to stop."

He shook his head.

"Cerulean!" Yelling wouldn't help. She knew that, but her frustration burst out of her. "Help me understand, then."

He shook his head again, but it was jittery, and when he spoke his voice shook too. "Hilda doesn't care that she killed her dad. He was bad. My parents were good."

A loud honk startled Vinnie, and she slammed on the brake, narrowly missing someone coming through the intersection where she'd just run the stoplight. Heart pounding, she pulled the car over to the side of the road. She needed to get Cer to Jory, but he seemed stable physically, and he was talking to her, finally.

"That wasn't your fault. They wouldn't want you to hurt yourself too."

His breathing had become heavy, and he rocked, slamming his back into the seat repeatedly. "I still see them." He shuddered, his whole body shaking.

"You still see them?" He couldn't be saying what she thought he was saying. Cerulean had told them he'd passed out and woke up in the fire, his parents already dead.

"Burning, I see my mom screaming and her skin is peeling away." He was sobbing now. "And I can't stop. The fire keeps burning and it won't stop. Then the fire comes for me, there's fire all over my skin."

Vinnie unbuckled her seatbelt so she could lean over and pull him close. What could she say to that? He'd told them he wasn't there. Was this something in his head, or had he been there? All she knew was she didn't want him to burn himself out using his power or overdose. "It's over."

He buried his face in her shoulder, his body shaking. "It's not over. I'm always burning. Every day I'm on fire. My skin turns black, and it won't stop."

Vinnie swallowed hard. Trying to find something, anything, she could say to him. He needed help, needed a therapist, but how do you get a therapist for someone who wasn't supposed to be free? Who was wanted for murder?

"I still see them. I couldn't save them. I was so scared and confused and I ran. My body burns, my skin is always burning off, to punish me. No matter how much good I try to do — I'm still punished."

"Oh, Cer. Sam." Her own throat was closing as tears pricked her eyes. "You aren't being punished. You didn't hurt anyone on purpose, it wasn't your fault."

"It hurts so much. It never stops hurting. I just want to stop hurting Vinnie."

She could barely get the words out. "I don't want you to die. Don't I count?"

His breath was shaky as he pulled it again, hiccupping lightly. "It hurts, Vinnie."

She rubbed his arm. "I know, but you can't give up. I need you. I would be dead now without you."

He pulled in a shuddering breath. "That was a pretty wicked fireball I threw."

"That *was* a pretty wicked fireball. You saved my life."

He sat up, wiping snot on his shoulder. "I did, didn't I?"

"You did, I'm so glad you were there."

His head bobbed in a way that almost looked like a nod and then his eyes rolled back, and he slumped, passed out. Vinnie put her fingers on this throat. Alive, just worn out.

The coffee cup in his hand was miraculously not spilled. She pulled it out of his grasp and put it in the center console before starting the car again.

Cerulean still hadn't woken up when she pulled the car into the carport.

Vinnie felt for Nell's power as she got out of the car. She opened the passenger door and pulled the power, allowing strength to fill her. The Stone energy couldn't erase her fatigue, but at least she'd be able to carry Cerulean. She slid her arms behind his back and under his knees, lifting him out of the car.

When she was halfway up the steps, Nell appeared in the

doorway. Oh good, mom was up. Now they just needed dad. As if summoned, Jory appeared behind Nell's shoulder. Vinnie almost collapsed with relief when she saw him. He could fix this.

CHAPTER TWENTY

Nell darted down the steps. "What happened?"

"Ice spike in the shoulder," Vinnie said as Nell reached under and through Vinnie's arms to take Cerulean. Vinnie released the power she'd borrowed just as his weight settled in Nell's arms.

Jory stepped out of the doorway to let Nell through. His haunted eyes coming up to meet Vinnie's.

Vinnie swayed forward, using the momentum of her fatigue to start her feet moving. Jory's hand brushed her shoulder as she walked into the house, and relief flooded her. He would forgive her. He was glad she was safe.

Nell had settled Cer on the couch by the time Vinnie got inside.

"Sit," Jory said as he brushed past her to look at Cerulean.

Jory put his hand on Cerulean's forehead, and Cer's eyes cracked open. "Preacher Man."

"I'm not a preacher." Jory kneeled, placing his hands on Cer's shoulders and closing his eyes. "You did a good job of stopping the bleeding. I'm just going to fix a few things."

"You should have been a doctor," Nell said.

Jory didn't argue, he didn't need to, because they'd all said things like that to him before. As far as the government knew, he was dead, but there were still databases with his name and fingerprints. Even if he could pass background checks, he said he couldn't take watching people die because he couldn't be too obvious. And even if he didn't have to hide, he couldn't save them all. His power was finite, like anyone else's.

At least he could fix Cerulean's wounds. Cerulean would be fine, despite what Vinnie had done. She'd thought she could help, that she could do something, but the killer was better than she was, could do things Vinnie couldn't do. Maybe she could learn them. She'd picked up what Will was trying to teach her easily enough. With time, Vinnie believed she could figure out how to stop this killer but seeing Cer hurt shook her. Did she even have time to learn with Maddie's life at stake?

"Talk," Jory said. The deep rumble of his voice was a balm, even though he was angry.

"I threw a fireball at the bad woman," Cer said. "After that guy we killed passed out."

"The guy we killed?" Nell said. Her eyes were luminous with fatigue and though the weather was still warm, she wore a baggy off-the-shoulder sweater that swallowed her slight frame. It would be easy to assume she was harmless and that the steel in her voice wasn't a warning.

Vinnie didn't want to be on Nell's dangerous side, so explaining wouldn't be fun. "Will. He wasn't dead after all."

"He's a Zee?" Jory asked.

Vinnie processed that for a moment. That made two people who took the stories of Zee coming back from the dead seriously. "He's a Mesmer." Might as well just get it all out there so they could be angry and yell. "He contacted me a few days ago and asked for help again, and I've been working with him." Nell opened her mouth, but Vinnie barreled on. "I helped him find the girl, Maddie. We went tonight to get her out. There was a woman there who was Mesmer, Dancer, and I think Ferr."

"That's not possible." Nell's hands clutched the back of the loveseat.

But it was. If Vinnie could hold multiple abilities and there were more people like her, then this killer could be Vasum. What would her ability feel like to someone who could detect it? "That's what I felt. She threw ice spikes. I guess that could be a water ability exclusively, but Will said there are more people like me out there."

"There are more like you." Jory's words were like one long exhale. His head drooped even as his hand moved to Cer's shoulder.

"So, this killer could have been pulling abilities from someone else," Nell said. "But you can only hold one."

The room tilted, and not just from the fatigue. Vinnie moved her rubbery legs forward so she could collapse in a chair. Nell didn't know how much Vinnie had learned. Her world had changed in just a few days, and she hadn't brought her friends along. Would tonight have gone differently if she had told them what was going on? Nell had said she was glad Will was dead, but she also didn't seem bothered by the revelation that he was alive. "Will showed me how to hold more than one. I used Ferr and Wisp magic together to search the city for Maddie."

"I guess that explains why your clothes are hanging off of you." Jory stood and turned. His whole body seemed clenched. "Not only did you take the chance by chasing a potential killer, you teamed up with someone dangerous. You don't know who he is or what he's capable of, and you didn't even tell us so that we could at least be on the lookout. Where did this reckless streak come from? A few months ago, you were content to keep your head down and stay safe, and now you think you're some kind of superhero? You're not. And now you've put Cerulean in danger too."

"I don't think I'm a superhero." Never mind that she had been thinking that she could do amazing things. "But I can do more than I thought I could. The killer was *right there.* If I understood my ability better, I could have stopped her. And a few months ago? I thought I was safe. I thought we all were safe, but we are not safe with people like that out there." Her chest burned and Vinnie rubbed it, trying to ease the constriction.

A few steps brought Jory close enough to place his hand on her forehead.

"Your sternum is cracked. Eardrums ruptured." He moved his hand to her shoulder and closed his eyes.

That would explain the dull throb in her chest that expanded to a full, fiery pain now that she was paying attention. The pain eased back into a dull throb.

"I think I'll leave the bruise," Jory said as he pulled his hand away. "We won't be safer if you put yourself in danger. It sounds like you were outmatched. She could have killed you both. I don't know why she didn't."

He paced away and sat on the loveseat that Nell stood behind. They seemed to be waiting for her to say something.

"I wouldn't have been outmatched if we had all been there."

Jory's head slumped.

"Could you have been wrong about her abilities?" Nell asked.

That was Nell, always looking for answers. If her ability was misleading her, how would she know? She didn't have a user manual and people didn't announce what they were so she could verify. "I don't think so."

Nell pried her hands off the loveseat and walked around to sit beside Jory. A loud snore from the direction of the couch punctuated her movements, and she cast a worried look at Cerulean before turning back to Vinnie. "You're working with Will Darrow and went to rescue this girl."

The words were a prompt, but Vinnie didn't know what else Nell wanted from her.

The front door opened and closed. There was a clop of heels, a shuffle, and then bare feet padding down the hallway. Hilda appeared in the archway wearing a slinky red dress. She had her heels in her hands and so much make-up on that she looked like someone else.

Morning, Cupcake. She leaned against the wall, folding her arms.

"Yes," Vinnie addressed Nell. Hilda could catch up by listening to what they said and thought. "Will and I went into the house. I used my ability to find Maddie, who was tied up in the master bedroom. I tried to untie her, but a woman appeared from an anomaly."

"Wait, an anomaly?" Nell sat forward.

"There was one in the room. She came out of it and attacked, knocking Will out fast. We fought, and she was about to throw another ice ball at me when Cer came in and threw a fireball at her. She threw an ice spike at him, but it gave me time to get the knife Will had brought—"

"How did she knock Will out?" Nell asked.

"An ice ball." Vinnie frowned. "Why did she throw a ball at him but a spike at Cer?"

"Because he's working with her," Jory said like it was the most obvious thing in the world.

"No," Vinnie said. "She threw a ball at me too, and I'm not working with her. Maybe she didn't think Will was a threat. He can hide his ability. I would look like I had no power, maybe, but Cer is a Wisp. She hit Will pretty hard with the ice ball."

"Another person out there like Vinnie?" Hilda said, trying to catch up.

"That's what it looks like," Jory said. "Vinnie felt three different abilities."

Will taught me to use multiple abilities at once. I didn't know it was possible.

Hilda's mouth twisted. *Wisp, that's why you're emaciated, and Ferr? You were searching for her.*

Yes.

Vinnie continued out loud. "I attacked her, drawing power from Cer. I thought I had her worn down. But…" The next part sounded even crazier than the rest, and she was less sure about it. "I think she was pulling power from the anomaly."

"No way," Nell said. "That isn't possible."

Jory grunted. "We've got a person like Vinnie, another person who can hide his own ability, what's one more thing?"

"Power is power," Hilda said. "We push the power back into the anomaly. Maybe we could pull it out too?"

Jory stared at his hands, which were on his knees, watching his fists clench and unclench. He looked like he was going to hit something.

Nell said, "You didn't sense any other Twisted in the area, did you? How did she get the other abilities, if not from the anomaly?"

That hadn't occurred to Vinnie, and it should have. "Maddie was Dancer and Will, and Greg are Mesmer so that explains that but not the Ferr. I didn't sense anyone else in the area that she could pull from, anomaly energy doesn't feel the same. Not outside a person anyway." But as Will had made clear, there was a lot Vinnie didn't understand. "I'm not sure how it would feel inside a person."

"We've got a killer who knows Vinnie's and Cerulean's faces, who can use multiple abilities and can possibly pull from anomalies and use that power outside his or herself." Jory grabbed his phone off the side table and dialed a number, put the phone on speaker, and set it on the coffee table.

After a few rings, TK's voice came on, sounding wide awake. "What did they do now?"

"Is it possible for someone to pull power from an anomaly?"

"Why are you asking me that?"

"Terrance." Jory didn't have to say anything else. 'Cut the crap,' was implied.

TK sighed through the speakers, the sound coming out as a heavy rasp. "Yes, probably, but someone would have to have a lot of power to begin with to do that unless they know something I don't. And doesn't everyone know something I don't? Now, are you going to tell me what this is about?"

"The guy from the amusement park is still alive and Vinnie was working with him. They found the kidnapped girl at a house in the suburbs, but the killer got away. The killer knows Vinnie's and Cerulean's faces now. The killer, can, apparently, use multiple abilities and the park man has taught Vinnie to do the same."

"What suburb?"

"What difference does that make?"

"Jory," TK Said in almost the same tone Jory had just used on him.

Out of everything he'd just heard, that seemed like a strange first question. "Anders Heights," Vinnie said.

"Money neighborhood," Jory said.

"We're doing this, then." TK had known Jory longer than any of them, except Cerulean. His response was not a question, and he didn't seem happy about it. They were going to help.

"What?" Nell, who had been sitting with her arms wrapped tightly around her middle, unfurled. "Cer and Vinnie could have been killed. We need to stay out of this."

"The killer knows their faces, they have power and possibly money, you think they won't come after Vinnie and Cerulean, who put themselves in the way?" Jory asked.

"Vinnie was already putting herself in the way." Then understanding dawned on Nell's face. "You didn't think Vinnie would find anything."

"No," Jory said. "I didn't think there was a serial killer. And no, I didn't think Vinnie on her own could find one if someone with more connections had already been looking. And no, I didn't think it would happen so fast if she did. But you were the one who was willing to help her a few days ago."

"I was helping with a computer, safe and legal."

"We're not safe now," TK said through the phone. "We've got their attention."

"Then we hide Vinnie and Cer. We keep them safe," Nell said.

Hilda snorted. "You haven't been paying attention, Nell."

Vinnie felt bands wrapping around her chest, threatening to suffocate her. "She'll kill Maddie. I'm sorry that I got us into this, but I can't just abandon her."

"And there it is. She won't stop," Hilda said, shooting Nell an 'I told you so' look.

"Don't be sorry, Lavinia," TK said. "You may think this is your doing, and it is, but it's also not. Something big is coming, it's been coming. The chances of us remaining on the sidelines were slim the minute Jory let me in his house four years ago. Do you think it's a coincidence there's one of each type of ability here? Things happen for a reason."

"Now you're a prophet too?" Jory growled.

"I work in news. I don't need to be a prophet I just need to pay attention. Things are changing, Jory. We are getting more and more stories trickling in of unexplainable things happening. Violence markers against Twisted are up. The world is restless."

Hilda pushed off the door frame, standing up straight. "That's not us, that's the world. That has nothing to do with us or The Holt. Your logic is off."

"We can turn it over to the authorities, Vinnie," Nell said. "You saw her tied up. They'll find her."

"Was Vinnie wrong about the killer's abilities?" TK asked. "Because my logic is irrelevant. The local police would be outmatched."

Hilda's hand slashed through the air. "We already know that's possible because Vinnie can do it. It's not something new or evidence of the world changing, just a killer who can do what Vinnie can do. That doesn't mean there are more people involved or that we have to get involved ourselves. It's just one killer with a vendetta against Twisted. That's the simplest explanation. Occam's Razor, the simplest explanation is probably correct." She glared at Nell. "Don't look at me like that. Just because I didn't graduate high school doesn't mean I'm not smart."

"No one said you weren't smart," Jory murmured, earning himself a glare too.

"Why are you looking at me?" Nell said. "I didn't say you were dumb. I agree with you. We need to stay out of it."

"That's not what I said," Hilda said. "I said it was one killer. We can take out one killer who is threatening our family."

Nell deflated. "What if it is more than one? One of the team members at the Warrior Games had a heart attack. I investigated because Vinnie asked me, and he had ties to Lambs Against Chaos. We already know there might be a connection to the games. It could be more than one killer."

"We'll kill them too," Hilda said.

Vinnie opened her mouth to argue that they weren't killing anyone and then snapped it shut. They were going to help. This is what she wanted. The rest of the argument could wait.

"I'll..." Nell hugged her arms around herself again. "I guess. We should wake Cer, and someone needs to talk to Shaw when she gets home."

"Let him sleep," Jory said. "We need to figure out where we go from here."

CHAPTER TWENTY-ONE

"Do you have a minute?" Jory stood in the doorway to Vinnie's room.

She was just shoving her feet into her shoes, the sign she'd prepared to put on the library door beside her. "Yeah."

"Meet me in the garden."

Before she could protest that she didn't have that much time, he was leaving.

By the time she'd gotten her shoes and got to the back door, Jory was stepping over the low fence to his garden, pruning shears and a basket in hand.

They'd come up with a tentative plan last night. He was going to find out who had been to showings of the house by talking to real estate agents he knew. Nell would find out who owned the house. It should be public record, so that was easy enough. Vinnie and TK would go to the house, and she'd show him where the killer and Maddie had been so he could feel their energy signatures and trace them. Then Vinnie, Hilda, and TK would go talk to Will.

Trying to read signatures at both places would likely wipe TK out, but if he still had the energy, they would go to the stadium.

186

Cerulean could boost him enough to search the crowds there. Will said the killer couldn't be an employee of the games because they tested them all, but if the killer was Vasum, the test might not catch them.

Jory was laying out a knee cushion and kneeled to weed and prune.

Vinnie paused by the fence. "I need to get my sign up before the library opens at nine."

"It won't matter if you're a little late."

"It matters to me."

Jory gave her a flat look. "Please." He pointed to the space next to him.

Guilt sealed her mouth against another protest. He was putting himself in danger because of her. The least she could do was listen. Besides, he was right. Not that many people came into the library at nine in the morning on a Saturday.

She stepped over the small fence and kneeled on the garden pad next to Jory.

He clipped a pepper off the vine and put it in a little basket between them. "I want you to keep Shaw and Cerulean out of this."

Vinnie had picked up the second set of sheers he'd brought and was about to clip a pepper. Her hands dropped to her lap, and she tried to tamp down her frustration. "They aren't children, they're almost my age. And we need them."

"They couldn't even talk to Will Darrow without giving him our names. They charge headlong into danger without thinking of what damage they might do. Cerulean could have been killed last night. And now you're being just as reckless. Maybe I should try to keep you out of it. You could have been killed last night, too. But you won't stay out of it and let us handle it, will you?"

Ouch. Vinnie couldn't deny that she'd made some mistakes. They hadn't seemed that reckless at the time — they'd seemed inevitable. Could she have chosen differently? Maybe, but she didn't think she would have. Jory had said before that Shaw and Cer were younger than their years. Is that what he thought of her, too? She ran her own business. Sort of. She'd traveled across the country on her own. So had Shaw. Yes, Shaw acted young, but she was a survivor. Cerulean had lived on the streets alone. They were all survivors.

"No, I won't stay out of it, and you won't keep them out either. It's not up to me. I'm not their mother. If you want someone to act like a mom, ask Nell. She has the temperament."

He slammed his clippers into the dirt. "They won't listen to anyone trying to parent them, but they idolize you. Who knows why, but they do. If you tell them to stay out of it, they might actually listen."

Another ouch. Vinnie didn't know if she should be flattered that he thought they idolized her or hurt because he thought she didn't deserve it. "It's going to take all of us. You didn't see what this woman could do. We need them, and you aren't responsible for what they do."

"I am." The anguish in his voice caught her off guard. "I am. I brought them into this house."

"And saved them from the street. You've saved us all. Is it so bad if we take that gift and give it to others? And Cerulean..." Her voice trailed off. How did she talk to him about what Cer had said about not wanting to live?

"I never wanted to take any of you in," Jory said. "I didn't want anyone else in my life. Everyone I care about dies. I had brothers, Vinnie. I had a dad and a mom. They took my older brother when I was three. My dad killed himself before they could test him, hoping they'd not realize the Zee ran in the family, and Mom moved us across the country, worked jobs that didn't ask for ID. Then, some men my younger brother worked with found out what he was and beat him to death. We were all Zee, my dad, my brothers. They had witnesses to prove what my brother was, so no one said a thing. The police would do nothing. So, I did something. I only killed two of them. There are three still out there."

There was no venom in Jory's voice when he mentioned the last three. If it had been Hilda, Vinnie would have thought that she'd be biding her time before going after the last three, but not Jory. He wasn't the same hothead that had gotten into that bar fight. Or maybe he'd never been the hothead to get into a spur-of-the-moment bar fight. "The bar fight, it wasn't impulsive, was it?"

He shook his head. "No, I didn't lose my temper. I went in there with a plan. Trying to find justice cost me my last years with my mom. She died of cancer when I was in the camps. Just another form of recklessness."

"I went in with a plan, too," Vinnie said. A sick feeling started in her stomach because of what she was about to say. She'd never told anyone this, but if he wanted to use the past to justify his position, so could she. "The girl in high school that got caught because of me? It wasn't an accident. She bullied my best friend so much she became suicidal. I had to stop her, so I waited for Lauren in the cafeteria and bumped into her, knocking her tray down. I refused to apologize, and when she started calling me names and threatening me, I pulled her power and made myself cry blood. Of course, Lauren was the first one tested. They took her away, and she died. Because of me. I can never take that back or fix it. But my friend lived. Others started doing better in school because they weren't afraid. Was it worth it? I don't know, but if I'd done nothing people would have continued to get hurt."

Jory cupped his hand around a tomato, still on the vine. His thumb gently pressed the flesh, testing its ripeness. "You've always been a crusader, then. I'm relieved it wasn't being here that broke you."

Anger flashed hot in her abdomen. "I'm not broken. Trying to help people isn't a bad thing."

"There are things you can come back from." He tugged the

tomato and released it. The vine bounced. Then he took his sheers and cut the tomato off. "And things you can't."

Vinnie shook her head in frustration. "Why did you take us in if you didn't want us, then? You didn't say no when I showed up on your doorstep. And Hilda and TK were here. I know you needed the money, which is why TK moved in, but you didn't have to take on the rest of us."

"I found Hilda asleep in the basement with a sword. Which she pointed at me and said she wasn't leaving." There was a smile in his voice at this. "I was afraid of her. I don't know what happened, but she was dirty and bruised, her hair wild. You don't tangle with feral creatures."

She almost laughed, ruining her righteous anger. Vinnie had seen Hilda's sword, though she would use the term sword loosely. It was one of those cheap decorative swords that high school kids bought to hang on the wall that would probably bend if you tried to stab anyone.

"You never told me that." There was more to the story that he wasn't saying because Vinnie was sure he and TK could have kicked Hilda out if they'd wanted to.

"Then you came in like a whirlwind, bags already packed. I thought maybe you could protect me from her."

Now she knew he was joking, even though his face was perfectly straight.

She'd been desperate and scared. Her dad had controlled every aspect of her life, and while she hadn't been as cut off from the world as Shaw, she didn't know how to survive.

"And then I started feeling the anomaly after Cer moved in. Then Nell showed up, and the only thing missing was a Dancer. We wouldn't have to call anyone else in and expose ourselves. It worked out so perfectly, almost like it was planned."

Again, he wasn't telling her the whole truth. He could have called the city. They may not jump to stop the crime in The Holt, but they would close an anomaly. Goosebumps had popped up on her arms. "I think he heard you."

He picked up his clippers again and moved to the next plant. "Who?"

"Harry."

"It's not alive."

"That's what you all keep saying."

He paused and searched her face. "You're serious."

"No. Yes. Maybe. I don't know. Could it be aware but not alive?"

"Like some sort of amoeba? Those have some awareness, right? That's a creepy thought, but is there anything that would be surprising anymore?" He clipped another tomato and put it in the basket beside him.

"People suddenly accepting us for who we are and not locking us up?" Vinnie said, half joking, but him saying he didn't want them there kept playing in the back of her mind.

Jory laughed, but it wasn't a happy sounding laugh. Then he sobered. "I didn't want to take any of you in, but I did, and now you're my responsibility. Shaw and Cerulean are impulsive and sometimes reckless. I thought you knew better, though. I thought you wanted to be safe."

She did. "TK is right. The world is not safe. It's only as safe as we make it. Cerulean knows this. If he hadn't come, I might be dead, and that's the only thing that — " She caught herself, unable to say that she thought Cer was staying alive so he could help. "He's hurting, Jory. He needs a reason to keep going. And Shaw…"

"Shaw just wants to be a dragon," Jory said. "Such a bizarre obsession."

"Dragons are big and powerful and can't be hurt easily. That's not bizarre to want to be strong."

"There are a lot of ways to be strong that she is capable of, but she chases something that's not possible," Jory said.

Even though Vinnie thought Shaw transforming into a dragon was improbable, hearing Jory dump on her dream got Vinnie's hackles up. "She saw someone transform into a dragon, it's not impossible."

"He was from a different world," Jory said.

She didn't know how to argue against that. Some people who came through the anomalies had the same abilities they did, but maybe there were things about those worlds that were different enough to make a dragon possible there and not here. "It's not impossible."

Jory put the clippers in the basket and looked at her. "Fine. Tell me something, Vinnie. If you had a choice between saving us and someone else, what would you choose?"

She could see the trap, but not how to stay out of it, so she tried to dodge. "Neither, I would save everyone."

"What if that's not a choice?"

There was always a choice. How could she not try to save everyone? She knew what he wanted. "I would save you."

"Good. I can tell Cerulean I need him for something on the day you go to the Warrior Games with TK. I'll keep him involved and helping in a way that keeps him out of danger, so he has a reason to keep going."

And there was the trap. Do what she could to save Cerulean because she'd just said that's what she would do. But it still wasn't a choice she was sure she had to make.

Tickets to the Warrior games had been sold out for weeks. They would have to stand outside the stadium, which would require more maneuvering. TK would need a boost from Cer to extend his range. "TK Doesn't have the range to search the whole stadium for a signature. I don't think it would be that dangerous for Cer to come."

"We don't know what he might do if TK finds a signature that matches. He doesn't always think straight. There are so many

Twisted there. You can draw power and give TK the boost if he needs it."

"There's too much power around the teams. It overwhelms me, I'll be useless."

"I need touch to heal someone." Jory reached out and put his fingers on her wrist. The ache in her knees from kneeling eased. "Hilda, TK, Shaw, and Cer can all use abilities that affect others at a distance. You can use my power to affect others at a distance. You should be able to use your power that way, control where it goes, how much it takes in."

Should, maybe, but it was untested versus something they knew how to do. Will had taught her how to hold two abilities in one night, and she'd learned a little about controlling her ability and focusing it. Maybe she could do this, but she wasn't sure. Plus, her body was still worn out from searching for Maddie. They'd decided that trying that again would be too much. Maybe filtering would be too much too. Vinnie didn't know how much it would take out of her. "I haven't figured it out yet. When someone's life is on the line doesn't seem like the best time to try something new."

"If you can't do it, we'll figure something else out." His face softened. "Please. I asked you to stay out of this, and you didn't. Now I'm asking you to at least keep Shaw and Cer out as much as possible."

Shame and anger roiled inside her. Shame that she'd gotten Cerulean hurt and anger that he was using that against her. The others were putting themselves on the line because they cared, and she'd backed them into a corner. Now Jory had backed her into one and she couldn't do anything but agree.

"Okay," she said at last.

CHAPTER TWENTY-TWO

Vinnie grabbed the super sweet tea from the van's center console and gulped some more down. She ran her tongue over her teeth, enjoying the sugary taste. Her body was recovering, so she shouldn't need to do this much longer. Unless she did something to wear herself out again. Like using Wisp power to boost TK from outside the stadium.

She slid the seatbelt off, wincing as the buckle smacked into the window. Her parking spot was a block away from the library. Vinnie grabbed the paper sign off the seat, took another swig of tea, and hopped out of the van.

The streets were busier than normal for a Saturday morning. The cold was coming, and people probably wanted to take advantage of the last warm days. Her hoodie wrapped around her like an old friend, keeping the slight chill off. She'd worn this hoodie the day she left home, and she'd worn it at the parade a few weeks ago when doing something good seemed straightforward. The nubby soft fabric against her arms comforted her.

Vinnie dodged a young couple holding hands while they walked. She barely registered the man standing leaning against the lamppost outside the alleyway that led to the library until he looked up. Her steps slowed as Conor's head came up and he saw her. A small spike of adrenaline shot through her.

What was he doing here? How had he found her? It had to be a coincidence that he was here now. He wasn't here because he or his friends saw her at the house last night, right? She wished she could read his expression behind his sunglasses.

Then he smiled, like the sun breaking through clouds, and her stomach flipped for a different reason. Ugh.

"There you are," he said. "The internet said the library opened at nine on a Saturday. I guess it was wrong."

"Have you been waiting here since nine?" That was at least forty-five minutes.

Conor's mouth parted and then snapped shut. He shook his head a little too emphatically. "Nope. No, that would be pathetic and desperate, and I would never."

"How did you know how to find me?"

"There aren't a lot of volunteer libraries in the city. I found the donation entry on Communities Caring." He cleared his throat. "I didn't go to a lot of trouble, honest. It wasn't hard. I wasn't sure this was yours, then you don't seem like the type to be late..."

She was a reckless idiot. She'd thought she could go talk to potential killers and everything would be fine, but she was so unprepared for ordinary questions, she'd told the truth. Now, here he was, the day after she'd run into a killer.

She folded the paper that said she was closing the library because of illness, not wanting to give him more information. But it was too late now. He'd found her and she was putting it on the door to the library where anyone could see. Vinnie held the paper out, showing him. "The library usually opens at nine. I'm shutting it down a for few days because a friend is sick."

His mouth tightened. "Must be a close friend."

Something about that bothered him. If the killer was Vasum, like her, it could have been him last night shifted into a smaller form, but that seemed like an unnecessary use of power. There was still the possibility of more than one person being involved, and so she still needed to be careful.

"None of your business," she said, putting as much coldness in her voice as possible, hoping he'd take the hint.

Vinnie left him standing there and went down the alley and took the steps to the basement two at a time. The tape she needed to hang the paper was in the back room. She unlocked the door, shoving it with her shoulder until it came free of the frame.

When she came back out of the back room after fetching the tape, Conor was standing by the front desk, eyes traveling along the ceiling around the room.

"Didn't you hear? The library is closed." Irritation warred with pleasure inside her. Vinnie opened her senses, relieved to find someone with Stone ability nearby. She could pull some power if she needed it. She wasn't completely helpless.

"I'm sorry." He scratched his head. "The other night when you came to The Roundhouse was tense. I was hoping I could make it up to you by taking you to lunch?"

He really didn't take a hint. "I'm busy."

"Right, your sick friend." He frowned at the paper in her hand. "Maybe a quick coffee?"

She stared at him in disbelief. "Why are you so determined? There are plenty of women who would love to have coffee with you. Why keep trying someone who isn't interested?"

"You... I...." He scratched his head again and looked away. "I don't believe you're not interested. I think you're scared." His eyes flicked to hers and away again. "I met your dad once."

Vinnie's hands clenched, the sound of crumpling paper loud in the quiet room. Here he was, standing in her library, no one else around. There were no tenants on the floor above. Zandia might come in soon, but what help would she be? She pulled the nearby Stone power and moved one foot toward the door before she caught herself.

"I'm sorry. I'm sorry," he said. "That upset you. I don't know your dad. I only met him once. I swear. I am not a stalker. Well, I mean, I thought your name was familiar and looked it up to confirm."

She felt coiled, every fiber tensed to run. "Then why bring it up? If you're looking for money or a sponsorship. I can't help you. I don't talk to my dad."

"No," he said. "It's not that. I'm sorry. I'm trying to explain why I'm here. You climbed a fence because you were looking for a friend of your sister's. Your dad is the CEO of the biggest telecom in the country and you're running a volunteer library in a basement that smells like..."

"Pickles," she said.

"Yeah." he scrunched his face. "That is kind of what it smells like. I'm not much of a reader, so I've never understood the whole smell of books thing, but the pickle smell is stronger than the book smell."

She crossed her arms. "You were saying."

"It's rare to meet someone with that kind of courage," he said.

How could she have been so stupid that she didn't consider that he might have met her dad? Here in The Holt, the likelihood that anyone would connect her to her dad was remote. The likelihood that anyone could name the CEO of any major corporation was remote. But her dad liked to pretend he was a philanthropist, and Conor's foundation would be right up his alley. Plus, with Conor being an athlete, he could end up at an event her dad was attending. She didn't think Conor was famous enough to be stalked by reporters but there were fan sites, all it would take was someone taking a picture of her with him and someone who knew her from her former life seeing it, and her dad could find her.

Conor's story of recognizing the name and looking her up sounded true. He'd pushed his sunglasses up, and his eyes seemed just as earnest as his words, but he could just be a good liar.

"That's a cool story, but if you only met my dad once, how did you make the connection?"

This was important because if his story was true and he made the connection, anyone could. She should have been more careful.

"Your dad was awful." He eyed her to see what her reaction to this was, but Vinnie remained frozen. "We were at a fundraising event for the Foundation. He was angry at the lack of progress in the research, and he took it out on the hostess, threatening to have her replaced. I made a comment to one of the other people at my table over dinner, and he said that Jonathan Forbes hadn't been the same since his daughter Lavinia disappeared. He was desperate to find you and was afraid Twisted had abducted you. He said his anger was part of his grief and worry."

Ha. Yeah. Her dad had probably been upset that he lost a powerful tool he hadn't even known he had until it was too late. Vinnie tried to force her body to relax, unclenching her hand. She laid the crumpled paper on the counter. "And what did you think of that?" Are you going to tell my dad I'm here? That's what she wanted to ask.

"He never reported you missing. That would have been big news, a CEO's daughter kidnapped. And I got a bad vibe off him." He stepped forward and smoothed the wrinkles out of her paper. "The story seemed fishy to me but, not my business and I forgot about it. In the parking lot, when you said your name was Lavinia, I thought it sounded familiar, but only remembered where I'd heard it last night. It was easy enough to find pictures of Jonathan Forbes's daughter on the internet. A missing girl looking for a missing girl."

"It's not the same." Vinnie's insides unclenched a little, and she watched his hands as he carefully smoothed the paper she'd crumpled.

"Because you ran away. Or left. I guess you were an adult by then. Most people don't run from privilege. Even if the privilege is killing them, they hold on to it with everything they've got, do whatever it takes, even if the person with the purse strings is horrible to them. But you left. For this." He waved his hand around, indicating the library.

"Don't let the pickle smell fool you. This place is amazing."

"It feels good to be in here. I can feel the love. That's not a joke. I swear. I mean it. But." He put his elbows on the counter and leaned closer, murmuring conspiratorially, "What's up with the hideous wallpaper?"

Vinnie snorted. "It was here when I rented the place. My lease doesn't allow me to make changes."

"Do they come check?" There was a mischievous glint in his eyes. "I could help you take it down. When your friend is better."

Vinnie shook her head. "Why would you do that? Don't you have a job to be doing?"

"Right." He frowned. "I could help you do that when your friend is better, and the season is over in a month. I'll have some time before I need to head home."

"Maybe you won't even like me in a month after you get to know me."

"Am I going to get to know you?" He'd rested his chin on his hand and was gazing at her. "It really is too bad you're so busy. Some ticket holders canceled tomorrow. You could go to the game, and then we could go out."

Vinnie crossed her arms as if that would stop her from liking him. Then what he'd just said sunk in. Ticket holders canceled tomorrow. He could get them into the game, where it would be much easier to search. That would be reckless again, wouldn't it? Accepting that invitation.

"Some of my friends have been wanting to see a game."

Something flashed in his face, disappointment or frustration, but hope replaced it. "You'll come? If I can get you and your friends tickets? Go out with me after? I promise to be respectful of your time."

This was exactly what they needed right now — a break. If she could get TK and Hilda close to him, then maybe they'd know for sure if he had helped the killer.

He was waiting for her to answer. She couldn't make that decision on her own, not after last night. What if it was a mistake?

"I'll talk to my friends and call you. Will that work?"

He grinned as if she'd already said yes.

CHAPTER TWENTY-THREE

TK let off the brake and eased through the next intersection. He'd been waiting for Vinnie when she got back home. Now he drove five miles below the speed limit, seeming to be in no hurry, which had given her plenty of time to tell him about Conor, but she hadn't.

"You drive like an old man," she said.

They were finally a few blocks from the house where the killer had been keeping Maddie. "Is there something wrong with being safe?"

TK reminded her of lava — placid on the surface, but something boiling beneath. Vinnie had never seen him lose his temper, and she hoped she never did.

"What we're doing is not safe, there's an anomaly and the killer could still be there or might come back."

He pulled to a stop at a four-way. No one else was coming, but he let the car rock back and paused before hitting the gas. "And that means I should drive like a maniac and risk us in other ways too?"

Vinnie turned her head back to the window. The driving

wasn't that important, she just wanted something to say. "Have we heard from Nell yet?" she asked.

"You know that's just busy work."

"You don't think knowing who owns the house is important?"

"I don't think the killer would be stupid enough to use a house they owned. She said Maddie's parents have finally reported her missing. And there were two messages in the online drop box asking us to look for her. Probably teenagers."

TK was supposed to have shut that down — Jory had picked up the physical one. "The drop box you were going to shut down?" And someone trusted them enough to ask for help. Vinnie almost smiled at that.

They'd come to the street where the house was, and TK pulled right up in front. "I forgot."

"You didn't forget." The words were out of her mouth before she thought about them, but it felt right.

"Why would I leave it open?"

That was the question, wasn't it? TK had no reason that she could think of to leave it open.

"Maybe we should park farther away?" she said.

"Best not to look like we're breaking in. You feel anything?"

Reaching out was almost automatic now. She'd pushed her ability wide open so often over the last few days.

"There's nothing." And there wasn't. No Twisted, no anomaly. Greg kept to what he said he was going to do and got some people to shut it down. Or someone else did. Vinnie had wanted to call Will this morning to make sure he was okay and ask questions about last night, but the others wanted to wait, talk to him in person. "Unless Will is in there."

"Creepy fucker." Even TK's curses were calm, like a monk saying, 'toast with butter,' but the monk had a knife under his robes and would stab you dead.

"A Norm could be in there." They should have brought Shaw. "Shaw would have been useful." Or Hilda, but what they wanted Hilda to do later would probably take a lot of her energy.

"Shaw is too erratic. Jory is right."

Said the man who left a drop box open he had agreed to close.

Vinnie pulled her hoodie up over her head and ducked as she pushed out of the car and approached the house. Her glance drifted to the for sale sign as she walked past. A smaller sold sign sat on top. Had that been there last night?

She went straight to the front door and tried the doorknob, remembering how Greg had unlocked it. They didn't have a plan — get in, get TK to the area where Maddie had been, see what he could feel.

"Back door," TK said.

So much for not looking suspicious. The only fences around the yards here were stone walls, maybe a foot and a half high. No privacy fence to hide what they were doing from the neighbors.

"Weekdays are the best days to break into houses because most people are at work. Kick the door, get in, get out." TK's face turned hard. "I never broke into anyone's house."

"I know that," she said. He'd grown up in a poor but loving family and didn't get into trouble. He'd been homeless briefly, but then he'd gotten a job at the news station and was promoted within just a few years to his current position.

They'd reached the back door. TK kicked the door just under the handle and it popped open.

"Alarm?" Vinnie said. "Your car is out front, someone is going to remember it."

TK strode into the house and headed toward the master bedroom like he knew where he was going.

"Why am I here at all?" Vinnie muttered as she followed him.

"Because there is a small chance you might be useful for a change." TK stepped into the bedroom.

For a change? "I thought you needed me to show you where they were."

He walked straight to the spot where Maddie had lain, crouched. "The stink makes that very clear."

And just like that, she was sure he had an ulterior motive. "And you knew it would, so why am I really here? Do you want to lecture me about getting Cerulean and Shaw involved, too?"

He stood and turned, taking in the room. "I told Jory you would be trouble."

Vinnie shook her head, tired. "Then he shouldn't have been surprised at your prophesies last night, because you were right."

He continued talking as he walked toward where the center of the anomaly had been. "I grew up in The Holt. I know trouble, you have too much power and not enough sense. Just like Sam."

Hearing Cerulean's real name was always jarring, reminding her they had a history that didn't include her, making her feel like she was an outsider. TK had wanted her to come with him today, and he still hadn't told her why, since he didn't seem to need her. "Jory thinks I'm unstable too. He would keep me out of this if he could."

TK's nostrils flared as he pulled in a deep breath to smell the air. His mouth pulled down, and he lifted his hand to wipe it as if he wanted to wipe the smell away. "Augh. Nasty." Then he shook his head. "He's wrong about that. I didn't say you're unstable. You're trouble, but at least you have some sense. You wanted to go to amusement park man, but you held back. Sam and Shaw didn't. They followed their impulses like the children they are. Your problem isn't that you don't think things through. It's that you think them through and come to conclusions that are way too rosy to stand up to reality."

Was that better? "You're complaining that I'm optimistic?"

He wandered back to the edge of the room. "There's optimism and there's delusion."

How would a person know if they were delusional? She didn't think Conor had anything to do with the killings, but everyone else seemed to disagree. None of them had met him, so she should have a better idea than they did.

Didn't admitting to herself Cerulean might be taking drugs again mean she was a realist? She wasn't trying to deny that. "I think Cerulean might be using again."

"Could be."

Was that a note of concern in his voice? "He said he hurts all the time. That he saw his parents burn."

His shoulders stiffened as his eyes roved the room again. Looking for something or just not looking at her? "Is that all he sees?"

"Isn't that enough?"

TK finally looked at her. "That's not the only people he's seen burn. Not the only people he's burned."

This was the first she'd heard this, and she'd known Cer for four years. "Who did he burn? Who else would he be seeing?"

"Someone who deserved it. And maybe some people who didn't, hard to say."

Vinnie bit back her anger. "Hard to say. Why?"

"I didn't see it, and I don't know all of them."

And yet, he was condemning. Maybe TK's views were too pessimistic to be reality. "Do you think his parents deserved it?"

"I don't like to speculate." There was a little less calm in his voice now.

"But you are speculating. You're saying he hurt people, but you didn't see him."

She wanted him to snap at her in return, but his shoulders relaxed. "Sometimes the worst things about people are things you can't see. You expect the best of people, but it blinds you to the danger. Sometimes you have to stop making excuses for people and listen to the small voice inside telling you to run, Vinnie."

"Cerulean would never deliberately hurt anyone." The pain that flashed on his face was gone so fast, Vinnie thought maybe she imagined it. He was wrong, though. "If you believe the best about people, they will rise to meet it."

He shrugged, "Maybe."

Vinnie didn't think he believed that. He was just done arguing. He'd given up on convincing her. She was just about ready to growl at him in frustration.

"Why are you telling me this now?" She thought back, trying to remember if he'd ever hinted he felt this way, and she realized he never seemed like he was close to Cer. Even though they'd known each other the longest, they rarely spoke to each other.

He began walking around the edges of the room, pausing now and then. "You wanted to know why I agreed with Jory."

That answer made Vinnie doubt her judgment more than anything else he'd said. Her voice was softer when she spoke again. "Are you going to tell me what happened someday?"

He met her eyes across the room. "Someday," he agreed.

"Conor Hahn was waiting at the library for me," she said. That was one way to get the words out. Just blurt them. "He offered us tickets to tomorrow's games."

To her surprise, TK smiled. "That's perfect. How did you manage that?"

Exactly what she'd thought. It was perfect. Tomorrow felt like too late with a life on the line, but they probably couldn't have done it tonight, anyway. "He just offered."

His enthusiasm dampened. "Maybe a little too convenient. Catch?"

"He wants me to go on a date with him after."

TK thought about that for a moment. "We can get you out of that." He paused by the window, leaning close.

"I didn't accept. I said I'd let him know. I didn't want to be reckless, or... delusional if he's the killer."

He turned back toward her. "Believing things will work out is not a bad thing. If I didn't believe in myself and my future, I wouldn't be where I am now. You have to make mistakes in life to figure out what works and what doesn't. I've failed, yes, but if I hadn't trusted myself, then I would have given up and been nothing. When you weigh the downside of going to the game, it's small compared to what we could gain. Going to see Conor the first time had a bigger downside because you made a potential killer aware of you. It was a bad bet, and that's what you have to think about. Risk versus reward. We can't turn that clock back. We can't weigh the options of the future based on what we should have done in the past, Vinnie, but what is here now. Where we are now is in danger and that's what we have to make decisions for the future on."

"People's lives are on the line. I don't want to make a mistake by assuming it's safe if it's not. If he's the killer or in with them and they see you and Hilda with me, then they know your faces, too. They know you're looking for them and you are both in the line of fire." And because Conor finding out who she was in a roundabout way was on her mind, so was the potential that someone would take a picture of TK because he was a news anchor and Vinnie would be in the picture, and someone else would identify her.

"Good, we'll put them on notice then. You don't mess with The Dragons. Besides, I think that ship has sailed. Our best bet is to catch them as fast as we can." He walked backward from the center of the room. "This magic was nasty, by the way. Our anomaly smells clean like ozone, but this, it's more like burning hair."

The abrupt change was disorienting — from saying she had too rosy an outlook to a rallying cry. He was confusing her. Was she too cautious or not enough? "I'll call him and accept the tickets. You didn't answer my question about why I'm here when you have this under control."

"So they don't arrest me for breaking and entering, of course."

Vinnie crossed her arms. "Do you think not answering the

question makes you clever? Or are you practicing so you can be a creepy fucker like Will? He hates answering questions."

If she expected him to be offended, she was disappointed. TK just lifted one eyebrow. "Let's get out of this room, and maybe I can teach you something, too. That's why you're here."

When they were out in the hall, he continued, "You've been in more places than I have. It's possible you can solve this before we even start."

He pulled a ring out of his pocket, gold set with a small diamond. It looked like an engagement ring. TK held it out to her. As he dropped the ring into her hand, he continued. "Not many people know this, but your body remembers everything you've encountered. Even if you didn't hold any Ferr power when you encountered the owner of this ring, the memory of it is still in your blood. What I want you to try is to see if you've encountered the owner of this ring, and if you can do that, you might be able to match the signature in the room to someone you've met, and our job will be so much easier. Go ahead and pull my power."

Vinnie did as he asked. The power didn't increase her sense of smell as much as it did for TK, but other senses kicked in and she could hear his heart beating just a little too fast.

"You know how to search in the environment," TK said. "Now, turn the power in and search inside yourself."

Turn the power in? Vinnie tried to focus on herself, but she only felt her own energy signature. "I don't understand."

"Can you hear your heartbeat?"

Vinnie's focus shifted. "Yes."

"Be the blood flowing through your veins."

She thought of Shaw telling her to put her mind in her body parts and ask them to change. What TK was saying seemed similar, and Vinnie used the memory of changing her body shape to focus on her blood. A smell came to her, sharp and acrid, not just burning hair, but charred flesh and rot like meat.

Her stomach heaved, and Vinnie covered her mouth and nose and ran for the door. She burst out the back door and dropped, gasping, onto the back lawn. The smells from the house clung to her body. Vinnie dropped TK's power, wishing she could scrub the memory of the smell from her mind as easily. Her stomach roiled again.

"That didn't go as well as I'd hoped." TK stood above her. He held out his hand and Vinnie put the ring in it as he grasped her hand with both of his and pulled her up. "Don't feel bad, it's hard. Let's get out of here before someone comes."

CHAPTER TWENTY-FOUR

"Seriously?" Hilda muttered from the passenger seat as TK pulled into the parking lot of Will's motel. Now that TK had the power signatures in his memory, they wanted to see if he felt any here. If they ran into Will, maybe they could get him to answer some questions this time.

Vinnie didn't want Will to be one of the bad guys because it would be nice to have someone who knew what they were doing on their side.

"Would it?" Hilda said. "He was pretty useless last night. Go in, get knocked out. The end."

"He taught me how to use two abilities, found Maddie, closed the anomaly."

Hilda twisted in her seat to look back at Vinnie. "He didn't know she'd been taken until you told him and doesn't think the murders are connected to the Warrior Games, even though he knows someone like you could pass any tests. How do you know he closed that anomaly? What if he's lying about everything?"

"When you put it like that, it is strange." He knew Vasum existed. "He doesn't seem stupid."

"Which means he has a different agenda," Hilda said.

"Or he has blind spots in his thinking," Vinnie countered. "He may have met a Vasum but I'm not sure he knows everything there is to know, so he might not know it doesn't show up in tests. And he doesn't know this city. I only knew about Maddie because one of my patrons knew her mom."

"If you two could focus right now?" TK said. "Unless you just want me to keep driving around and around this parking lot."

Now that you mention it. That's a big coincidence you met someone connected to the disappearance, Hilda said.

She was right, but so was TK. They needed to get on with this.

Between one breath and the next, Vinnie had opened her senses. Her skin felt raw, and she scratched at her arm. She'd left herself open so much lately she was beginning to feel as if she couldn't close off again.

"Nothing," she said.

After a few beats, Hilda said, "I don't hear them. There are only two people. One in the main office and one in a room."

"Only one person? Weird," TK said.

Three cars were parked at various intervals in the parking lot.

"Someone could have left their car and gone off with friends," Vinnie said. Will and the people who worked with him could block Vinnie's ability, but she didn't know if they could make themselves invisible to Hilda.

"What do you sense?" Hilda asked TK.

TK went still. "Two energy signatures from the house are here. I need to get closer to tell how long ago they were here but, I don't think they're here, now."

"Will and Greg's signatures," Vinnie said. "None of the terrible smell?" People underestimated Ferr, usually more worried they would convince them to do something against their will, but Ferr couldn't do that. Not exactly. They were hoping whatever ability Will had to block Vinnie and Hilda, he couldn't also block TK's ability.

"Why would he want to hide his money by staying in a place like this?" Hilda asked.

Vinnie unbuckled her seatbelt. "What makes you think he has money?" She'd thought the same thing when she met him, but she didn't remember Hilda saying she thought the same.

Hilda's chin tilted down. "He just seems like someone with money."

"You seem like someone with money."

"Because I know how money looks and acts. Most people don't think about it."

"Maybe you could teach me that," TK said.

Vinnie shook her head. Hilda had only met Will once. She couldn't possibly know if he was rich.

"Let's go talk to the front desk people, we can get some intel." Hilda was out of the car and halfway to the front door by the time Vinnie and TK got out.

"Looks like we're going to talk to the front desk people," TK said as he closed his door. Hilda had paused by the front door of the motel. When they were almost to her, she pulled it open and went in.

They had planned to see if Will was there and try to get a reading from outside the hotel, then talk to him. Hilda hadn't mentioned wanting to talk to the front desk people.

The interior office was clean but shabby. A worn rug sat on top of a worn carpet. A middle-aged man with tidy blond hair sat behind the computer reading a magazine and wearing way too much cologne.

Hilda cleared her throat as they approached. His bored eyes came up. When he saw them, he sat up straighter, alert.

Vinnie managed not to roll her eyes. Barely. TK hung back by the door and concentrated his focus on the generic art on the wall.

"Hi," Hilda said. "We're looking for a friend, but we've

forgotten what room number he told us and he's not answering our text messages."

The man slumped a little. "I'm not sure how I can help."

"Can you tell us what room Will Jones is staying in?" Hilda placed her elbows on the counter and leaned in.

He fluttered. Vinnie wasn't sure what else to call it. "I really can't tell you where anyone is staying. Privacy. And I'm sure you are who you say you are, but..."

"Of course," Hilda pouted.

Anything? Vinnie thought at her. Out loud, she sighed. "We're not even sure this is the right place. Maybe you could..." she scooted a little closer, looking at him from under her lashes and biting her lip. "Maybe you could just tell us if he's staying here? That way, we don't waste time loitering in the parking lot if it's not even the right place?"

Remind me not to ask you to flirt. You're terrible at it. No reaction to the name. "Please," Hilda leaned over the counter and touched his shoulder to get a better read on his thoughts.

"The name doesn't ring a bell," he said.

Truth. Hilda said. "Maybe his friend checked him in. Greg?"

The guy frowned and sat back a little, thinking. Hilda let her hand drop away.

That was weird, Hilda said.

Vinnie waited a beat, but when Hilda didn't elaborate, she said, "Maybe they checked in under different names?"

"That's illegal!" The clerk was sweating, even though it was cool in the room.

Hilda turned to Vinnie. "Maybe they just lied to us!"

"He wouldn't." Vinnie gave an exaggerated frown. "Would he?" She turned back to the clerk. "He's about six feet tall."

"5'11", tops," Hilda murmured.

"Dimpled chin, Superman lips," Vinnie continued.

The clerk shook his head. "I don't know —"

"I have a picture," Hilda dug into her purse and pulled out her phone. A few taps on the screen, and she turned it toward him.

The clerk shook his head again, shifting in his seat.

Vinnie's hand snaked out to grab Hilda's. A picture of Will walking into the old west area of the amusement park filled the screen.

What the hell? And when had she even taken that? Vinnie didn't remember seeing her get out her phone.

He was crazy gorgeous. At Vinnie's look, she added, *And I wanted a picture so I could search. And ask hotel clerks questions.*

Hilda's mental voice sounded faint, even though they were right next to each other.

Vinnie pushed a trickle of worry away — Hilda could handle her own ability. She leaned on the counter. "What about his friend, he's hard to miss? Six and a half feet tall, probably. Big square jaw."

"I haven't seen him," the clerk said dully and then shook himself. "I'm so sorry. I wish I could help." He turned away. The beads of sweat covering his body made him look sick.

Hilda grunted and lifted her hand halfway to her head before dropping it and straightening. *He's seen them. I get flashes and then his mind goes completely blank. No one's mind is ever completely blank.*

Like the name triggers the missing memory?

"Yes," Hilda said. She was looking a little ill, too.

They had known Will or Greg could change what Hilda heard, but they thought they had blocked her actively at the amusement park. What it sounded like Hilda was talking about — planting a trigger that kept someone from remembering something only when it was activated — was beyond anything she'd ever heard.

TK stepped closer to the counter. "I think it's time."

See if you can get the key to the room. Use what we practiced.

Plan B. Vinnie hadn't had much time to practice what they wanted her to do next. They'd wanted her to try it on Will.

Vinnie was almost glad he wasn't here because the thought of trying something like this on him scared her.

She pulled TK's power, pushed it down and held it, and then pulled Hilda's, leaving some so Hilda could keep tabs on the clerk's thoughts. The buzz on her skin increased, and Vinnie fought not to scratch at her arms.

"That's okay," Vinnie said. "We'll just go home. If he wanted us to meet him, he should have answered his phone."

The clerk smiled. "Yeah, I would never do that to you."

Vinnie felt her heartbeat against her skin. TK had said she needed to create understanding and connection. She wasn't forcing the clerk to do anything or affecting him at all. Her own body was what she changed. His heart thumped in his chest, and she sped hers up to match. Listening carefully, she matched her breath to his. Not something he would notice consciously but would signal his mind to trust her.

She used Mesmer ability to find his scrabbling thoughts. He liked Vinnie and Hilda but was worried he would lose his job. Vinnie tried to implant a thought in his head that he wanted to help them. "Will can be a little forgetful sometimes, but he loves Grace," she pointed at Hilda. "If you give us the room number, he'll think he gave it to us. No one will know."

A few moments ago, you said he might be lying to me and now he loves me? Hilda's inner voice was barely a whisper.

Shhh. Hopefully, the clerk wouldn't notice the contradiction.

She already knew the room number. That wasn't the point. The point was to get him to agree to something small first.

The clerk's shoulders tensed, but he said, "I'll look, but those names aren't familiar." He turned to his computer, tapped a few keys and frowned. He tapped the keys again. "I'm sorry I seem to have a computer glitch. I know the rooms were at least eighty percent filled, but I'm showing no guests at all."

Vinnie didn't need to fake her surprise. "What? He's supposed to be here!" She leaned over the counter to peer at the screen.

"It was room 129," Hilda breathed. "I remember now."

The clerk's look was apologetic. "I'm sorry, miss, your boyfriend is gone."

"Can we have a look?" Vinnie asked. "If no one's there, it wouldn't be violating any rules, right?"

He brightened. "Let me get the key." He grabbed a key from his drawer and opened a locked box on the wall behind him, pulled out another key, and froze. His thoughts became murky and confused.

"I..." the clerk said, his voice coming out breathless.

"We'll rent the room." Hilda put a twenty on the counter. "This is a deposit. We'll go look and bring the key back if we decide not to rent it, but you keep the money."

"Okay." He set the key on the counter and slumped back into his chair.

"Thanks." Hilda grabbed Vinnie's elbow and pulled her toward the door. Her fingers dug in tighter and tighter until they stepped out of the building. Then she let go and fell back against the wall, grabbing her head.

"Okay?" TK said.

"It was like swimming through molasses." She pulled a little orange pill out of her pocket and dry swallowed it. "That was so wrong. Like someone set up a trigger that automatically erased his memory when you asked. It was there, and then it was gone. Not like they'd just taken it away, but set it to be gone only if someone asked. Will is the devil." Hilda sunk down, clutching her head.

"We already know he's strong," Vinnie said. "He can block all of our abilities. That doesn't make him evil, and I don't think he was trying to hurt you."

"Why are you always trying to defend him?"

"Why are you always trying to attack him?"

Hilda's eyes were wet, the pain making her eyes water. "You

should try calling him again. See if you can figure out where he is, make triple sure he's not in that room."

The clerk's thoughts had been strange when he'd tried to give them the key, like he also had a trigger not to give it out, even though the computer said the room was empty. "I don't have a phone," Vinnie reminded Hilda.

"Really, Vinnie." Hilda stood, wobbling, and fished her phone out of her pocket. "Just get a phone and if your dad calls, tell him to fuck off. It's not safe not to have a phone." She slapped her cell phone in Vinnie's hands.

Vinnie dialed the number. It rang and rang without an answer, just like it had the two times she'd already tried to call today.

She gave the phone back to Hilda. "You should go to the car and rest. We'll check out the room."

Hilda closed her eyes. "Fine."

TK and Vinnie made the short walk to Will's room near the middle of the lower floor of the motel.

Vinnie unlocked the door, and they stepped into an empty room. The bed was made, the trash was empty, and there were no belongings anywhere.

TK grunted and lurched for the trash. His puking was loud in the silence, and Vinnie's stomach turned.

She forced herself to walk further into the room, eyes scanning for anything left behind. There was nothing in the bathroom, nothing under the bed, nothing in the drawers. When she'd completed her search, she joined TK on the sidewalk outside.

"He didn't underestimate Ferr," TK said.

"What happened?"

"Some kind of power signature bomb, to confuse my senses."

Which meant Will had done it on purpose — he had thoroughly erased himself. He'd gotten her to find the killer, and then he'd disappeared like he had never been there.

CHAPTER TWENTY-FIVE

The change in the level of the mattress pulled Vinnie out of a light sleep. An arm wrapped around her from behind and snuggled up against her back. Shaw buried her head against Vinnie, seeking comfort.

"What's up, little sister?" Vinnie murmured.

"Everyone was so upset."

Vinnie grabbed the hand that was on her stomach and squeezed. Last night had been difficult, and things had been so busy today she hadn't checked on Shaw, who was so sensitive to all their moods it hurt her when they were angry. "We all made up. Everyone feels better."

"Not Jory," Shaw said. "He hurts."

Vinnie scrunched her eyes tight thinking of their argument earlier. He wanted to keep them safe, but he couldn't. "He's worried he's going to lose us, but we're all still here. We can all be okay."

Shaw tightened her grip and curled her body tighter like she wanted to make herself smaller. Her breathing became shallow.

"Shaw?"

"I felt you die." Shaw was almost hyperventilating now.

Vinnie pulled out of her grip and rolled over, stroking back Shaw's hair. Tonight, Shaw's cheeks were rounder and her eyes wider. She wasn't trying to look innocent this time — Vinnie wasn't even sure she was aware she was doing it, but the change made her look like she was twelve if you discounted her adult sized body. "Hey, I didn't die. I'm right here. I didn't even come close to dying. Just some ice to the chest."

Even if she had, Shaw had been too far away to feel anything at all. How would she even feel someone dying? Maybe a loss of the sense of their emotions?

Shaw's breathing had relaxed a little, but she was still tensed next to Vinnie. "I felt it."

"How did you feel it?"

"Here." Shaw rolled onto her back and faced the ceiling. She massaged her chest with the palm of her hand. "I felt it here. I know you were too far away for me to feel anything, but it was so real. I was asleep, and you died, and I felt it. I'm not crazy."

Shaw couldn't have felt her die because she hadn't, not even close, but that didn't mean that her power or even mind hadn't made her think Vinnie had died. "I don't think you're crazy." Will said that Vinnie using their power would bring them to their full potential. Could this be something new about Shaw's power? If so, what? "Are you sure it wasn't just a nightmare, you felt someone else's emotions and got confused?"

"It is confusing. Other people's feelings feel like my feelings. This was different. Real, but not."

"The feeling was real, but my death was not."

"I guess." Shaw's body relaxed a little more.

"Cerulean took an ice spike to the shoulder. He was closer to dying."

Shaw closed her eyes and her breathing slowed, becoming deep and even. Vinnie thought maybe she'd fallen asleep. "No," she said finally. "He wasn't. Jory wants me to stay out of it."

Shaw couldn't know that Cer wasn't close to death, not in any way Vinnie understood, but her words eased something inside her. "Do you want to stay out of it?"

"You died."

Vinnie fell back and pressed the heels of her hands into her eyes. "I'm still here."

"What if one of you died because of something I did?"

That was Jory's logic — don't do anything because one of them might get hurt. "What if someone lives because of something you did?"

Shaw rolled away from Vinnie and curled up into a ball. "I think I want to go home. I've tried to be a dragon and I can't even come close. I thought maybe it wasn't possible in our world, but I'm just not smart enough. I'm not smart enough to save anyone."

She looked so small, or as small as someone who was nearly six feet tall could. Maybe it was a protective mechanism. Being out in the world after years of just being with her parents and brothers must have been a shock, and she turned inward. Shaw had been strong to leave home. The thought of doing something amazing — becoming a dragon — had given her the courage, but that courage was wearing out.

The dragon had said she needed a vessel. Vasum — that's what Will had called Vinnie. When she'd searched the internet for the term, hoping to find hints of others like her, she'd found it meant vase. Her ability was like being a vessel.

"Even the smartest people need clues, and the help of other information to figure out things that seem impossible. There is rarely such thing as a lone genius. They have people helping them and still can take thousands of tries to do something that hasn't been done before. We know there are people like us on the other side of the anomalies. We just need to figure out what your dragon has that we don't or what no one on our side has thought about."

"That's never going to happen, Vinnie," Shaw mumbled into her knees. "I can't increase my mass. I'll never be able to."

Shaw hadn't been in the room when Vinnie had told the others that she learned how to hold two abilities at once. "Nell can, though. And I can hold both. Will taught me."

Uncurling, Shaw turned back to Vinnie. Her mouth parted in surprise. "Could you?" Her voice was barely a whisper. "Maybe that is a clue."

Vinnie's heart sped up before her mind caught up to what she was contemplating. Her body still felt weak from the search for Maddie and the fight last night, but Shaw was giving up. Maybe she could give her some hope.

Vinnie ran through it in her mind for a moment before scrambling off the bed and stripping her t-shirt off.

Shaw pushed up and wrapped her arms around her knees again. Her face was flat, not excited but not as sad looking as she had been a moment before.

Vinnie breathed, centering. Maybe mass first? She reached for Nell, pushing aside all thoughts of fatigue and worry over whether they were going to get to the killer in time. A deeper breath to dig deep into her core for the strength, and then she pulled from Nell, letting the power settle into her abdomen. She'd borrowed Nell's ability for strength but had never used it for mass.

You can't make something from nothing. Imagine the air around you filling you up, Hilda said.

You should be resting.

Pot. Kettle.

Shaw had shifted on the bed, arms dropping in defeat.

"Don't give up," Vinnie said. She imagined the air coming into her, but nothing happened. Nell couldn't manipulate air. Maybe it wasn't air. Maybe it was power. Could power live in the air?

Hold on. Hilda said. *Nell says it's like a magnet. Power in the body attracts power outside the body, but you need to pull the magic from natural objects. Earth, wood, stone.*

The floor under her feet was wood. *If I pull from the floor, will I fall through?*

No, you're pulling power to create mass, not pulling physical mass.

The power inside the body was a magnet. She knew how to pull power into her body, that's how her ability worked. Now she needed to make Nell's Stone power do the same.

The power flowed through her. Vinnie focused on what it felt like and found something similar in the wood under her feet. She pulled and felt the magic flow into her. Put your mind in your body part, Shaw had said. Would Stone magic work the same? Vinnie focused on her shoulders and arms and was rewarded with the feeling of them expanding.

"Yay, you're big," Shaw said without enthusiasm.

Shaw had seen Nell do this, so it wasn't impressive. Vinnie put Nell's ability deep in her core, then reached for Shaw. Wings seemed like the easiest thing to try. If she could make wings without decreasing the size of any other body part, that would be progress. Something moved in her and she could feel her back twitch, but the look on Shaw's face said nothing had happened.

Nothing had happened except Vinnie felt like she was falling apart from the inside. The power tore at her shoulders, so she stopped focusing on wings.

Maybe she needed Jory's healing ability. If she could hold two, she should be able to hold three.

Vinnie put Shaw's energy next to Nell's and tried to pull from Jory. White-hot agony flared through her brain, and the rush of noise from holding all the power started. The impact of her knees on the floor startled her. Her legs had grown too weak to hold her up. Shaw scrambled off the bed and was coming toward her. Vinnie held up her hand to stop her and stumbled to her feet. She didn't know how to use Jory's power to help her heal.

You're going to hurt yourself, Hilda said without heat. *Jory has studied anatomy and physiology and who knows what else, to focus the power.*

I don't have time for that.

You only need general regeneration. Imagine light. Little light balls flowing through your body. That's not what happens, but that's what Jory sees, only more specifically, but you don't need specific.

Vinnie planted her feet to keep from swaying and imagined light flowing through her body. "Keep going," she told the light, frowning at herself. Power couldn't talk. "I might be delirious."

Shaw stood, hands hanging at her sides, face frightened or awed, Vinnie wasn't sure.

Vinnie didn't know how much more she could take, but something had shifted in her from wanting to make Shaw feel better to a desire to prove she could do this. She set the intention of the light flowing and continuing to heal, and then instead of imagining wings growing slowly out of her back, she imagined them snapping out, powerful muscles holding them in place, a membrane under each to catch the wind.

And then she felt it — the weight of the wings pulling on her back muscles.

"Holy shit!" Shaw said. "You did it!"

Laughter came from the door. Vinnie turned, her wings almost hitting Nell as she walked into the room to get a closer look. Jory and Cerulean were also in the doorway, and Hilda leaned heavily against it.

Jory's eyes were watery, his face full of awe. "I didn't think it was possible, even though I've seen the video of the dragon a few years ago. And Shaw's account. "

"Dude, that's creepy," Cerulean said.

"It's not creepy." Shaw inched closer to Vinnie. "Can I touch them?" She didn't wait for an answer but reached out.

Vinnie tried to pull the wings in closer to her body, but her back was already aching, heart pounding with the effort.

Shaw's fingers trailed lightly along the top of one wing, sending tingles across the surface.

Drop it before you pass out, dumb dumb.

She wanted to hold it a little longer, to revel in what she'd done, but her vision was graying. She dropped the power, and her knees buckled. An arm went around her as Shaw caught her and lowered them both to a sitting position on the floor.

"That was amazing," Nell came forward. "Are you okay?"

"Just a little tired." That was a lie. Vinnie felt like she was breaking apart inside. She tried to pull Jory's ability, but nothing came.

"You used my mass…" Nell said

The room spun, and Vinnie had trouble making her tongue move. "Jory's physiology altering and Shaw's shape altering."

"If you can do that, think what else you could do?" While Nell's words were positive, something on her face was off. Fear, Vinnie realized, but what was she afraid of?

Hilda shook her head. "Think how easy it would be for her to kill herself. Cer, can you get Vinnie some water and carrots?"

"Do you always have to be so negative?" Nell said. "We can figure this out. We'll be a badass team." But there was still that uncertainty in her voice.

Shaw stood. "That's right. We won't be the Twisted. We'll be the Twisters." She lifted her arms in the air and spun. "Watch out world, we are the storm!"

The storm. They were the storm. Vinnie tried again to pull Jory's power to heal herself, but nothing happened. She'd overexerted herself.

Jory shook his head, a small smile on his face. He walked forward and put his hands on Vinnie's head. His smile turned to a frown. "Vinnie?" He was on his knees in front of her, her face cupped in his hands.

She couldn't get enough air to answer. Her body was too tired to breathe, too tired to use her ability.

Then the numbness eased, and air flowed into her lungs. Jory still had his hands on her face, eyes closed. The pain in her back eased.

Jory opened his eyes. "Idiot. You almost killed yourself." He took his hands off her and she collapsed backward.

"But I didn't," she said. "And I didn't pull Wisp and waste myself away more."

Cerulean was scooting along the floor with a bag of carrots and a glass of water.

"No, you just found a different way to hurt yourself. Help her eat," Jory snapped before storming out of the room.

CHAPTER TWENTY-SIX

The tickets Conor had gotten them led them to a booth surrounded by plexiglass walls in the middle of the stadium bleachers. Several booths were lined up in the same row, and theirs was the second one in from the main aisle.

Not plexiglass, Hilda thought. *Glass-clad polycarbonate. Bullet and blast resistant.*

I thought VIPs were usually closer to the action. She'd thought they'd be closer to the center where TK would have less distance to search.

Too dangerous for important people to be so close to the Twisted. We aren't searching the crowds. Here, we're closer to the teams and Twisted Crews.

TK opened the booth door and allowed Vinnie and Hilda to go in ahead of him. There were five other people inside the booth and seven empty seats. An older woman with heavily plucked eyebrows and a too smooth face sat up a little straighter when she saw them.

"Goodness, Terrance Kent, I'm so impressed to be in your company today." Her voice said she was anything but. "Who's the lovely?" Her eyes went to Hilda, who was dressed in a cream-colored pantsuit.

Vinnie almost wished she'd worn something nicer than her hoodie and jean since TK had also dressed nicely in a pale green oxford and gray dress pants.

TK reached out to shake her hand. "These are my friends, Hilda and Lavinia."

Vinnie really needed to talk to her friends about using her real name. It was too distinctive. Thankfully, the woman had already dismissed Vinnie.

The woman grabbed the tips of TKs fingers and then let go. "Friends. I see. I'm Alice Huburg, I own—"

"Huburg Vintage Wines," TK finished for her. "Pleasure to make your acquaintance. I'm also a fan of yours." His voice also said he was anything but.

Oh brother, Hilda thought. She inspected a seat in front of Alice and her companion before perching on the edge.

At least the booth smelled clean. To her, anyway. Vinnie wondered what places like this did to TK. Vinnie made a mental note to ask him and sat on the edge of her chair too, straightening her spine to make herself taller so she could get a better view of the field.

"It'll play on the monitors," TK said.

There were two large monitors attached to the low wall in front of the booth. Both were playing advertisements.

"What's the fun of that? If I wanted to watch the game on a screen, I could have done that at home."

Hilda laughed. *It's not about watching — it's about rubbing noses with the gentry.* She turned and smiled at Alice. "I'm a huge fan of your Shiraz, and a lot of your wines, actually, but that's my favorite."

Alice beamed. "It's very popular. What do you do, dear?"

"I'm in banking."

It was Vinnie's turn to choke back a laugh. Banking.

Alice leaned forward, her head close to TK. "Who are you rooting for?"

"Hush." He said as he continued to stare off into the crowds.

Vinnie's head whipped around in time to see Alice's shocked face. "Sorry, he's a big fan of this event."

Alice pursed her lips and sat back in her seat, pointedly ignoring Vinnie.

What's gotten into TK? Vinnie asked Hilda.

He says she works for La Mafia. She owns a wine business, but they were in the red, so she rents warehouses out.

The screens shifted to a view of the fields and an announcer came on, welcoming them to the games. Then there was some chatter with another announcer as they discussed the teams.

For drugs? The city surely wasn't big enough to need warehouses for their drugs, were they?

I don't think they keep people in crates long enough to need a warehouse.

Did they really keep people in crates?

Hilda bumped Vinnie's arm and pointed at the arena.

The dull roar of the crowd diminished as the ground-level doors slid open. People wearing various colors of robes with crystals attached to their foreheads strode out. There were six in each group, four groups in total. When they had made it to the center of the arena, they stood in a circle facing outward, hands clasped together and raised in the air. These were the Twisted who made the obstacles the athletes had to go through. A woman with golden hair with an orange gem on her forehead tilted her head back. A beam of light shot out and then dissipated. The crowd cheered.

Wisp. That wasn't light, it was fire and dangerous as fuck. If you watched the monitors instead of craning your neck like a four-year-old, you would have known that.

After a few moments of listening to the cheers, the Twisted crews left the center of the field. When they had arrayed themselves along the edge of the arena, the crowd quieted again. Vinnie shifted her vision between one breath and the next, surprised at how easy it was becoming to see the power. Power sparked between the teams like it was ready to explode from them. The first teams competing today were the Atlanta Lizards and the Los Angeles Sloths. As the teams poured onto the field, the cheers grew louder. People leaped to their feet, shouting as players in skintight suits entered the arena. The players had some other equipment attached to their suits, but Vinnie couldn't quite see it.

Look at the monitors, Vinnie.

Vinnie pulled her eyes away from the spectacle. On the monitor in front of her, the camera had zoomed in on one team, but she still couldn't make out what they were wearing.

"Backpacks, they're full of gear," Hilda breathed.

I can't see the power on the monitors. Vinnie looked back at the field just to make sure she hadn't accidentally let go of the vision — the ease that she could use it was still new to her.

A referee stepped onto the field and stood in the middle. His voice came through the speakers in the booth as he talked about rules. Human teams could not interfere with each other, only the Twisted could. 'Human Teams,' as if the Twisted were not human.

When the referee finished talking, he blew a horn, and the teams dashed onto the field.

The ground on the arena floor erupted as a large hill rose in front of the Sloths. A few of the team members dodged around the obstacle, but two went over. When the first one reached the top of the hill, the center sunk away, sending him into a deep pit. His teammate stopped, pulled off his pack, and had a rope coiling down to him, seemingly within seconds.

Meanwhile, the team members that had gone around faced winds, blowing them back down on one side while a wall of fire erupted on the other.

"Holy shit," Vinnie said. "How are they doing that?"

"It takes all of them," Hilda said. "Well, not all of them, but there are probably several crews working on each obstacle. They coordinate some of it beforehand, maybe most of it, but they also have a Mesmer pulling the teams together, one for each crew and one or two for the interwork. It takes a lot of practice."

"I didn't know you were such a fan."

Hilda shrugged, one elegant shoulder lifting. "The achievement is fascinating. Just think what they could do if they put them to work on actual problems."

Alice snorted. "You can't trust their kind."

Hilda's back straightened, and she rolled her neck like a prizefighter about to step into the ring.

Now is not the time, Vinnie thought at her, hoping Hilda would listen.

Alice opened her mouth to say something more but snapped it shut and sat back.

A small smile tugged at Hilda's mouth. *Did you do something?* Vinnie asked her.

Hilda's posture relaxed. *Not at all. Shouldn't you be pulling some Wisp energy to boost TK?*

Vinnie's eyes had drifted back to the monitor so she could see what was going on but refocused on the field. The sheer amount of power being thrown around made her stomach twist with anxiety. Her skin crawled with the power, and she hadn't even opened up her ability yet.

This would have been so much easier if we brought Cer.

On the field, a medic team scurried out from a side entrance. They ran onto the field and a tunnel of air — it looked like air — sprang up to protect them as they lifted a Lizard player onto a stretcher. Vinnie hadn't seen what happened, as she'd been focused on the field closer to them.

Two of the Sloths had made it halfway across the field and now faced a manticore made of fire and dirt.

She opened her power carefully. Now she just needed to focus it, but her nerves jangled and the crowd around her seemed especially loud.

A sudden silence descended around her, and Vinnie could hear her heart pounding.

Does that help?

Hilda, of course it was Hilda. No need to panic. *When did you learn to do that?*

About five minutes ago. Sound travels through the air. If you block the sound waves, no sound.

Hilda had seen what the Mesmers on the field had done — making a tunnel of wind — and learned. If only Vinnie could do that.

It's not natural to your body. We grow up with our power. You don't have to teach your mind to think. It can do that on its own, within limits, of course. Things like critical thinking take understanding and practice. You have to learn to read, but you don't have to learn how to learn. I don't need to learn to harness my power, I just need to learn the ways it can be harnessed. You are not a Mesmer, even though you can use my ability. You have to learn to learn, which makes it harder.

What was natural to Vinnie's body was seeing the energy, feeling it, borrowing it. If Hilda's theory was right, this should be easy.

She was afraid after what had happened the last time she'd been around so much power, but she'd filtered the power when she was working with Will. She could do it again. The field was almost pure white with all the power, but a few threads of color here meant it wasn't all combined. Mesmer energy flowed around and through the main block of white. As she watched, a flash of earth energy flared in one area, shaking the ground so hard that the players in the area stumbled and fell. Flashes of Mesmer and Dancer in another area created a wall of water. Two players dove in and were spit back out.

There were so many lines of energy, some stronger than

others. Vinnie picked one of the medium strength orange threads and tried to feel that and only that with her power. Warm Wisp energy flooded her. She hadn't even tried to pull, but now that she had the power, she tugged it deeper, letting it coil up inside her. Then she pushed it at TK.

He flinched and cleared his throat.

Hilda snickered. *He said that was like being bludgeoned.*

I know. There must have been so much power in the air that she was picking up residual energy from other abilities because she also knew that Hilda was worried, and a little scared.

You got me figured out. Now I have to kill you.

Vinnie couldn't pull her thoughts together well enough to respond. Separating out the Wisp power didn't feel natural or easy. All the power around her wanted to come along and she had to focus to hold only one and push it toward TK.

She narrowed her focus to the stream of Wisp energy flowing through.

Hilda's mental voice, when it came again, sounded distant. *You can let go. TK has searched the entire stadium. There's a similar signature, but it's out in the clubhouse, not on the field. He said if it's someone on the teams he should be able to get close to pinpointing them when they come on the field, or when we go with you to meet Conor afterward.*

Something hissed along the line of power Vinnie still held. The urge to send the power out to the field pressed into her head.

Vinnie?

The line of orange Wisp magic had taken on a red cast. Ferr. Vinnie needed to—

The line of power cut off with a pop. For a moment everything was silent, then a boom sounded on the field below and the crowd surged to their feet.

"Fire."

"What happened?"

"Are they okay?"

The monitors showed charred ground where one of the Twisted crews had stood. Some Twisted were outside the scorched earth, but Vinnie didn't know if it was the crew that had been standing there.

"What did you do?" Vinnie realized she had spoken out loud and clamped her mouth shut. She hadn't cut the power off — it had felt the same as when Hilda blocked Vinnie from taking her power.

I didn't do that. Something was trying to influence you. I saw it in your mind. I had to cut off the power.

Vinnie eyed the field. The explosion was in a different location from the power she had pulled. The backlash from Hilda cutting the power flowing to Vinnie hadn't caused the explosion.

You cut me off from the power.

Someone was trying to use you. I just blocked them.

Hilda had cut her off from any ability. It was bad enough that she was helpless unless someone with power was around, but now Hilda could prevent her from using her ability at all. And if Hilda could, any Mesmer could.

"Vinnie," Hilda's voice was agonized. "I had to."

TK reached out and squeezed Vinnie's hand just as the announcer came on, asking everyone to remain calm.

CHAPTER TWENTY-SEVEN

"It seems like the same thing to me." TK leaned against the wall by the stadium entrance, drinking from a water bottle. He'd taken an iron pill, and they were waiting for him to recover a little.

After the announcement, curtains had come down from poles suspended between the crowds and field, shielding the field from view. Then, stadium and Warrior games employees had evacuated everyone from the stadium.

"It wasn't the same," Hilda said. "At the amusement park I broke a circle, and the power lashed back at Vinnie. This time I just cut off the power flowing away from a Wisp. That wasn't a backlash."

Vinnie stood a few feet away from them. She could support Hilda's story because she knew the power hadn't come from the same place, but she wanted to be as far away from Hilda as possible right now. She'd cut off the power without asking, just did it.

Conor had texted that The Roundhouse was in chaos, but they were welcome to come over. She'd said she needed a few

234

moments to compose herself. That wasn't a lie. Soon she'd need an excuse not to go out on a date. Trauma was a good one.

"Could you please tell Vinnie to stop pouting about it?" Hilda said to TK.

He took a sip of his water. "I'm sure Vinnie could have handled the situation without your intervention."

Hilda folded her arms and looked away.

"Vinnie," TK said. "We have bigger fish to fry right now."

"I'm not pouting." She had a right to be upset over control being taken away from her.

He pulled down his sunglasses and looked at her over the top, raising one eyebrow.

Vinnie sighed and moved closer. "They said no one was seriously injured. Do you think that included the Twisted crews?"

TK, who looked like he needed someone to hold him up, shrugged. "We can't change the world."

"I think that security guard wants to change the world." Hilda nodded her head at a man in a uniform who was giving them a thousand-yard stare.

"Maybe he thinks we're reporters who are going to sneak past the curtain and take pictures for the morning news," Vinnie said.

"That's what we get for bringing a reporter," Hilda said.

"Anchor. I don't go out on the streets looking for stories." TK shifted his weight, pulled his phone out of his pocket, unlocked it, and frowned at the screen. "I should be recovered enough by the time we get over there. The power signature should be obvious enough that I won't have to exert myself."

The parking lot was crazy with the mad rush of people trying to get out, so they decided to walk to the clubhouse, which felt like it took forever but was probably only five minutes.

The guard inside wasn't the same one she'd met before. This one looked a little grumpy.

"We're here to see Conor Hahn," Vinnie said.

The guard held up his phone and snapped a picture. After a few texts, he waved them through.

Vinnie led them down the short hall into the main room.

Conor stood a few feet away from the entrance to the Tiger hall with Kara and Lou.

His face lit up as they approached. As soon as Vinnie was close enough, he pulled her in a quick hug, like they were old friends or something.

Okay, he's like sunshine in a bottle, I get it, but still. No.

Vinnie ignored the comment. "These are my friends Hilda and TK." She pointed at them.

Hilda put a hand on her shoulder and shoved playfully as she reached out to shake Conor's hand. "A pleasure," she purred.

Hilda was stunning. Just standing there next to her, Vinnie could feel eyes looking at them, but Conor barely glanced at her as he took her hand and then released it.

"It's good to see you again, Terrance," Lou said, which effectively cut off Vinnie's next thought.

"Louann," TK said.

Why does he know her? Vinnie asked.

Wipe the anger off your face, Vinnie. Neutral, Hilda responded. *She was on his morning show. He thought we watched his morning show and knew this.*

"I hate that name. Please, just call me Lou."

"Now that everyone has been introduced but me," Kara said, sticking out her hand to TK. "I'm Kara."

TK took her hand.

"You're here looking for Conor," she said. It didn't sound like a question.

TK's face went blank for a moment before he recovered. "I'm not here on business, but if he wanted to give an interview, I wouldn't complain."

Amusement glinted in Conor's eyes. "I think she meant you were here to see me, but we might arrange something. I'm jealous

Lou got to be on TV without me. I'm sorry you didn't get to see a full game."

Vinnie wanted to ask TK why that was, and why he hadn't mentioned it. He could have asked questions or got one of them into the studio to talk to her. She said, "Are the games always so dangerous?"

Lou laughed. "She doesn't even watch. There were issues in the beginning, but we have them well controlled these days."

Well controlled. Vinnie would never get used to how casual some were about controlling others.

Hilda's voice was icy when she said, "Well controlled?"

TK cleared his throat. "The master Mesmers that coordinate the crews are lifers. The most obedient and well behaved."

"They also wear shock belts if they get out of line." Kara's voice was full of barely suppressed rage. "It's cruel, both the way they are raised and the way they are treated now. Maybe if they were treated more like human beings, we wouldn't have to worry about them attacking us."

"Not treated like human beings?" Lou scoffed. "They are pampered and given special privileges. They have better lives than most humans."

"Except the freedom to choose their own lives," Kara snapped.

Conor shot Vinnie an embarrassed look. "Guys, is now the time?"

Lou snorted in disgust. "It's always the time with her, she's always picking fights." She threw up her hands and walked away.

"Sorry," Conor said. "They're saying it was sabotage, and of course, if that's the case, then it had to be a Twisted. Some of the Sloths were injured and it could have been any of us."

"And how many of the Twisted crew were injured?" Hilda asked.

"All six," Kara said. "Two are in the hospital. That's all we've heard. The two whose abilities appear to have caused the explosion were also injured. For this to happen, the master Mesmer would have had to have been involved or compromised."

Notice how your guy didn't even think about people like us? TK says it's him, by the way.

He sabotaged the teams? How—

Not that. He has Maddie's energy all over him.

Sunshine in a bottle, Hilda had called him, and Vinnie agreed — the golden hair and sun warmed skin. Even as solemn as his face was now, he looked like he could smile at any moment. He already had the beginnings of smile wrinkles on his cheeks. That was the face of a killer? How little conscience would one need to have to smile all the time and then go murder people? They'd talked about other people being involved, but she hadn't really thought it could be Conor.

If she were braver, she'd try to open her ability, brave the chaos, and see for herself. Out loud she said, "What about Ferr?"

"Ferr?" Kara's head tilted, and her voice came out low.

Vinnie squared her shoulders and looked Kara in the eyes. "You said the master Mesmer had to be involved, but can't some Ferr influence others? The games use strong Twisted to run the obstacles. Isn't it possible one could hold more influence than the Mesmer?"

"I don't think so," Kara said. Her sharp eyes bored into Vinnie. *Ferr?*

"Why not?" Vinnie asked. "Their job is to hold the team together. They don't directly create obstacles. If they are binding the powers together, they could also tear them apart."

Anger flashed in Conor's eyes for just a moment and was gone. "That's a scary thought."

A team member walking by with water bottles paused, offering drinks. Only Conor took one.

There was a Ferr influencing the team. Vinnie told Hilda. *Ferr power was wrapped up in the Wisp power that caused the explosion.*

That was one of the abilities the killer had. Conor has a strong motivation to sabotage the Sloths. They are winning the games.

Vinnie had seen the anger a moment ago, but she'd also seen his kindness, the way he was always apologizing, the caring he'd shown in the library.

You need to be thinking with your head, not other body parts, Hilda said.

She didn't think she was being irrational. *What is he thinking about? Did he have anything to do with the explosions?*

"A Ferr can't make anyone do something they don't want to do," Kara snapped.

That was what everyone believed, that a Ferr's influence was like hypnosis. Some people could be influenced, and some couldn't, and the influence wasn't strong or lasting. TK agreed with that, but Vinnie had seen too many impossible things lately.

"That's what they want you to believe," Conor said, echoing her thoughts. He wrenched the cap off his water bottle and took a swig.

He's thinking about punching some guy in the face. Nice, he's a real sweetheart. Nothing about the explosion.

What would Vinnie do if she believed he was the killer? She needed to find Maddie before she died, and TK said he had her energy all over him. Even if he wasn't directly responsible, he had to know something. Vinnie needed to get him away from here so she could use Hilda and TK's ability to see if she could find Maddie.

I need to get him out of here to use your abilities together. I'm getting better at filtering, but don't trust myself enough in here with all the power flying around.

"I've never seen any proof of any Ferr making anyone do anything against their will," Hilda said. *We agreed that was too dangerous.*

We agreed it was dangerous for me to go alone. I won't be alone. I can handle this, just like I could handle the power earlier. Out loud she said, "Just because you haven't seen it doesn't mean it's not possible."

Hilda glared at her. *No.*

Kara huffed and threw her hands in the air. "It would be a hard thing for a Ferr to do. It's far more likely it was Amanda, the Mesmer. She's been grumbling for months. Rightly so, but the simplest answer is usually the correct one."

"Occam's razor," Hilda said.

Kara smiled and put up a fist for Hilda to bump. "Exactly."

TK cleared his throat. "As fun as this conversation is, I believe Vinnie and Conor had plans, and Hilda and I have some work to catch up on."

Hilda turned her glare on him. *Congrats, Vin, TK agrees with you and doesn't care what I think.*

"We did have plans. If Vinnie is still willing?" Conor scratched the back of his neck and looked at her from under his eyelashes.

Well, isn't he the cutest? Hilda thought.

It's amazing that I can hear your sarcastic tone even when you're thinking at me. "Sounds great, ready?"

"Always," Conor said. He placed his hand on her elbow and started toward the door. "I know just where I want to take you."

He's awfully eager to get you alone.

Easier to kidnap and kill me that way. Even though three other people know I was with him, he knows no one would ever suspect him because he's semi-famous and everyone knows semi-famous people never do anything bad.

Brat. This is not the time for joking. He's a murderer.

They stepped out of the building and Vinnie took a deep breath, glad to be out of the crowded room. *Let's hope I can get the information out of him, then.*

CHAPTER TWENTY-EIGHT

Slow him down. Kara wanted to talk to TK about scheduling an interview, Hilda said.

Vinnie paused by the passenger door of Conor's car. "Are you sure you want to do this, right now? There was just an explosion in the arena."

"It's — " He stopped, considering his words. "There's nothing I can do. I want to get out of here more than anything. Are you okay?"

Was she okay? Vinnie hadn't stopped to ask herself that in so long. Everything that had happened the last few weeks flashed through her mind. She was not okay, not remotely okay. Seeing that explosion barely registered in her brain, it just felt like one more thing.

The door to The Roundhouse opened, and Hilda and TK emerged.

"I'm okay," she said and got in the car.

Conor went around the front of the car and climbed into the driver's seat. He flashed a quick, shy smile as he started the car.

The car flowed out of the parking lot and down the street, the smooth ride a stark contrast to any vehicle she'd ridden in the last four years. Even TK's car, which was a nice older model, had some bumps and shakes.

TK and Hilda were a few cars behind. Vinnie could feel them like an itch in her mind, and she reached out to pull Hilda's power. Nothing happened. Panic flashed through her.

"Are you sure you're okay?" Conor asked.

Vinnie tried again and then realized her senses weren't actually open. She was feeling TK and Hilda without her senses being opened. She opened them and pulled some power from Hilda. "You seem to surround yourself with people who don't like Twisted."

Vinnie listened to Conor's thoughts tumbling around in his head: fights, Lou, Alice... he knew Alice?

"I have nothing against Twisted. I don't agree with Lou that they're evil, and most of the players are more neutral."

"But everyone who works for the games, except the Twisted crews, has to be tested, so you don't have to be around Twisted."

His thoughts were discomfort, uncertainty. He wanted to be a good person. That didn't prove that he was. Most people thought of themselves as good. "Yes, they have to be tested or have an ironclad certification that they aren't Twisted. Maybe if I were around them more, I would be more comfortable."

What counted as ironclad certification? She would look that up later. "There was a woman in your booth who also seemed to hate them."

Different women flashed through his mind. "Who? It's not my booth, the others were there for other team members."

But she knew he'd at least met Alice. "Alice Huburg?"

"Ah," he said. "Lou's cousin. She's obsessed with the games. She's at least one game in every city we go to. Not a pleasant woman, but she is the reason we're here in this city. Maybe I should thank her since I met you?"

A frisson of excitement went through Vinnie. Alice traveled around with the games. Had she been the right size? No, but Lou was almost certainly the right size to be the killer. "How is she the reason you're in the city?"

"We have sponsors for the games. They choose the location of the next games based on who'll pay for us to come to their town."

Vinnie processed that information. TK said Alice rented warehouses to La Mafia because she had no money, but she had money to sponsor The Warrior Games?

Hilda's voice in her head was soft, distant. *Where are we going, Vinnie?*

Vinnie had been so focused on the conversation and trying to make sense of Conor's thoughts, she hadn't noticed their surroundings. They'd left the city, the car whispered over a highway road.

"Where are we going?" she asked.

"I'm taking you to my murder cabin." She sat up straighter and he laughed. "I'm kidding, of course. I know it's a little weird, but there's a small lake outside the city. A pond really, but there is something I really want to show you."

"Why?" *We're going to a lake.* There were only two lakes near she knew of. No wait, there was one to the south too, but that's not the direction they were going.

He glanced at her and then back to the road. "To impress you, of course. You'll be so blown away you'll see how amazing I am. I had a good feeling about you."

"Like you had a bad feeling about my dad?"

"Something like that. This will sound nutty but, I get hunches, usually about people. I feel like you're important to me. I'm not always right, but it makes life more fun to just go with it sometimes."

"That does sound nutty." Or like latent ability.

He barked a short laugh. "Blunt. I like it."

And she liked him, how she wished she didn't right now. She needed to figure out how to shift the conversation back to something useful, but if Alice was involved maybe she used the warehouse for more than drugs. That was something they could look into, at least.

He turned the car onto a gravel road and pulled up to a gate. The gate had a code box, and he leaned forward to punch in the code.

Crap, Hilda, and TK wouldn't be able to follow without that code. She leaned forward to see.

4-9-2 are the last three numbers, there are two before that.

The last three numbers?

Hilda's thoughts were too distant. How had they gotten so far away?

There's a gate, you'll need the code.

No response from Hilda and the chatter from Conor's mind had stopped. Hilda was too far away. Vinnie tried to focus, narrowing her ability in the right direction, but only got a hint of Hilda and TK. The whisper of something beside her caught her attention. Dancer, and it was coming from Conor. The sense was faint, almost like an echo. A sick feeling settled in her stomach.

That could be Maddie's power. TK said her energy was all over him. Would that be what her power would feel like if she had been pulling from someone else? She wished she could ask Will.

She hadn't gotten the sense from his mind that he had anything to do with Maddie's disappearance, but that didn't mean that much. Right now, it looked like she was headed to an isolated location with a killer.

He was not stupid. People knew she'd left with him, so if she disappeared, he would be the prime suspect. Unless he was a Vasum and knew how to use Mesmer ability to erase memories. That was a lot of people, and he wouldn't know how many people knew. Hilda and TK could have told someone else. Too risky. She was probably safe.

The car rolled out into a small clearing and there was a body of water. There were no cabins. Houses dotted the edges and there were a few small docks into the water.

Vinnie followed Conor to the edge of the pond, where he stopped beside a small boat sitting on the shore, and nodded to it, expecting her to get in.

She imagined him taking her out to the lake and pushing her into the water. Accidental drowning. If he were helping with the killings, he would know she was looking for him. He would have a motive for killing her, even if he thought she had no ability. Vinnie couldn't reconcile the thoughts she'd seen with someone wanting to kill her. His liking seemed genuine, but there had been that anger.

"You're not afraid of the water, are you?" He seemed concerned.

"I've never been on a boat."

He held out his hand to her. "It'll be worth it, I promise."

She looked out at the dark water. How could anything out there possibly be worth it? "It's just a pond."

"But it's not." He stepped closer, taking her hands in his. "Remember I told you about hunches? Trust me."

All her reassurances to herself that it would be too risky to kill her weren't doing her nerves any good, but she was already here. Vinnie took his hand and stepped into the boat.

The boat had no motor, so after Conor pushed it into the water, he picked up some oars and began to row, muscles rippling under his pale t-shirt.

Tearing her eyes away, she looked out across the calm lake. "You had a feeling about me, huh?"

"No laughing at me."

He was serious. He thought she would laugh. "I'm not laughing. You get feelings about other people. Did you get any feeling about Maddie? Do you think maybe she ran away too?"

He stopped rowing, looking intently at her. "It doesn't work like that. You knew her better than me. Did she seem like someone who would run away?"

Right. Maddie was supposedly friends with her sister. Her sister that he knew she didn't have since he'd looked her up and knew who she was.

"I never met her. And Shaw's not actually my sister."

He'd draped his hands over his knees. "Found family is sometimes more real than biological family."

Warmth spread through her at his words and the intensity of his eyes. "That's true."

He pointed at the sky. "We're here."

The pond looked the same, just an ordinary pond in the late evening. A lot of stars, but she'd seen stars before. "You're right, this is amazing."

"Smart-ass." He looked up. "It hasn't started yet. May I?" He pointed to the bench beside her.

Her heart thumped. "Yeah, sure."

He stood, but instead of sitting beside her, he dropped to his knees and reached into the box behind her, pulling out a blanket. He draped it across the bottom of the boat and sat with his back on the bench beside her and looked up at the sky again.

"Is your dad the reason you don't have a cell phone?" he asked.

His shoulder was pressed to her knee. Too warm, it was way too warm. "Cell phones are bad for the brain. You get addicted and live your life staring at a screen."

"But what if some serial killer took you to a lake in the middle of nowhere? You can't call anyone."

That was the second time he'd said something about a serial killer. Vinnie reached out for Hilda again. Still nothing. She forced a laugh. "Please, the odds of two serial killers being in the boat right now are astronomical. How is your cell reception, by the way?"

"Ha. Touché. Reception is bad out here." He tugged on her knee. "Come down?" His eyes shone in the fading light.

That seemed dangerous. Not because he might be a murderer, but because she wanted to so badly. What difference did a few inches make? She scooted down, settling in beside him, and he draped his arm over her shoulder.

She couldn't reach Hilda or TK, but what did she have? Vinnie opened her senses again. There were no other Twisted close enough for her to borrow their power. She refocused on Conor and found that same whisper of Dancer energy. What had TK said at the house? The body remembers everything that it encounters. That sounded plausible enough, and she could tell the difference between her friend's power and that of a stranger. Could she remember what Maddie's felt like?

Conor's hand on her shoulder tensed. "It was my mom," he said. "The reason I feel so uncomfortable around Twisted. After my dad died, she met a man, and she was so happy. I'd just see her smiling for no reason, humming. Then I came home early one day from school, and she was crying over something he'd said. She told me he was always saying awful things to her, and she'd just forgive him and then when she was away, she'd realize and feel humiliated. She wouldn't leave him. Nothing I said convinced her. Then he left her and took all her money. He'd done it legally. She signed the paperwork. Lawyers said there was not much we could do."

The Dancer energy had grown as he talked, but it was still almost imperceptible. This wasn't Maddie's energy. This was the energy he naturally had. Will said everyone had some, and she'd been able to feel people around based on that, but that had slipped her mind over the last few days. Conor had his own Dancer energy, too weak to be detected by tests.

Conor continued. "I just went to try to reason with him. He said he'd done what was best for my mom and I almost believed him. I started to walk away and then this rage welled up in me."

He swallowed heavily. "I think I would have killed him." His voice broke a little. "I hit him and knocked him down and climbed on top and hit him a few more times. He defended himself the only way he could. It was self-defense when he stopped my heart, but that didn't change what he was."

"Ferr," Vinnie said. He was hurting, so Vinnie didn't point out that her dad had manipulated and controlled her. Anyone with any kind of power could do that, whether it was money, political power, or emotional manipulation. He wasn't wrong that a Ferr could do it more easily.

"I'm glad he stopped me, and I'm glad that he will never get out of prison."

Vinnie squeezed the hand that was on her shoulder.

"It's starting," he said, scooting his butt forward and leaning back so he could look at the sky without craning his neck.

The sky hadn't changed. "What am I looking at?"

"Just watch."

Still nothing. Minutes ticked by. Vinnie shifted uncomfortably, wanting to ask again what she was supposed to be seeing. His hand tightened on her shoulder as he stared raptly at the sky.

Vinnie scooched down so she could put her head on Conor's shoulder as they stared up. Just when she thought he must be crazy or pulling her leg, the brightest shooting star she'd ever seen shot across a narrow space in the sky and disappeared.

"What...?"

"Shhhh."

A pale blue light appeared in the circle and poofed outward, followed by red and green and yellow, starting as small dots and going out in waves. Then more shooting stars, more colors. It was an anomaly, way up in the sky. It had to be. Vinnie relaxed her attention, trying to see the power and there, maybe just the fuzzy edges of something more in the black sky.

Just as suddenly as the lights had started, they stopped, the fuzzy edges of the power collapsed in on themselves and were gone.

"What was that?" Vinnie asked.

"I think it was an anomaly," he said.

"It closed by itself." Too late, she realized what she'd just said. Would he realize she could see it? "I mean, the light stopped." Did his arm tense again, or was she imagining it? "How did you know it would be here?" Her head turned toward him, and Vinnie leaned back a little.

His breath caught for a moment before he said, "I'm not Twisted, but I sense the anomalies sometimes, and I think people are opening them on purpose, in places where they won't cause...." He turned toward her. "Harm." The last word was just a whisper of breath on her cheek. "You are so beautiful," he said, and his lips came down to brush against hers. He pulled back. "Sorry, that was presumptuous."

Vinnie reached out her hand, cupping his jaw, and bringing him back to her.

Conor's hand came up behind her head, holding her while his mouth pressed against hers, soft and firm at the same time.

VINNIE! Vinnie jerked away, startled at the sound of Hilda's voice in her head. *For fuck's sake, what are you doing? Get out of there.*

What? I haven't found anything out yet.

"I'm sorry. You—" Conor started.

Vinnie held up one hand and put the other on her head as if it hurt.

Oh, is that what you were doing? Trying to find out about his lips? Something has happened. Have him bring you back to The Rope.

Hilda?

Just get out of there

CHAPTER TWENTY-NINE

Conor stopped his car in the street in front of The Rope. The bar was tucked into a strip of buildings, with the only parking on the street. Even on a Sunday night, all the nearest parking spots were taken.

"Are you sure you'll be okay?" Conor asked.

Vinnie wasn't sure of anything. Hilda had been frantic but refused to tell Vinnie what had happened. Vinnie had told Conor she had a headache and then had to stall so Hilda and TK could get to the bar first.

"The headache will pass," she said.

He eyed the bar dubiously. "Call me?"

"I will," Vinnie said as she got out of the car.

The interior of The Rope was dark and grungy, and Vinnie was never sure if the smell of whisky came from the bar or the pores of the patrons. TK and Hilda stood out like beacons in their nice clothes. Hilda turned from the bar as soon as Vinnie opened the door. They could only have arrived just before Vinnie and Conor, but Hilda had a glass in her hand.

TK was absorbed by his phone. Hilda just put her glass on the bar and headed for the door, and Vinnie waited until TK noticed and followed.

Neither said anything on the way to TK's car. Neither said anything as they pulled out of the parking lot.

Finally, Vinnie asked, "What happened? Why did you pull me out of there?"

TK glanced in the rear-view mirror. "They found Maddie's body. Probably been dead since Friday."

Vinnie heard the words, but they didn't make sense. She couldn't be dead. This couldn't have been for nothing.

"How did she die?" she said.

"That's an incredibly stupid question," Hilda snapped.

Was it? Maybe the question was dumb, but she needed someone to confirm what TK had just said because it couldn't be real. Vinnie pressed her lips together, holding back all the other questions. How did they find Maddie? Where did they find her? What did they know? All the questions tumbled over and over in her mind. But the most important was — if she had done something different that night, could she have saved her?

"I have work in the morning." TK's voice broke her out of her thoughts. They'd stopped in front of the house. "Call me, let me know what I need to do from here," he continued.

"You're leaving?" Vinnie asked.

"There's nothing I can do right now."

He could be here with them. But Vinnie couldn't get those words out.

Hilda was halfway up the steps when she noticed Vinnie hadn't moved. She turned and stalked back to the car and jerked the car door open. "Get. Out."

She didn't wait to see if Vinnie complied. The front door had banged open before Vinnie pulled herself out. Her limbs felt heavy, and she had to close the car door twice because it didn't latch the first time.

The sound of TK's car backing out was too loud as Vinnie trudged through the front door, pressing it closed behind her.

They were waiting, the low murmur of their voices carrying down the hall from the kitchen. Vinnie fought the urge to go up the stairs instead. All she wanted was to curl up in her bed, but she followed the sound of voices.

Nell stood when she entered, took two steps, and wrapped Vinnie in an embrace. "A friend called me, they haven't released it to the public yet." She let go.

Following her back to the table, Vinnie sank into a kitchen chair.

"I'm sorry, Vinnie," Jory said.

Sorry. "Why didn't you just leave me out there? We need to find out now more than ever."

Hilda said, "We were locked out. We couldn't contact you, couldn't reach you at all. You could have been dead out there."

A spark of anger pushed Vinnie to her feet. "Then at least you would have known who did it and could stop him."

Hilda, who had been leaning against the wall, pushed herself up. She stood there, her nice clothes torn and stained, mouth parted in surprise. "You. Selfish little brat. I had to run through the trees and brush to get the message to you. We didn't know what was happening out there, just that he needed another victim."

Vinnie swallowed and dropped her eyes. Hilda had run through the woods in clothes that cost way more than she could afford to get a message to her. She hated what she was about to say, but it was important. "He's not the killer. I don't think he's involved at all."

"Of course you don't." Hilda slid down the wall, falling into a crouch. The hands that came up to cover her eyes were shaking, as she ground her palms into the eye sockets.

"Hilda?" Jory said.

Vinnie wished she knew what was happening in Hilda's mind right now. She'd never seen her like that.

"I had forgotten something Will told me," Vinnie said. "Everyone has a tiny spark of what makes Twisted, Twisted and I can read that energy. I can compare it. Conor was not at the house with Maddie that night. Even if he was Vasum and could somehow shift into a smaller form. He's not Vasum, though. He's Dancer."

"TK said he had Maddie's energy," Jory said. "They could be working together."

"Yeah, TK..." Nell looked away.

"Spit it out," Jory said.

Nell shrugged one shoulder. "Why is TK not here so he can explain exactly what he felt? He should be here with us."

"And do what? There's nothing he could tell you he didn't already tell me," Hilda said. "He said the feeling was strong. Like he was just with her."

"But Conor couldn't have been just with her," Nell said. "They found her this morning, and she'd been outside that warehouse since Friday."

"Warehouse." A shot of excitement went through Vinnie. "There was a woman in the booth with us — Alice Huburg. She's a cousin of Lou's and she goes to the games in the different cities. She has a warehouse she rents to La Mafia."

"I can check to see if it's the same warehouse," Nell said. "I didn't have any luck finding out who owned the house. It's owned by a holding company."

"Why would a holding company own a house?" Jory's fingers were tapping on the table.

"Alice wasn't the right size to be the killer — though she could have shifted to a different shape — but Lou is," Vinnie said.

Hilda drew a shaky breath and pushed herself back up to standing. "But TK would have been able to match them to the crime scene. He was right next to both at one point."

Vinnie squirmed, excited. They were finally getting somewhere. "At the hotel, Will used something to confuse TK's ability. When we were at the house, he had a similar reaction. There was a strong odor for him. They may have done something similar to throw us off the trail."

"Whoever it is, we need to figure this out." Hilda took a few steps and was at the table, looking less confident than Vinnie had ever seen her. "They've killed one victim. They'll be looking for another. I can talk my boss into giving coupons for free massages to the Tigers. If I can get Lou in. Maybe I can find something. People let their minds roam when they're getting a massage."

"I don't suppose there's any chance they'll just leave us alone?" Nell said. All eyes turned to her, and she drooped. "I guess not. I can also see if there are more missing persons that look likely. It's a long shot."

No one had said anything about Maddie. No expressions of horror and grief. Did they feel it? They must feel something, but they were already springing into action. Maybe action would ease the pain but Vinnie had nothing left to do. She could ask Zandia if she knew of any other missing teenagers, but as TK might say, that was busywork. Knowing Will was the only advantage she'd had, and he was gone.

"We can ask TK to check the drop box," she said. "The online one."

"It shouldn't take him long to reactivate it," Hilda said.

"He never shut it down." Vinnie felt a little like she'd just betrayed him, but he hadn't said it was a secret.

Nell hissed a breath through her teeth.

Jory stiffened. Then he nodded. "Okay. Any other ideas?"

Vinnie couldn't help but think of Conor again. She didn't think he had anything to do with the murders, but he'd been around Alice and Lou, which seemed like their best lead. Or maybe she just wanted to get close to him. She expected a snarky comment from Hilda, but there was nothing.

Are you mad at me? Vinnie thought.

Hilda didn't react — no twitch of muscle or change of expression.

Vinnie waited another beat, and another idea came to her. Jory wasn't going to like it, though. Both because they didn't want to do anything that would cause police to take notice of them and because Shaw or Cerulean would be the best person to try it. "Shaw looks young enough. Will said he talked to the girl she skipped school with. We could go to the school and see what we can find out about her, or who she went with, or if anyone else saw anything strange. We also haven't tried talking to her family."

Nell said. "If you're caught asking questions, you could end up being investigated. Especially now that she's dead."

"Lives are at stake," Vinnie said.

As if on cue, Vinnie felt Shaw coming up the front steps. She hadn't opened her ability and wasn't trying to find Shaw. Just like in the car, she was aware of them all without trying. Almost as if they were extensions of her awareness.

"You said you'd help me keep them out of it," Jory said.

"You can't keep people out of life," Hilda said. "It always comes for you. No matter how far you run to hide."

"OH. Kay," Nell said. "But I would prefer it if they stayed safe."

"You're talking about me," Shaw said from the doorway, surprising Jory and Nell.

Jory opened his mouth, but Shaw cut him off. "What happened?"

Vinnie half stood, ready to rush over to Shaw. "Maddie is dead."

Shaw nodded and her eyes met first Jory's and then Nell's. "I was her age when I saved a dragon. I'm much older than that now. My parents didn't get to decide what I did with my life and neither do you. How can I help?"

"This is way out of our league," Nell said. "It's not a dragon with a few guys chasing him."

"Way to be condescending, Nell," Shaw said. "Bravo. It wasn't just a dragon with a few guys chasing him. Any one of those people could have kicked your ass blindfolded."

Nell's mouth fell open. "They could not have," she growled. "I'm—" She cut herself off and growled again. "This is still way out of our league."

Shaw started to respond, but Vinnie cut her off. "It's not out of our league." She thought of the colors of power at the Warrior Games, all swirling together to create something that was so much more than any of them could do individually. "Have you ever watched the Warrior games? The things they can do are amazing, but they don't do it alone. The obstacles and the coordination are too difficult for just one Twi — Magiera. The things they do wouldn't be possible without a full crew. Will wasn't looking for me. He was looking for us. The killer was fast and strong, but she was only one person. If there are more, we can deal with that, but as far as we know, there was just her and we can be faster and stronger than she is, but only together."

Jory stood, his chair scraping back. "If you need me, you know where I am."

After he was gone, Nell said, "That's a nice speech, Vinnie, but we don't have the practice those teams have. Maybe someday this wouldn't be too much, but now? We really should all be staying out of this."

"Screw that," said Hilda. "They don't get to kill kids and get away with it." Despite her words, she sounded tired, defeated.

"No one has to be involved if they don't want to," Vinnie said.

Shaw shook her head. "I think it should be all of us or none of us. Like you said, we're a team."

"The police will look into the murder," Nell said. "They're going to put their resources into it now."

Hilda scoffed. "And they've all done so well so far? In all those other cities where Twisted were being murdered? We're close."

Nell's head drooped. "I've already said I'll do what I can. Maybe we should practice together, too. We'll need somewhere safe." The last part was said almost to herself.

"It's settled," Hilda said. "Shaw will go with Vinnie tomorrow. Nell will... do Nell things, and Jory can find us a practice location. We can ask TK more about what he felt from Conor. Maybe he can stop by the spa when I'm talking to people and see if he detects any obvious energy signatures on any of them. They won't be expecting him, so if they were using some kind of obfuscation, they won't be prepared."

The numb helplessness Vinnie had felt earlier had eased. They couldn't bring Maddie back, but maybe they could stop anyone else from getting hurt.

CHAPTER THIRTY

The only light was the sliver glowing under the small, square door. A wall pressed into her lower back, and another brushed against her arm. The space was too small. Vinnie tried to stand from her crouched position and her head bashed into a ceiling that shouldn't be there.

"Hey, kid?" said an unfamiliar man's voice. "Where are you? Come on. You forgive me, right? I promise I'm not going to hurt you."

He sounded jovial, but her heart sped up and the muscles in her scrawny arms tensed. She lifted one arm in the dim light. It was too small to be the arm of an adult. She was a child.

The cabinet door opened and a pale man with thinning hair grinned at her. "Gotcha!"

Her fist shot out, smacking into the man's nose.

Vinnie jerked awake, body twitching as if she'd been the one to hit the man. She tried to sort out the dream. The man had seemed familiar, but that was just dream logic. She didn't know him and didn't know why she was dreaming of hiding in a kitchen cabinet.

No, wait. She replayed the dream in her mind. The ice-blue eyes, the pale hair. She recognized the features, if not the person.

That hadn't been a dream. She rolled off the bed and stood for a moment, debating.

Hilda was in the basement. Vinnie could feel her down there. Everyone else was still in their rooms. Something about today had thrown Hilda off-kilter, and she was sending memories.

Vinnie rubbed her weary eyes and started for the basement.

She moved as quietly as she could, trying not to wake the others. The basement door creaked as she opened it and padded down the stairs. Hilda sat with her back to the wall, her sword across her knees, staring into Harry. "You can just turn right back around. I don't want company."

A breeze brushed Vinnie's hair across her shoulders, tickling her. "Then why did you send me your thoughts."

Hilda's head swiveled, a moment of confusion flashing in her eyes before she turned away again and slumped. "I didn't."

Vinnie walked the rest of the way into the basement and slid down the wall to sit next to Hilda. "Was that your dad?"

The hand on the grip of the sword tightened and released, tightened and released. Images flickered in Vinnie's mind, a playground, a swimming pool seen through a fence, the sword on a wall above a fireplace.

Did Hilda know she was sending her thoughts?

"I'm moving out," Hilda said.

The sudden crushing feeling in Vinnie's chest caught her off guard. She'd failed when she failed to save Maddie and now here was another failure that felt almost equal in magnitude, followed by guilt that someone's death only felt marginally worse. "You can't," she said, knowing how ridiculous she sounded. "When?"

"Soon. I just decided tonight."

"It's because of me," Vinnie said, wanting Hilda to confirm that it was her — that she was to blame for this.

Hilda shifted. "It's everyone."

Vinnie got images of laughter and silly games. The others hugging, patting each other on the back, taking turns cooking, arguing over the TV remote. "You're still projecting your thoughts."

The wind in the basement kicked up and then died down again. "You have to take care of Harry for me, make sure no one hurts him."

"It's not alive," Vinnie said automatically.

She expected Hilda to laugh, or at least smile, but she repeated. "It's not alive, but you need to keep him safe, anyway."

"Why?" Vinnie just wanted to keep her talking, to see if she could figure out why she wanted to leave. Convince her not to. There was a quick flash of memory — of a man with a bloody lip and a gun, and then it was gone.

"Because this is our secret weapon," Hilda said. "It's something the government thinks they have control of, something they think we can't have, something they think they can use to keep us in line. This is knowledge." She waved at Harry. "If they keep us away from this, we can't understand our power as well because it's all inside people, but if you can look at this you can see the way it works. I can see how power works when it's not in a flawed individual but only its raw self. Harry lets us see possibilities and if we see what's possible, we may not take their oppression anymore. They don't want us to know. Knowledge is power, Vinnie. If you have power, you don't give it up."

"You have power here with us, but you're giving it up," Vinnie pointed out.

Hilda tapped her on the forehead with one finger. "You're. Not. Listening. People are imperfect. The power is flawed when it's housed in emotional bodies."

Realization replaced Vinnie's sadness with cold anger. "You're leaving because we diminish your power."

Hilda flopped back, shaking her head. "No."

"That's what it sounds like."

Hilda shifted, so she was staring at Harry again. "I don't care what it sounds like."

"You can't just bury your emotions, it's unhealthy," Vinnie said and realized she was doing the same thing by attacking instead of expressing her hurt. "I don't want you to go, we're family. Tell me why."

"Exactly," Hilda muttered. "You were out there, and I couldn't do anything about it, and I made a mistake, could have exposed us all. I can't be powerful if I act stupid."

That sounded like exactly what Vinnie had said — Hilda thought they were a liability. She had to protect them instead of becoming powerful or whatever. "And here I thought you wanted to help out of the goodness of your heart."

"Those assholes hurt a little girl and they are going to pay for that."

The image of the little girl, Hilda, hiding in the cabinet popped into her head again. She would help with this thing and then leave, and she wouldn't even talk to Vinnie about it or listen. Her frustration flared. "If you could stop projecting your memories, that would be great."

"If you don't like it, cut it off. I'm too tired."

"I can't cut it off. If I could cut it off, you wouldn't be in my head all the time."

Hilda pressed the heels of her hands into her eyes, the way she had in the kitchen. "Fuck's sake, Vinnie. You can see the power."

What was she trying to say now? Why did everyone have to be so difficult? "Just because I can see it doesn't mean I understand how it works."

Hilda's lips parted. "You're not doing it on purpose, projecting your thoughts at me?"

"Of course not. I—" she thought of the emptiness when Hilda didn't respond to her thoughts. She wasn't doing it on purpose, was she?

"People who don't even know how their power works," Hilda muttered. "I learned to block by seeing it in your mind, but you seriously don't know how you do it?"

Vinnie tried to process that. "How could you learn by watching me?"

"I can see how people think about things when they use their power."

Think about things. "They don't have to think about it. It's part of them, they just do it. The power knows what to do."

Hilda coughed and then caught herself. She made a choking sound for a few moments and then, as if she couldn't help it, she laughed. "The power doesn't know what to do. It's not alive, just like Harry is not alive. Who told you that?"

"Everyone." Maybe not everyone, but they seemed to use most of their abilities without a lot of effort. "It makes sense. It's a natural part of them, like breathing. I don't have to tell my body to breathe. And you said it yourself. It's part of you, you don't have to learn to learn."

"Hm." Hilda sobered as she thought about that. "I don't think you understood. The power is there and because I live with it, some things will seem to be natural. Like walking. You had to learn to walk, but you don't remember, so it feels like something you always knew how to do." Her knees flopped down so she was in a cross-legged position, and she sat forward, animated. "I guess I could probably see how people's minds think about walking too because some part of the mind has to be thinking about it. And martial arts! Anybody could theoretically do martial arts, but they don't take the time to learn. I guess most people are like that with their power, too. And how would they learn? Who out there has explored the limits of what our powers can do? We would need to share and teach each other to make learning faster."

"I'm sure there are more organizations like the Warrior Games who have learned different ways to do things." There had to be. There were also plenty of countries that didn't sign the Treaty of Vancouver, which prohibited the use of Twisted in the military.

"Mm," Hilda's eyes were unfocused, staring into Harry.

"You were telling me how I block off my power," Vinnie prompted.

Hilda refocused her gaze on Vinnie. "When you use your power, you imagine a wall against your skin, or a shell, like a suit of armor. You've only got it set to block your ability. Which is just about the stupidest thing I've ever heard, blocking your ability."

"It's not stupid. You do the same when you block out thoughts," Vinnie pointed out.

"Yes, but that's different. Hearing every single thought will drive you mad."

"Using someone else's power without meaning to isn't so great either." She'd only accidentally gotten someone taken once, but it wasn't the only time she'd pulled power without thinking.

"You're not a child anymore, and the mental energy to maintain something like that... but you're not anymore." She put her palm on Vinnie's forehead, a line appearing between her eyebrows. "Is that why you can hear me? You're taking my power? No... your shield is still there. It's different. Think about lowering the shields."

Vinnie opened her senses, and Hilda's power blazed in front of her, and her thoughts ran through Vinnie's head.

.... *not down completely... there are parts... colors and they have flavor...*

Hilda pulled her hand away, and the voices stopped. "You've incorporated us into your shield so you can use our power without having to think about taking it down."

"I can feel you all the time now. If you're close enough, I know where you are."

"Useful," Hilda said. "If you can block awareness of other's powers, which stops you from using it, you should be able to reverse it, and stop it from being used on you, which would keep your thoughts from being projected at me and vice versa."

Which wasn't as helpful as it sounded. If she wasn't aware of how she used her power anymore, how could she figure out how to reverse it?

Hilda sagged. "Just listen to your thoughts. It's not that hard."

That wasn't true. It was extremely difficult, even though she'd been meditating for years and should theoretically be able to do it.

An image of her with her eyes burned out popped into her mind. This was Hilda's thoughts again and everything she'd been saying earlier about not being able to do anything and people being imperfect clicked into place. "It's not really about the power. You don't want to be sad if something happens to one of us. You're leaving because you don't want to care as much as you do. You're scared."

"Good job, Freud. Please, just leave me alone."

"I'm going to be fine. We'll figure this out."

"Leave." Hilda made a shooing motion with her hand.

What could Vinnie do? She wouldn't stay when someone had asked her to leave, and she couldn't find any words that would convince Hilda to stay.

CHAPTER THIRTY-ONE

"No feeling sorry for yourself," Vinnie muttered. She finished tying her shoes and stood, trying to push the thoughts that she had failed out of her head. It still didn't seem quite real that Maddie was dead.

Shaw was asleep, curled tightly on top of her blankets, shivering. Vinnie grabbed her own blanket and draped it over her. They'd go to the library later, but she had something else she needed to do, and she might as well get it done.

The smell of bacon drew her down the stairs to the kitchen. Jory was putting the last of the slices on a paper towel lined plate. Vinnie watched him for a moment. He'd taken her in when she ran away from home and never asked questions. He tried so hard to protect all of them.

"I'm going to Walt's to buy a phone," she said.

He opened the carton of eggs sitting next to the stove. "Have some breakfast first. Need some money?"

She shook her head before realizing he wasn't looking at her. "No, I have some saved that I was going to use to fix the door to the library." She always stated to library donors up front that part of the donations were for living expenses, but she always felt guilty using them for that purpose. She helped pay the bills for the house and food, but those were necessary. A phone felt frivolous, and she hadn't wanted one anyway, but Hilda was right — she would be safer if she had one.

"What door?"

The bacon still sitting on the counter drew her closer. "The outer door has been sticking."

Jory blew out a breath and shook his head. "I could have fixed that easily by now. Why didn't you ask?"

Because she felt like she was always asking for things. Of course, Jory could fix the door. Vinnie grabbed a slice of bacon and shoved the end in her mouth and left the kitchen. "I didn't want to bother you," she said from the hall.

"Take the van!" He called after her.

Vinnie paused on the porch and looked at the van. Her thoughts were roiling in her head, and Walt's wasn't that far. She could walk, clear her head, and maybe she'd have some brilliant idea about how to find the killer.

Fat chance.

The door to the house opened again just as she reached the front gate.

"We're coming!" Cerulean came down the steps.

So much for clearing her head. "You're up early."

"I'm up late," he said.

"You haven't slept at all?"

"You can sleep when you're dead," he said in the monotone voice that meant he was repeating something he'd heard.

The door opened again and Shaw, looking half asleep, leaped off the porch and joined them in the yard.

"You need to sleep, too," Vinnie said.

Shaw rolled her eyes. "We're coming."

Vinnie opened the gate. "You don't even know where I'm going."

"The van?" Cerulean glanced back over his shoulder.

She wouldn't have as much time to think with them along, but Vinnie still wanted to walk. "I need to clear my head and could use the exercise. You probably could use the exercise too."

He had filled out a little. Must not be using his ability as much. Still, his breathing was already a little heavy by the time they made it to the end of the block, but so was Vinnie's. Her body wasn't getting enough time to recover from using power.

"Where *are* we going?" Shaw asked. "We were going to go to the library later. It's not later."

"To buy a phone," Vinnie said.

Cer pumped a fist. "Yeahhh, we can play Land of the Dead together."

"She's not getting it to play Land of the Dead." Shaw said. "She's getting it to call her boyfriend."

Her boyfriend. Conor was not her boyfriend, but the thought of him filled her with warmth. "He's not my boyfriend. I'm getting it so you guys can contact me and not worry."

"I want to text you," Cer said.

Shaw reached over and shoved him. "Dork, you can text her when she gets her phone." To Vinnie, she said, "You don't think Conor's the killer. What are we going to do about the serial killer?"

"I could light him on fire," Cer said.

Vinnie stifled a shiver. "Her."

"Them," Shaw murmured.

Cerulean deflated. "I don't like 'them.' That's too many."

Shaw kicked a rock off the sidewalk. "What's the plan, Vinnie?"

The plan. "I can get Carla's number from the library database and call her and get Maddie's parents' number from there." Or not, probably not. Carla seemed unlikely to give her the number.

"They just found out their daughter is dead," Shaw said somberly. "We were going to the school, right? Maybe we should start there. You said she was in the picture Conor showed you. Do you have the picture?"

The picture. Conor had said he would email it to her, but she'd never gotten it. "I can ask Conor to send it to me again when I get my phone."

They were out of the residential section and onto one of the main roads, where the streets were lined with businesses.

"TK wants me to ask people about the wine lady," Cer said.

Vinnie stopped walking. "What?" He couldn't mean TK had asked him to talk to people in La Mafia. Nell was looking for information about the warehouse. Cer didn't need to put himself at risk to do something Nell was already going to do.

"I know people," Cer said. "People might know if the bad guys knew the bad lady at the house and the one with the wine."

"People at La Mafia might know the killer," Shaw translated.

Why would TK say that? He thought Cer was dangerous and shouldn't help, but he sent him to talk to La Mafia? And they still had other options to explore. Did TK dislike Cer so much that he didn't care if he got hurt?

"That seems like a waste of time," Vinnie said. "Why would a serial killer be working with La Mafia?"

They stopped at a stoplight and waited for the walk signal.

Shaw's eyes went wide. "You don't think they're after us, do you?"

"La Mafia or the Serial killer?" Vinnie asked. Both had reasons to come after them, but Shaw hadn't been there for those discussions.

"They could both be after us." Shaw's voice was filled with awe, not fear. "The woman saw what Cer could do, so she knows, and then we helped shut down something was bringing La Mafia money. Maybe they're ganging up to take us down."

"We're dangerous." Cerulean reached out and slapped a sign as they walked past.

They were dangerous. Vinnie had seen what was possible

watching the Warrior Games crews. They weren't on that level, but they could be. "They are more dangerous than us. I don't think you should go alone, Cerulean. You can help us talk to the kids at the school."

He shrugged. "I know people. I'm used to them, and they are used to me."

He still knew people. She'd hoped he didn't have contact with that crowd once he'd moved in with them.

"He does," Shaw said. "He knows how to talk to them. He's a hooligan."

Cerulean gave Shaw a flat look. "It's easy to talk to people. You just talk."

They'd arrived at Walt's, a dingy little convenience store with one gas station pump out front — out of place in the heart of The Holt. It sat on the corner, freestanding amidst more utilitarian brick and gray buildings, the long-winged roof a throwback to an earlier era.

"You should come with us then." Vinnie wasn't sure she liked the idea of bringing Cer. People loved him once they got to know him, but it could take a while to get past their initial reactions. She just didn't want Cerulean going off to talk to dangerous people on his own. Is this what Jory felt like? "You can come with us, then we'll go with you."

Shaw had pulled open the door and was inside before Vinnie finished talking. They didn't seem to be listening.

Vinnie nodded at Manny, the morning cashier, and owner, before heading to the phone section. A decent one would take most of the cash she currently had.

Shaw reached out and picked one up. "This is what I have. You'll like it." Vinnie stared at it."He can't trace you. You don't even have to give them your name when you activate it."

"You buy cards for minutes," Cer added. "Cash."

He should know since he was wanted. Did he know he was wanted for murder? But Vinnie was so used to thinking of her dad as all powerful. He could find her somehow through a phone not attached to her name. She was sure of it. Even the library lease was in Jory's name.

Maybe she was overreacting. Her dad was cruel and used her, but he wouldn't have done her permanent harm, would he? And if he found her, she was an adult. He couldn't control her anymore.

She took the phone to the counter, paid for it, and they were back out on the street.

Vinnie dug into the packaging.

"I'll go talk to people. Text me!" Cerulean didn't wait for an answer.

"Wait." Vinnie started after him. "You shouldn't go alone."

He moved fast, and she didn't know if she had the energy to run or yell. "Shaw." Vinnie nodded the direction Cer had gone. "I thought we were going to talk about this."

Shaw watched Cer go. "That's his world, Vinnie. We don't belong there. We'd just get in the way.

"He'll be asking dangerous questions. Why would TK say he should go on his own?"

"Maybe he knows something. I think he knows people in that world too."

That didn't make Vinnie feel any better. If TK knew something, why wasn't he sharing it with the rest of them?

"Do you want to go home first or straight to the library?" Vinnie asked.

Shaw pointed her finger into the air. "To the library!"

CHAPTER THIRTY-TWO

"He's fine," Shaw said for the fourth time. It was late afternoon, and they were almost home, but Cerulean wasn't with them.

Shaw had texted him and he'd agreed to meet them back at the library, but he hadn't shown. They'd eventually given up and started the long walk back to the house.

Vinnie stopped by the front gate and pulled her phone out again. Cer had wanted her to text him, but he hadn't responded to a single one she'd sent. She shoved her phone back in her pocket.

TK's car was parked outside, and she could feel him in the kitchen. Hilda was home too, but Jory and Nell weren't.

"He'll be home soon." Shaw could have been talking about Cer again, or Jory. They'd come home because Shaw wanted to talk to Jory. Vinnie couldn't say she felt the same. Facing them all right now felt a little like facing a firing squad.

"Cerulean is fine," Vinnie said.

"Yeah." Shaw's voice was soft. Maybe she didn't believe he was fine any more than Vinnie did.

Shaw pushed past Vinnie, going through the gate and up the walk, but she paused at the door, waiting.

Vinnie joined her, and they went into the house together. Two days ago, Vinnie would have believed Cer was fine, but the knot of worry in her abdomen wasn't going away. Two days ago, she'd believed she could save Maddie, in spite of the long odds. She could see how unlikely their success was now, especially after the day they'd had. They'd found nothing at all. Students wouldn't talk to them, Carla wouldn't talk to them.

Shaw headed straight for the kitchen where they found TK stirring something in the pot on the stove.

Vinnie peered at the stove, where there was a meaty red sauce bubbling away. On another burner, water boiled, and TK dumped some spaghetti in the water as she watched.

Her eyes told her he was making spaghetti, but her brain denied it. "What are you making?"

"Spaghetti with meat sauce." He tasted the sauce and nodded before putting a lid on the pot. "Needs to simmer."

"You hate pasta," Shaw said. A small frown line appeared on her forehead.

He scoffed. "Everyone loves spaghetti."

TK did not love spaghetti. If there was one pasta TK hated above all kinds of pasta, it was spaghetti. Vinnie backed away from the stove. "Is someone coming over?"

TK hummed as he moved to the sink to rinse some dishes he'd been using to cook. "Don't think so."

"Terrance Kent," Shaw said. "Why are you making spaghetti?"

He looked at her like she was crazy. "To. Eat."

Vinnie felt Jory coming down the hall before he appeared in the doorway dressed for work in jeans and a button-down shirt. He took in the stare down between Shaw and TK. "What's going on?"

"TK is making spaghetti," Shaw said.

"You hate spaghetti," Jory said to TK.

TK's face was blank for a moment before he smiled. "They brought some to the studio last week. It was good, surprised me too. You can't spend your life avoiding things because of the past."

"That's a lie." Hilda's voice came from the hallway. As she walked into the kitchen, she held her body loose, but her lips were tense. "I think. Let me see." She took a few steps closer to TK.

TK took a step back, holding up his hands. "Oh my god, a man can change his mind. It's just spaghetti. It was my favorite when I was a kid."

"That's true," Jory said. "Maybe you guys should chill?"

TK shook his head and turned back to the counter, where he'd laid out some vegetables on a cutting board.

"That's not the only thing he did!" Shaw said.

Jory stopped and waited for Shaw to continue, but she just stood glaring at TK.

Vinnie said, "he told Cerulean to go talk to people in La Mafia and find out if anyone knew or gave permission to the killer to use the house, and now Cerulean isn't back. He was supposed to meet us."

"You let him go to those people?" Jory's voice was low, and his eyes were on Vinnie.

Before Vinnie could protest, Shaw said, "Cer's an adult Jory. So am I. You treat us like children, but we're not and we can think for ourselves. What I would like to know," Shaw said, turning to TK, "Is why TK put the thought in his head in the first place. Telling him to go talk to them."

The knife clattered to the side and TK seemed flustered for a moment before scooping up the cutting board and carrying it to the stove. "He's navigated that world for a long time. He'll be fine. Or he'll get high, we'll see him sometime tomorrow and he'll still be fine."

The onions and peppers sizzled as he scooped them into the heated pan.

"You don't even care," Shaw said.

"Shaw—" Jory started.

Vinnie's legs were shaking from all the walking she'd done. She pulled a chair out from the table and sunk into it.

TK clamped his eyes shut. "You can't have it both ways. You're either adults and can make your own decisions, or your not. He's the only one who can do it. He'll find her and we'll all be safe."

"Who does Cerulean need to find?" Hilda's voice was low, dangerous.

TK opened his eyes. "The killer, if he finds her then we'll all be safe."

"Has his mind been tampered with?" Vinnie asked Hilda.

"What?" TK said. "Maybe you should all just go. I need to do this." He stirred the pot of sauce.

Hilda shook her head. "Not that I can see. He's thinking about eating his grandma's spaghetti when he was a kid."

Shaw took a deep breath. Her hand was rubbing just under her heart as if it hurt. "He's scared."

"I'm right here," TK said.

"What are you afraid of?" Jory's voice was gentle.

TK just hung his head. "I don't know why I told him to talk to them, but he'll be fine."

"He said he'd come back," Shaw whined.

"Has he ever done that before?" TK asked.

They all knew the answer to that. Cerulean did this all the time, said he would be somewhere, and then wasn't.

"He isn't going to become more responsible just because there's a killer out there," TK continued.

"What I don't understand is why there being a killer out there made you less responsible," Hilda said. "First Shaw and Cer, then Vinnie, and now you. You've all lost your minds. You can do good without being stupid, you know. Cer is not the only one with contacts."

TK flinched. "What's that supposed to mean?"

"I think you know what it means," Hilda said. "I'll get my shoes. Since you lost him, you should know where to find him."

"I did not lose him. He's probably just out there high somewhere."

Jory, who had been standing with his arms crossed watching the exchange, released them. "I'll go with you. I might also know some places he would be."

Vinnie stood. A wave of dizziness washed over her, and she braced her hand on the table.

"Stay," Jory said. "In case he comes home."

She could help. She hadn't told them she could sense them all now. She could help.

TK rubbed his face. "I hate pasta. The noodles should be done soon. Just mix it all up."

"I'll take care of your stupid spaghetti," Shaw said.

"I can help," Vinnie said. "I can tell all of your magic from other people's. I can sense him too."

Jory sighed. "That sentence barely made sense. You need to recover, you're skin and bones. If we don't find Cerulean tonight, you can look tomorrow. He's probably fine."

He pulled his keys back out of his front pocket and left. Hilda followed.

"He's going to be so pissed we interrupted whatever fun he's having," TK said and took a last look at his pasta and left, too.

Shaw's sigh was weary as she stood. "He's fine. TK is probably right."

"You don't believe that," Vinnie said. She wished she knew what to believe. There was a killer out there who knew Cerulean's face. If it was someone at the Warrior games who she met, they could follow her back to him. If La Mafia was involved, then he'd gone straight into trouble. But TK was also right, Cerulean did stuff like this all the time.

"Augh." Shaw covered her mouth and stepped back from the pot of sauce she'd been about to stir. "Come smell this."

In a few steps, Vinnie was at the stove. She leaned over, smelling the sauce, and gagged. The meat TK had used was rancid, and some hair must have fallen into the pan with the vegetables because it was burning.

CHAPTER THIRTY-THREE

Light burned into her eyelids. Vinnie groaned and pulled the couch pillow over her head.

"Sorry," Nell said. "Why are you in the living room?"

Vinnie sat up, rubbing gunk from her eyes. "I wanted to know when everyone got home." But she hadn't woken — she could feel them in their beds, Jory, Hilda, Shaw, but no Cerulean. "Why are you so late?"

Nell sat on the other end of the couch by Vinnie's feet. "I feel useless. I can't find him. I can't read minds or emotions. My ability doesn't help with anything at all. All I've got is my job."

There was something Nell wasn't saying. Maybe she realized her job hadn't helped much, either.

Nell shifted from side to side and just when Vinnie was about to break and say something, Nell said, "So I waited until the higher-ups left for the day and I broke into the deputy police chief's office."

"You did what?" That was not what she'd thought Nell was going to say. Vinnie was wide awake now.

Nell's cheeks were twitching, trying not to smile. "He's an

idiot. I figured he'd have his passwords written somewhere in his office. I had to use his computer, of course."

"Nell." Vinnie was torn between admiration and fear. "The station was still full of people. Someone could have come in. Or seen you. That was risky."

The smile Nell was holding back broke through. "Yeah, but Vinnie." Her nostrils flared as if she was smelling something, and she frowned, opening her mouth to say something. Then she shook her head, and whatever she'd been about to say was gone. "Will was right that there's a serial killer. We kind of knew that, but I like confirmation. He was wrong that there is no one looking. It just goes way higher than is normal. I guess that makes sense if we're dealing with a powerful Twisted. Most of that is beyond my boss's security clearance, too. But I found notes. The police are supposed to report to the Federal Investigations Department if they see certain things. Young people who may be Twisted turning up with burned eyes, drowning in their own fluids, no blood, etc. And they are not supposed to engage if they think the killer may be in their area. There are hints if you read between the lines that it started in a retraining camp. I followed crumbs and I think I found the right case, though there was no official connection to any investigation for a serial killer the MO matched."

The retraining camps, the ones where they took older Twisted they thought could still be productive members of society with proper training. None of that seemed helpful to Vinnie, but what Nell had done took courage.

"The camp was in Michigan," Nell said.

Vinnie went cold. Michigan. Home. "Which one?"

"Linden," Nell said.

Vinnie didn't need to ask when. Will had told her when — four years ago. "Who? And how do they know?"

"I couldn't get a name. The official story was she died escaping, but someone had drained the blood from her body. It's her, isn't it?"

Nell was asking if it was Lauren, the bully Vinnie had framed. "The timing is right. Blood drained. Because she was Ferr."

"There's no such thing as a coincidence when you're hunting a killer."

"What does it have to do with me?" Vinnie said.

"I don't know," Nell said. "Had to be an inside job, though. Or someone who had access."

"Who has access to retraining camps other than employees?"

"I'm not sure, but I think they have contractors for some things. It depends on the camp." Nell made a choking sound and covered her mouth, and frowned again. "I did find something else. This was easier since it's property and banking records, but it still took some digging. The holding company that bought the house the killer was using—the owner of the holding company is Gina Delgado."

"Delgado?" Vinnie repeated. "Related to Nieves Delgado. Head of La Mafia?"

"Wife," Nell said. "Ex."

"How could they have anything to do with this? They're a local... what do you call it? Syndicate?"

Nell lifted one shoulder in a shrug. "Organization. Whatever. They are local, but they have to have contacts outside of the city. Maybe suppliers in common. That woman in the booth was connected, too, right?"

"Connected to La Mafia and the Warrior Games," Vinnie agreed. "She's Lou's cousin."

"What if the Warrior Games were just a front for criminal activity?" Nell's voice seemed awed. "Criminals probably have ways of getting people into retraining camps."

Weariness overtook Vinnie, and she slumped. "We just need to find Cer and then maybe we should stay out of this."

"The invincible Vinnie, admitting something may be too big for her. Never thought I'd see the day."

"You guys tell me often enough, maybe I'm starting to believe you." She scooched down farther and closed her eyes.

Nell patted her leg and winced. "Gah, what is that smell? I thought I was imagining it when I came in, but I'm not, am I?"

"TK tried to make spaghetti with rotten meat."

"TK again." The tone of Nell's voice was the same as it had been last night when she mentioned TK — wary, irritated.

Vinnie cracked an eyelid. "What aren't you saying?"

"It's probably nothing. He came to talk to me the day you guys went to the games. He wanted to know if they'd found Nieves Delgado or had any leads. I said we didn't. Then he wanted to know if I had access to the financial records and could find out who owned the holding company. That's what put the idea in my head. He was disappointed I didn't have access."

He'd brought them the case and it made sense that he wanted to know how the investigation was progressing. But he had said that what Nell was doing was busy work, so why was he so concerned about who owned the house? "That seems reasonable."

"But Vinnie," Nell said. "When he said he was disappointed — he was lying."

"Didn't you say body language lie detecting techniques were iffy?" Vinnie said.

"Yeah," Nell was shifting again. "But my power isn't as iffy. Sometimes I can tell when people are lying. I don't know how long I've been able to do it, but I started noticing in January. People sound different when they aren't telling the truth. Something in their voice. I can't explain."

"I think my brain is going to explode. You didn't mention you could do that."

Nell snorted. "You sound like Cer.I don't want to make people uncomfortable. People lie all the time. That's why I wasn't sure at first. The only solution would be to not talk to me at all. I don't want that."

That made sense to Vinnie, but she still didn't like that Nell hadn't mentioned it. "Do I really lie all the time?" Nell patted her foot. Vinnie guessed that was a yes. "Why wouldn't TK want you to know who owned the house?"

Nell shook her head, shoulders shrugging slightly. "He's been acting strange since the night you and Cer were attacked."

He hadn't seemed that different to Vinnie. "I only noticed when he made the spaghetti. I guess going to the games with me and risking exposure was a little out of character but these last weeks have been crazy. He's not the only one acting strange."

"Yes," Nell agreed. "You've also been acting weird."

A surprised snort escaped Vinnie. "Me? Why did you go hacking when you didn't want to be involved in this in the first place?"

"I have proof now that the proper authorities are looking into it, don't I? You all are saying they don't care, and they won't do anything, but they are. There's a lot of prejudice out there, but people are not heartless. Most people would not be okay with people being murdered, no matter who they are."

Vinnie grunted, her fatigue returning in a rush. "You wanted evidence to get us to stay out of it, then."

Nell's eyes flashed with anger or frustration. Vinnie wasn't sure which.

Nell stood. "Get some sleep."

CHAPTER THIRTY-FOUR

She hadn't been able to fall back asleep, and so Vinnie had gotten up, dressed, and sat on the front porch. She pulled her hoodie tighter and wrapped her arms around herself. The sky was marginally brighter than when she first came out. The neighborhood slept, and she wished some lights would turn on and the houses would show some signs of life. Maybe if it did, then Cerulean would also appear.

Her phone sat beside her, but she hadn't even bothered to unlock it. Her fingertips touched the surface and she considered calling Will. She hadn't tried to contact him since they'd found the motel room abandoned. He had been right about the serial killer. He knew things he shouldn't have known. Would he have any clue where Cer might be?

What did she have to lose by calling him? Vinnie tapped in the passcode to unlock the phone and several text message notifications appeared on the screen from Conor. He'd lost her email address, and could she send it? He'd sent the messages late last night. The last time she had a phone, those would pop up even when the phone was locked, so she hadn't even checked. What if Cer had tried to text her? She wouldn't have even known.

She typed in her email address and hit send before switching to the phone function.

Her fingers hovered over the numbers, uncertain. Vinnie was about to put the phone back down when it rang, Conor's name popping up on the screen.

She answered.

"Hey," he said. "You're awake."

"Rough night, couldn't sleep."

"I just saw the morning news. Your sister's friend was on it. I'm so, so sorry."

Maddie. She'd pushed that to the back of her mind in her worry about Cer. "Thank you."

"Is there anything I can do?"

Tell me who did it. "Send the photo."

There was a long pause. "Right, sorry. I'll do that. Sorry to bother you."

Guilt settled in her abdomen. This wasn't his fault. "I'm sorry. I didn't mean to be short with you. I have another friend who's missing. He didn't come home last night."

"Oh," he said. "Oh... you don't think...? Shit. Can I...?"

Was he offering to help again? He hadn't completed the sentence. "Are you busy this morning?"

She could feel her friends in the house behind her. Jory said they'd take her to look, but they'd come in late. He could sleep in, and Hilda had some of the team coming into the spa today, including Lou. She would need to work. Jory could go with TK again. If they split up, they would cover more ground. Maybe it wasn't a good idea, but right now, Vinnie didn't care. She wanted to find Cer.

"No," he said. "Light training late this afternoon, but we don't have another game until the weekend."

"Can you help me look? Just drive me around?" She wouldn't be able to explain how she could find him without getting out of the car, she realized. Too late.

"I'd love to help."

———

SHE'D PUT on her shoes and scraped her hair into a ponytail. The short ends fell on her neck, tickling her as Conor's car pulled up to the house. Hilda had woken, and they'd bumped into each other in the kitchen. Now she stood beside Vinnie on the porch.

"He's a little uncomfortable, and worried about you," Hilda said.

"Clear?" Vinnie asked.

Hilda wanted to see if she could see any malice in his mind. Fair enough. She unfolded her arms and turned back to the house. "Yep."

Vinnie walked to the car, settled in the seat next to Conor.

"Your friend stayed the night?" he asked.

She forgot that their living arrangement was a little unusual. "A few of us live together, it helps keep costs down."

"Ah," he said. "Where to?"

"Go toward the library," Vinnie said. She knew what direction Cerulean had started walking from there. While she could feel her friends without thought, she would have better luck opening her power up as much as possible, so she did, extending her range as far as it would go.

The low ebb of Conor's power spark caught her attention. Vinnie tugged at it experimentally.

Conor grunted and rubbed his stomach.

"What is it?" Vinnie asked.

"I think my breakfast is disagreeing with me," he said.

No one else said they felt anything when she pulled from them. Hilda could tell, somehow. She'd never really asked how. Was it because he had so little magic, he had nothing to give?

She was so focused on the mystery that she almost missed the signature. "Stop here." Cerulean was nearby. Could it really be this easy?

Conor pulled into a parking spot near the alleyway that led to the library door.

"You think he came to the library?" Conor asked.

The feeling was coming from across the street. Vinnie shook her head and got out of the car. The morning traffic rush had started — people trying to get to work, but she didn't need to wait long to cross the street. Traffic was never heavy here.

She followed the sense of Cerulean to the old gym that had shut down last year when someone stabbed the owner outside his house in the Heights. Vinnie stopped outside the building for a moment before ducking around the back of the building.

The alley was empty of people. She walked a little farther in to peer around some trash bins, just to be sure.

Conor followed behind her. "Did you see something?"

"No, I just thought —" She stopped, looking at the mural on the side of the gym. She'd seen it a hundred times, but she'd never paid much attention. The sense of Cerulean was coming from the painting. Stepping back, she took the whole thing in. The mural showed people working out in a rural setting. Strange. Technically, it was a good painting, and now, looking at it with her senses open, she realized it felt not just like Cerulean, but also TK.

Something in the corner of the painting caught her eye, and she almost laughed. There, just at the painting's edge, was a tiny pig with wings. The pig was cerulean blue with swirls of gold and silver. Cer had painted this. Had he painted the entire thing? It wasn't his style. Vinnie reached out her hand to the painting, tracing her fingertips across a line.

"Pretty," Conor said, though his voice said he was being polite.

"Yeah," Vinnie agreed and started back for the car. "He's not here."

Conor continued driving her around the city. Every time she felt Cerulean, she asked him to stop the car, and she found another painting.

After they found the third, one of a man with fairy wings feeding flowers to a unicorn, he asked, "Why are we looking at paintings?"

"My friend, Cerulean, painted them."

He tilted his head. "They're… whimsical. Except for the first one. Was he paid to paint them?"

"I don't think so," Vinnie said, but she wasn't sure.

They were quiet after that, but after another hour, Conor asked her what her favorite color was.

"Green," she answered, and asked him about his favorite song. They drove, alternating asking each other questions for another hour, stopping periodically to look at the paintings.

They'd circle back around and were moving toward the house again. Vinnie was trying to ignore the sinking in her abdomen that said they wouldn't find Cerulean when she got another ping on her senses.

She knew this place well and knew they would find another painting and not Cer.

"Stop here," she said.

"This is a sad little park," He said as he pulled into one of the four parking spaces that faced the street.

Vinnie pulled off her seatbelt with numb fingers. She'd never been back here.

"What's your favorite vegetable?" Conor asked.

"Zucchini, you?" Vinnie got out of the car.

"Weirdo, who has a favorite vegetable?" Conor stepped out after her.

Any other time, she would have laughed.

Conor was right. The park wasn't much. Two swings creaked in the breeze in the middle of a patch of dirt scattered with rocks.

A lopsided slide sat off to the side near a junk shop that had a bright yellow sign with peeling black letters. Still, it was a tiny oasis that seemed out of place with the surrounding buildings. If the park had been in the heart of the city instead of The Holt, they would have bulldozed it to make room for an office building long ago.

The park was broken down and dirty and she expected to feel residual fear from the first time she'd been here, but when her feet touched the grass, she felt comfort. This was where she'd first met Cerulean, and that had led her to the others — her family.

There was a bench on the other side of the park, almost tucked against a nearby printing and copy store. The bench was made of wood, much warmer to sleep on in the cold of winter than the metal benches dotted throughout the city. The painting on the wall of the copy store seemed to shimmer as she approached, but that was probably just her memory.

The blue painted cat had spirals of different colors rather than the gold and silver of the pig, and most of the other creatures Cer painted. Large black dragon wings studded with white sprouted from its back. The colors seemed duller than her memory made them. Only the green of the cat's eyes was still bright. One tip of the dragon wings was flaking, and Vinnie ran her fingertip along the wing.

"This one is more special to you than the others, isn't it?" Conor asked.

Vinnie nodded and tried to swallow the lump in her throat. "I was eighteen when I ran, almost an adult. I got on a bus and just rode until I felt like stopping. When I got off the bus here, in The Holt, it felt right. The problem was, I had been sheltered. I knew what things cost, sure. Some things anyway. It wasn't easy to get money from my dad in a way that he wouldn't notice, but I'd save up a few thousand. I thought it would be enough until I could find a job. But I wasn't careful, and the money started to run out and one night I slept here. It was raining. I had put a blanket I'd stolen from a hotel over the bench and was huddled under it. I was cold and miserable and crying. Then I looked up and there was this guy." She snorted, remembering. "He scared me. Bright orange hair and half his face was blue. I screamed, and he said, 'Don't scream, you look cold, I can build a fire.'" And he had, despite the rain, because he was a Wisp. "He huddled under the blanket with me and started a fire. Probably could have gotten us arrested. We started talking. He lived on the streets, taking work where he could find it. He told me to go home. I said I didn't have one, and he said he knew a place, a guy who would take in people who needed a place to stay, but I wasn't going to ask strangers if I could live with them. I told him I'd been having nightmares, and he told me to wait. He came back with paints, in tiny little bottles. He painted this and said that it would get rid of my nightmares. I fell asleep by the warm fire and when I woke, he was gone."

"I got a job, but it was going to be a long time before the first payday. I lasted a few days before going to the house he'd told me about. The days I slept here, I had no nightmares. Later, when I was settled, I came back to find him. Even with face tattoos, he wasn't easy to find. People don't want to talk." Hilda had been with her, though. "But much easier to find than someone without."

"And you've been friends ever since?" Conor said, a note of pain in his voice. "Is that why you keep ditching me, you already have someone?"

She shook her head. "It's not like that. He's more like a little brother and he's had problems with drugs. He took away my nightmares, but he can't take away his own.

"You're a big-hearted person, Lavinia Forbes," he murmured.

Vinnie didn't know what to say to that. "I have to find him."

"Do you think the disappearances are related?" Conor asked. "They say police are stumped about your sister's friend."

"My other friends think he may have just gone on a bender. He was clean for years, but lately... maybe not. I just..." Her voice caught, and she remembered Will saying sometimes people knew things they didn't know they knew. "One of my friends works in the police department. She said there has been a rash of killings following the Warrior Games. It's been kept quiet."

"Bullshit." Conor had been leaning against the back of the bench, but he stood up straight now. "They couldn't keep something like that from us. We would have noticed."

Did he believe that? If the news didn't make a big deal of them, then would anyone on the teams have noticed there were similarities in a story reported in two minutes on the late news?

Vinnie hung her head. How did she ask him if he'd seen anything strange if he denied anything was going on? "He probably is just on a bender, but with Maddie..."

He reached out to rub his hand on her back. "I get it."

Impulsively, she turned and wrapped her arms around him, pressing her face into his chest. He held her tight and for a moment, everything felt like it was going to be okay.

Then Conor cleared his throat. "It's a long shot, but could he be avoiding your calls? Out of shame?"

Vinnie pulled away and wiped the small amount of moisture that had collected under her eyes. Would Cer have avoided them from shame? He hadn't wanted to talk to her about the drugs, avoiding the question, and if he was high, maybe he didn't even notice his phone, but he had to come down sometime, right?

"Maybe," she said.

He fished his phone out of his pocket and handed it to her. "Try mine. He won't know the number."

The first thing she'd texted to Cer was that it was her. He'd wanted her to text. Trying Conor's phone seemed like a long shot, but what could it hurt? Vinnie took Conor's phone and pulled her own out to get the number.

She dialed. After five rings, it still hadn't gone to voice mail, and she was about to hang up when the ringing stopped.

The sound of soft breathing came through the phone, but whoever had answered didn't say anything.

"Hello?" Vinnie said.

"Hi." The voice was Cerulean's.

CHAPTER THIRTY-FIVE

"Cerulean?" Vinnie asked, even though she recognized his voice.

"Stranger Danger." His voice sounded groggy, like she'd woken him.

She was torn between relief and frustration, and a little embarrassed that she'd dragged Conor all over the Holt. He sounded like he was fine. "It's Vinnie. Why haven't you been answering your phone?"

"You said you would text me," he said.

"I did text you. Shaw texted you. Hilda called you. You didn't answer."

There was a shuffling on the other end. After a few moments Cer said, "Oh, those are you. It says Vinnie."

No apology, nothing. He just sounded confused. "Where are you? We were worried. "

"Don't know."

"Did someone take you? Hurt you?" If someone had taken him, why would they leave him his phone?

"I bought some off Jody, and then I was here."

Bought some. Drugs. Vinnie sat on the park bench. The

others had been right. He was fine, they'd been panicking for nothing. Almost nothing. Cer doing drugs again was a problem.

"He bought drugs," she said to Conor. To Cer, she said, "Are you coming home?"

There was a groan, like he was stretching. "No car."

"Take the bus."

There was a rustle of cloth, and Cer's breathing became raspy. "I don't think there's a bus."

No bus? What did that mean? "Where are you? How did you get there? Give me an idea, a landmark or something."

More rustling. "I think it's the place we came after we killed that guy. After we didn't kill that guy."

"Nell's house?"

"Nell lives with us."

He'd been exhausted when they went out there and must not have heard that she owned the house. "How did you get out there?" she repeated. That was over an hour's drive, and he didn't have a car.

Another long pause, then he said. "I thought we could party out here without being busted, but they left me."

"I'll come get you. Stay there!" Vinnie jabbed the off button and shoved the phone back at Conor. Cer had just been getting wasted, causing them all to worry. She could go home, get Hilda's car. "Can you take me home? I'm sorry for wasting your time."

She pulled out her phone and texted Nell that Cerulean was okay, and she needed the address to her house. It had been dark before, and she wasn't paying attention.

Conor, still holding his phone as he watched her, said, "I can take you."

The relief was instant. She was still so exhausted and the thought of making that drive felt like too much, but everyone else was busy with more important things. She had a twinge of embarrassment that he was seeing her messy life. She'd never really thought of it as messy before, just happy. How did it all fall apart so fast? "You don't have to do that, it's a long drive, over an hour."

"It'll be an adventure." And he sounded like he meant that.

HER STOMACH HAD GRUMBLED before they made it out of town, so they'd stopped and bought donuts. No amount of wiping with a paper napkin had gotten the sticky, powdery feeling completely off her fingers, and she wasn't about to lick them in front of Conor.

"You should have gone for the filled, unfrosted ones," Conor said after she wiped her fingers on her pants for the fifth time.

She laughed. "You were right. Too bad I don't have a sister to blame for my misdeeds."

"Mean!" he laughed. "I was eight." He'd been keeping her entertained on the drive as they exchanged childhood stories. Vinnie had to dig deep to remember positive things, but she'd held her own.

Conor took the turn to Nell's house, and Vinnie struggled not to wipe her hands on her pants again. What would he think of Cerulean? Cer was a lot to take in. She didn't think Conor would be condescending, but people often surprised you — in good ways and bad.

There were other houses set back from the gravel road that led up to Nell's she hadn't noticed the first time. A large expanse of fields separated the houses, but they could still see each other — though not well.

The first house they passed was a mobile home with a few old appliances in the front yard, the next a well-tended small box of a house with a blooming garden. An old mailbox with a painted-on number sat next to the turnoff for the long driveway up to Nell's grandma's house. Conor made the turn and as they crested the small rise, the house came into view.

An old truck sat to the side of the house, with tall grass and weeds growing around it, but other than that, there were no vehicles.

A scrap of color in the road caught her eye as they approached the house. When Vinnie realized what it was, she sat up straight. "Stop."

"Is that a body?" Conor's voice was full of horror.

Cer. Vinnie sprang out of the car, a small rush of adrenaline allowing her to overcome her fatigue and sprint over to Cerulean.

His head rolled toward her as she approached.

"Are you okay?" Her eyes scanned him for injuries or blood.

In one fluid motion, he was on his feet. "Yes. Are you?"

Vinnie sagged in relief. "What are you doing laying in the road?"

"The grass has stickers in it." He waved his arm. Then his eyes snagged on the car. "You shouldn't have brought him. Send him away."

His eyes seemed clear. His voice wasn't slurred. He was acting like he always acted, but Vinnie wasn't sure if she'd know what someone on drugs acted like.

"He's our ride. If I send him away, we are both stranded."

Cerulean stood there, frozen, as she'd seen him so many times. Blank gaze on the car.

Conor shifted, and his hand reached for the handle.

"It's okay. I've got this," Vinnie called out. She took Cer's arm. "Let's go home."

Cerulean slipped out of her grasp. "I left some stuff in the house." He shuffled away.

Did she even want to know how he'd gotten into the house? Vinnie followed him.

After a few steps, he paused. "Let's go home. It's not important stuff."

Had he left drugs in there? "What stuff is it?"

His face scrunched. "My shoes. It's okay. I don't like them anyway."

She looked at his feet. Sure enough, he was only wearing socks. Vinnie shook her head and started toward the house, with Cerulean trailing after her.

The front door was off, hanging on a hinge with scorch marks on one side near the handle. That answered the question of how he'd gotten in.

"Nell is going to be so pissed," Vinnie said. "Why did you burn it?"

Cer had stopped on the steps and was shuffling from foot to foot, eyes on the door.

"She'll get over it, let's get your stuff," Vinnie said.

Cer stood still, staring at the door with his lips parted. He swallowed. "We should go. It's not safe."

Goosebumps popped up on her arms. "Are there people still here?" If she had access to some power, she wouldn't be worried about a few junkies. She did have Cer, and she could use his power if he didn't.

"No." Cer swallowed again, adam's apple bobbing.

Vinnie opened her senses, looking for power or people. He was right, there was nothing.

"Why are you afraid of going in?"

Cerulean swayed on his feet. "There were bad people."

She breathed a sigh of relief. Just a memory. She needed to calm him down so they could go in. "Yeah, they left you here. Let's go around, make sure they're gone."

He sneaked his assent as she went down the steps and around to the side of the house. She peered in the first window, noting the darkened kitchen where nothing seemed to be disturbed.

"They were bad people," Cer said weakly as Vinnie peered into another window.

She continued around the house to the back sliding door that opened into the sunken living room of the split-level house. This room also appeared to be empty.

"Vinnnieee," Cerulean wailed.

Goosebumps traveled up her arms again as she put her hand on the back handle and tugged, not surprised to find it locked. "Are your shoes in here?"

He didn't answer. He didn't look at her. He didn't so much as twitch.

She started back around the house. "You stay outside, and I'll go get your shoes."

Cerulean followed her to the front but stopped at the bottom of the front steps.

"Where are they? In the back room?"

His shoulders hunched, but he didn't answer.

She would just have to find them. How hard could it be?

"Okay, go wait in the car with Conor." Vinnie took out her phone, texted Hilda, and then pulled Cerulean's power close, just in case, before climbing the front steps again.

She scooted the door aside and stepped in, listening for sounds of movement.

She felt Cer following her and held up a hand for him to be quiet, which meant nothing to him because he said. "We should go."

Why didn't he want to go back there? Had he done something he didn't want her to see? TK had said that he'd hurt more than just his parents. She hadn't wanted to believe him, but from the way Cer was acting, she wasn't so sure. "You need your shoes. Whatever else is back there, we can fix it."

She hoped.

His face twisted in anguish, and Vinnie reached out, putting her hands on his cheeks. "We can figure this out, okay? It's going to be okay. Wait here."

Vinnie went through the kitchen to the back living room, unsure what she might find.

Stopping just inside the entrance to the room, her gaze swept from corner to corner, searching for anything amiss. She spotted Cer's shoes by the back door, but there was nothing bad. Vinnie took a step toward the shoes.

A shuffle of movement beside her drew her attention, but before she could turn, a hand grabbed her arm.

"Don't move," Kara said.

CHAPTER THIRTY-SIX

Images flashed through Vinnie's mind of her friends screaming in pain, calling out for help. She knew they would be hurt if she didn't do as Kara asked. She felt the truth of it deep in her body.

Vinnie stopped on the threshold of the room, unable to move.

Kara still held her by the arm. "You can take four steps forward."

Vinnie took four steps forward. Kara released her arm and stood in front of her. She was smiling.

"So glad you could finally make it. What took you so long? Don't you even care about your friend enough to text or call before he's been missing for twenty-four hours? Geez, Vinnie."

Vinnie wanted to protest that she had texted Cer, and they'd called, and he hadn't answered until today, but Kara had told her not to move, and talking would mean she would have to move her mouth. She needed to do what Kara told her to do, and everything would be fine.

"You know what?" Kara said. "Come on into the room."

Vinnie started forward, almost pitching forward at the first step.

"Watch your step." Kara took her arm again, and nausea washed over Vinnie.

The steps loomed. She took one careful step, then another, relieved when her feet touched the floor. Dread made her stop for a moment, but the compulsion took over, and she walked to the middle of the room.

"Already fighting the compulsion. Hm." Kara said.

Kara was a Mesmer. No, that wasn't right. She knew deep down that she needed to do what Kara said. Her senses told her that Kara was Ferr. Why hadn't she been able to sense Ferr from outside? She could sense her now. Kara was Ferr or Kara had stolen Ferr from someone. Kara was the killer. Her mind scrabbled, trying to latch onto something other than standing in the middle of the room as she was told. But no, Ferr couldn't make you do something you didn't want to do. Kara was —

"I finally did it." Kara put her fingertips to her mouth, and her eyes danced with excitement. "Do you know how long I have been looking for you? All the pieces I had to put into place to get you here? It took a lot of skill and a little luck. Thankfully, you are just as dumb as Lauren said you were. Although, that stupidity got in the way a few times." Her face scrunched. "What kind of idiot takes off with a guy when her friend just told her he is a murderer? Lavinia Forbes, that's who."

Vinnie's mind had spun out at the name Lauren, and she had a hard time focusing on the rest. Lauren had died in a retraining camp and Kara was the killer. How? She couldn't think straight. It didn't matter how Kara had killed Lauren. Right now, she had Vinnie immobilized and would kill her, too. At least Cer hadn't followed her back here. Cer. TK. TK had said Conor was the killer. Kara had taken his hand and told him he was there for Conor. Was that all it took? How? Vinnie mentally shook herself. She had to stop thinking about how and think about how to get out of this.

"Just one question, and then we need to get going," Kara

continued. "Do you feel bad about Lauren's death? You are the one who sent her to jail."

A burning started in Vinnie's middle and rushed up to her cheeks.

"You can answer that," Kara said. "Don't take things so literally. When I said don't move, I meant don't attack me or try to get away."

"No," Vinnie lied. "Do you?"

Kara shook her head. "Lauren was what psychologists affectionately term a 'psychopath.' We both did the world a favor. Trust me."

"How did you meet Lauren?" The chattering panic in Vinnie's mind had slowed but she needed more time to figure out how to stop Kara. Keeping her talking might give her that time.

"We were in the same facility."

Kara had no identifying tattoo, but Vinnie had already known that. Nell's theory about her working there must be correct.

Kara, as if noticing the direction of Vinnie's gaze, lifted her hands with the backs facing out. "I wasn't a prisoner. I'm not stupid. But, enough about me. Let's get you out of here before someone comes. I'll have to deal with Sam, and then we can go."

There was no car. Vinnie had walked all the way around the house. However Kara planned to get her out of here, it wasn't by car. You never let a kidnapper move you to a different location. Vinnie had heard that somewhere. She needed to stall, give herself time to think.

"Did you kill Maddie?"

"That was the fluffy-haired girl? No, not intentionally," Kara said. "I try not to kill them, but they all die. It isn't like I wanted her to die. I take their power, and they die."

Every question, every exchange, only made Vinnie more confused. How did she take their power? Vinnie heard movement behind her, but she couldn't turn.

"Get away from her Vinnie, run," Cer said.

"Sam," Kara said. "I told you not to come back here. Oh well, she was much easier to subdue than I thought. So, you being here is better."

"You said you wouldn't hurt her," Cerulean said.

She shrugged. "I said I wouldn't cause her pain. Are you hurt, Vinnie?"

Vinnie needed to get Cerulean out of here. She had his power, which she'd forgotten in her panic. The power didn't require her to move to use it.

"I'm sorry, I'm so sorry, Vinnie," Cerulean sobbed. "She said she'd make the pain stop. She promised she wouldn't hurt you."

"Addicts," Kara said, tsking softly. She reached out and put her hand on Vinnie's shoulder. "Don't take my power. That is what you do isn't it? Poor Lauren didn't know what hit her. Step one, pick a fight with her. Step two, make blood appear all over your skin. Step three, they test her. You know what happens after that."

Choked sobs were still coming from the direction of the door.

"You should go outside, Cer," Vinnie said. Cer still had his phone. He could call the others, let them know. He could get Conor out of there. "I wish you'd called me sooner," she called out, hoping he would understand. "You can always call any of us for help."

"I can't answer the phone," Cer said. "People will come, and she'll hurt them."

That was why he hadn't been answering. He'd been trapped out here with Kara, but part of him was trying to keep them safe. Conor had been right. He didn't answer any number he recognized, which meant Cer knew that had been her texting and calling. "Maybe you can just go home, then. Go to the highway, hitch a ride."

"Stay where you are, Sam," Kara said. To Vinnie, she said, "He won't call for help."

"Because you coerced him not to?"

Kara's eyes shot daggers in Cer's direction. "Wisps are the most resistant to my charms. Ferr can't make anyone do what they don't want to. Your friend doesn't want to hurt, but that hasn't been as strong a lever as I thought it would be."

A lever. Vinnie had a vision of her friends hurting when Kara came in. She wanted to do what Kara told her to do because she didn't want her friends to be hurt.

"Get out of here, Cer. Run," Vinnie said.

Kara looked her dead in the eye. "Stop talking to him."

Vinnie looked right back at her. "Run, Cerulean."

Rage burned in Kara's eyes, and she moved close, putting her hands on either side of Vinnie's face. "I'm going to rip every ounce of power out of him, and he will die screaming if you don't shut up."

The images of exactly that flashed through Vinnie's mind, and she knew Kara would do it, but maybe if she distracted her, Cer would run.

"You're the psychopath. Lauren was just a bully," Vinnie said.

Kara stepped back. "I'm a visionary. I'm trying to save us all. If a few people have to die, then so be it. You're not one to talk."

She meant Lauren again. Shame made Vinnie's tongue thick. "I never wished Lauren dead."

"That's a lie," Kara said.

Vinnie squirmed. Maybe she had imagined her dying, but she'd never really wished it, had she? "She made our lives hell. I wanted her out of my life, but I didn't want her to die." At least, that's what she told herself.

"And that is why our kind are still locked up and used. People are too afraid to break a few eggs to get the omelet. Lauren was just as awful locked up, you know. She continued to make people's lives hell because you didn't stop her. You think just because she wasn't hurting you and your friends anymore that it didn't count? That those people's misery didn't count? You are wasting your power because you are too afraid of what might happen if you used it as it's meant to be used. But I'll figure out how it works and finally put it to good use."

Vinnie wriggled her shoulders again before realizing that was movement. She could move if she didn't think about it, but how could she not think of moving? She needed to keep Kara talking to give herself time to figure this out. "You already have the same power. Aren't you like me?"

"Sadly, no. I'm Ferr." Kara tapped the crystal on the pendant around her neck. "I can use this to take someone's power, but I can't keep it. It's horribly inefficient. I take the power, they die, I lose the power. I will figure it out, and then I will save us all."

A sick feeling lodged itself in Vinnie's abdomen at the thought. Kara talked about killing people as if it was nothing, killing them and taking their power. She took their power with an object, something Vinnie hadn't known was possible. She'd been way over her head from the beginning, just from the lack of knowledge.

How was she going to get Cer out of this? Vinnie could still hear him there, whimpering. Maybe if she could nudge him, he'd go. She used his power to send a rush of warmth at him.

"Objects don't have power and can't take it," Vinnie said.

Kara shook her head, disgusted. "You have no imagination. That's why you live in a slum, barely scraping by."

Cerulean moaned and Kara started to turn.

Vinnie needed to keep distracting her. "How did you find me? I haven't had a phone or used a credit card. Is facial recognition from street cams a real thing? My friends can't seem to agree on that."

"Whoa," Kara gave her head a disbelieving shake. "I knew you weren't very smart, but really? You are a PERSON WITH MAGICAL POWERS, and the only way you can think of for someone to find you is mundane means?"

Kara was Ferr. She could have tracked her. "But you didn't have anything of mine to find me. And it's a big country."

"You're wasting my time," Kara said.

Vinnie turned her head. Turning her head wasn't moving. "You're wasting mine. I think it's time Cerulean, and I got out of here.

"I can't go," Cer said. "She can make the pain stop."

Vinnie couldn't talk to him, but she could talk to Kara. "You're going to make the pain stop by killing us, aren't you, Kara?"

Kara took two strides and backhanded Vinnie.

"You said you wouldn't hurt her." Cer pushed off the wall.

Kara pushed her lips up in a caricature of a smile. "I won't hurt her again, but she needs to behave."

His head shook again, waving back and forth as if he wanted to shake something out. "Are you going to kill us?"

The look Kara gave Cer seemed almost sad. "I need your power, but I wouldn't kill you on purpose."

But he would die anyway. She'd said earlier when she took their power, they died. Trying to convince Cer to leave wasn't working. Kara hadn't even restrained him, so she was confident he wouldn't leave, that he'd stay, and she could take his power.

"Let's get this party started," Kara turned away, took a wide stance, legs spread, arms in the air like a big X. Her breathing grew heavy, tortured.

The air in the room changed as the power of an anomaly filled it. She'd created an anomaly. Just created an anomaly out of nothing. There was no car because she was going to take Vinnie through an anomaly.

Kara had collapsed to her knees, panting. A few drops of crimson hit the carpet under her head.

Cer's snuffling had stopped, and his fists clenched. She'd never seen the rage she saw in his eyes now, but she knew what it meant. He was going to attack. Vinnie caught his eyes and shook her head. Why wouldn't he get out of there like she'd told him to?

His brow crinkled and his lips pursed. He leveled his gaze at Kara. As if she could sense his eyes, Kara threw her arm out and Cer crashed into the wall, his head banging hard, and he slumped.

Air. She'd used Mesmer power she'd gotten from the anomaly. Vinnie had been right. She was pulling power from an anomaly. Kara wobbled a little as she as she got to her feet and turned. Blood dripped from one earlobe and splashed onto her shirt. The look she gave Vinnie was malevolent, all humor was gone from her face.

Without thinking, Vinnie was moving toward her. She needed to stop her, or her friends really would get hurt.

"Don't," Kara said. "I need you alive, but I don't need you to have all your limbs attached." She held one hand out in the anomaly's direction, a silver bracelet on her hand flashed as light reflected off of it. "I will flatten you."

Vinnie stopped. She'd overcome the compulsion, but she was still overpowered.

She reached out to Kara's Ferr power, but she couldn't pull it. How had she gotten herself to move? Vinnie shifted deeper, so she could see the power. Colors flared to life. Mesmer and Dancer energy flowed into Kara. The pendant glowed faintly with Wisp energy. There was power in the bracelet, too, but it was too weak for Vinnie to identify.

Kara had only told her not to pull her power, but the Wisp, Dancer, and Mesmer powers weren't Kara's. Vinnie took a few steps back as if she were retreating and reached out and tried to pull the Wisp power from the pendant. Nothing happened.

A small frown turned Kara's mouth down and she dropped her arms, then pointed both at Vinnie. Black energy flowed from them.

Vinnie leaped to the side, but the power curved, smashing into her, and making her limbs vibrate with pain. The black arc connected her to Kara, and she felt as if she was being pulled apart. Her vision blurred until she could no longer feel her limbs. There was nothing in her awareness but pain.

When the pain stopped, there was a white expanse above her. The ceiling. Vinnie was on the floor, staring at the ceiling.

Kara's voice came from the haze outside her immediate awareness. "Interesting, I can't find your ability. I know it's there. I'll figure it out soon enough."

Her boots were in Vinnie's line of vision, but that's all Vinnie could see of her. She could no longer feel or see the power. If she ignored the echoes of pain, maybe she could do something. Anything. Get the pendant off Kara, so she would just be Ferr.

"All that talk about saving the Twisted and you're killing them. You're a hypocrite." Speaking felt like trying to shove her voice out of her lungs.

Kara crouched — her sharp nose pointed at Vinnie. "I know I've said it before, but you still really don't get it, so let me say it again. You are shortsighted and unimaginative. And you're a coward. Like most people, you just accept that they enslave us and use us as you run and hide with your friends." She leaned closer, close enough that Vinnie imagined she could be like one of those action movies and smash her nose with her forehead. If only her body would move. Kara continued, "We are powerful, but there aren't enough of us. And they have guns and weapons. The only way we will ever free ourselves is if we learn to use our full potential. For me to figure it out, means some people have to die. Like you. I'm not going to cry over it."

Vinnie tried to calm the residual ache in her limbs so she could focus. She forced a chuckle from her lungs. "You expect me to believe you want to help people. You're a psychopath and bully, just like Lauren. A selfish bully, who lives to hurt people."

The pain roared through Vinnie again, so loud she couldn't hear her own scream, but she felt it as it scraped her throat.

It stopped again. "Nia, Nia, I have to say, that's a very satisfying sound. It's true, I want to hurt them, and you, as much as they hurt me."

Kara's head snapped up toward the door.

A shout came from the front of the house. "Vinnie?"

Conor.

CHAPTER THIRTY-SEVEN

She needed to warn Conor. Tell him to run, get away. "Conor," she croaked. Vinnie swallowed the dryness in her throat to try again, but before she could open her mouth, he came through the door.

"Kara." His shoulders sagged in relief. "What are you doing here?"

Kara slunk a few steps to the side to put herself between Conor and Vinnie — one hand pointed backward as the other fiddled with her necklace. "Conor. What are *you* doing here?" Her voice was full of fake cheerfulness threaded with anger.

"I brought Vinnie..." His voice trailed off when he saw Vinnie on the floor. He took an automatic step back.

"You're not supposed to be here," Kara said.

Vinnie's skin felt like spiders were crawling all over it and little shocks kept going through her body — the after-effects of whatever Kara had done to her.

Conor's eyes roved the room, catching on Cer, still slumped against the wall.

"She killed Maddie," Vinnie wheezed.

"Kara?" he said, taking another step back.

A wall of air hit Vinnie, and the breath whooshed out of her lungs.

Kara shrugged. "I never deliberately kill anyone. Except," She looked up at the ceiling, thinking. "I did kill people who deserved to die, and I have taken some power, from others which caused them to die, but I used it for you. You didn't think you had all those wins without help, did you?"

Conor took a few steps back toward the door, keeping his eyes on Kara. "You're just a trainer. Not even Twisted, everyone working for the games is tested."

She looked at Vinnie. "You see. Just a trainer. Everything I've done for him and I'm just a trainer. This is why I need the power, because people don't appreciate us, and they don't deserve us." Her head swiveled back to Conor. "And you really shouldn't have so much trust in systems. It's easy enough to fake paperwork that says I've already been tested and found not to be Magiera — that's the proper name for people you so derisively call Twisted."

Magiera. Vinnie had only ever heard one other person use that word and hearing it from Kara was like getting a bucket of ice dumped on her. The shot of adrenaline was enough to help her shake off the disorientation and give her enough clarity to know that Kara was still holding the Dancer and Mesmer.

Pulling the Wisp energy hadn't worked, but that was in the pendant. Vinnie tried the Dancer energy, and it flowed smoothly into her.

Conor was afraid. She could feel it now, but there was a hard core of something else, like a dark knot in his center. He was backing up through the doorway, glancing at her on the floor and at Kara.

If she could distract Kara, maybe he could get away.

"Conor?" Vinnie waited for him to look at her. When their eyes met, she said, "Run." She used the Dancer energy to roll to her feet, and send a blast of sorrow at Kara.

Kara flinched and turned to Vinnie. Her face looked disappointed rather than sad. Conor ran.

Emotion was tricky, but Vinnie had felt Shaw's soothing enough that she'd thought that would work.

"What was that supposed to be, Nia?" Kara held her hand out, palm down in Vinnie's direction, and an ice ball coalesced and flew at Vinnie too fast for her to dodge. The ice knocked Vinnie off her feet again. She fell backward, head crunching into the end table before she hit the floor. Blackness edged her vision. She couldn't let herself pass out. All her focus became about not letting go of consciousness. She still felt it when Kara jerked the power away from her.

"He'll be back, you know," Kara said. "You didn't save anyone. He has the heart of a hero, pity he's normal. Tricky girl." Kara turned from her and bounded up the two steps to the higher level. She crouched to examine Cerulean.

Vinnie rolled to her hands and knees on the carpet, trying to will the vertigo away and see what Kara was doing.

Kara's palm hovered above Cerulean's chest, her back tensed, and orange magic flowed from him to her. Cerulean screamed, his body twisting, writhing.

Vinnie pushed against the floor, fighting the pain and fatigue to get to her feet.

Conor reappeared in the doorway, just as Kara said he would. He lifted his arms straight out, gun in his hands. "Stand up and put your hands above your head or I will kill you."

Vinnie closed her eyes. Conor was dead. If he was going to shoot, he should have done it immediately.

When she opened her eyes again, Kara had her hands in front of her, rage twisting her face.

There was a loud bang as Conor pulled the trigger.

Kara froze, blood blooming on her shoulder. "You shot me."

"Turn around and stand up," Conor said.

Smart, if her back was to him, she couldn't aim the power at him.

Conor gasped, choking. He put one hand to this throat, the other tried to hold on to the gun. The gun banged again, shot going wide, and then it fell limply from his hands.

Vinnie reached out and pulled all the Dancer energy. Conor leaned forward, coughing up water.

Kara stood, the orange power still flowing from Cerulean to her hand. As she pulled her fist up, the power seemed to tug out of Cer and wrap around her. He collapsed, limp.

"No," Vinnie rasped.

She'd taken his power, which, if Kara had told the truth, meant Cerulean didn't have long to live. Vinnie needed to move.

Conor pulled in a breath and coughed.

"Conor, Run," Vinnie meant to shout, but her voice came out a husky huff.

The moment Conor's eyes latched onto the gun, the next sequence of events played in Vinnie's head. Before he moved, she pushed her body into motion, but the Dancer power didn't make her faster.

Conor lunged for the gun. Kara pulled up a fireball between her hands and, just as his fingers touched the handle, the fireball hit him in the chest. Kara lifted her hands, palms up, and his clothes ignited. He fell to the ground and rolled, trying to put out the flames as Vinnie reached him.

She'd never manipulated water, but she knew there was water in the air. Drawing the water close was just like pulling the surrounding air to make herself invisible. She drew as much water around Conor as she could find.

"You little minx," Kara snarled. The Dancer energy left Vinnie and Kara sent an ice spike whirling at her.

Vinnie pulled fire from Kara and held up a palm. The point melted off, but the rest crashed into her, and she went down.

After the initial whoosh of air out of her lungs, her breath seized as Kara took away the air.

How much power could Kara hold that she could throw those ice spikes? There was no way Vinnie could beat her unless she could pull all the power away from Kara or pull from the anomaly.

Vinnie pulled Mesmer power and increased the air around her, sucking in a breath. Then she pulled as much Wisp as she could, shoving it deep down. If she could boost her own power, maybe she could pull from the anomaly.

Kara appeared over her. A rivulet of blood dripped off her chin, plopping onto Vinnie's forehead. Crouching, Kara touched the blood on Vinnie's forehead. "Let go of the power you've taken and from now on you cannot take my power."

In her mind, Conor died, screaming in agony, and her dad laughed and told her she should have listened to him because now she was going to be in a cage for the rest of her life.

All the power left Vinnie in a rush, and she knew she was dead. There was nothing left she could do. Cer was dead, Conor might be dead and all she could do was lay here, letting it happen. She was just as useless and helpless as her dad told her she was.

Kara kicked, her boot slamming into Vinnie, knocking her back a few feet. The crunch in her chest let her know something was wrong before the pain radiated out from her center.

"I want to kill you for attacking me, but I need you alive," Kara said, stalking toward her. "Fortunately." She paused, frowning. When she continued, her voice was thoughtful. "And unfortunately, you probably won't live long. I need to at least try to keep you alive until I figure the power out." She crouched again. "You could just tell me — how do you hold on to the power?"

Vinnie tried to think around the pain. She couldn't keep the power. Not if the person it came from was not there, could she? Kara hadn't put a compulsion behind her question. "If you tell me how you create the anomaly and take its power I'll tell you how to hold it." She could see the power now, even though she was no longer trying. She'd always thought it was an effort to see it, but now she could see that she had it reversed. It was an effort not to see the power. Maybe Hilda was right, she'd been blocking it all along. She'd blocked the power for so long she wasn't even aware she was blocking it, but the pain had exhausted her, and Vinnie's mind no longer resisted seeing how it flowed to Kara in a continuous stream.

Kara shook her head. "Of course, you can't make this easy. I need to get you out of here before someone comes looking." She looked at the place where Conor collapsed and sighed. "And I guess I'm going to have to wipe his memory in case he lives. Or try too. He'll probably die."

A shot of panic went through Vinnie, and she tried to spring up, but a wave of vertigo set her flopping down again.

"Nice try!" Kara crouched and smeared more blood on Vinnie's face. "Don't move a muscle."

A shiver went through Vinnie. She wanted nothing more than to do what Kara said. Her body froze, including her lungs. Were lungs muscles?

"Oh, good grief, breathe," Kara stood. "And blink. Stay there. I'll erase his memory and then we can go."

Erase his memory in case he survived. The thought echoed in her head and she wanted to scream. Vinnie couldn't move her body, she couldn't pull power. She was helpless — helpless and trapped.

Let me in. The voice in her head was male, and though it lacked the smokiness of the owner's real voice, she recognized it.

Will?

Yes, let me in your mind and I can imprint the pattern. I can show you how to fight her.

Vinnie swallowed and closed her eyes, feeling the world go dark around her, hearing the click of the lock on her room as her dad locked her in. Did she have another choice? If there was one, she couldn't see it through the inky blackness in her mind. Kara had used the term Magiera, just like Will had. They could be working together and this could be a ploy to get inside her head to figure out her power.

I already know how to use your power. Let me show you.

The bundle of power that was Kara hovered over Conor.

Vinnie was out of options and time. *Okay.*

And then she was in a room with dark paneled walls, expensive wallpaper, and curvy Queen Anne style furniture. Vinnie was still lying on her back, and her own face hovered above her. No, it wasn't her face. The chin was rounder, face softer, and the eyes were a warm, rich brown, and bigger than Vinnie's.

"I've got it. Let me show you," the other woman said. She leaned over and kissed Vinnie on the forehead.

Colors burst into Vinnie's mind. Patterns of power, complex and varied. So many lines and connections, like a vast web that just kept getting bigger and more complex.

And Vinnie didn't know how to use any of it.

Allow me, Will said, or the woman said. Vinnie couldn't tell. Her eyes flew open, and her body shifted and pushed itself up. Every bit of her screamed in protest. It hurt and if she had been in control, she would have collapsed.

But she wasn't in control anymore. *What are you doing?*

Sorry. I'll have to do this. Her body turned toward the anomaly. It had appeared as a white glow before, but now she could see there were different colors in the white, making it look pearlescent.

The pain eased.

Vinnie watched as her hands lifted, palms out. *Let me go. You said you were going to show me.*

I didn't realize you were under a compulsion. You can't do this.

The power flowed toward her body, filling her up and making her feel cold and hot and wet and dry. Vinnie would have gasped, but she no longer had control of that.

Her hand shot out toward Kara, who crouched over Conor, so intent she hadn't noticed what Vinnie was doing. Will used the power in Vinnie to lift Kara's body straight up into the air. Her face was a mask of fear, mouth gaping at Vinnie. Then Will flung her to the side.

She hit the ground, landing in a heap before she rolled gracefully to her feet. "I don't know where you learned that but—" Kara gasped, clutching at her head. Then her fingers moved around to her mouth, tugging at the lips, fingernails raking at the edges, but her mouth wouldn't open.

Will was choking her.

Stop it, you're going to kill her. Vinnie's body strode across the room, hopped up on the steps to get closer to Kara, and looked down at her.

That's the idea, Will said.

Kara struggled to get up, blood leaking from her eyes, nose, ears, and Vinnie felt ill. She tried to push Will out, but where was he?

She won't stop. She will kill all your friends like she's killed so many others, he said.

We just have to get the pendant off her, and then we can have her locked up. She tried again to find him so she could push him out.

That worked so well with Nieves Delgado.

There were deep gashes in Kara's chin now, her eyes were pleading. One bloodied hand reached for Vinnie. Will jerked Vinnie's body back.

She is still trying to compel us.

Us. The word echoed in her head as Kara's eyelids fluttered. Will wasn't in her body. Kara couldn't compel them both. The thought echoed in her head. He wasn't in her body, so she couldn't push him out. A shield, Hilda had said. Will wasn't inside of her. He was using his power to make it feel like he was, and Vinnie just needed to block him, block out his power.

Stop! She said to him.

She will kill you.

He'd partially healed her body and restored some of her energy. Vinnie thought about what it felt like when she couldn't sense the power around her. She began moving her power, shifting her molecules to block him out.

There was a roar of white noise in her head as Will tried to maintain his hold. *We have to stop her before she hurts anyone else.*

It's not your choice to make. The last bit of wall of power snapped into place, and her body collapsed.

Kara gasped, letting out one audible sob.

Vinnie. I can't save you if you don't let me help. Will's voice was soft, distant.

Get out of my head!

The power Will had pulled from the anomaly was a deep swirl inside her, now roiling, threatening to tear her apart. The compulsion kept her from moving, but she already had the power.

"Ferr," she said aloud, not sure what she meant. Power thrashed inside her, making it hard to think.

"Bitch," Kara said. "I should just kill you." Her words were slurred, and she pushed herself up. As Vinnie watched, the bleeding on her chin stopped.

"Ferr," Vinnie repeated, trying to pull together her thoughts.

Kara swayed, wiping the blood from her mouth. The cuts on her face from her fingernails closed. "Now we should go."

She reached down, grabbed the front of Vinnie's shirt, and hauled her to her feet.

"You're going to behave now." Kara pulled Vinnie behind her as she started toward the anomaly.

I saved you. Vinnie couldn't seem to open her mouth as she stumbled along after Kara. She needed to pull all the power together, somehow. The map of how to use the power Will had given her was gone, along with his mind.

Kara pulled up short, her face incredulous. "Saved me? You

were trying to kill me. I don't know why you stopped. Stupid. Stupid people like you shouldn't have the power."

Vinnie couldn't disagree with her at the moment, with the power inside her feeling like it was shredding her very being. She didn't dare let it go. It was all she had for protection. They were almost to the anomaly, and Vinnie knew if she went through it, she might never come back out.

Hold on, we're coming. Hilda said.

Help was coming. It should have been a relief, but it wasn't.

It's too late. Cer was probably dead. Conor was probably dead. She'd be dead herself in a minute.

It's never too late as long as you're breathing.

Jory? Why could she hear Jory?

Kara's left foot disappeared into the anomaly, and she tugged Vinnie after her. Now or never.

Vinnie tried to bury all the other powers and separate the Dancer. but there was so much noise and energy screaming through her she couldn't. She tugged anyway, trying to spin away and push Kara toward the anomaly with her knee. She stumbled back, pulling Kara with her, and they landed in a heap.

"Maybe it really would be easier just to kill you and find another way to learn what I need to learn," Kara snarled as she pushed herself up. She gathered power around her, and her eyes lit up with an inner glow.

Let us in! Hilda shouted in her mind.

Like she'd let Will in. Fear made Vinnie numb. To lose control of herself like that...

We won't hurt you. You know this. Nell. She could hear Nell. And Nell was right. Her friends wouldn't hurt her. Her family.

We know how to use the power inside you. Let us in. We can control it, Hilda said.

They knew how to control it because they'd been working with anomaly energy at home. They could do this together. Vinnie wasn't alone. "Okay," she said.

Kara growled. "Okay?" Weight settled on her, crushing her.

And her mind cleared. Her friends separated the power into it's components. They held it like that for a moment and then Hilda tugged on the others, guiding them to reform the power until Vinnie was Stone, supported by Dancer.

Here we go, Nell said, and Vinnie's body launched up off the floor. She had only a moment to notice Kara's startled reaction before her fist punched into her face, sending the other woman flying backward.

Kara almost hit the ground, but something propelled her back up and she righted herself.

I've burned the compulsion out, TK said. *Can you get the power away from her?*

An ice spike rushed toward her, but Shaw bent Vinnie's body to the side, dodging just under it. Vinnie grabbed the power in Kara and pulled, but it was like mist, and she couldn't get a hold.

Except for the Wisp power. That was Cerulean's, and it was solid, rooted inside Kara. The air around her disappeared and Vinnie gasped, struggling to breathe.

Nope. Hilda said as the air returned to normal.

Snarling, Kara launched herself at Vinnie. As her hand touched Vinnie's shoulders, Jory took over and Kara crumpled.

Vinnie reached inside her, grabbed Cerulean's power, and pulled it out. Every last drop. Kara screamed and writhed, but between one shake of her body and the next, she had rolled to her feet again.

"You think you can — "

Vinnie's fist hit her face again, and she fell back toward the anomaly. She started to right herself, and Vinnie knew she wouldn't quit. She wouldn't stop fighting and Vinnie couldn't get the power away from her. Their only hope was to get her into the anomaly.

You can't close it, she'll just come back ou, Hilda said.

Can't? Vinnie could close it.

We can, Shaw said. And Vinnie spun, her kick sending Kara through the anomaly.

The crystal. Vinnie pulled Wisp power. She moved so fast it was as if time slowed. Her hand grabbed the pendant around Kara's neck, even as she was pulling on the power from the anomaly.

She sucked the power all into her body. She felt the necklace give way and she let go, getting her hand out of the way just as the anomaly snapped shut.

Vinnie swayed on her feet. She could feel every molecule of air, feel every cell in her body.

Let go of the power before you kill yourself, Hilda said.

CHAPTER THIRTY-EIGHT

*C*onor *and Cerulean.* Maybe Hilda would understand that Vinnie couldn't let go of the power yet because she still needed help. She had to save Conor and Cerulean, but she didn't know how. All this power and she couldn't heal them because she'd never learned how to heal.

Jory could heal them. He needed to take over and use the power.

Jory? But there was silence in her head. She couldn't hear them anymore. *Jory! Hilda? Help.*

No response. Her senses stretched wide, but she couldn't feel them, either. Hilda said they were on their way.

Vinnie stumbled toward Conor, the room tilting around her. His body was burned, his entire chest was a mess of melted skin and clothes. She crashed to her knees beside him. He would be okay. Jory would be here soon. As she watched, his breath shuddered and stopped.

"No, hold on," Vinnie tried to separate some of the Zee power, but it was so hard to think. After a few moments, she almost got some Zee power separated, but how did she use the power to heal? Light. Imagine light to heal and then push it like she'd dumped the power at the amusement park.

Grabbing hold of the Zee power, she shoved.

Conor's chest arched off the ground and slammed back down. He pulled in another shuddering breath, and the room tilted around Vinnie. He was going to die. Both were going to die if she didn't get them to help. She couldn't do this.

.... Dragon...

Was the voice in her head Shaw's or her own? What good would being a dragon do?

Dragons were fast, surely. Faster than cars. She'd transformed her body before. She could do it again. Her friends were on their way. They had to be on their way. Why couldn't she feel them?

How far! She thought as hard as she could, but there was silence.

A dragon. She could be a dragon. She could fly fast. She needed to use all the power. The map Will had given her showed how it all worked together, but she couldn't remember. It's all there, it's in your body, Will said. And TK said. She was Vasum. Maybe if she could connect the pieces, follow the trail, she could find the map. Vinnie thought about the woman she'd seen in her mind.

"I've got it," the woman said, and she smiled a manic caricature of a smile.

The map of the power appeared in Vinnie's mind.

"I've got it," Vinnie repeated, but the map seemed fragmented. Parts of it were clear, but other parts were faded like memory seen through a haze of many years. It would have to do.

She stood, stepping back from Conor. The power of an anomaly was inside her. Kara had ripped into the fabric of the universe and freed the power, and now Vinnie was the power.

Vinnie knew what it felt like to grow wings, and Will had given her the means to hold it all together.

Stone for mass. Dancer for transformation. Mesmer to stabilize and understand. Ferr to keep it flowing and keep it all together and convince all the parts to cooperate. Wisp to power it all up, and Zee to heal the constant damage.

Her body wanted to be a dragon.

Distantly she heard clothes ripping and knew they were hers, but the power was making her body thrum as it rushed through her.

Her back grew heavy with wings. The ceiling was pressed against her and then it wasn't as the roof ripped open. Vinnie lifted her long neck to the sky and roared, and it felt good.

Vinnie pushed her wings against the sides of the remaining ceiling, shoving it outward so that debris didn't fall on the two men inside.

She was free. Vinnie ducked her head back into the room. With gentle claws, she lifted first Cer and then Conor, trying to make a cage so that she wouldn't press into Conor's wounds.

How did a dragon fly? Her thoughts tumbled over each other, trying to find purchase.

Push off with your back legs, flap the wings, the voice that might be Shaw said.

Vinnie bent the back legs to get leverage and then pushed. Her jump cleared the roof, and she flapped her wings. Gravity was strong, and this body was too heavy. She landed hard outside the house, just missing Conor's car.

Scoop the air, push the earth away.

And use Wisp power. The second voice was Cerulean. Of course, she needed the power and not just the physical dragon body.

She was strong, the Stone power inside her made her strong. Mesmer power made her light. Use the air to lift. Fill with fire. A helium balloon.

Vinnie jumped again, flapping the wings. When she came down this time, the house was a dot behind her.

Not enough. It still wasn't enough.

She was power, she could do this. She was air, fire, water, blood, bone, and earth. Vinnie jumped, feeling the air currents beneath her wings, the fire in her belly, the lightness of her bones. Gravity was nothing to her. The wind brushed every part of her, and she soared.

The highway stretched below her. Vinnie beat her wings, taking herself higher so anyone below couldn't see what she was carrying.

Small pinpricks of warmth entered the edges of her senses before she spotted the white of Jory's van. The driver must have spotted her too because the van whipped onto an off-ramp and barreled toward a small town.

Vinnie banked left and followed, soaring above the buildings. She followed the van past the town until it turned down a gravel road and stopped in a field. She slowed the beat of her wings, descending toward her friends. The ground rushed up too fast.

Vinnie beat her wings, trying to slow her descent, but it had little effect. She pulled the men in close, trying to prevent the impact from jostling them as her back legs slammed into the ground. Her body skidded and came to a stop in the field.

The van screeched to a halt. Jory launched out of the passenger side. "Let go of the power before you kill yourself!"

Distantly, Vinnie thought about all the potential bad that could happen just releasing all that power, but she noticed what she hadn't before — her body felt like it was ripping apart. As gently as she could, she put Conor and Cerulean down and let go, trying to shove the power into the earth like she had at the amusement park.

The earth tilted and moved, but she couldn't tell if it was the ground moving or her.

"WAKE HILDA," TK said. "See if she can block us from view. Shaw, see if you can use fear, keep people away."

Vinnie's fingertips became aware of grass, then her hands. The blades cut into her skin. The ground beneath her scorched her back. Her stomach heaved, and she tried to roll, but her body wouldn't move. Liquid filled her throat, and she choked, unable to move.

Sudden searing pain flared in her shoulder, and her body shifted to the side.

"Get it out." They were words. They vibrated in the air, but she couldn't tell if it was a man or a woman who spoke, much less who it was.

Something thumped into her back, sending an earthquake along her torso and out to her limbs.

"Vin—" The rest of the words were garbled as Vinnie's stomach heaved again and the liquid in her throat pushed out, coating her teeth and lips. The taste was familiar.

"..... Blood... Can you..."

A hand on her head. The pain eased by the tiniest sliver.

"All I can do." This time she recognized the rumble of the voice was male.

The ground was under her back again, and Vinnie opened her eyes. She hadn't realized they'd been closed.

Shaw, who had been leaning over her, jumped back. "Shit, your eyes." The blue of Shaw's power vibrated around her. Intermixed with the blue were all the other colors, sparking and dancing.

"You were a dragon." Shaw's voice was thick with emotion.

Vinnie's eyes shifted to the darkening sky, which also sparked with power, blues and grays, and yellows. Rain was coming.

"Conor? Cer?" Vinnie's voice was a deep rumble, rattling in her chest.

"Jory's looking at them. You need water." Shaw disappeared

and Vinnie tried to push herself up. She made it up onto an elbow before sliding back down.

"Be still," The voice was female, nearby. Nell appeared in her line of vision and draped a long, thin coat over her, covering up her naked body.

Shaw returned with a bottle of water. She reached under Vinnie and helped her sit up. The water burned painfully as she swallowed.

"Rain," Vinnie rumbled.

"You sound like a man," Shaw said.

"It's not raining," Nell said.

But it was going to. "Help me stand."

"You need rest," Shaw said.

"Cerulean." She could still feel his power bouncing around inside her. The power had stayed when she pushed the rest into the ground. Cerulean needed it if he was going to live.

"I've got her." Nell slid an arm under Vinnie's shoulder and lifted, bringing them both to their feet. The coat slid to the ground, but Vinnie didn't care.

Jory's green energy pulsed in the deep grass some distance away, barely distinct from the browns and greens shimmering around the grass and earth. A small amount of blue ebbed under him. Conor.

The green shifted as Jory stood and turned toward her, his eyes bleak. "I can save him."

Why the sad eyes? She thought at him and frowned. She had no air power. She couldn't talk to his mind. "Cerulean?"

"I don't know what's wrong with Cerulean," he choked. "I might be able to figure it out, but Conor doesn't have much time."

A fat drop of rain fell on Vinnie's nose and slid down.

"I can't save them both," Jory said. He looked at her, expecting her to say something.

"Cerulean is one of ours," Nell said.

But Jory was looking into Vinnie's eyes. He knew, deep down,

ELLE WOLFSON

he knew he couldn't save Cerulean, that something was missing that he couldn't put back. He wanted her to absolve him of the decision. He would try anyway if she asked him to, and Conor would die.

"Conor," Vinnie said. "Save Conor."

Nell's arm left her waist so abruptly that Vinnie stumbled and would have fallen if Shaw hadn't caught her.

"You're not going to listen to her!" Nell yelled after Jory. "Cer is one of us." She rounded on Vinnie — eyes full of rage. "You think he should save your boyfriend over one of your oldest friends?"

The image of Cer crying popped into her head. *She said she'd take the pain away.* She'd known Cer was in pain and had done nothing.

"Jory can't save him. But maybe I can."

If it was the loss of power that would kill him, maybe she could put it back. A drop of rain plopped on her shoulders.

"You think you're so awesome, now?" Nell said. "You're the reason he's like that."

"Nell," TK said. "You're not helping."

Her jaws and her fist clenched. She turned on her heel and stomped back to the van.

TK draped the coat back over Vinnie. "Turn off the rain, Shaw."

"I'm not doing that," Shaw said.

"I can see magic." Vinnie saw it everywhere, in everything. Her stomach was threatening to heave again, and her legs were shaking. "It's everywhere. I can put it back."

"You are half dead, yourself," TK said. Ferr magic swirled around him. His was a lighter red than Kara's.

She frowned. She'd never noticed the nuances before.

"I have to try."

He nodded. "Of course you do, Shaw, help her over. I'll check on Hilda."

326

Vinnie closed her eyes and swallowed. "Hilda?"

"She overexerted herself and passed out," Shaw said.

That's why the communication had cut off. Vinnie couldn't bring them to her to help her use the power, but Hilda could.

"Come help me," Vinnie cut in.

As long as she had his power, he had to be alive. Kara said when they died, she couldn't hold the power anymore.

Vinnie took a step, all her muscles protesting, and wobbled. Shaw's arm tightened around her midsection, and together they hobbled toward where Cer lay in the tall grass.

The tattoos that had covered half his face and body were gone. Everything except the dragon on his wrist. She hadn't realized the tattoos were part of the power. Had he chosen them?

"I never noticed he had freckles," Shaw said.

Vinnie had, on the one clear side of his face, smattered just under his eye. He looked so fragile without the tattoos. They'd made him look fierce. Now he looked like a frail young man.

"Help me down."

Shaw kneeled, taking Vinnie with her. TK had returned and kneeled on the other side of her, reaching out to take her hand. The rough warmth of his fingers soothed her nerves.

Vinnie closed her eyes, calmed her mind, and reached out, feeling the power around her and within her. When she'd pulled the power from Kara, she could tell what was Kara's power and what was not. The power inside her felt different. She couldn't tell where she began, and it ended.

The power was indistinguishable from the rest of her. There was no center where it rooted, as it had in Kara.

TK's arm came up to catch her as she slumped forward. "Vinnie?"

She wanted to scream in frustration, but only managed a whimper. A soothing balm washed over her. Shaw, trying to help.

She'd used TK's power to hold the different powers together inside her. Could she use it to pull them apart? Vinnie pulled in

Ferr power, and the coppery taste of blood filled her mouth. Swallowing the discomfort, she sent the power through her body, trying to see the connection, but she was the same. The power was homogenous.

If she were outside herself, could she see it? If she reached into others, she could feel it. She could feel it in herself. Vinnie retraced the sequence, remembering when the power had flowed into her. She could almost remember how it had connected.

Cerulean's breath stuttered and stopped.

Vinnie was out of time. Hilda's power could help with her memory, but Hilda had already used too much. There was no time to think of something else. Vinnie pulled on the Mesmer energy. It was only a trickle, Hilda's power almost gone. A sharp spear of pain went through Vinnie's brain, and she gasped. She remembered. She pulled a tiny trickle from Jory and her muscles seized, but her body remembered.

Shaw counted softly, "1-2-3-4," as she compressed Cerulean's chest.

Vinnie could see the roots of the power within her, so tiny, so easy to miss. She grabbed them and tugged, ripping a scream out of her body along with the power. She pulled again, and the world went white. She could see nothing behind her eyelids, and she couldn't think.

She had to think. Her toes didn't hurt. Vinnie focused on her toes and tugged again. Everything went dark with the pain, but she had the power. Now she had to give it back — just a push when she usually pulled. But Cer wasn't there anymore.

Her eyes cracked open. Through the haze of Vinnie's vision, Shaw was still doing CPR, but Cerulean wasn't there.

He wasn't there anymore. No colors sparkled around him. His body was there. Vinnie lifted the power, feeling it in her hands, and shoved the power into Cerulean's body.

Cer gasped and his eyes opened. The irises were no longer blue, but a flaming orange. He smiled and his eyes turned blue again. Then his body went limp, and a soft puff of air escaped his lips.

A drop of water hit Vinnie on the forehead and trickled down to her ear. "What?" Why did he still look dead?

Shaw put her fingertips to his neck, checking for a pulse. She shook her head, and a hitching sob escaped.

"I gave it back," Vinnie whispered as another drop of rain hit her cheek. She swiped it away. "I gave the power back, and he woke up."

Vinnie searched for the power inside Cerulean, but it wasn't there. Her eyes scanned the ground for the power.

TK put his hand on Shaw's shoulder, and his head dropped.

"I can try CPR again." Shaw's voice broke.

Vinnie shook her head. "I gave it back." The pain must have addled her brain. It was so hard to think. So hard to think. He had to be okay. She gave the power back. "He woke up."

TK wrapped his arms around her and pulled her close. Vinnie tried to pull away. She had to find the power. Maybe it was still inside her. She held up her hands, staring at them.

"Let go," TK murmured.

Vinnie buried her face in his shoulder, fighting the burning in her eyes, fighting the pain in her chest so she could breathe. She didn't need to cry. She'd given the power back, and Cerulean would be fine.

"Let go," He repeated.

"No, I have to..." The rain began to pour, cold water soaked into the back of her shirt. A distant thought told Vinnie they needed to get Cerulean out of the rain.

CHAPTER THIRTY-NINE

The woman in the blue dress seemed out of place among the somber colors of most of the mourners.

Two weeks since Cerulean had died, and the ache in Vinnie's abdomen refused to fade. The metal chair she sat on creaked as she shifted. She didn't know who had brought the chairs, but she was grateful. Exhaustion seemed to have taken up permanent residence in her bones.

The cemetery was tucked into the far corner of The Holt, at the border between poor and almost middle class. The surrounding buildings hid it from view of the street. The building in front of the graveyard had been a church, which was probably why the graveyard was here.

TK had arranged everything. A death certificate with a fake name. A burial with a headstone that said Cerulean. Sam Chabanik was gone, disappeared into the void and no gravestone would ever mark his resting place. Nell had raged about that, but she raged about everything now. Vinnie no longer recognized her.

They'd had no formal speech at the gravesite, no announcements in the paper, but people came — some climbing over the low chain-link fence that surrounded the small cemetery and some coming through the gates like civilized people. Some were wild-eyed and ragged, some dressed nicely, some appeared to be lost.

Had Cerulean known this many people?

The woman in the blue flowered dress caught Vinnie's eye again. She crouched by the open grave and grabbed a handful of dirt to toss in before standing. The boy with her, who appeared to be somewhere between five and nine years old — Vinnie couldn't tell kids' ages — wrapped his arms around her waist and buried his face in her abdomen.

A few chairs down from her sat an old man with a sunburned scalp. The rest of the chairs were empty.

Vinnie felt Jory approaching before the chair beside her creaked and the heat of a body was next to her. Familiar hands appeared in the periphery of her vision, but she couldn't bring herself to look at Jory.

"I wish I could change your mind, Vinnie." Jory's fingers were intertwined in a prayer position in his lap. "I don't want you to leave. I would never blame you for what happened."

"You should." She already had her apartment rented. Jory had helped her with that since she'd barely been able to get out of bed. He'd helped because she asked, even though he didn't want her to go. She'd had just enough for a security deposit and the first month's rent, but she would need to get another job fast if she didn't want to be on the street.

"This is not your fault," he said.

"Nell disagrees with you."

"She's angry and hurt, she'll get over it."

People could hold on to their anger for a long, long time. Nell had done everything she could to avoid Vinnie, even leaving the house if Vinnie came out of her room.

"If I'd stayed out of it, he would still be alive."

"Cerulean made his own decisions."

331

"But, as you said, his brain wasn't mature enough to make the right ones. You can't change your mind about that just because you don't like the consequences."

Jory's head dropped, chin almost touching his chest. "Leaving won't bring him back. It just splits us up."

The woman in the blue dress had moved away from the grave and was talking to TK. As Vinnie watched, he wrapped his arms around her shoulders, cocooning her in his arms.

"She was looking for me, Jory. Me. Specifically. She used Cer to get to me. If I hadn't been there, he'd be alive. If I hadn't been who I am... If I hadn't gone after her... If she knew about me, others might know about me." Especially since she'd flown over the highway as a dragon. "I don't want you guys getting caught in whatever happens."

"It took all of us to take her out, and she was just one. With an artifact. How is that even possible? To put magic in an object?"

"Exactly. I can't protect you all."

Jory's hand clenched on his knee. "It's not your job to protect us."

"If I'm not near you, you shouldn't need protection."

"You're stubborn. Family sticks together."

Her heart twisted. Family stuck together. Not any family she'd ever known. "I'm not falling off the earth. I'm just down the street. And I have a phone, you can call."

A soft chuff, almost like a laugh, escaped him, but he wasn't smiling. "What then? You're just going to spend the rest of your life not getting close to people?"

That had been Hilda's plan, but Vinnie didn't know if she was still planning to move out, too. Vinnie hadn't told Jory the apartment was her first stop. She needed to get as far away from the people she cared about as possible. Maybe if she learned to use her ability, she could come back.

"Maybe," she said, answering his question. "Who's the woman?" Vinnie pointed at TK and the woman in blue.

"Gina Delgado."

Adrenaline sparked through Vinnie. "The one who owns the house Kara used?"

"What?"

Nell hadn't told anyone else what she found. In all the drama and excitement, it had slipped Vinnie's mind. "Nell, she found the owner of the company that bought the house. It was Gina Delgado."

"Gina," Jory said. "They're old friends. She was also close to Cerulean a few years ago. She and Nieves had a falling out, and she left town and hadn't been back as far as I knew."

The house contract would have happened around the same time they set up Nieves. "TK knew when he sent us after La Mafia."

"I'm sure he had his reasons," Jory said.

Vinnie watched as the boy pulled a toy out of his pocket and held it up to TK. "Gina was TK's lever. That's what Kara used to coerce him into saying Conor had Maddie's energy on him at the games. He thought she was capable of hurting Gina. She'd already knew where I was and who my friends were by the time she took Maddie to Gina's house, and she had a backup plan."

"Contingencies upon contingencies. Taking Maddie was probably not an accident either. She needed someone connected to the library. Was Carla acting strange the day she told you about Maddie?"

Vinnie tried to think back. Had Carla been acting strange the day she told Vinnie about Maddie? She didn't know her well enough to know. TK had said the coercion made him feel confused. He couldn't tell them what had happened and some part of him had thought making pasta would help them figure it out. Cerulean had thought not answering his phone would mean they wouldn't find him. Had anything about Carla's behavior made her seem like she was trying to resist a coercion? She had refused to tell Vinnie much of anything about Maddie. Maybe she was fighting off the coercion, or maybe that was just Carla. "I don't know."

"Have you heard from Will?"

"No." She hadn't tried to contact him again either, after what had happened at Nell's house. She had tried to contact Conor, though. She'd called and texted Conor, but the only response she got was from Lou. Lou had made it very clear he wanted nothing to do with Vinnie anymore. At least he'd survived.

"Will just shows up, gets us involved in this, and then disappears." It was an old refrain by now. What had Will been up to? What was his end game?

"He seemed to have a special hatred for Kara. Maybe he got what he wanted." She'd said this many times, too. Jory never seemed to believe it.

More people came through the front gate. One was a girl who looked about fourteen, carrying an armful of flowers.

"Who are all these people?" Vinnie asked.

"Fans, mostly."

"Fans?"

Jory pointed at the mural on a nearby building, one of Cerulean's, and the largest she'd seen except the one on the gym. This one was a woman with white hair with daisies on her cheeks. Her hand rested on a pink lion's head. The woman and the lion both had wings. Cer rarely painted anything without wings.

"There's a website dedicated to his art," Jory said. "People take photos when they find one and post them, speculate on their meaning, post maps of where to find them."

She didn't know her friends at all. "Did he know?"

Jory shrugged.

The mural on the building was pretty and whimsical, like all Cer's paintings.

A tall figure stood under the tree by the mural. Hilda's head was bent, looking down at her phone. The sunlight through the trees made patterns on her pale blond hair.

"I have to get back to work." Jory stood, pulled something out of his pocket, and held his hand out to her, palm down. "You should keep this, put it in a safe place."

Vinnie held her hand up, and he dropped a piece of crystal into her palm. The bottom half of Kara's necklace. The anomaly's snapping shut had sliced it cleanly in two.

"Come home any time," Jory said.

Vinnie watched his retreating figure for a moment before turning back to the mourners. She should go too. She'd wanted to see all the people that came to say goodbye to Cerulean, thinking it would ease the pain, but it hadn't, and she was so very tired.

Vinnie stood and waited for her legs to steady.

A flash of red hair out of the corner of her eye startled her. It wasn't Kara, of course it wasn't. Just a young girl carrying a carnation toward the grave. This wasn't the first time she'd thought she saw Kara, and it probably wouldn't be the last.

Hilda still stood by the tree, staring off into nothing. They'd barely spoken since the confrontation, and Vinnie wondered if Hilda was also avoiding her. She didn't seem to be angry, just vacant. The dark shadows under her eyes almost looked like bruises, and every spark and snarky comment that had made Hilda who she was, seemed to be missing.

Maybe time would heal them all, or maybe they'd never be the same.

Vinnie convinced her feet to move. There was no way she'd make it to the apartment on foot, but there was a bus stop not too far from here.

"Vinnie, wait!" Shaw pulled away from a group of people and jogged toward Vinnie. "I have something for you. I'll be right back."

Shaw disappeared. Vinnie leaned against the fence, longing to sit down. When Shaw reappeared, she had something clutched to her chest.

She held out the small, black, book to Vinnie. There was nothing printed on the cover, no clue about what it was, and Vinnie just stared at it. She should open it, see what it was.

"It's Cer's last sketchbook," Shaw said. "Something to remember him by."

Vinnie looked into Shaw's eyes. They were glassy from crying but looked clear right now. Vinnie had the almost overwhelming urge to apologize or shove the book back at Shaw.

"Don't," Shaw said gruffly. "Just take it. I have three others."

Vinnie held the book to her chest as Shaw had, and swallowed heavily. She wanted to say thank you, but she couldn't get the words out.

INCOMING.

Vinnie had just settled into her seat on the bus when Hilda's voice burst into her head. Hope pulled her head up. Hilda hadn't spoken to her mind to mind in so long, but it wasn't Hilda getting onto the bus.

Will wore a baseball cap that looked out of place on him, and some sunglasses that suited him just fine. She'd taken a seat in the middle of the bus and sat closest to the window so no one would have to get past her if they wanted to sit in the same row. Her consideration left her trapped. He would sit next to her, and she wouldn't be able to get away. She didn't think he would hurt her, but she wanted nothing to do with him.

Will didn't sit next to her, though. He sat in the seat in front of her and turned sideways, taking up two seats so he could look back at her. "You can leave if you want, but all I'm asking is that you give me until we get to your stop."

He took off his sunglasses and tucked them into the collar of his too white t-shirt.

"Why are you wearing that? You look weird."

A tiny crease of confusion appeared between his eyebrows, and Vinnie wanted to take the words back. They sounded too friendly, like banter, and she did not want to be friendly.

"I'm trying to blend," he said.

"Try not looking so shiny and perfect next time."

"Next time?" he said.

"Not the next time you talk to me." Again, she'd sounded like she was bantering. "The next time you try to blend. Unless it's at a country club or something."

"I've never been to a country club."

Sure he hadn't. "Whatever it is you're selling, I don't want it."

"I wanted to apologize for saving your life."

Anger that Vinnie had been tamping down roared to life, and she leaned forward. "I think maybe what you're trying to say is that you're sorry for taking control of my body without my permission and trying to use it to kill someone."

His nostrils flared with his own suppressed anger. "Yes, that's what I meant," he said, voice flat.

Vinnie flopped back. "You don't mean that."

"I don't mean that. I'm sorry for the damage that it's caused between us, but I would do it again to save you."

Vinnie thought of the woman she'd seen in the vision. She'd meant something to him, and she looked a little like Vinnie, but she didn't know this guy. "Look, I'm flattered, but you're not my type."

He looked surprised for a moment, then recovered. "Vasum are rare," he said. "You shouldn't be flattered. If I could find another like you, I wouldn't have even worried about it. I would have let you die since you were trying so hard to, going out to the middle of nowhere with no backup when you knew someone might be trying to kill you. Vasum are rare and I still need your help."

Her breath hissed out, and she leaned forward again. "Keep your voice down. Now who's being stupid? This is public transport."

But no one was looking at them. That didn't mean they weren't listening.

"I made sure no one can hear us," he said.

"Great, so I can tell you to fuck off, because I'm not going to help you anymore, and no one will hear me."

His face hardened. "I think you should reconsider. You've painted a target on your chest with your stupidity. A dragon? And then you close the anomaly, which is the only explanation there was for the dragon being in this world. I've already taken steps to help you and can continue to do so."

Vinnie felt sick inside. She'd known that the dragon was stupid. It was all over the internet, including some grainy video. It was on the news — speculation about whether the dragon was of this world — that some Twisted had figured it out, or if it was from another world. The official line was that an anomaly had been opened and closed from another world. That happened from time to time. The vigor with which the news reported that it wasn't someone from this world and couldn't possibly be had surprised her.

Then there was Maddie's death and Kara's disappearance. Investigation ongoing.

But what made her the sickest was the memory of someone taking over her body. "I was born with a target on my chest, and I didn't ask for your help. Not there and not here. If you wanted to help me, you'd tell me how you found me. Then maybe I could stop anyone else from finding me. Or my friends."

His green eyes glittered, cold. "You think your friend is the only one who'll die if you try to solve this on your own?"

"Solve what? There's nothing to solve. She's gone." But there could be others, that's why she was getting away. People would come after her. They'd be looking for her and she wanted to keep everyone else safe. Turning into a dragon had been stupid, even if it saved Conor's life, but she wasn't so dumb that she didn't think there were more people out there who would want to use her as Kara had, as Will wanted to.

"You think that's it?" he said.

She didn't, but she wasn't going to give him the satisfaction of knowing that. Vinnie relaxed her body and turned her face to the window, hoping he'd get the point that the conversation was over.

"You can't take this on alone, Vinnie." His voice was almost gentle now.

Vinnie wanted to retort that she wasn't alone, but she was. She was because she chose to be. There was no other way that she knew to keep her friends safe since she obviously couldn't protect them.

"Where were you?" The words came out of her mouth before she could stop them. "Where were you after we fought the killer at the house? You were gone."

"I'm ill," he said. The anguish in his voice was enough to make her look back at him. "I shouldn't have put myself in danger like that. And after that, I needed treatment. It's complicated."

She didn't think he was lying, but there was something he wasn't saying. "You say you want to help, but you won't even tell me the truth."

"I can help you stop anything like this from happening again," he said.

That she did not believe. As much as she was responsible for what happened to Cerulean, so was he. He'd said he learned what he knew by doing research. She could do the same.

"I don't need your help. You didn't save me out there. I did that with the help of my friends."

"What you did was almost kill yourself."

"Maybe I'll do a better job of it next time, and the people I care about will be safe."

He blanched. "You'll risk your life just to spite me?"

Would she? He knew things that might take her a long time to find on her own, but this whole horrible chain of events had started when he walked into her library.

"What can I do to convince you?" he said.

"Nothing." The bus lurched to a stop. "This is where I get off. You're out of time."

Vinnie stood, her legs less shaky than they had been in weeks, and walked off the bus.

ACKNOWLEDGMENTS

Big hugs and a thank you to my husband James, for all your love, support, typo wrangling, patience — especially the patience.

And a big, big thank you to Julia J. Simpson for your advice on so many things, for helping me fix messes. And for your patience. (Seems to be a theme)

ABOUT THE AUTHOR

Elle's favorite books are books with magic in them so that's what she writes. She believes there is real magic in the world for those who seek it.

She loves adventure, peanut butter, and colorful things like yarn, fabric, and crayons. Shiny things also catch her eye.

She might be a crow, but she is definitely not a werewolf.

The Magic is out there.

CPSIA information can be obtained
at www.ICGtesting.com
Printed in the USA
BVHW080902100921
616514BV00006B/78